MW00396119

TAKE WING!

INTERESTING THINGS

THAT HAPPENED

ON MY

WAY TO SCHOOL

...and having writ, moves on

Edmunds
Grey
Dimond

The assaye so hard:
so sharpe the conquering.
The lyfe so shorte:
the crafte so long to lerne.

Thanks for your gift to
The Ginny Fund

Also by E. Grey Dimond

Paul Dudley White: A Portrait (edited)

Paul Woods Revisited (edited)

More Than Herbs and Acupuncture

Inside China Today: A Western View

The Reverend William Whitehead
  Mississippi Pioneer: His Antecedents and Descendants

Ed Snow Before Paoan: The Shanghai Years

Letters From Forest Place
  A Plantation Family's Correspondence 1846-1881 (edited)

Patrick Dimond/Diamond/Dimon
  Eighteenth Century Migrant: A Survey of His American Descendants

The Story of the Originals

Essays Of An Unfinished Physician

...restless, questing, hopeful people

Shaping Wood

Milepost 80

Milepost 85

TAKE
WING!

INTERESTING THINGS

THAT HAPPENED

ON MY

WAY TO SCHOOL

by E. Grey Dimond, M.D.

Revised Edition with Preface by Dr. Malinda Bell

Copyright ©1991 by E. Grey Dimond

Copyright ©2005 by Diastole-Hospital Hill, Inc.

ISBN 0-932845-53-3

All rights reserved. No part of this book may be reproduced, stored in a retrieval system, or transmitted in any form or by any means, electronic, mechanical, photocopying, recording or otherwise without the prior written permission of the publisher.

Printed by Anundsen Publishing Company, Decorah, Iowa

Original printing by The Lowell Press, Inc., Kansas City, Missouri

Published by Diastole-Hospital Hill, Inc., Kansas City, Missouri

Order additional copies directly from Diastole:

2501 Holmes Street
Kansas City, Missouri 64108

Preface

*"A school is like a glass of wine.
A nice stemmed glass helps, but it's the wine that makes the memory."*

Dr. E. Grey Dimond, Provost Emeritus
1996 Silver Anniversary Gala
University of Missouri-Kansas City School of Medicine

I WAS THE FORTUNATE recipient of an extraordinary medical education and Dr. Dimond is largely responsible for the vineyard that is my alma mater, the University of Missouri-Kansas City School of Medicine. Though he doesn't take all of the credit, he is recognized as the founder of the UMKC-SOM and the architect of its nontraditional educational plan.

Dr. Dimond's credentials are readily verifiable and quite impressive, but they provide no personal details about a very private man. Try to locate interviews of Dr. Dimond, and with few exceptions, these were granted during one phase of his life and for one purpose: he was going to revolutionize medical education. Though he accomplished this goal, it represents only a fraction of his pursuits and lifetime.

He is internationally recognized and respected for his many contributions as physician, scholar, diplomat, author, and teacher. He is a charismatic leader whose determination and imagination both inspire and inflame. His passion for an idea and his subsequent skillful implementation has been revered as genius and reviled as arrogance. Dr. Dimond's autobiography *Take Wing!* allows readers a view behind his curtain.

Take Wing! was originally published in 1991 with a limited press run intended for family, close friends, and colleagues. Persistent persuasion has resulted in this reprinting. *Take Wing!* is not merely his story, it is our history. Dr. Dimond's life review is complemented by a kaleidoscope of people, politics, and process spanning nearly 75 years. His recollections and interpretations of various events provide an insightful, first-person commentary on the realities that were our community, our nation, and our world. Significantly, it is the only record of the UMKC-SOM history by an original source.

One would be mistaken to think the process of starting a university-affiliated medical school is as simple as filling a building with students, bringing in teachers, and collecting tuition. If it were that easy, it wouldn't have appealed to Dr. Dimond. In fact, when he was asked to come to Kansas City to start a medical school, his response was predictable: Only if he could do it his way.

The UMKC-SOM educational plan changed the course of medical history by inspiring curriculum changes elsewhere and improving patient care everywhere. Dr. Dimond believed the making of compassionate, capable doctors did not come from rote memorization of textbooks in stuffy classrooms. For UMKC-SOM graduates, the essence of physicianhood was imparted at the patient's bedside under the tutelage of a role model-mentor-docent. And, though his detractors believed it was wrong to select and admit students immediately after high school, he considered the vitality and idealism of still malleable youth to be the key ingredient. To critics, he has held fast to the same reply: Judge the product.

When he retired as Provost of the UMKC-SOM in 1979, Dr. Dimond wrote:

> "If what we have done is a real truth and clearly results in graduates who leave their medical school years with an open, enthusiastic, un-cynical attitude, with a motivation towards serving people, with a commitment to meeting the honor given them in being called Physician—then it must be those graduates and the patients they serve who will identify and perpetuate this distinct approach to medical education."

To conclude that *Take Wing!* is only the saga of a medical school would be to miss the opportunity it presents for life lessons from a life-time teacher. While autobiography has the obvious limitation of affording only one perspective, I believe *Take Wing!* to be an honest representation of the man I have come to know. But my opinion is superfluous; to quote the master: Judge the product.

Dr. Dimond has remained on the Hill overlooking the Medical School, surveying the vineyard and the products. He is a proud papa, confident of the graduates' futures and their success as citizens and physicians. Today, his patience and penchant for planning is most visible in his pastimes of sculpting and gardening. There is every indication he reads vigorously, writes daily, and welcomes correspondence. I close with a toast to Dr. Dimond and an invitation to readers to drop him a line ᶜ/₀ Diastole.

Malinda H. Bell, M.D.
Class of 1985

Dedicated to

Sherri Grey
Lark Grey
Lea Grey

And the Graduates of the
University of Missouri-Kansas City School of Medicine

Acknowledgments

MY LIST OF ACKNOWLEDGMENTS should be to all of those with whom I have so thoroughly enjoyed this life. It has been a happy trip, with sufficient stress and black moments to make clear the sweet value of all the good things that came my way.

For this book, I recognize the professionalism and good humor of Jim Soward. Jim is an "original," one of those who came with the medical school at the beginning and gave his talent generously. He founded the Office of Educational Resources (OER) and it is that department that took my manuscript and carried it to completion. Jim and Lisa Zimmerman and Laura Patterson edited the manuscript, and the finished product truly reflects my thoughts and style, controlled and guided by them. My thanks to Perry Hunter, a second-generation star in OER, for his good taste, professional skill, and knowledge of print production, all of which played a major role in the look and feel of the book. And to Todd Hanna of OER who handled much of the newer photography in the book and the dustjacket, and to Barbara Rauscher of OER who took the cover photo, my thanks as well.

My years with the University of Missouri obviously have been considerable. Through the difficult years of the School, the curators of the University never interceded or faulted the effort. James Olson and George Russell, in their role as chancellors and presidents, have been major protectors and supporters.

Three deans have guided the medical school: Richardson K. Noback, Harry S. Jonas, and James J. Mongan. Each man brought a unique strength and the appropriate talent needed during his tenure.

And it would not be right to not acknowledge and thank those students (and their parents) who came to this new, untried school in its experimental years. You gave the most: your trust and faith. My cordial, warm acknowledgment and appreciation.

Introduction

I HAVE LED A LIFE of defined objectives, which is too bold a statement to be the truth. For no one has control of all the variables, and what I may claim was a defined objective, can just as easily be recognized as chance. Perhaps I, therefore, should say that when chance presented an alternative, I often was willing to try a path not taken before, and to leave that path by my own terms. That is what I mean by defined objectives. Someone wrote, "Chance is a fool's name for fate." I don't believe that at all. Chance is chance. The use of it is a life.

I have written this book for certain reasons: Does not everyone feel the need to justify an autobiography? In his superb autobiography, *Old Men Forget,* Duff Cooper gave his answer: "I have written this book, and enjoyed writing it, because I wanted to set down some of the memories before they faded. Nor can the dearest and most secret of them be included."

One cannot improve on that, only modify it to suit a less glamorous life. First, and the truest of the reasons, is that it will give me satisfaction down through the years, years without my presence, for my daughters and their children to have not only a chronological stream of how I used my time, but some awareness of the people I knew and the things we did. I have published books about my own ancestors and enjoyed tracing family roots. Although I could trace their paths of migration and who begat whom on what date, I found myself wishing I knew how the man or woman thought and the why behind their actions. In this book I try to tell my "whys" and yet know well that one man's "whys" may not be the truth, but the justification that made the action livable, livable for one's self.

For much of my life, I have been a teacher; others, therefore, were my students. Even in the years when many would have said I was an administrator, the reality was that I was very much a teacher, trying hard to offer a course on medical education and a physician's duty. Students are influenced by the words of the teacher, but also by the conduct, the personality, and the performance of the teacher. In such a life, one inevitably influences the lives of others, good or bad, right or wrong. My instincts tell me I have an obligation to many of them to tell more of what went on in my own head and what were the reasons, rationalized or not, for changes and actions in my career.

It would give me pleasure to write a book with the excitement and charm of Hans Zinsser's *As I Knew Him* or with the poetry and mystique of Axel Munthe's *San Michele*. Both men had drama and theater in their lives, which I did not have, and my own potential to be dramatic is one I have controlled. At any given point, when events opened for me the large window of becoming a public figure, I have quickly moved to assure my continued privacy. One of the messages of my book is that although I have led a life which was often quite public, my inborn instincts always were to remain private. This is not meant as claim to modesty; modesty is a virtue. I was motivated by a wish, a need, to remain a very private person.

I have written about some of the people with whom I worked; and, at the same time, have not spoken at all about some with whom I have shared much. In part, this has been because there has been a mainstream that has guided my choices; but, equally, there is no need to tell their stories, some quite personal. If they read this book, please know I remember—and you were not forgotten.

PART ONE

Chapter One

DAD WAS BORN IN WINONA, a small Mississippi town of about 5,000, equally divided between blacks and whites. Mom was born in St. James, Missouri, an even smaller town, although she was inclined to claim St. Louis as her birthplace.

I was born in St. Louis essentially by chance. Dad and his pregnant wife were there visiting. Mother went into labor and was delivered by a Dr. Rhodes at 3917 Lexington Avenue. Five days later we returned South and my residence in St. Louis ended.

Dad came from Anglo-Saxon people who were here by 1650 and were planters until the end of the Civil War. By the 1700's and 1800's, part of the family had a strong Baptist orientation with a series of fairly prominent Baptist ministers. (After the War between the States, the family moved to the Methodists, Presbyterians and Episcopalians.) This had no influence on Dad, and I have no remembrance of our family going to church a single time. When I was 10 or 12, Mom had a brief moment during which she felt it important that I go to Sunday School. This lasted about three Sundays. I went to a nearby United Brethren Church, and then this urge died out and we were able to sleep in again on Sundays. The brief religious spurt had ended.

I have no remembrance of prayer or grace at meals and, I don't think I ever met or spoke to a minister in all those years. Although a prayer was not said at mealtime, Mom was unremitting in having me learn and say, as I went to bed, "I lay me down to sleep and I pray the Lord my soul to keep," ending with, "God bless Mommy and Daddy, Granddaddy and Uncle Lark. I promise to be a good little boy and mind my mommy and daddy. Amen." Mom's instruction included a detailed warning that this prayer was the best way to stay out of hell, and she spoke of hell and heaven as real places. I held to this bedtime prayer faithfully until I was 19 and in Purdue, when I decided to experiment and see what would happen if one stopped this heavenly request. After a few nights of uneasy guilt but no disaster I learned to go to bed without supplication.

There was a huge family Bible that had belonged to Dad's parents; it was never opened. It was kept on a lower shelf in the linen closet. I now have it and treasure it because of the record of birth, marriage, and death.

Dad's family, for several generations, had been more than ordinarily prosperous. From the mid-1600's they had been owners of large tracts of land and slaves.

His great-grandfather was not only a businessman, a plantation owner, but also the first Baptist minister of the State and one of the founders of two of the original counties of Mississippi. His grandfather, Edmunds Grey, was the presiding officer for the founding of Carroll County, Mississippi; the family owned 14,000 acres of land in that county.

When the Civil War ended plantation life, the family opened a large, (large for Winona), general merchandise store, Dimond and Whitehead, backed a local bank, and weathered well those difficult years. One member of the family went to law school at Ole Miss and when very young went off to see Mr. Candler of the Coca-Cola Company; with a partner, he bought world rights to bottle Coca-Cola. The two partners agreed to buy syrup only from Mr. Candler and he agreed they had the only bottling rights any-place in the world. This arrangement continued for many years and the family was able to establish foundations that are still active in the South.

After the Civil War, the men stopped being planters and entered the professions. They became lawyers, doctors, brokers, and three of the immediate family graduated from pharmacy school.

Dad's childhood was probably a happy one, at least until he was 15 years old. He perhaps would have lived a steady, satisfactory life if he could have remained within his Southern family and their inherent support system. He was the youngest of five children, and, in one dreadful year, 1910, his mother and the only two sisters died. Dad was then put in a military boarding school and the brittle, sassy streak in his personality showed itself. The hazing, so natural for such a school, was not tolerated by this youngest son of a prominent Mississippi family. One evening at the dinner table, the demands for sitting square, eating square and the full hazards of traditional hazing, broke through Dad's precarious temper control. As he told me, years later, "When we were at dinner and he persisted in making a fool out of me, I simply picked up the water carafe and laid the bastard out cold. I was expelled." This was Dad's last exposure to the military, and it was good that it ended.

Still, if he had stayed in the South, surrounded by family, all would have been better. A migration from the deep South to the Midwest was an unusual pattern in those years. He moved among strangers.

His touchy, sensitive, very quick personality was well-masked by wit, humor and joking. But the prickly Southerner was just inside, not always well-contained. When I was 12, he came close to trouble. He played golf every weekend, played for money, and on the final hole, while trying to make a winning putt, one of the foursome came up from behind and made a loud raspberry sound. The putt was blown, and Dad attempted to use his putter on the man's head. This attack was compounded by a choice collection of Southern profanity, in which he was expert. I was caddying, and there was no doubt Dad had meant to brain the man, one of his best friends.

There was also a combative streak that made it impossible for him to take much personal kidding. He was inclined to brag about how dangerous it would be to provoke him. His friends would try to make him laugh and get his mind off whatever was the problem but, even if he weighed only 150 pounds, they were very cautious about his temper. He never liked to be physically touched and they had to learn that he was not someone to drape an arm over and not someone to give a playful swat.

Dad had most unusual cold, green-gray eyes. Recently, I was looking through old papers and found his driver's license. Under eye color, it indicated gray. Gertie's (my mother's) eyes were big and brown with green flecks—"root-beer eyes," she liked to say.

My parents met in St Louis. Mother was an employee of the telephone company and Dad was just finishing college and working after school in a drugstore. Mom's mother, Angie Morrison, was born in St. James, a small town in east-central Missouri. Angie was a divorcee, a rather rare role for the time. Her marriage in St. James to a German immigrant from Prussia had ended, and she moved with her little son, age 5, and her daughter, age 2, to St. Louis. They moved in with Angie's cousins and it was one of these cousins to whom Mom fled for several months during my junior high school year. I never knew my German grandfather, and Angie died when I was 1, so there are no memories or associations for me with Mother's parents. Later, when I traced the roots of my four grandparents, I found Findley Morrison in Virginia before 1750. His son, Hugh, was in the Revolutionary Army and earned a veteran's land bonus in Kentucky, setting in motion the typical westward movement of Americans. His son, John, moved on to Missouri in 1811.

One of my mother's family became a preacher and was in at the beginning of the founding of a church college; he became the first president of Anderson College in Indiana. He wrote an excellent autobiography with the strangely moving title, *As The River Flows*, and again, as with my Dad, none of this religion had much effect on Mom. At the very end of her life, when she was dreadfully ill and dying in a strange town, Muncie, Indiana, she became frightened and wondered if she had done the right thing and questioned if there was a hereafter which she would be denied. The last months of her life were awful, and she needed help wherever she could find it.

An only child is equated with a spoiled child, and it is accepted folklore that this nasty behavior carries into adult life finely honed qualities of petulance, whimperishness, and arrogance. The only-child adult is in a difficult position; almost any attempt to explain the evil predictions do not apply to him is greeted by knowing nods, yawns, and condescension. Adult behavior such as momentary irritation is met by placation: "O.K. We understand. It's hard for someone with your background to accept normal reversals." Or, most painful, there is no response at all, but you have a nagging feeling that the other person is *thinking* it.

It gives me pleasure to assure anyone interested that I am, thoroughly, completely, enthusiastically, an only child. Let me hurry to claim that other dubious status: I was a mamma's boy, if "mamma's boy" means that one's mother devoted herself to a son. If the user of the term suggests this role includes being a sissy, and someone inclined to being a bit delicate in behavior, then we have a variance in meaning. Mom believed in masculine boys and men. I came home crying one day, age 6, with the story I had been hit by a neighbor boy. Her response was quick. I was shoved out the door and told to go find him and "beat up on him." And the door slammed. When I was 13 and formed a club which met in our basement, she was all for it when she learned we were playing poker and shooting craps, but she hooted when I told her the group was "The Woman-Hater's Club." She advised me, in no uncertain terms, that our problem was that we didn't yet understand what life was all about. Later, when I did discover girls and what life was about, Mom was all smiles, and quickly made Margie into her best friend.

Mom saw one of the problems of my woman-hater's club was that none of us knew how to dance; she assembled us in the living room and taught us the fundamentals. The fundamentals did not stop with dancing, but also included how you open doors for ladies, which side you walk on, hats off in elevators, and all the other basics that now are considered inappropriate conduct, and even a means of arresting a woman's development. Mom's enthusiasm for my dating, learning about girls, romances, and other exercises of youth, kept her busy—busy trying to find my diary, find notes exchanged in school and finding out what I thought about various dates.

She never lost her affection for Margie; and, as I began to learn how big the world was, and Margie and I went separate directions, Mom held on to Margie, treating her as a combination of daughter and best friend.

Mom's enthusiasm for swimming, golfing, skating, bowling, and roller skating naturally caught me up in these things, and some of the best memories I have are of summer evenings, my friends and I—and Mom—roller skating on the wide sidewalks around Sarah Scott Junior High School. I remember one evening when some high school fellows thought she was a cute new girl in town and tried to date her. I was embarrassed, but she enjoyed telling the story. I remember Mom standing on my shoulders at Isaac Walton Lake and doing a somersault into the water, and of playing golf, playing golf, playing golf. A city-owned golf course was nearby our home, and one could play all day for 25 cents. On several days I played 54 holes. I became obsessed with seeing how many holes one could play in a day and stripped the equipment down to a two-iron and a putter and ran between shots. I developed a hook that became a danger to a player on any fairway to the left of where I was playing. I haven't played since I was 18.

Mom was called "Gertie" by all my friends. She was a pretty, big-brown-eyed girl (remember, she was only 31 when I was 10 so I do remember her well). Her hair was shiny black and her smile big with good, white teeth. She was 5 feet 3 inches (Dad was 5-foot 11) and she weighed about 120, but she fought hard to keep from gaining. As she would say, "My bottom fills out too easy."

Her clothes sense was good, and in the 1930's women wore perky little hats, of which she had a large collection. She liked jewelry; and, other than her pearls and her wedding ring, none of it was good. Costume jewelry and rhinestones gave her pleasure. To add to my burdens of spoilage, I not only had a devoted mother and a perfect early romance; I also had a superb boyhood friend all through primary school, junior high, and high school. He must be added to the list of a childhood of happiness.

Vic and I were together essentially every day from ages 6 to 18; and then because of war, schooling, marriage and careers we, practically, never saw each other again. I say "practically" because we never again had the exact, perhaps precious, relationship we did in those formative years. We certainly have remained friends, and if someone insisted on the identification of my "best friend," my response, without hesitation, would be Vic. Yet, we both know that the bond between us is based upon those early unfolding, exploring years and not upon any fundamental understanding of what our adult development may have been.

Vic became a lawyer, a successful man, very well-arrived in our home town and home state. He graduated first in his class at Indiana University Law School, was severely wounded in combat in

Europe, and attained the rank of Colonel in the Reserves. On the rare times we are together for a few hours, we descend into muffled chuckles, jowl-shaking laughs, not one moment of which makes sense to others. We have never talked about it, but we both know, know quite clearly, that the other boy-man we knew is there, would do anything on earth for the other; and, equally clearly, we know we don't know the adult other. Complicated? Not at all. We both know the other's fabric. We know how the other man was formed, what shaped him, what our antecedents were, and our comfort level, one to the other—is not needing a review or new assessment.

A major part of my pre-18 years, therefore, was a combination of being an only child, but with additional values, the values of a young, enthusiastic mother, a happy romance with a first girl, and a childhood-long friendship with Vic.

It adds a little to say that Vic was also an only child; and, although our moms were certainly different, his was as absolutely supportive of him as my Gertie was of me. Our mothers were very different, and with no intention, even slightly, of suggesting either background was the right one, my Mom was urban, a city girl, very modern, very socially active; Vic's Mom was from a rural, southern Indiana background, a schoolteacher early, but home-based during our childhood years. Cletie B. was an intelligent, sensitive woman. She truly could cook, and enjoyed it. My Mom was not in the least capable in such tasks, and was never interested, remotely, in canning, preserving, bread making, pie making, or cake baking. Vic's mother was skillful and enthusiastic in all of these areas. My Mother took an interest in our learning to dance and our table manners; Vic's Mom was interested in getting homemade biscuits in front of us, with plenty of eggs and bacon. It adds another dimension to understanding Vic when I add that his Dad was different. Big Vic was a retired Big League pitcher. He had been with the Chicago Cubs and the Pittsburgh Pirates, and had won two games in the 1925 World Series. After retiring, he got a law degree and became a State Senator. Little Vic was my buddy; Big Vic was an extra dividend.

There was still another factor that made my childhood not only completely happy, but also healthy. My Dad, because of his education in the pharmaceutical industry and because of his employment with Eli Lilly and Company (a very first-class company), was well informed on the importance of diet, fruit, vitamins, cod-liver oil (awful stuff that came in fish-shaped bottles), meticulous hygiene, fresh air, vaccination, clean bedclothes, sanitation, good medical and dental care. My spoilage included an unusual standard of health care for the 1920's.

When the Depression came along, we essentially did not experience it. The steady, unfailing strength of Eli Lilly kept the Depression out of our lives, and from birth until I was almost 16, there just was no great concern about money. All about me, there were fathers who did not have jobs for years. Terre Haute was no isolated pocket of depression, but it had the full devastation of those years. Classmates, good and with potential, were in make-do clothes, and when we reached the eighth grade, numbers of them left school. Others transferred to the technical high school, trying to learn a craft that would bring in some money.

Although the Depression was not a nightmare for us as it was for so many, it did take a decided toll. In 1927, my grandfather died; and with his inheritance, Dad bought a great deal of General Motors stock, all on margin. When the market came crashing down in 1929, his great adventure in the stock market was cleanly wiped out.

I was born in 1918, just when running water, indoor toilets, central heating, electricity, telephone, and automobiles were becoming available; however, they were always a part of our home. I can't tell painful stories of kerosene lamps, of chopping wood, about digging a path in the snow to the outdoor toilet—any kind of an outdoor toilet was on Dad's unsanitary list. It is true that until I was 10 we had ice delivered every day, and there was a drip pan beneath the icebox. That drip pan and hauling out the ashes from the furnace are the closest I can come to talking about the old days. Even those touches of proof that I had a work-ethic childhood were partly wiped out by Dad's enthusiasm for the new device, the electric refrigerator, a Westinghouse. He considered this invention a great boost for sanitation and further justified it by keeping it stocked with a full supply of vaccines. Because of his relationship with Eli Lilly, much of our refrigerator was packed with Lilly's Iletin, their special name for insulin.

Later, when the Roosevelt era ended Prohibition and beer returned, Dad promptly sold our Westinghouse and bought a Kelvinator. Why? Beer bottles were too tall to fit upright on the shelves of the Westinghouse; and, with Prohibition over, cold beer was high on Dad's value list. He believed beer bottles should stand upright, in case the beer had sediment. The Kelvinator provided this dimension.

This was not the first time beer had been a determinate of our way of living. All through Prohibition, Dad had been convinced that, as a pharmaceutical chemist, he certainly could make beer, not just beer, but a great beer. But this skill was missing from his make-up, and we lived through a series of brewing efforts, including moving to a different house so he could have a bigger, better-ventilated basement. He bought all the equipment, and when the brew did not brew, he bought larger, better gadgets. At each stage, he failed. The large earthenware crock in which he placed his carefully measured, carefully washed ingredients somehow would fail to rise up and brew. There were a series of bubblings over, small bursts, one or two master explosions; and when he finally reached the bottling stage, again with all equipment scrubbed and sanitary, there were other explosions, first one bottle at a time, then a large cascading sequence of eruptions with beer-smelling fluid dripping from the basement ceiling.

When the day came to try the finished product, he made a performance. He got his tray, cheese, and crackers ready, pulled the beer bottle forth from the Kelvinator with a stylish flourish, wrapped the bottle in a towel because of the potential explosion, flipped the cap off—and out came a cascade of green liquid, a green fluid with a most unpleasant color. With his audience: Mom, Runt the dog, his son, he poured it into his pre-chilled, frosted stein.

He was trapped; and, with a reluctance that made his face flush, he took a single sip. He put his substantial nose over the stein, inhaled, and announced proudly, "Damn! It smells like the real stuff." He then poured a little in a saucer for Runt, who circled the dish, put his tongue in, and refused to go further. Dad took a long draft of his creation, choked, and fought it down. He grunted and his face froze in a grimace.

For about an hour he stood at the sink, head averted, opening and pouring the strange, green-brown, foamy liquid down the drain.

One of his best friends successfully made a good beer all through the Prohibition; and, although Dad drank it with joy, he always mumbled that it was made under unsanitary conditions and should be used as a culture medium. This perhaps was close to the truth. Dad's brew was so sanitary it just did not have enough energy and creativity to make beer.

Dad was a complex collection of intelligence, charm, enthusiasm, energy, quick temper, and neurosis. To help understand life with Father, I need to tell about the two pets who were a central, shared warmth.

The first to come into our little three-person home was Bobby, a Hartz Mountain canary. This cheerful, golden singer gave Dad deep pleasure, and keeping Bobby happy, well-fed and with a clean, tidy cage was a daily event, with Dad murmuring soft Mississippi sweet talk and whistling, whistling especially, "St. Louie Woman with all those Diamond Rings." While Mom got breakfast on the table, Dad had his Bobby time; and then, carefully, he moved the cage and its stand to the morning sun and would demand our attention when Bobby gave forth with what I still remember as spectacular trilling and warbling.

Dad felt Bobby's happiness would be complete if he had a mate; and one evening he slipped in the back door and popped Dickie, a female counterpart of Bobbie, into the cage. He did it so quietly that Gertie and I did not notice it. By bedtime, he was pouting (Dad, not Bobby) and stomped into the bedroom and called out that we were blind and insensitive. After adequate smoothing, soothing, and urging, he returned and we followed him to the kitchen and noted the two birds in Bobby's cage. We gave an adequate performance of ooooohing; he was placated.

For the next several days, we enjoyed sharing our observations about the newly married couple. For the first few days, Bobby's singing exceeded his past variety. Then he stopped singing and Dad hovered over the cage, fretted over the diet, put some cod-liver oil on the bird food, boiled the drinking water, and accused the new bird of having brought a disease into the house. Mother was first to notice that Bobby was repeatedly tearing up the paper in the bottom of his cage, placing little pieces of it in a corner. Each day the cage was cleaned and Bobby started over, tearing up paper and fussing with it in the corner. It struck home that Bobby was about to be a father; Dad was energized. Books and telephone calls made him an expert in short order. He cut an end off an oatmeal box, padded it with a bit of flannel, wired it securely to a perch in the cage, and placed string, thread, white tissue paper, etc., in the cage. A special cuttle bone, said to make strong eggs, was obtained, and after a thorough washing, was wedged in the cage wires.

He kept notes to record the big event and when five eggs appeared, his joy was tempered only by the demand that no one make any disturbance or noise—he had read that if young, first-time parents were frightened, they could abandon the nest. The kitchen became a sanctuary, and we ate our meals in silence. The fact that Bobby no longer sang was forgotten, and Dad assured us that there would be a host of birds all about the house singing when the babies arrived.

To be brief, the babies did arrive and they all survived. Dad was filled with pride and gave them every attention. Finally, when he began discussing where to put the five new cages and how he would know which were females and at what rate they would breed, Mom warned him that his canary-bird ways were excessive. In conversations not heard by me, it came to pass that Dad refused to look at the birds again, that Mom and I cleaned the cages, an ad was put in the paper and, one by one, $10 each for the young, $15 for the mother, and $25 for Bobby, they went to new homes. All except one. One of the babies died, and Dad personally put it in a metal cookie tin, dug the hole and buried it to the left of the back door.

As this bird chapter ended, just at the right time, on December 7, 1928, a telegram came from Winona, Mississippi from Dad's brother, Uncle Alf. It was addressed to me and the message was simple: "Jack! Happy Birthday. Surprise for you in baggage car C&EI train arriving Terre Haute, 7 a.m. December 8."

The birthday present was a 10-week-old male Manchester Terrier. The baggage-car master was Uncle Alf's friend and the little pup had been hand-carried—the train goes through the center of Winona and overnight later, through the center of Terre Haute. We learned it was the runt of a litter of 10 and we, therefore, named him Runt, a name of no dignity, but this was never a burden to him. He grew up to be 10 pounds of constant love. His arrival was announced in the newspaper, much to Vic's irritation. His dog, Sylvie, never made the paper.

If one lists the attributes of a childhood, then a wonderful dog must be there. I could have an equal enthusiasm for a cat; some of my adult years have been made fuller by the special ways of a Siamese. But my childhood story relates to a dog named Runt. He filled the home, all comings and goings were events, no one napped alone, the house was never empty. There was Mom, there was Dad, there was Runt. That was my nuclear family.

Having told of Dad and the canaries, you can assume that he was not likely to turn away from the "genuine Manchester Terrier from Mississippi," his favorite full-flavored description of Runt. Incidentally, the article in the paper had somehow confused Mississippi with Mexico; and, to this day, Vic insists that Runt was a genuine Manchester Terrier from MEXICO.

Dad declared the baby dog's nutrition was critical, and he would personally attend to it. Carefully selected round steak was ground by Dad, stirred by him in a saucepan, a bouillon cube added to "pep up the flavor," brought to a simmer, and then he supervised the blowing to get it cooled before placing it before the dog.

Runt was essentially of that size and breed that makes the best circus performing dog. Now, 60 years later, when Vic and Margie and I speak of him, we speak of his intelligence. We taught him no tricks. He selected manners and conduct fitting the occasion. He enjoyed sitting up. He carefully placed himself on Dad's right at the table, sat up, laid his ears back on his head, and turned his large brown eyes on his fellow Mississippian. Dad was defenseless. With careful precision, he would, with knife and fork, remove a choice piece of meat for Runt and, with sweet, Southern murmuring, give a careful toss to Runt, still sitting up, who daintily caught and chewed it.

Although Runt had no instruction, such as heeling, staying,

etc., he had an enormous vocabulary. We were positive about it. At least, he taught us how to communicate, and his ability to pick up the most minimal suggestion that someone might take him for a walk or a ride or that there might be some ice cream brought home, always brought forth from Dad, the declaration, "That Runt is the smartest man I ever knew."

I have mentioned the sports I enjoyed with Gertie; Dad was a graceful, slender man and on summer evenings he enjoyed putting on a glove and pitching hard ball back and forth with me. He had a fluid, limber way of throwing and could never resist a few moments of "burn out," gradually raising the vigor of each pitch and hooting with pleasure when I complained. I saw him in a swim suit but once, and his body was so white and pink that he looked strange—perhaps why he avoided swimming. He played par golf, played with the same foursome for all those years. He and I played a few times, but his joy came from playing and betting on the game; playing with his son was too tame. This desire to gamble was a deep theme and cards were a part of the weekly social pattern of my parents' life. The stakes were minimal, but the idea of winning stimulated him.

From my birth, this good life continued almost 20 years. Then it ended. There was no growing old and mellow for them and me, growing wiser and putting grandchildren on their knees; there was no completed story.

The three members of this family were born in 1895, 1897, and 1918. Dad was 23 when I was born, Mom 21. The story of our years together would find them 33 and 31, and myself 10 when the Depression began in 1928, and, in 1938, when our home ended, we were 43, 41, and 20.

The location for our family was also constant, Terre Haute, Indiana. Dad joined Eli Lilly when I was 3, and we came to Terre Haute in time for me to enter the first grade at age 7, obviously a little late. We had lived in Mississippi, Louisiana, and Texas until then. One hint of my only-child status is that Mom put off sending me to school as long as possible. When I finally was stood upon the toilet seat and had my hair vigorously parted, snarls combed out, ears doubly checked, Mom was in tears and painfully sobbed about losing her only child. The blow must have been softened a little—elementary school was only one block away; I did come home for lunch, and school was out by 3:15 p.m. But even then, she usually came by for the morning recess, chatted with the teachers, and made sure I wasn't hungry.

The next 12 years were a steady sequence of going through the school grades, one through 12, essentially with the same classmates, and with all of the regularity that makes those school days seem to have been eternal—so much longer than 12 years. The pattern of summer vacation, back to school, marbles, tops, kites, baseball, swimming, each at its time, and the normal cycles of school pageants at Thanksgiving, the Christmas carols, the Easter season, Halloween, fireworks on the Fourth. Church and State may have been separate, but we certainly had a thorough indoctrination in the Christian calendar. The only evidence that there was another world was the odd absence of Jewish classmates at some strange Christmas and New Year time they observed.

We all moved forward in school together, no one got "double promoted" after the second grade, and only a few were held back a year. We learned to spell by sheer hard drill, and learned math the same way; except, I must admit, something slipped up in the sixth grade and I never did learn how to do a square root.

Strange as it seems, given this childhood in the midst of basketball country, I never have played a game of basketball and cannot remember even taking part in the constant action of "just shooting baskets." It was a sport that had no appeal for me, either to play or to watch. Vic was outstanding in basketball. This still did not motivate me.

There were some variables but they seemed so much a part of life that it never occurred to me that they were an exception. Some restlessness kept my parents stimulated into moving. Even though we remained in Terre Haute the entire time, we packed, a moving van came, and we changed addresses 13 times during those Terre Haute years. The security of a loving home is such a buffer that it never in the least occurred to me that this was disruptive; the important issues of parents and classmates were not altered. Repeatedly, we went to Mississippi or to St. Louis to see family: long, exciting auto trips, complete with Runt. Was that whole time just 12 years?

But, there are small remembrances that now tell me they were important warnings. We got fully packed for a vacation in the South, into the car and started to leave the curb, when, suddenly, Dad refused to go on; and with silence and hushing motions from Mom, we unpacked and the excitement of the trip was over. Mom never hesitated to talk about such times with me and made it clear that the problem was "temper" and the strange way of Southerners.

When I was 11, Dad became convinced he had serious heart disease. He treated himself and sought advice from all of his doctor friends. Finally, he was put to bed for two months. He began a reading burst that had Mom going to the lending library for five new books twice a week. One of his best friends, a doctor, was convinced that Dad was simply neurotic, and, with heavy-handed therapy, had a hearse come to the house and ask for the body—Dad's. Finally, Mom got the invalid on the train, and they went to the Mayo Clinic and saw the great Dr. Arlie Barnes. I stayed home, took care of Runt, and fed the fish. After 10 days at the Clinic as a bed patient, Barnes very skillfully convinced Dad that he was well, that his problem was extra systoles, and that he was a very healthy man. Dad never mentioned his heart again, but there were always other little frettings about his health. He found only a few foods he "tolerated," and perhaps Mom's inability as a cook was just the result of serving meat loaf and Jell-O several nights a week.

In addition to golf, Gertie had a collection of "girlfriends" who began each day by getting on the telephone and each phone call would begin with, "What's new?" These calls were made daily to three or four friends, all who lived in the same town and did the same things. "What's new?" could not have amounted to much. Yet, this routine used an hour or two, which included the morning Coke and a cigarette, and was done immediately after calling in the grocery order. One or two afternoons a week these same ladies played bridge, rotating from home to home, and one night a week their husbands joined to play hearts or poker. The Lammers, the Fitches, and my folks played cards on Friday nights for the full span of these years.

Other than the card-playing evening and going out to dinner on

Sunday, we were at home, listening to the radio, doing jigsaw puzzles, playing games, and reading. From age 10 or 11, I found pleasure in reading the national columnists carried by our local paper, and O.O. MacIntyre and Arthur Brisbane convinced me there was a larger world out there waiting to be explored. I remember one column of MacIntyre's (his given name, Odd, was also a hint of something exotic), in which he stated that he remembered when he wore ready-made shirts. The idea of tailor-made shirts was fascinating and sinful to me. Forty years later when I had shirts made in Hong Kong, I still felt guilty. Westbrook Pegler was enjoyed by Dad, but I felt he wrote with such a bias that I instinctively disliked him. The name, Westbrook Pegler, seemed so improbable to me that I wasn't quite sure if it was a man or a place.

Other reading, sustained reading, included the *National Geographic* magazine, which was originally subscribed for me when I was born (one 1918 issue has survived and is in my collection), and it gave a fertile source of world view when I was young. I could spend happy hours with the *Geographic* maps, and this stimulated Mom into finding a bedspread and wallpaper with a world map design for my room. I was immersed in the world, literally.

Because of Dad's work, the *Journal of the American Medical Association* was always in the house, and, far beyond me though it was, it carried me into a medical world, a medical vocabulary, and the weekly editorials by Morris Fishbein were not about medicine but the social scene and travels of Fishbein himself. They were good reading and had a sustaining interest for me.

Before I was 12 I did what most American boys did, I polished off the entire Horatio Alger series. On and on they went, always with the same sequence of awful trials and nineteenth-century English cruelty and always with a complete, splendid final triumph by the young hero. Penrod and Sam, and the Tom Swift series went into my reading hopper, too. It is painful to admit that I did not really enjoy Tom Sawyer. He and Huck and their adventures on the river were just a little too melodramatic for my pleasure.

Music, any kind of music, was not a part of my parents' interest and although popular songs were enjoyed from the radio, there was no introduction to classical music, to opera, to chamber music. These were not within the range of our family's education, background, interest, and I am sure, talent. For six long years I took piano lessons, wearing out one teacher after another, and never gaining the ability even to entertain myself. When I was about 12, the then teacher, Mr. Fidlar, arranged a recital by his students before an audience of parents. It was fitting that I was assigned to perform "Plantation Melody." This single simple presentation was my trusted moment. The other 10 students rendered three complex classicals each as the program droned on. Mom's single comment when it was over was, "I certainly enjoyed the shortness of your piece."

My lack of piano talent was sharpened into pain and jealousy when two friends, Bob Rhodes and Woody Suttle, with minimal lessons, proved able to play any popular tune upon hearing it once. With a rollicking flourish, they could make the piano jump and sparkle.

Mom and Dad certainly considered themselves to be the epitome of loyal, democratic Americans. Neither of them hesitated to speak harshly about other races and religions, and affirm their concern about what might happen to the country if "they" weren't watched. One school year was disturbed for me because Dad transferred me to another junior high school when he learned "colored" students were being admitted to my original school. My own freedom from prejudice (but who is free from prejudice?) is as much from a personal belief as it was a reaction to my dad's pure bigotry.

Dad's job required him to be out of town each Wednesday night, and I do remember how difficult Mom found it to get up early on Thursday mornings. One teacher, Miss Peterson, finally figured out that my absences from school had a Thursday morning pattern, and, as soon as she awakened, would telephone Mom and remind her to get me to school. Gertie and Miss Peterson were the same age and, during the Flapper era, both were stylish and coached each other on the Charleston. Both took up smoking Raleighs at the same time. Mom was never able to inhale, but enjoyed her cigarette and Coke as she made her morning phone calls. Dad insisted the only reason she smoked was because of the Raleigh coupon, which offered dividends. This was perhaps true.

During Prohibition, Dad kept a bottle of bottled-in-bond Old
Granddad in his top bureau drawer, which he obtained by prescription from physician friends. In a sense, this was honest because he always used it to make hot toddies when he thought he
was getting a cold. He was hypochondriac enough to need frequent replenishment of the prescription. When I was 12 I pulled
the cork out of the bottle, touched it, the cork, to my tongue and
almost jolted to the floor. Whiskey had crossed my lips. I was
reading Indian stories at the time, and I was impressed by the accuracy of the words: fire water. He did have one recipe that required clean snow. In the bottom of a tall glass, he put several tea-
spoons of sugar and extract of mint, then a few ounces of
bourbon. He would give me a nickel to go outside and pack the
glass full with clean snow. He used a glass straw and called it a
Northerner's excuse for a mint julep.

Sports were a big part of life. Not hunting and fishing—except
a single time. The one time Dad's golf foursome persuaded him to
join them on an overnight fishing trip, he came home with a live
six-inch fish and our single bathtub was filled with water at just
the right temperature. The fish lived there for two days until Dad
found time to slip out to a country creek and put it back in nature.
He ordered us not to tell his friends.

He did have a revolver, and this he felt I should know how to
use accurately. The four of us (remember Runt) drove to country
lanes and pot-shot cans at 40 feet.

He also considered boxing, genuine boxing in the Gentleman
Jim style, necessary, and for years would get us both laced up in
regulation gloves with discussions of left jabs, right hooks, and
footwork. It was something he evidently had enjoyed in his
Winona youth; and he was a bit of a dandy as he pranced around,
bouncing on his toes, snapping his gloves together, and chortling
when he caught my guard down, announcing, "Son! You are careless! I could have cold-cocked you! Your chin was wide open!"

When I was 13, a muscular boy a year older than I gave me a
very thorough whipping in a fist fight. Both of my parents were
shaken by this, and I was enrolled in a local boxing gym for serious lessons. This coincided with that wonderful, phenomenal
growth which occurs just as manhood is turned on, and by the

time I was 14, I was six-feet tall and enjoyed going to the South for a series of private lessons from an Asian who was famous, or infamous, as a martial arts specialist. Dad called it "Jooie-Jitsu" and extolled that "a Jooie-Jitsu specialist could kill you with a single blow to the neck!" Whether such exposures should be given to a young boy is debatable, but there was a serenity, a calmness, which came from these exposures that stayed with me.

Each season had its sport, and as we moved into junior high school, Vic and I found ourselves maturing faster than our classmates, and therefore, able to dominate the sports. By high school, we were ready for the teams. Vic won his letter in track, football, and basketball, and I was lettered in track and football. Our close companionship was noted by the sports writers and we were described as our school's Damon and Pythias. Neither of us quite knew what this meant, but we liked it. We both enjoyed the smug feeling of being big men on the high school campus, and it is only in retrospect that I can voice regret that I put so much time and effort into a sport, football, which had no carry-over into adult life. Partly, this was because of the Depression and a lack of organized tennis, swimming, and golf instruction. Mainly, it was because the value system made it important to be on the football team.

I do recall one or two teachers with affection, but recall more who were simply inadequate. In primary school, I worked hard enough to be placed in the rather elite Section One (as was Vic) when we moved to the seventh grade, to Sarah Scott Junior High School, a circumstance which today would call forth a demonstration and protest against elitism. In junior high school I made grades adequate to remain in Section One and do remember some exceptionally able teachers. Section One also meant six years of Latin.

One of the junior high school teachers, Edith Silverstein, was definitely different and an alive, real woman. She brought a breath of interest even into Latin; and I remember her as someone fresh; even in teaching a language of the past, she was very much of the present. She and Gertie became good friends. I also remember Miss Brown, who enjoyed power and authority as the seventh-grade homeroom teacher for our Section One. We were not allowed to forget we were an elite, and she made it clear that we were expected to be exceptional. This was probably good for us, but Miss Essie Brown also divided Section One into those who were her favorites and those who were questionable. I was in the latter group; she never quite saw my merits. I never made her inner team. I may be telling myself something now that I did not know then, but I was more aware of her as someone to avoid rather than someone who could further your future. But, I also remember the quite special fact that she had a gentleman friend who, in his Cadillac, came each day at 3:10 p.m., parked just below her classroom, awaiting 3:15 p.m., and drove her away. He was Mr. Katzenbach, manager of the local Grand Theater; and, seventh grade or not, Vic and I knew we were seeing something quite fancy.

Also, the teacher in the classroom next door, Miss Georgia Brewster, who taught us English and literature, did not see my unique ability and made life miserable by accusing me of plagiarizing a poem. She had immersed us in the cadence of "Over the hills of Habersham—down the valleys of Hall...," which meant little to me, and then she assigned us the task of writing our own poem. I came out with, "I'm the proud owner of a rattly old bike— never in this world have you seen the like...," and she gave me my first large experience of embarrassment by announcing to the class that I had, by using the same cadence, plagiarized "Over the hills etc...."

Each Friday, everyone returned to their homeroom for the special purpose of hearing the live broadcast from New York City of the symphony orchestra, narrated by Walter Damrosch. His voice was alert, enthusiastic, and, with skill, he reached out across the country with this cultural effort. Deep in Indiana, deep in Terre Haute, deep in Sarah Scott Junior High School, his voice became a powerful anesthetic. Few could stay awake. Whispering and note exchangings were forbidden, and this made the program even more sleep producing.

In my recitation of the good things about the good years, I omitted one other circumstance that gave an emotional closeness: I was born on my mother's birthday. This happenstance equated my arrival with the thought of a living birthday gift, and was made especially significant because, just 13 months earlier, a son was born to them and died at one day of age. Our shared birthday was a large event in our small family, and from my youthful, selfish view, caused a superb harvest of gifts.

On my 20th birthday, when she knew her time was limited, my mother had her wedding ring made into a man's black onyx and jewel ring. This stone had been one of a pair of earrings from Dad's mother. I wore the ring, the only ring I ever had, until I lost it in the sea off Scripps pier, La Jolla, scuba diving, in 1962.

All through those years we exchanged birthday cards, and when I first had odd jobs and made some money, very small money, I tried to buy her a gift, of some elegance, by my standards. One Christmas, when I was 10, I was employed by a local store to sit in the display window and run the electric train, keep the wind-up toys going and wave at friends. This was both a horror of a job and a joy. Every toy in the place was at my disposal and I was paid to have fun. But the sense of exposure, of being on stage, of feeling almost naked, was not a happy one. Vic, of course, made it worse by standing outside the window making faces, and trying, in any and every way, to goad me. My pay for doing this two Saturdays after Thanksgiving was $2. I was paid in cash and walked through the store looking for the right present for Gertie. I settled on what my taste told me was a thing of beauty. It was a bright-red, glass-hinged container, shaped like an egg. The red outside was decorated in silver and gold sparkles. When you opened it, it contained six small shot glasses and a tiny decanter. It cost exactly $2. It was awful looking. Mom gave a tremendous display when she opened the package and tried her best to explain how she needed it.

The next day we went back to the store and exchanged it for a lamp.

Another time I was on stage was the local competition for the yo-yo championship. I won. I did 20 tricks in two minutes, at least it said so in the paper. I could have done more, and had a grand finale trick involving leaping in the air and throwing the yo-yo through my legs. But I was ruined by the new, unusually full knickers Mom made me put on for the evening. My splendid leap-and-leg trick was ruined, the pants were so baggy that there was no space for yo-yoing. But I still won.

Another remembrance of showing off was the Halloween for
which Vic and I did Martin Johnson and Darkest Africa. We won
first prize at elementary school. We then entered the citywide parade. I wore a khaki outfit and cork hat, but Vic was quite spectacular in a gorilla suit that his mother had made from some kind of
very shaggy velour material. The outfit included a full face and
head. My rather mild role was to walk down Wabash Avenue in
the midst of the big parade, snapping my whip, with a metal chain
around my gorilla's neck. We started out well: Vic was superb as
he leaped at the spectators, roaring as he assumed a gorilla would
roar.

For the first block, he was a splendid wild animal and enjoyed
himself immensely. By the second block, problems began. First,
he realized that no one knew who the gorilla was, whereas I was
readily recognized and getting complimented. Second, it became
intensely hot inside the heavy suit. Vic advised me he could not
breathe, and finally, that he could not go on. At that point, the
beauty of my role began to dawn on me. With the chain around
his neck, and the whip in my hand and a rebelling gorilla, I responded to the new opportunity with vigor and jerked my gorilla
along by his neck, snapping my whip at his rump. Vic began
jumping up and down in a very realistic gorilla-like manner. The
crowd loved it, and I thought we were certainly going to win the
competition. However, before we could get to the judges' stand,
Vic kicked me a very hard human kick, jerked his head off and
beat me with it. We left the parade, Martin Johnson pursued by
his wild gorilla.

No report on an American boyhood is complete unless one reports his success as a Boy Scout. Becoming a Boy Scout was an
exciting time for me. I looked forward to it and was an enthusiastic Tenderfoot. I read the Boy Scout Manual thoroughly and repeatedly. I memorized the Boy Scout code and on any occasion,
including this moment, could rattle off the fact that a Boy Scout is
trustworthy, loyal, helpful, friendly, courteous, kind, etc. Vic and I
mastered the semaphore code, and one year, at the big Scout
Jamboree in Terre Haute, he and I were put up on two towers at
opposite ends of the field house and charged with transmitting
messages to each other with our flags, by semaphore. His first

message to me was S-A-P, Sap! I promptly sent back to him N-U-T, Nut!, and from then on we were off on a series of insults which would have amazed the audience. Also, we were laughing so hard and enjoying showing off waving the flags that about 90 percent of our waving had no relationship to semaphore.

To move forward in the Scouts, you earn merit badges; this was my downfall. For one of the merit badges, Mom bought me one of the kits for starting a fire without a match. It consisted of a bow that wrapped about an arrow, and by stroking the bow rapidly back and forth you generated friction at the arrow tip, the friction ignited wood shavings, and with careful blowing, you had a fire and thus could go into the deepest woods and survive. I put long and serious effort into this plan and even caused smoke but never, remotely, a fire. To summarize my Scout status, I reached the humble level of "Second Class" and there my enthusiasm (and ability) stopped. I still think I would have enjoyed the Boy Scouts and did have a two-week summer camp the year I was 12. But for the record, I am a Second Class Boy Scout, a fact that I have not quite spelled out in my curriculum vitae.

I ended my career as president of the woman-hater's club and life became a mix of sports and dating. Books, homework, and grades all became distinctly a secondary reason for being alive. Try as I may, I cannot remember a single evening of doing homework. In high school, however, I can remember hundreds of evenings dating. Perhaps the teachers in high school were able and the flaw was my lack of attention. Or, perhaps, I was devoting my energies to the special study of girls. Either cause, high school was a time of girls and sports. I ran the 220 and was co-captain with Vic of the track team. I still feel a glow in the remembrance of the joy of running full out on the final curve in the 220—lightness almost like flying with power of legs and long stride, and sometimes winning.

In our senior year, a new level of experience came to our football practice. Wiley had a single coach, and offense, defense, punting, passing, blocking and all positions were coached by this burdened man. One day a new person appeared, John Eckhoff, a huge man, or at least his 240 pounds seemed huge to us, who had just finished playing college ball at Purdue. He volunteered his help to teach us more about tackling and blocking. He promptly made it clear that he considered football a violent, physical sport and that aggressiveness was the basic ingredient. He offered a phrase "You've got to play pants-cracking football." That phrase was related to football, obviously, but so many times later in life, I found the intent was just as applicable to many tasks one takes on.

As I became an obviously able-bodied young man, my dad's thoughts turned to why I could not work for money on weekends and during vacations. For several weeks I had a manual labor job at the large Ann Page factory that made jellies, peanut butter, and other foods for a large national company. The initial assignment was to unload boxcars of burlap sacks of granular sugar. The sacks weighed 200 pounds each; and, with a man on each end, it was no simple task to move even one sack, much less keeping it up for an eight-hour day. There is little doubt the foreman used this project as a small testing ground and a bit of stress for the summer help. With the Wabash Valley humidity and heat of a July day, and with the escaped sugar gradually coating you with a syrup of sugar and sweat, one quickly discovered the limit to what you previously considered a good physique. The first week, the actual grip in the hands was the first thing to go. After an hour, grasping the ears of the bag and jerking, simply pulled your exhausted hands free. As you and your equally destroyed young partner fought through the day to get some results, beside you, working smoothly, effortlessly, were the permanent roustabouts who took pleasure in walking slowly by your crumpled forms sprawled on the bags, one man carrying one 200-pound bag—and singing.

A full summer of this did little for my intellect but I developed a tremendous handshake. My next job was no physical effort but it was also essentially without pay. The thought was that I was getting experience. A friend of Dad's, with the considerable name of George Emery Sylvester Wilson, hired me to clerk in his new drugstore. The store's prosperity is indicated by the fact that on any day during which we were able to put $50 in the cash register, we each had a free fountain Coke—and those days were rare. I clerked in the store, ran the soda fountain, and, with my bike, made deliveries. It seems impossible, and the reader will believe I am trying to expand how awful it was in the old days, but for an eight-hour shift I received all the milkshakes I wanted, and 25 cents in cash. In these same summers, Vic had a quite desirable job assisting on a Coca-Cola delivery truck. All of us were jealous of this high-level work.

Terre Haute's population in that decade was 52,810. Don't ask me why I remember that. The little town was good to me; and, although I well understand its limitations (I am speaking of more than 50 years ago), I am grateful for the steadiness of daily life and the value of growing up among the same classmates who make up your whole society over a period of years. We were a heterogeneous group, mainly Anglo-Saxon, but with an influential, stimulating group of Jewish students, some classmates who were Syrian and, in high school, "colored" students, as they were identified. We began together in the first grade, an infusion of other students came as we moved into junior high school, and still another infusion as we moved into the tenth grade. The pace of the additions was just right, and stimulated and added a zest to the mixture. Now, from a long distance and looking back, the education that counted was that gained from the classmates and not from the books.

The town was divided into the north side of Garfield High School and a south-side school, our school, Wiley. This gave a useful we-they sense of competition, mimicking much of life. The main intersection was Seventh and Wabash, and these streets were also U.S. 41, the main national north-south highway, and U.S. 40, the great American highway connecting the East and West. Many times I stood at that corner and dreamed of following both highways to the end. My desire to see the world began right there. Reading license plates from distant areas destroyed my ability to be happy in Terre Haute.

We graduated from high school and Vic was predicted in the yearbook as a future lawyer and myself a physician. We both did as predicted but my route was suddenly in jeopardy.

The year I graduated, Dad was placed on probation by Lilly because of drinking and gambling. He had always enjoyed gambling, but from my junior year on, he was truly compulsive. He was in a horse bookie place every day and up to Chicago to the

race track, Arlington Park, weekends. Money was pouring out
and debts moved in. In a major effort to shake him into better behavior, Gertie went away the whole summer of my junior year.
She spent the summer with her aunt in Albuquerque, and I feel
sure would have sent for me and remained there if there had
been sufficient money. She came home in the fall and nothing was
improved. My senior year was a combination of happiness in all
the things that make a high school life happy, and an increasing
disaster at home. As families do, Mom and I held this to ourselves
and the face we gave the world was the same happy, cozy-family
face our friends expected from us. My closest friends heard none
of the real problems. Dating and teams and clothes and peer
world were the real values; what was happening at home was too
real to be reality. To gambling and drinking were added absences
from home, phone calls from taverns asking us to remove him.
Drinking, even a little, made him belligerent; and, on one occasion, he was arrested. I remember Mom's hurt and disgust when
we went down to the jail to get him. There were no AA programs
in those days and no concepts of rehabilitation care. Lilly gave
him every thoughtful latitude and finally gave him the warning of
probation.

I graduated in June 1937 with no exact plan for how I was going
to do it, but with every expectation of beginning premed that fall.
In July, Dad paused at breakfast one day and told me that I would
have to postpone going to college because he just had too many
debts. I can't look back now and remember exactly what was my
response. I do remember some crying by Gertie, but she had
been bursting into tears often in the last two years. It would be
unfair to leave an image of a boo-hooing, depressed woman. Mom
was, day by day, positive, cheerful, and steady. We continued to
live together in our comfortable apartment and, still, I told none
of my friends about my troubles.

Chapter Two

AGE 18, THEREFORE, WAS A turn in the road for me. The family began to splinter. Even the support system stopped: Runt died that year. Vic left for college. Margie and I parted, and it was 45 years before we again chatted.

Vic did go away to college, but I got a job working in a factory, driving a truck, and discovered that a strong high school athlete was a soft potato compared to men and women who labored away their lives in factories, on production lines, in warehouses, moving boxes, sacks and bales; and in trucks, pounding the highways. Eighteen months of this gave me a small amount of cash, and when I was offered a Purdue football scholarship, I was hard, tough and knew that getting an education was the way to get out of the trap.

I admired the ability of the people I sweated with in that dismal factory, but the grimness of their days and the range of their interests was the largest, lasting lesson from any of my schooling.

My transition from boy to man did not happen entirely at the factory. There is a fine degree of focusing that comes from adversity; for the first time in my life, I was personally the victim. Gertie had been bearing the disaster of Dad's deterioration, and, although I certainly knew and saw what was happening, I continued my happy high school days right up until graduation. The events pouring in on Gertie did not break through to me, break through in their true dimension, until I personally saw that I did not have a means of getting an education, that I was going to sink or swim, and the choice was on me, not Mom, not Dad. The issue became basic, mine, no one else's.

A good friend of my adult years, Bern Dryer, has a way of expressing this issue. His aphorism is, "I have been rich and I have been poor. I have found that, rich or poor, it is best to have money." I put in that eternal truth not to be facetious, nor to be crass.

I went to Purdue University and never returned to Terre Haute.

That first fall brought Gertie's cup of bitter tea to its brim. In October, Gertie and Dad drove up to West Lafayette on a Sunday afternoon to tell me that she was to have breast surgery the next day. It was cancer and it had spread. There followed irradiation and hope and then a recurrence in the other breast. Gertie kept her positive attitude, and, in a letter to me, which I still have, wrote, "Don't you worry about the old boy and his drinking or my trouble. What's important is for you to get your education. Then you and I can get out of this mess and have a new life."

That is not the way it happened. They had to sell everything they had. He lost his job, and the next job, and the next one, each a step down. They ended up in a room in Muncie, Indiana, living from one day's pay to the next. Gertie died when I was in my third year of medical school. Dad drifted on down, with lesser jobs, drifted on down; and for the last 20 years of his life, we did not see each other. He drifted on down, job by job, drink by drink, to Chicago's skid row, dying there. Mom never had the good years.

I did not leave boyhood and become the adult because of the factory. The factory told me that life should be lived for other values. The destruction of my family, first Dad, and then Gertie, clarified for the young man that life is lived alone. Help and love and strength come from others, but in the end it is a solo journey.

When I think of Dad's tragic end, I also think of one of his stories he enjoyed telling, when I was young and all was well. He used it more than once, perhaps to test my reasoning sense or, perhaps, because he enjoyed the rhythm of the final line.

He told it like this: "A man was being guided by the warden through the penitentiary. The warden gave a capsule history of each inmate as they passed the cells. At one cell, he related that the inmate had come from a respected family, was well educated, and drink had been his problem. The visitor stood outside the cell for some moments, he and the inmate staring at each other with no change of expression. As the visitor and the warden moved on down the long corridor, the visitor said, quietly and gently, almost to himself, 'Brothers and sisters have I none, but that man's father is my father's son.'"

The story was told to me for the sake of its intricacy and Dad never used it as a moral lesson. Even today, I pause as I think through to the answer. When he taught it to me, we, of course, did not know our future.

Security stopped, the protection from both parents was gone. Without brothers or sisters, the aloneness was painful.

From birth on, all through those Terre Haute days, my parents, my friends, even my school records, identified me as "Jack." This nickname was easier for everyone than Edmunds Grey Whitehead Dimond, Jr., and I am sure I agreed. The family was saturated with Edmunds Grey's. Dad was called Eddie. A cousin with the same name was called E.G. Still another cousin with the same name was called Grey, while another cousin was Edmunds. Two sisters were given names with the initials E.G.

The Edmunds name had entered the family in the late 1700's when my great-great-grandfather had married an Edmunds from Virginia, and she, Susannah Edmunds, named her second son, Edmunds Grey. The Grey did not come from mustard, Riesling wine nor Earl Grey tea, but from the English statesman.

With the end of the life in Terre Haute and a new life in college, I, at once, without a pause, left "Jack" behind and became Grey for the rest of my days, and to friends who gather close, E. Grey.

Jack matched me well for 18 years; Grey has been just right for the remainder. I carefully placed the name as a marker among my offspring. There are now daughters: Sherri Grey Dimond (Byrer), Lark Grey Dimond (Cates), Lea Grey Dimond (Guettar), and grandchildren, Lawrence Grey Dimond, Kelly Grey Allenbaugh. Surely from all of that seeding there will come another Grey?

There are two problems with my name, neither soluble. The first is that the world is incapable of spelling my family name. There is a universal determination to put an "a" in Dimond. I first became aware of this when I was very young. Mom took me on her shopping trips and I have vivid memories of her directing the salesperson that, "The name is D-I-M-O-N-D. No 'A' please!" Then when the employee blithely put an "a" in the name, Mom's irritation would burst out, "I said, clearly, no 'A'!" Mother had been born Schmidt and the First World War had made this name a burden. Upon marrying, she became devoted to establishing the correctness of her new name.

A lifetime later, I accept failure. Nothing will convince people that there is a non-diamond Dimond.

For most listeners the name is heard as Gray Diamond, obviously the name of some ballad singer or casino entertainer. I am blinded to this interpretation simply because the name has been E-d-m-u-n-d-s G-r-e-y D-i-m-o-n-d for several generations.

Purdue was a two-year chapter. I enrolled in the School of Pharmacy, majored in pharmaceutical chemistry, and began assembling the needed credits for premed. I knew I was in the wrong university for a future medical student, but the scholarship made Purdue possible; and even with 90 percent of my classmates aiming towards careers in engineering, it was a useful two years. However, I understood that such a system: technical college, pharmacy, fraternity, did not fit me. But I also knew it was the only way to get from here to there. Essentially, in those years, all premedical education was done in colleges of liberal arts and a premedical education in a pharmacy school was not a well-regarded pathway for medicine.

But Purdue and pharmaceutical chemistry offered a value which perhaps saved my neck. All through high school, school work had been easy, so easy that there was never a thought of studying, homework, or assignments. Even by loafing, I came through with a B average. When I hit Purdue, or when Purdue hit me, things suddenly became very serious. The work load was an immense shock to my *laissez faire* scholar's approach. Not only was there an immense increase in actual work load, but the added use of time required by the large number of lab courses. Each three hours of real time earned only one hour credit in a lab course, and pharmaceutical chemistry was, indeed, a lab-course education. Almost every course had a lecture in the morning and a three-hour lab course in the afternoon.

On top of this, was the seriousness of college-level football.

Three years of high school football had given me no clue to the requirements of the sport in the Big Ten. Practice required three hours every evening, fall and spring. This was really pants-cracking football. The caliber of the players made it a quantum leap from the pleasant sport we had enjoyed in high school. Purdue, like all other schools, actively recruited from all over the country. I weighed 175 and had left high school quite convinced I was a large, strong man. I had never seen 225-pound men who could run like sprinters. Our high school team had a single coach and he watched over all aspects. At Purdue, there was a host of coaches. I played End; all candidates for that position were given intense scrutiny, guidance, and criticism by our own coach. The physical conditioning was at an entirely new level, and I straggled back to the fraternity house after dark, exhausted, bruised, and sore to face hours of desk work. Without exaggeration, I can say that the two years at Purdue were so stressful, so physically demanding, and such a painful combination of academic load, lack of money, deterioration of Dad from drink and Mother from cancer, the physical requirements of football, and later boxing, that the rest of my life has been relaxing. Medical school was easy in comparison.

Fraternity life at Purdue was probably useful for me. As an only child, I had no experience in the kind of communal living which a larger family might have prepared me for, and, therefore, the dormitory for 50 sleeping men and a large shared toilet, were perhaps an exposure I needed. I am hesitant in this endorsement for I have little evidence that there were any such rewards. Purdue introduced me to the kind of group living one goes through in college. Return to a private, personal dwelling did not come until six years later. I do remember with absolute enthusiasm the superb food at the Sigma Alpha Epsilon house. My Gertie had never been a kitchen enthusiast and the cooks at the SAE House gave me an entirely new concept of good food. My roommates were, over the entire six-year period, Purdue and afterwards, diverse, and interesting. Again, although I cannot specifically identify what they contributed to my development, I suspect each added some new bit of information and required some additional adjustment in my behavior.

This immersion in group dynamics did not make me into a gregarious adult and I came out just about "as in I went:" one inclined to being alone and with no instincts for clubs, mixers, booster groups, foursomes, cards, alumni organizations, etc.

One weekend, my roommate, H.L. Freyn, and I hitchhiked to Chicago. Our reasons were simplistic. We just wanted to "get away." On Sunday afternoon, we began the hitchhike back to the SAE house; we were picked up by a young couple, out for their Sunday ride in their new Packard. Today they would be called yuppies. They were Eve and Ralph Linville. It was a lovely April day and they chose to take us all the way home. As we left them, I picked a bouquet of irises from the fraternity house garden and gave them to her. Later, from my mother's things, I mailed them a stein to express our thanks for the lift; in their car we had talked about a German beer hall H.L. and I had found in Chicago. They, too, knew the place and we had laughed about the large steins used at the hall. The Linvilles will appear again in these pages.

At Purdue, I worked all out and had so little money that I could not get into the happier side of fraternity and sorority life. There were a few memorable, unmentionable moments, but those were not years of wine and roses. I worked hard, and when I played, I played very hard. The void in life which needs a companion, a sympathy, began to be filled by Margo, also a graduate of Wiley, and then a student at DePauw, a good Indiana college.

I boxed as a light heavyweight on the Purdue team and can remember keenly the stage fright of standing up in the center of the field house, in the ring, in essentially my underwear, boxer's shorts, the ring brightly lighted, the field house darkened, and hoping I did not make a fool out of myself. It was the risk of embarrassment that motivated me, not any instinct for boxing. Fortunately, my nose was broken in an early bout and I could give up that sport. We fought only three rounds, three minutes each per match, but the physical demand of boxing was more severe than any sport I attempted.

I had one major exposure in 1939 to what one could call the "arts" of a university education. A series of panels were held, campuswide, not quite in a debate format, but with three or four students before a large audience, taking sides on a subject of general interest. One of these topics was the subject "propaganda," chosen because of the great notoriety of Hitler's "propaganda machine." I took the viewpoint, argued for it, that all societies have propaganda machines, that the concept is not new or wrong, but the cause for which it was used is the critical issue. I found that I had an ability to handle this kind of cerebral argument, and gained a clue about myself which I had previously not known.

I had a full involvement in a social issue at Purdue; the episode was a fairly good sample of what my life would be like, although I certainly did not know it at the time. At Purdue, I developed a friendship with a young man from Indianapolis. He seemed just the kind of personality for our fraternity. He wanted in, and I put his name up for membership. For the first time, I ran into the unwritten rule, unwritten, but therefore stronger than engraved granite: Jews were not admitted to the SAE fraternity. My friend was Jewish.

With not the slightest intent of being a social reformer, but feeling, knowing, that the unwritten code was unfair, I took on the personal campaign of getting him in the fraternity—and did. Now, 50 years later, I have not seen nor heard from the man since I left Purdue, and I have no way to know if I did him a favor. Or, did I expose him to hurt? Then it was important to me to help him achieve his desire—against the system.

When Vic and I were in the ninth grade, we had led a different but somewhat similar campaign about a classroom injustice, and the teacher, loudly and critically, said we were "Bolsheviks." It was true that we were rebelling against the system, and, in her rigid world, she gave us the right name. When we were in our senior year in high school, our chemistry teacher was so obviously hovering on senescence and incompetence that we took on the task of going to the principal and seeking his removal. Again, against the system.

Now, writing all this down and knowing the subsequent career, much of what I have spent energy on was a sequence of discrete issues where I thought change should be, could be, done. Almost the last words my mother said to me were, "Be careful of The Establishment. You will always be outside of it."

As I ended my second year at Purdue, I knew the time had

come to transfer into a liberal arts college. A regret of those years was the total absence of any mature counsel. I began a pattern which has stayed inherent within me: holding problems and solutions within. For better or for worse, and certainly now too late to have any rectification, my pattern, my style of life, has been one of keeping problems, worries, and even successes, held close to my chest. This, of course, is contrary to advice enthusiastically poured out by psychiatrists who have encouraged the "let-it-all-hang-out" era. My own belief has been, and is, that it is better to shut up, analyze, weigh, and decide inside, alone. Laundry washing is different than serious life.

In the 1930's and early 1940's medical schools required three years of premedical education, a total of 90 credit hours. I had graduated from high school in 1937, missed the school year of 1938, and was in Purdue in 1939 and 1940. Those were nervous, ominous years. Germany marching; France falling; England beleaguered, and China trying to survive Japan's invasion. The world was at war; and, although our country was not directly involved, every young man my age knew that our days as college boys were at risk. All of us had friends who had joined the Canadian Air Force or who were ferrying planes to England. It was an exciting time, and a very personal time, for all of us who were prime prospects for the military. I calculated there was a window open for me to get into medical school, and it could close the moment this country went to war. Then my chance at a medical education would be delayed by years and perhaps lost.

Chapter Three

As soon as school was out in the spring of 1939, I moved to the YMCA in Indianapolis, a useful, dismal place, and got a job washing windows, mopping floors, and emptying waste baskets at Eli Lilly's main factory. I am sure the good years of Dad's employment helped me get the job and it made just the margin of difference. Factory conditions were high quality, and the employees a happy group, but, again, as it had been in the year I had not gone to college, it was clear to me that the factory was not where I wanted to end up. I saved every penny and was able to work there during the breaks in the summer, spring, and at Christmas vacation. My frugality was impressive. I ate my meals at the plant, had no car, and moved out of the Y and into Blackwell's Funeral Home, where I shared nighttime call, in return for a free room, with a group of medical students. When the fall of 1940 came, I was enrolled at Indiana University in Bloomington. I moved in with a group of premed and freshman medical students and began acquiring the culture of medical student and medicine, something missing at Purdue.

I carried 18 hours of credit courses, all lecture courses, no lab, no football, no fraternity, and it was a breeze. Indiana University and liberal arts were so much easier that I almost felt dishonest. For the 18 hours, I had 15 hours of A and three hours of B. I was short a foreign-language requirement, and I took first- and second-semester French at the same time, alternately reading the front and back half of the textbook. This foreign-language requirement was never of any remote usefulness to me in any phase of my career.

It is painful to say that much of the premedical requirement was, in reality, an impediment to an education. This conviction never left me, and was one of the pieces of life that I was responding to when, later on, I was able to fashion another way of educating physicians.

In October of that year, Margo and I were married; in our youthful enthusiasm, we somehow thought this would be a strength and give us both a support mechanism. Eleven months later a daughter was born, and any probability of emotionally strengthening each other was lost forever. We were divorced when the baby was six months old, and Margo remarried a month later.

A fair question is to ask: "Why this marriage?" If one ever becomes objective about subjective actions, it surely can be accomplished with the passage of 50 years. My analysis, 50 years later, is to remind myself of my degree of aloneness. The family home was gone, my parents fragmented, there was no brother, sister, cousin, grandparent. My explanation of the marriage would be that I was trying to create a lost security. It was a premature, desperate, wish.

When the year ended and interviews for medical school were done, I was judged short nine hours for premedical requirements. Many of my Purdue pharmacy courses were denied as inappropriate for medicine, an interesting thought. The dean of the medical school, a tyrant of some fame, told me somberly that I just did not have the required courses of embryology and comparative anatomy. I extracted a pledge from him that he would reconsider me at the end of the summer, just four weeks before medical school began, providing I took embryology and comparative anatomy and did "well." He meant all A's, of course.

I had never been to summer school, and that was an education. The campus becomes a mixture of play and heat. The quarries around Bloomington, Indiana are famous swimming holes; and there is, or was, a cool, shaded bar downtown made famous by Hoagy Carmichael and his song, "Stardust."

I never got in the water or the bar. It was a busy summer, with both courses requiring lengthy lab sessions. I also tutored a premed friend from high school days, Stan Hoffman. As soon as the summer session ended, I was back at the Dean's door with my A's and the Caesar went down my credits, one by one, and suddenly snorted with pleasure. He could not find any credits for the required course in biology! He was hanging me and he was delighted. I was sunk and equally angry. Biology was a requirement for taking the two courses I had just finished in summer school, both with an A. To me, it seemed reasonable to assume he had permitted me to take these courses with the intent of waiving the biology requirement, and I had proved adequately that I had enough Biology knowledge when I had sailed through the more advanced courses. But I was trying to be logical and the Dean was not.

This experience also never left me and was prime stimulus to what I did when, later on, I formed a new medical school. I could have enthusiastically throttled the Dean. I thought of Dad, the carafe, and military school with more sympathy.

Then I remembered something which I had totally forgotten. The year after high school, when I had worked at the factory, I had made a desperate stab at beginning college in Terre Haute by enrolling at Indiana State Teachers College. I had signed up for nine hours but had to drop six hours because I needed to work. However, one of the courses was at 7:30 a.m.; I had seen it through for one semester, and dropped out of school completely the next semester. The one course was biology; I had made a C. I had never put it on my transcript; I had not even been sure that a C from a teachers college would be well accepted on a medical school application. I asked the Dean if a credit from Indiana State was acceptable and he huffed his way into a "Yes." I hitchhiked to Terre Haute, got a certified transcript verifying this three-hour C credit in biology, and was in his office the next day.

When medical school classes began September 1, 1941, I was there. A classmate from high school, Pat Duffy, and I roomed together; and we were at our desks on Sunday morning, December 7, 1941, studying anatomy, when the announcement of Pearl Harbor came in over our radio. I had made it through the window into medical school by a very slender margin.

Pat and I were well matched; he was a solid scholar and a good influence on me. We had a small apartment in a retired couple's home. Their niece, a university student, also roomed there.

Two remembrances remain, among others. One was the evening banking of the furnace by Mr. Cox, our landlord. He used this time (we finally made the diagnosis) as a moment to relieve himself directly into the furnace. The heating was by coal and hot air. From the moment of his descent into the basement until the ammoniacal whiff came up through the register, became a period in which Pat and I stopped all study and took bets on how many seconds would pass before the pungent signal reached our room.

The niece's name was Margaret, and as people do with medical students, she turned to us one evening when she had a headache. As freshman medical students, we were altered by our status, and a devilishness came out. We supplied her with two methylene blue tablets, assuring her this was a valuable headache remedy. Our study room was next to the shared bathroom. We sat poised long into the evening waiting for the moment she discovered her urine was vivid blue. Medical students are different. These two uriniferous stories from almost 50 years ago are evidence.

The freshman year of medical school was hard and from 120 of us who began, there were less than 100 who finished. I had the money I had saved from working at Lilly's. Mom sent me $10 a week and, again because of the good days when Dad was whole, a physician in Terre Haute was willing to sign a bank note for $300. I lived a spartan, frugal life; and, if I had a date that year, I cannot remember it. My days as an athlete were ended and, as the saying goes, my attention was focused. I did nothing but study, figure out how to buy a meal, and get enough ahead for rent, tuition, and books. I cut corners on textbooks as I could, and probably handicapped myself in the laboratory courses by buying a $10, over-aged microscope. For the first time in my life, I saw most clearly the difference between the haves and the have-nots. I had no car; my clothes were the ones I had; there were no beer busts, and my eating was skimpy. Of course, the whole country was having a stringent time as the war effort closed in.

I had left Purdue weighing almost 180 and enjoying various large muscles. I ended the first year of medical school about 20th in the class, weighing 165, a pale, amuscular remnant. Thinking about it through the years, I realize that the main gain from the first year of medicine is the acquisition of the language of

medicine, surely as much a foreign language as any. Much of
what we were put through was a form of scholastic hazing, of
overloading, of testing our willingness to carry out unending
tasks of memorization. I well remember some classmates who
would have made superb physicians but who could not tolerate
the process of getting there.

I think every member of my class will remember our sense of
excitement when Dr. Khalil Wakim gave our lectures in cardiovascular physiology. The otherwise dreary, lecture-intensive year was
lifted by his spirit and enthusiasm. Of course, we all went through
the required initiation rites of the tedious, macabre, strangely ir-
relevant dissection of the formaldehyde-soaked cadaver.

The war was on full blast and the faculty began to be drafted.
This did not affect the freshman-year faculty because most of
them were senior and not physicians. Our second year, we moved
to the medical school main campus in Indianapolis; here, the decimation of the physician faculty was apparent. Initially, I shared an
apartment with three classmates, Dick Davis, Bob Witham and
Glenn Irwin. About this time, or shortly thereafter, Pat married.

The hospitals were shorthanded and this proved to be a bonanza for me. I got a job at the University Medical Center with the responsibility for keeping oxygen tanks at the bedside. This was before the day of oxygen piped in to the bedside. My job began at 5
p.m. and continued until 7 a.m. The pay was $50 a month, but the
real reward came from a free room, free meals, free laundry service, and, because I did not have a car, the chance to actually live
on campus was a godsend. I was on call every night, and, once or
twice each night, was called by a nurse to bring a fresh tank of
oxygen to a bedside. Indiana University Medical Center was a
large place with many buildings and wards. I became expert and
proud of my ability to lean a tank on edge and roll it down the corridor with one hand. One might say I became a dashing wizard of
distributing oxygen and eyeing the student nurses.

My luck continued, and I was able to take on the additional job
of running the cashier's desk from 5 to 7 p.m. This paid an additional $50 a month. Things were definitely improving. And then
the break of breaks occurred. A notice appeared on the elevators
that the medical center's cardiologist needed someone to read

medical journals to him for two hours an evening, two evenings a week, and the pay would be $200 a month. I hurried over to the medical school registrar, Gracie Blankenship, and asked for details. I learned that the full-time cardiologist of the medical center had an eye condition, uveitis and retinitis, and had lost his central vision. Central vision is critical for reading, not only for reading journals, but for reading electrocardiograms. The cardiologist was Dr. Harry Baum, a likable, wonderfully homely man in his 40's who was well-liked, respected, and because of his eye problem, had developed his ability to use the stethoscope to a widely admired level. He was not married. He lived in the hospital and a recent exacerbation of his disease had resulted in this job offer. He was especially valuable to the medical center now that war was on and the staff was being drafted. With his eye problem, he was beyond the draft. I got this job and, essentially, a career.

Another large variable had entered the life of medical students. With the declaration of war, the government began drafting manpower, but at the same time acted to protect those who were in training in critical fields. All medical students were put in the Army as privates, in uniform, while completing their medical education. A similar program was offered by the Navy. Part of the motivation was to protect us from the draft, but, also, by putting us in uniform, it was felt we would be protected from public criticism as slackers. Of course, it also gave the Army a sure way to control our services.

This program, the ASTP, Army Specialized Training Program, was also designed to hurry up our education. All vacations were stopped, and we went from one school year to the next with no break. This was called the 9-9-9-9 plan, a nine-month period for each school year. We were inducted at Fort Harrison, Indiana, given our private uniforms, and every morning we lined up by platoons in front of the medical school, counted off, had roll call, and resented the presence of a somewhat scrawny sergeant and a commanding officer who seemed suspiciously like an alcoholic. We were ordered to police the grounds and pick up cigarette butts; we were marched about the large campus, somewhat enjoying the march as we passed by the student nurses. In fact, these two student groups became the basis of each other's social lives.

We were fairly well confined to the medical campus by our school rotations and the war, and the nurses, even more so, because they lived under strict scrutiny in their residence hall. Propinquity brought about logical results and doctors married nurses.

The 9-9-9-9 calendar for an academic year proved to be no burden; and, here again, I made a note about the value of intensifying the education pace when one is dealing with a profession such as medicine, where intensity, discipline, persistence, and dedication are basic ingredients of the way of life for which you are preparing. Thirty years later, such a calendar was a part of the medical school in Kansas City.

The ASTP program paid us a monthly stipend, and this, plus my jobs and reading for the near-blind cardiologist, eased all financial burdens. By the end of my senior year, I had to ask myself when ever again would I be so prosperous: free room, free laundry, free food, free uniform, free tuition, and about $600 a month income. Graduation was a financial blow.

The job as a reader proved to be superb. Even more than a job, it made clear that my career should be, must be, in cardiology. By my junior year, I could read electrocardiograms of any complexity. My awareness of what is the medical literature, how to access it, how to analyze an article and to know what journals are of quality was a lifelong fringe benefit. The cardiologist took me to see each of his consultations; and, with his constant instruction, I mastered the use of the stethoscope. Because of his vision deficit, he could not use an ophthalmoscope. I sought out a close friend who was in training in ophthalmology and gained thorough instruction, and, thereafter, always enjoyed using this lovely piece of equipment.

I went to Harry Baum's quarters each Tuesday and Thursday, 7:30 to 9:30 p.m. He sat in a comfortable lounge chair, feet up on a hassock. There was no light by his chair, and, even in this shadowed area, he kept his dark glasses on. I sat on his left, facing him in a straight, upright chair. I found my ability to read clearly and to control breathing was helped by sitting severely upright. I had a single bright light, goose-necked down on the reading material. Medical literature was simpler then, at least there was only one heart journal, *The American Heart Journal*. We read it cover to cover, including the advertisements. With the articles, I identified the title, then the authors, their titles, and the place where the work was done. Again, the heart world was simpler; there were only a few distinct centers and each had a single well-known cardiologist. It was a world of small fiefdoms for training and research and each had its tribal chief. As a hopeful young cardiologist, you would try to get into the inner circle of one of these fiefdoms, spend time there, and the rest of your days you were identified as a Wilson man, a Levine man, a Roy Scott man, etc. In 1941, these well-known chiefs and places were (I will forget some) Sam Levine at the Brigham, Paul White at the MGH, Harold Feil at the Cleveland Clinic, Roy Scott at Cleveland General, Johnson McGuire at Cincinnati, Frank Wilson at Ann Arbor, Louis Katz at Michael Reese, Helen Taussig at the Hopkins, George Herrmann at Galveston, Arlie Barnes at Mayo, William Kerr at San Francisco, Charles Wolferth at Penn, and, of course, a few others. My main point is that there were not many, and what are now very famous heart centers just had not come into existence. Dr. Baum commented about the absence of a really great center even in New York City, and much of the country was a Sahara in cardiology.

In addition to the *American Heart Journal*, we read the *Annals of Internal Medicine*, the *Archives of Internal Medicine*, and *JAMA*. The only foreign journal, and it was not a monthly then, as I remember (perhaps because of war) was the *British Heart Journal*. From all of this, I learned who was where, what Dr. Baum knew about the authors and institutions; and, because the reading was serious and could be tedious, I learned how to change voice, inflection, cadence, and how to, in essence, teach.

Illustrations and electrocardiograms I described verbally. Each wave on the electrocardiogram was described: "The P wave is smooth, upright, one and a half millimeters tall and 0.1 seconds long, the PR interval is 0.24 seconds...," and at that point Dr. Baum would interrupt and say, "That is prolonged, the normal PR interval cannot be more than 0.20 seconds," and we continued in this manner for the full two hours. Neither of us had a Coke or beer, and, when the two hours ended, my voice was tired and my back kinked.

Dr. Baum's use of his senses: hearing, palpation, and percussion was impressive; under this apprenticeship, one teacher and one student, I acquired an ability and a satisfaction in the art of physical examination of the human body which, through my years of practice, gave me more pleasure than any other phase of medicine. To step to the bedside and, with your fingers, eyes, and ears, analyze the state of health or disease became the skill in which I took my greatest pride.

I came to the medical center in 1942, and six months later came under the aegis of this cardiologist. For the rest of the sophomore year, all of the junior and senior year, and through 18 months of house officer training, I was essentially privately tutored in cardiology.

Medical school education in those years had no clinical experience. Almost all of the instruction was in the lecture hall, lab, or morgue. The only way we saw the living patient was from our seats in a large classroom, and a patient was brought in and examined in front of us by a professor. Some of us were 30 or 40 feet from the patient. For only one month of our senior year was a new event introduced—we were given a month of rotation through the outpatient clinics. While my classmates were having this didactic, sterile experience, I was every evening seeing disease at the bedside, taking histories, reading electrocardiograms and X-rays, and examining the living patient, not the corpse in the morgue. One more conviction came to me—medicine must be learned from the living event. Books, yes. Knowledge, of course. But to understand and learn about the pathos, travail, and complexity of the sick human, the learner must not be far separated from the bedside.

Chapter Four

THE WAR, A LACK OF money, and my parents' problems left such a shadow on all of those college and medical school years that I realize I carry a permanent scar, almost a bitterness, about the use of those years. What would it have been like to have gone to a small, good-quality liberal arts college; to have taken leisurely the full four years of liberal arts education, perhaps with a year in Europe; to have played college football in a smaller arena for fun; to have learned to sail; to play tennis; to ski; to have had a car; to have had spending money; to have gone to medical school when the full faculty was there and the summers were open for travel and new experiences?

Bitter? Yes, but also with time and maturing and substantial exposure to some men who did have those good breaks, I was able to see that full, generous years used that way may just as well lead to a career of no success. Bitter the experience was, hurried all of us were through medical school, shadowed constantly by the war; still, the pace and continuity of it was a real preparation for the life of a physician.

One thing I had to learn by experience, something all of us learn who carry the M.D. degree, is that the practice of medicine is a physical, emotional task, an unremitting demand beyond anyone's expectation. Being a physician is absolutely hard work and for years, decades, of a career, there is little surcease. Medical school needs to prepare one for this, and four years of a gentle collegiate education with long summer vacations are a misplaced preparation.

Is this the rationalization of a pawn of his own experience? Very possibly. No one has two views of life; one can borrow from the experience of others, but the only road that had all the bumps, felt and sensed, is the road you took.

Gertie died in my junior year. They had moved to Muncie, Indiana and it was a bleak nightmare. For the first time, I was sending her money. In June, a telegram came, "Come at once, I need you...Mom." I got an official leave from the military and took the bus to Muncie. Gertie was in Ball Hospital, using nasal oxygen; and, even though I was but a junior student, it was obvious she was very near the end. She had sent for me knowing this, but perhaps even more so, because she was frightened, among all strangers. Dad was a useless, failed support and, as happens when pain closes in, her world had come down to a very personal dimension of caring, caring about one thing: "When is my next shot of morphine?" Gertie was being exposed to that miserable failure of the hospital system, a dying patient whose only release came from morphine, and the attendants reciting the dogma of routine, "I'm sorry, your next shot is not due yet."

Gertie died a week later, and, again with leave, I took her home to Terre Haute. I had Dad in tow, and Mom's brother, Uncle Lark, met us in Terre Haute for the services. I buried her at Roselawn and years later moved her to the family grave in Winona, Mississippi. In her purse was single poem which she had often read to me, "Living and loving and dying / Life is complete in the three." She had completed the trilogy.

Dad stayed sober until that evening, and I took him on the interurban back to the medical center. We parted; he got a job in a drugstore in Indianapolis. A year later when I graduated, he came to commencement, neatly groomed, and sat there tall and straight, a lean, dignified white-haired man, 48 years old. This was but an intermission. He left Indianapolis and went his tragic way.

Internships in wartime were but nine months long and mine was further distorted by my determination to get on with special training in cardiology. I took rotations in internal medicine, pediatrics, and surgery, and skimmed very lightly over obstetrics, not even delivering a baby. I carried on at the same time the role of Resident in cardiology, in both adult and pediatric cardiology. Again, remember how much simpler cardiology was at that time. Hypertension had essentially no treatment; Irvine Page's group was experimenting with intravenous nitroprusside, and a drastic surgical removal of the sympathetic nerves was being tried in a few centers. Coronary disease treatment was a matter of nitroglycerin. If a coronary occlusion occurred, it was six weeks in bed, with absolute bed rest, and the man not even allowed to shave himself. All such patients were doomed to the bedpan during the whole time. Congenital heart disease was divided into blue, or not blue, and it was not important, for there was nothing to be done. The treatment of acute rheumatic fever was salicylate and bed rest, and there was no treatment for the scarred valve of rheumatic fever except the use of a very painful injection of mercury, in an attempt to lessen the dropsy (edema).

With, essentially, a lack of any form of therapy, we became experts at diagnosis, and even though we had nothing to offer in effective treatment, we gave considerable effort to placing exact labels. This label, or diagnosis, could not be confirmed by anything such as echocardiography or angiography, nor by inspection at open heart surgery. The morgue was where the lesson had to be acquired, and a part of every day was to get to the autopsy. The telephone operator would page us, "Dr. Rokitansky, please come to your office," and we all knew this name of a famous, long-deceased European pathologist was our in-house code word for an autopsy.

Skill in handling the patient was a very real ability and Harry Baum was good at this art; however, he did not hesitate to declare the local master in this skill was Dr. Robert Moore. I made arrangements to make rounds with Dr. Moore on Sundays on his private patients at Methodist Hospital, and readily declare him the master of my lifetime in this bedside art. Dr. Moore was in his early 60's at that time and had no real concern with the nuances of the electrocardiogram nor any concern with the most recent literature. He was simply a magnificent physician, magnificent in bringing cheer, optimism, solace, and hope. Many patients came to him who were bedfast because of hypochondriasis, or, equally often, from the burden of a wrong diagnosis or the conservatism of the referring physician. Dr. Moore's ability to bring the patient back to his feet, to convince him that he was again a whole person, to get a pale invalid fully upright and productive—that ability was not only great, but was a vast pleasure to watch as it was applied. Throughout this levitation of the sick, never once did Dr. Moore cast a shadowed fault on the referring physician. He taught the art of the bedside, but, equally, he gave me a lasting lesson in the role you play as a consultant. I learned a great deal of cardiology from superb cardiologists, but the master of the art of medicine was Robert Moore.

When I finished the nine-month internship, I next had a nine-month straight residency in cardiology. By this time, I was carrying the entire electrocardiogram service for the medical center. I was a licensed physician, and with Dr. Baum to guide me with the difficult problems, I had a heavy nine months of full-time cardiology. I enjoyed pediatric cardiology and Dr. Baum, essentially, turned the pediatric consultations over to me. These were, in the main, questions of acute rheumatic fever, and the chairman of pediatrics, Lyman Meiks, tolerated me even though I was obviously unfinished. I became fond of this able man. He had a kind of Tom Mix appearance and was inclined to declare at the slightest chance, "Ah hell, I don't believe that!" and kid and tease closely. Still, he was able, honest, extremely well informed, and I respected him.

Harry Baum had been older when he went to medical school. He had taught earlier at a boys' school, perhaps Deerfield, Wisconsin. He never married, and, never in the years I knew him, had any female contacts. One did not speak of closets and coming out in those years, and none of us felt that he was perhaps a hidden-away gay. Interns and Residents are an observant, alert, even suspicious group and 40 or 50 of us shared the intern quarters; it would have been difficult to have odd trysts for any of us, heterosexual or homosexual. Yet, by the time I ended my training at the medical center, it was obvious to me that Dr. Baum was a very troubled person and barely containing latent odd desires. He carried his visual handicap with courage and even humor, yet there were many days when he was sunk in an emotional pit and almost unable to function. When I left for the Army in September 1946, it was with a sense of relief. I was not totally surprised when, a few years later, he ended his life.

My several years of observing student nurses at the medical center brought results, and in April 1945, Audrey Stone and I began what was to be 22 years of happily married life.

Indianapolis was in the Fifth Military Command, and the regional headquarters, at least as far as the Medical Corps was concerned,

was Dayton, Ohio. In August 1946, I put on my uniform and reported there to the medical officer in charge of my destiny. Specifically,
he had the task of interviewing you, deciding what your level of
medical usefulness was, and then, with an almost imperial wave,
consign you for the next two years to any place he considered appropriate. The military, of course, has always had this almost para-
lyzing power; and, on the day I reported to the headquarters in Dayton with about 20 other Medical Corps first lieutenants, we each
awaited our turn, stressed and numb, knowing we would come back
out of that office no longer in control of our futures.

The war had just ended and every physician on military duty
was pouring back into civilian life. Men who had been gone four
and five years were heading home, and we new military doctors
who had been spared from conflict, were their relief. We recent
graduates were being called in by the hundreds.

The first several of our group came out of the colonel's office,
staggered out, under orders—orders to report for duty in Kiska,
Fiji, Gander, places where the long-suffering physician was being
sprung free as fast as possible. My turn came, and, as I shook
hands with the tall, lean, balding, sandy-haired man, I noted the
wooden name plaque on his desk: Col. Johnson McGuire, M.C. A
considerable light blinked in my head. This was one of the names
from my journal reading experience with Dr. Baum. Could it be
that the famous cardiologist from Cincinnati was now the chief
medical officer of the Fifth Military Command? He immediately
put me on my guard as he scanned my record. "What kind of
training is this? You haven't had even a residency in internal
medicine, and you have already been in training in cardiology?
Explain it! And do you know Robert Moore?" I hurried into a description of Harry Baum's eye problem, and tried to give him an
idea of the amount of cardiology I had been exposed to and why.
He interrupted me and said, "Tell me about the Wolff-Parkinson-
White Syndrome." For the next 10 minutes, he fired eponym
questions at me, especially in electrocardiography.

When he was done, he whistled and said, "I don't know if you
know anything else in medicine but you certainly know cardiology. You don't have enough formal training for me to classify you
as a specialist and you don't even have the right training to be list-

ed as a generalist. I'll declare you as a "cardiologist by experience," whatever that is, and you are assigned as cardiologist to Crile Army General Hospital near Cleveland, Ohio. We'll watch your performance and, as short-handed as we are, you will probably be the only damned man in the Army who can read electrocardiograms. Tell Bob Moore that he is a great physician."

For the next six months, I was the cardiologist at Crile General, and military service could not have been more interesting. Crile General was a huge hospital, loaded with wounded and healing soldiers. I saw an entirely new kind of cardiology, especially heart problems associated with toxins, with infections, and a large number of men brought back from Europe with heart block, due to diphtheria. Of course, I also learned how the Medical Corps functions; and, again, just like studying medicine, it was a matter of learning a new vocabulary.

The head of the medical service was a dark complexioned, hawk-nosed man, with a bristling butch haircut and a carefully waxed moustache. I had never seen a waxed moustache and the sharply twisted, upright ends were impressive. His name was Mahlon Delp, a Kansan who had spent a full five years in the service. He had chosen to not take his earned return to civilian life until he had gotten his full colonelcy. He had a vinegary personality and, in the whole six months, I never saw him really laugh. He kept a pipe clenched in his teeth and, if directly asked a question, would choke into bursts of coughing. He ran a superb Department of Medicine but, to a great extent, ran it by intimidation. He kept most of us frightened, but the man's dedication to work and his own willingness to put in long hours, day and evening, kept our spirits up. He also saw to it that we had an active education program, and the weekly teaching rounds, plus grand rounds, were well-done. I actually was the cardiologist of the place and ran the consulting service as well as the Heart Station. This was an exciting responsibility for someone with nine months of formal residency. All the other physicians were awaiting their discharge time, and I was the only one in the department who was just entering the service. I enjoyed every minute of it.

At the end of six months, hundreds of the new graduates were gathered in San Antonio, Texas for our formal six week officers' training school. We represented, from all over the country, the ASTP program. We were the fair-haired boys who had been spared military duty when the war years were serious. Most of the men training us had little use for the special status we had enjoyed. It was a wasted six weeks, but it was made considerably better by the pleasure of life in San Antonio. On the day the training ended, we had a graduation ceremony, and then rushed to the bulletin boards to see our new assignment. It was truly a grab-bag; and, if the 20 or so of us who had been together in Dayton six months earlier had felt empty, this moment in San Antonio was made even more dramatic by the fact that there were 600 or 700 of us, all being assigned by a roulette grab-bag system. I drew the Far East Command. Privately, I had been told that I was to be assigned to Walter Reed in Washington. Such small mistakes occur in the military.

More than 150 of us reported to Seattle, and we were shipped out on the S.S. Stetson Victory, packed five bunks high in the bottom of the ship. It was a cold, dreary 13-day voyage. We were taken by the Great Circle route and sailed up the coast of Alaska, then just below the islands of Attu and Kiska, always a little seasick and a little queasy. I had brought a fifth of gin, with visions of being a gentleman officer having an evening martini. The thought of a martini was impossible; the gin bottle, as well as food, remained untouched.

We came ashore in Yokohama and spent two weeks in tent camp. Each day a few of us were sent off to our permanent assignment. Japan was under military occupation and the majority of the group were assigned to be general medical officers for troops in the field, most under fairly basic conditions. Finally, 15 of us, all who had had a part of a residency, varying from pediatrics to obstetrics to surgery, etc., were assigned to the 42nd General Hospital in Tokyo.

This was the only General Hospital in the Far East—and I was to be cardiologist to the Far East Command, a considerable thought for a 28-year-old partially trained novice. We were taken in a convoy of jeeps from Yokohama to Tokyo, through forlorn miles of devastation; broken-off factory chimneys were the recognizable part, all else was flattened. As we got into Tokyo, very infrequent taxis chugged by, running on wood-burning apparatuses built into their trunks. One pulled to the side and the driver scurried out with a small log and threw it in the stove.

At the road intersections, Lister bags of chlorinated water were hung dead center; small queues of Japanese, weighted with water containers, stood silently, waiting their turns.

One of these bags was in front of the Kabuki Theater, spared by its proximity to St. Luke's Hospital. In 1989, I attended the Kabuki in this same theater, and sleek Japanese automobiles pulled up, out stepped equally sleek, chic, young Japanese women; but, because Kabuki is a deep vein of Japanese culture, the older women were often in kimono. The play, as seen in 1946 or in 1989, was unchanged. Why should a war and a few decades change a thousand-year-old custom?

The 42nd General Hospital (later named the 49th General Hospital) was housed in the missionary Episcopalian hospital, St. Luke's, which was the loveliest of buildings. The hospital had not been damaged by the bombings, and had been spared for this very purpose—to be the referral hospital for all Army problems north of Shanghai, including Korea and the islands south of Japan. The cardiologist who had been with the hospital during combat gave me a swift handshake, handed me the keys to the heart station, and ran laughing out of the building. I was also made chief medical officer of the 40-bed officers' general medicine ward. This latter responsibility gave me exposure to general internal medicine, which I had skipped at Indiana University Medical Center.

The patients assigned to this officers' ward included high-ranking civilians; consequently, I met many of the lawyers who had come out for the war-crime trials, many of the reporters and newspaper people covering the occupation, and others who came down with a medical problem. One patient was brought in from Shanghai where he had been a civilian wartime prisoner of the Japanese and had suffered grave damage to the circulation of his feet. He was John B. Powell, who had spent a lifetime running an English-language newspaper in Shanghai. He was the beginning of my education and the original stimulus for my interest in China. From him, I learned that he had been Edgar Snow's first employer when Snow arrived in Shanghai in the late 1920's. I did not know Snow, and Powell was not at all complimentary about

Snow's already famous book, *Red Star Over China*, for Powell had no kind words for the Communists. He began my awareness of the complexities of the Orient; and, many years later, I had the pleasure of knowing and working with his son, Bill Powell.

I read up to a hundred electrocardiograms a day and handled the consultations in cardiology, literally, for the Far East Command. A Japanese physician was assigned to be the EKG technician. His name was Nobuo Ito. We developed a very reserved, quite stiff, but mannerly relationship. This relationship withstood time, and he spent many years in my laboratory in Kansas and La Jolla. On my 70th birthday, he flew to Kansas City; and, with himself in kimono, and myself in dinner jacket, we exchanged deep bows, a quick handshake, and within a few minutes he was gone. Within ourselves, we each cherish the other but this formality has never varied.

A very senior cardiologist, Colonel Charles K. Berle, was chief medical officer for the Eighth Army, and he was delighted to provide me with mature backup when I saw something I did not know how to handle. He was lodged at the old Imperial Hotel, and over many a martini there, he and I became fast friends. We remained so to the end of his life. He also introduced me to caviar, which he obtained, in an unlimited supply from his medical counterpart in the Russian forces of the Occupation. Colonel Berle had been trained by Dr. Paul White at the Massachusetts General Hospital, and, as our friendship grew, he explained to me why I had to go there when I got out of the service. He cabled this information to Dr. White; and, before I left Japan, I had a toe-hold on an appointment with Dr. White.

My exposure to the original Imperial Hotel and architecture of Frank Lloyd Wright was stimulating and later on resulted in my gathering a substantial collection of material by and about him. An enthusiasm for architecture has always been barely repressed in my make-up.

The hospital was a full general hospital, complete with surgery, orthopedics, obstetrics, medicine—everything. In addition, it was not only the hospital for the American military in Japan, but also for the increasing number of civilians coming to participate in the complexity of the occupation. Economists, lawyers, engineers, businessmen, journalists, Red Cross workers, church staff, wives, dependents, in addition to military personnel, were all patients in the hospital. Because the chapel was intact and not destroyed as were other churches in Tokyo, and was such a handsome building, the allied forces and families living in Tokyo came for religious services.

The Sunday services were expanded into three faiths. The Episcopalian service was incorporated into a good utilitarian single Protestant service. Then, in a matter of minutes, the altar was rotated, a new group of worshipers moved in, not only on the chapel floor but patients were brought in from each floor of the hospital onto large balconies that projected out into the chapel; and, suddenly, the church was a synagogue and a rabbi chaplain took over.

Another rotation of the altar and the third service was Catholic. Chaplain John Lerhinan, captain, was the Catholic priest assigned to the 42nd General Hospital. Tall, 6 feet 3 inches, trim, pink faced—a face which glowed with a smile—sandy-haired, in uniform except when in robes for Mass, a voice which moved in mellow brightness, with an up-and-down cadence, and a little mixture of Irish brogue and New York State accent. Lunch followed the three services and Father John and I ate together. His opening remark was often, "Well, how did I do today? Did you feel an urge to come forward?"

Our friendship found its way between his lifelong commitment to his Church and my unbelieving path. We never avoided the subject and often reasoned with each other, through an easy banter, but often through mutual analysis of our reading, or through good conversations about world affairs.

We had a lifelong friendship, seeing each other in Boston, New York, Washington, Kansas City, and, when he was called to high office in the Redemptorist order, in Rome. His friendship was a special lifetime dividend of my time in Japan. It continued until his death by coronary occlusion in 1988. We had had a joyful reunion in Kansas City just two weeks before his death.

The 42nd General Hospital was a very civilized, well-run facility. The officers had a private dining room with starched tablecloths and flowered centerpieces. The dining service, by tiny kimonoed Japanese girls, was meticulous. We, the staff, were young, all partially trained, all enthusiastic about getting out and finishing our training, but it was a good, serious group, all giving their best.

The nurses, on the other hand, had all had much time in the service, some making it a career, and professional enough to make up for some of the doctors' inadequacies. At the end of the day, we adjourned to our club, complete with orchestra, pool, and excellent food. Father John enjoyed people, conversation, and was well-read. His table at the club was a center for good fellowship, laughter, and a gentle confessional.

When men talk about their military service, it usually is a recitation about how bad things were and what a waste it was. I have to remain quiet. My two years in the Army were the best years of training imaginable. One of the reasons they were so good is that I was being stimulated to the maximum of my ability. I was never underused or misused, and the fact that I was expected to know what I was doing undoubtedly caused me to find out how to do it. One quick route to maturity is responsibility.

I came out of the Army even more convinced that there is no medical-school book equal to the real, living textbook. Nothing can synthesize the human circumstance in all of its complexity.

Others can provide details of what it was like to be on the medical staff of General MacArthur. Roger Egeberg, for one, has written a delightful book. I took care of, as a physician, several of his general staff, and was on the periphery of their social set; but I was not in the very inner sanctum of the General's movie-viewing group.

The physician to the whole American Embassy and Headquarters group was Colonel Douglas Kendrick, an extremely likable, very handsome physician, perhaps in his early 40's. He often worked with me in getting patients into the general officers' ward, for which I had responsibility; and, on several occasions, I was his guest at the Embassy. I especially enjoyed the superb pool there. Other bits of hobnobbing with the "high brass" included a tour of northern Japan, to the Japanese Alps and the Kegon Falls, in the private rail car of headquarters. Military living at the very top becomes very grand, imperial, and delightful.

Several of us from the hospital became friends with a nearby Japanese family, the family of Yoshio Hamada. We aided them with food and medical care and they often had us for dinner. This proved to be a lasting contact. Their youngest daughter later came to the University of Kansas, married an American, and his work with IBM has allowed them to live in both countries. The eldest daughter came to live in our home for a year in 1958, and was there when my youngest daughter was born. The Hamada family provided my personal schooling in the Japanese ways of family life, of food, of manners, and a bit of the language.

The beauty of the small trained trees, bonsai, caught me and Father John and I made many trips in his jeep (chaplains had jeeps, physicians did not) to see exhibits, famous trees, displays—and this affection for these living sculptures stayed with me. I never became good enough to even hint at bragging, but have enjoyed the company of my small forest.

I came home by air, the plane island-hopping to Wake, Johnson Island, and Hawaii; and I was made into a civilian at a base outside of San Francisco. I hurried into San Francisco and bought loafers, gray flannel slacks, and a genuine camel-hair sportscoat. I remember the emphasis on "genuine." It was September 1947, my military time was over, I had money in the bank, there was a GI Bill of Rights, and I was ready to get on with a career as a cardiologist.

In addition to my camel-hair coat, I became the proud owner of a gleaming new Buick, with a cash payment-in-full of $1,850. It was satisfying to stand there in the showroom and count out the real money.

Audrey had kept our apartment while I was overseas; we were fortunate to have it because housing was critically short.

There were thousands of us in similar positions, ready to get on with our careers in medicine, and almost all of us needed more training before we settled down to practice. The war had created a backlog of need for refresher courses, for finishing interrupted residencies, for fellowships. The university centers were overloaded with men trying to get on with their education.

I was in contact with Paul White and he said he could not take me into his program before July 1948; and, even then, he could not promise me a clinical fellowship. He said I should come on as a postgraduate student and he would see what he could work out. We agreed I would come in July 1948; and, in the meantime, I would pick up my residency at Indiana University Medical Center.

The cardiac service had changed, and Harry Baum was no longer there; but there was a considerable cadre of men in training and an active teaching program with several older men back from the military. I had a stimulating seven months and enjoyed the cross teaching we accomplished, all working together, and all discussing the literature and telling war stories.

The techniques of 12-lead electrocardiograms, of vectorcardiography, of phonocardiography, were just developing, and we all learned about them together, teaching each other. I made rounds with Dr. Robert Moore each Sunday.

The medical center was just beginning its immense postwar build-up; but, of course, cardiac catheterization and open-heart surgery were not yet possible. That exciting new world was just opening. Patent ductus ligation was done, and we were all stimulated by the reports of surgical cure of coarctation of the aorta. We knew the details of the Blalock-Taussig shunt for Tetralogy of Fallot; but the cardiovascular surgeons were not yet spread out over the country, the flood of progress was poised, but not yet at tide. The importance of restricting salt in the treatment of hypertension was new; and Kempner at Duke University, who combined a rice diet with a messiah conduct, was a lively topic for our journal club. The sympathectomy for hypertension was in a boom time; we read and talked about Smithwick, Peete, and Adson and we did a few of their operations at the center. We spent hours analyzing the merits of digoxin versus digitalis, and were there unique values in ouabain, and how to use veratrum viride.

Still, cardiology was a stethoscope, fluoroscope, electrocardiogram, digitalis, and nitroglycerin. There was a sense of change, of excitement, but the future had not yet come. For me, it was a time to read thoroughly the literature, which was beginning to buzz with the research work of the talent that had returned to the universities. I read, in preparation for Boston, cover to cover, Paul White's book, *Heart Disease*, which was the great reference textbook of the time. The seven months free of daily patient responsibility and night call gave me time to put into place the patient experiences I had poured into my head, strengthen it by reading, and place it in context. I also read hard the full range of internal medicine, for I intended to take the Internal Medicine Board, even though I was avoiding a formal residency.

We took a happy two weeks to get to Boston, going up from Indiana to Green Bay, Wisconsin, across Lake Michigan, across Michigan, through Canada to the Niagara Falls, and across New England through the Berkshires. We arrived in Boston on a glorious June afternoon. The drive along the Charles River, the glow of the golden towers of the Harvard dormitories, the sculls and sailboats on the Charles, and the hugeness of Massachusetts General Hospital all told me I was in the right place. We had done the right thing to stop the comfort of our cozy life in Indianapolis and the prospects there of joining a successful private practice. The last cord to Indiana was cut.

PART TWO

Chapter Five

WE HAD NO PLAN AS to where we would live and had no remote idea of neighborhoods, traffic problems and other things which should guide one. Instead we drove through Cambridge, Concord, and Arlington, and when we saw a huge white New England home on Pleasant Street in Arlington, surely from the 1700's, perched above lovely Spy Pond, we simply went up to the door and asked if they had ever considered having guests. It worked. The owner was Donald McJannet, an administrator at Tufts and the proprietor for more than 20 years of a highly respected school at Annecy, France. The war had driven them to the United States, they had found this superb three-story house built in 1750, and we would be most welcome in a third-floor apartment. We had ended our search for a place to live at our first stop. The McJannets were gracious, energetic internationalists who were a dividend to the Boston experience.

MGH was everything one could have hoped for. Each of us who has gone there over its long life has, undoubtedly, felt the same sense that it was just the right time to be there. I have not had experience at Hopkins or the Brigham, but I would imagine there is the same almost euphoria of being at the hub, the very hub of medical science. MGH combines this feeling with a phenomenal stuffiness and conviction that all other institutions are secondary. But for those who have the privilege of having been inside the system, it is an experience from which one does not recover. As one of my colleagues said who was with me there: "At our home medical schools, our teachers use the best textbooks available for our education. Here at MGH, the teachers are the authors of those books!" It was true; at grand rounds at Friday noon, the front rows were occupied by Means, Aub, Fulbright, Butler, Jones, Cobb, Mallory, Cope, Churchill, Lipmann, White, Smithwick, Sprague, Castleman and others, names I had first learned of in the reading sessions with Harry Baum. The excitement of simply being there was compounded by the quality and earnestness of all those around you. The employees at all levels knew they were working in a great institution; the postgraduate students, Residents and Fellows all felt this, too, and therefore the whole system sustained itself at a higher than required level.

Expectation of the best caused the best to happen. Oh yes, there was the stuffiness factor, the elitist patina, and it was very easy to be either in or out.

I returned to MGH in the early 1980's for a summer. Nothing was changed. It was still the gathering place of talent, talent well arrived and talent on its way up. The place still moved with a quickness, an enthusiasm, and everyone was still crowded into any space possible to snatch. One characteristic of a vibrant, creative medical center is that no small cubbyhole is left unused. No closet remains a closet, but becomes someone's lab or office; no basement is a basement, but instead is fought-for space. MGH in 1948 and MGH in 1980 were different by a factor of 10, perhaps, in size, but the vast growth had not kept ahead of the need. Most research workers out over the United States would find it hard to believe that the high-quality research coming out of MGH often comes out of what was a side corridor in a back basement.

This cubbyhole, grab-space and hold-on tactic was the first thing to be noted when one finally found the great Paul Dudley White's Cardiac Lab. MGH had its beginnings in a gray-stone building, the Bulfinch, built in 1823. The fact that the Bulfinch is very much alive and used to the present is a bit of Bostonian frugality and charm. As one watches the destruction over the country of hospitals, schools and public buildings because they are "old" and were built 50 or 70 years ago, the memory of Dr. White's stuffed, crammed, nested, famous laboratory in the Bulfinch Building makes one smile and salute the old Brahmins who set the tone and standards.

The Fellows and graduate students in the Cardiac Lab were my immediate world, and from them came colleagues and cardiology contemporaries who went on to major careers over the entire world. The 15 or 20 of us who were there at the same time remained a nucleus of friends and, of course, a bit of competition. Much of my professional social world was encompassed in these friendships. Through the years, I saw again Mariano Alimuhrung, Shreenivas Shreenivas, Tim Counihan, Sean O'Toole and Constantine Ferrero, all in the postgraduate course that year. From the Residents, J. Willis Hurst and I brought through a relationship which maintained itself, although we basically had such different personalities that it was never possible to work well together. Menard Gertler, Gordon Myers, and Ed Wheeler were junior staff men with whom I maintained longtime friendships.

I was assigned two projects, the first to appraise the results of the Smithwick sympathectomy procedure for hypertension on patients selected by Dr. White and operated on by Smithwick, himself. The second was to work on the metabolic ward on patients undergoing severe sodium restriction for their hypertension, many of whom were on Kempner's Rice Diet. The first project I did working directly with Dr. White and the second working with one of the younger consulting cardiologists, James Curren. After a few months, Dr. White made me a clinical Fellow, which gave me direct access to the clinic patients, and, with a Massachusetts license, I was able actively to participate.

One of the junior staff men, Gordon Myers, had just returned from the Johns Hopkins Hospital where he had been sent to learn the very new technique of cardiac catheterization from Richard Bing. He invited me to join this first team being assembled at MGH to develop catheterization. We transported a few dogs at night to the radiology department and worked up a team with Gordon as the principal. We then did the first patients to have this procedure at MGH; and, on one memorable occasion, we were all quite startled, alarmed, and excited while catheterizing a small child to see the catheter go through the right ventricle, out the pulmonary valve and the suddenly turn down and head straight down towards the diaphragm. We quickly recovered from our shock over this peculiar pathway as we realized we had passed through a patent ductus arteriosus and the catheter had left the right heart circulation and was in the descending aorta. Every case was an adventure, an education, a victory. It was a time of high excitement in cardiology as, for the first time, the cardiologist was actually inside the heart; and new methods, new facts, new abilities to diagnose poured out from new teams all over the world. It was this ability which set the stage for the era of open heart surgery. For the first time congenital heart disease was not just a matter of blue or not blue, but with this new precision of diagnosis the stage was set for the great achievements of cardiac surgery.

Dr. Edward Bland, Dr. White's deputy, conceived the idea of having a surgical production of an atrial septal defect as a means of releasing the deadly lung pressure behind a rheumatic mitral stenosis. The study of Olivia, the first patient, by catheter, before and after, made me realize I was now on the side of those writing the literature, not just reading it.

I had left Indiana University Medical Center with a serious commitment to a group of colleagues, who, like myself, were back from the military, finishing up their training and making career plans. We were general surgeons, obstetricians, ophthalmologists, urologists, radiologists, internists, and myself, cardiologist. We had spent many nights planning how we could form a major group and where was the best place to base this new clinic group. I had come to Boston with the tacit understanding that the ophthalmologist, Fred Wilson, and I would lead off for this planned group and set it in motion in Austin, Texas after I finished my time in Boston.

Several things happened which began to make this plan insecure. As I realized cardiac catheterization was the next great movement in cardiology, I began to wonder how I could extend my skill. At this very time, all of us were becoming aware of a young English cardiologist who, upon his return from military service, had entered into a whirlwind of productivity. First from the Hammersmith, then from the National Heart Hospital in London extremely exciting articles began pouring out. Much of this work correlated the new findings by catheter with bedside auscultation and electrocardiography. This work was the transition from the conservative cardiology of tradition to the new dynamic intervention cardiology. Through articles and then through a great new textbook, this man had quickly established himself as the premier of the new era of cardiology and his training program had become the mecca, attracting talent from all over the British Empire. His name was Paul Wood.

I asked Dr. White to write Wood on my behalf and a cable came: "Can accept Dimond July. Catheterization facilities available." This presented Audrey and me with the honorable dilemma of could we afford it. We had a small reserve from our military savings, she had practiced nursing for the two years I was away and was now on the nursing staff at Cambridge General Hospital. Could we stretch all of this into a year or two in London? Would the time in London remove me from the American scene? Could I find a way back into cardiology in the U.S.A.? Remember the world was much larger in the age before trans-Atlantic jets, and all of the large medical centers which came later and offered unlimited opportunities had not yet been built. Stranded and forgotten in England sounded like a quite real issue.

Dr. White reached the age of 62 during the time I was at MGH; and, facing the strict MGH rule of retirement at 65, he elected to resign and open a new office for private practice over near the Boston Garden. Dr. Bland was appointed his successor. In February, Dr. Bland invited me to his office and in his very soft-spoken gentle way asked if I would like to stay on as the Resident in cardiology for the next year. The pay would be $150 a month.

Now I was deep in opportunities and, equally, deep in a financial dilemma. What a difference a few thousand dollars could have made. MGH was well-known as an institution in which not all of the staff actually needed the work. Dr. Howard Sprague was one of Dr. White's most brilliant associates and would have been a prime candidate to succeed him except for the fact that Dr. Sprague always stopped work in the late spring and went off to his sailing and a long summer holiday. One of the young staff in the heart group had a lovely home, several large cars, a great old home at the Cape, five children—and practically no practice. His allowance took care of everything. Lest I seem soured by the bitter grape of jealousy, I must add that many men were in positions similar to mine and scrambling with everything they had to build careers and pay their bills.

I took my problems to Dr. White who, although well known to have not the remotest concept of money and was a worry to everyone as to how he, himself, would afford retirement, was wise in a way which was not encumbered by pretense or ego. I told him about Wood, about Dr. Bland's offer and fully about my friends from Indiana and our agreement to set up practice in Austin, Texas. Dr. White had a bright cheerful approach to all problems, and although you were never certain he had fully understood how visceral the issues were to you, immediately said, "The right way to be a physician is to practice medicine. You know all the cardiology you need to know. Go start your new group. The School of Aviation Medicine at Randolph Field has just contacted me to ask if I could send them someone to teach electrocardiography at the flight surgeon's school. Do both! Go try practice and go try your hand at teaching. You can't lose. I am going to be the first director of the new National Heart Institute and, if you want, later you can help me."

We ended our Boston time with a happy party at the Buzzards Bay summer home of the Currens, celebrating the 25th anniversary of Dr. and Mrs. White. The two of them appeared in the clothes they had worn at their wedding, surely good evidence that cardiologists practice the leanness they teach. Doctor and Mrs. White read poems they had written—light, graceful, witty poems—while standing on the steps of the big old home with all of us ringed about on the grass.

Audrey and I headed south, enjoying the Smoky Mountains, the Appalachians, the Skyline Drive, on our way to Austin, Texas. I can't claim I knew I was doing the right thing. The charm of Boston and New England had encumbered my thinking.

We met Fred Wilson and his family in Austin and began our plan. We set up office together, Eye and Heart, and went about building a practice in the true sense of the word. We had no foothold in the area, no special entree; but it was still the postwar era and there was newness, motion, it was an adventure time for many Americans, not only physicians. We quickly fitted into lovely Austin and began making a living. Fred Wilson was a delightful companion, and I could not have had a more enjoyable colleague in what was essentially an exercise in free enterprise. The medical community soon learned that we were the advance guard of what was intended to be a major group practice. This hazed the welcome of some, but the hospitality of the "Austiners" made up for that. Fred quickly was successful and did well almost instantly. My practice was slower and my dollar reserves more limited. But we staggered along and were soon out into the community looking for a large building or old home that we could make over and have ready for the next increment of our group, due to arrive the second year.

Three days each week, I drove to San Antonio and gave an organized, very intensive course in electrocardiography to the flight surgeons. The special course for them was six weeks long and, therefore, each six weeks I had a new chance to improve my style, delivery, and information. The flight surgeons were not an audience of toleration. They were expecting useful information. All were young and many knew a considerable amount of cardiology from their own residencies. I honed and sharpened my ability to face such an audience, to take a difficult subject, and through clarity and a careful choice of visual material, trained myself, in essence, how to be a teacher of the graduate physician. This became the arena in which I spent my professional career.

The School of Aviation Medicine offered excellent help in audiovisuals setting a standard for me that I carried through my career. The school also offered advice and instruction on how to teach. From this, I learned how to begin and end a lecture, but I never quite mastered the technique of having well-placed jokes to offer when you needed to lighten the teaching. I remember the lecture notes of one of my colleagues which had boldly printed in the left margin: "GIVE JOKE ABOUT DOG and HUSBAND. TELL IRISHMEN AND WHISKEY STORY."

A considerable event at the School of Aviation Medicine, and one not at all well known generally in the United States, was Operation Paperclip. This term obscured well a major post-World War II effort, the lifting up physically, out of conquered Germany, the best of their scientists and spiriting them off to Texas. Day by day, laboratory by laboratory, I began to discern an impressive cadre of German scientists, busily working away on research projects. One example of Operation Paperclip was the head of our national space program, Werner von Braun. In my own field, I found a former member of the German high-altitude physiology unit, Kurt Reissmann.

Reissmann was the classic Teutonic: blonde, blue-eyed, Aryan, complete with a dashing dueling scar. He was trained in internal medicine, hematology and physiology, and was involved in developing an instrument for measuring the vigor of the heartbeat, a torsion ballistocardiograph. The patient was placed on a bed supported by a single metal bar, and the bed twisted with each heartbeat about this metal support bar, a torque bar. The twisting movement of the bed was recorded as a repetitive series of waves.

The best-laid plans of mice and men come upon unexpected events. At Christmastime, Fred and I informed our colleagues that we were encouraged, and they could come on and join us with some expectation of success. The first shadow came from our general internist. He had just about decided to go to Iowa! Then the obstetrician indicated he would be slower in coming to Austin than anticipated. The enthusiastic effort by the two of us to get a building and be ready for the others began to look like we might have a large white elephant of a building with no productive partners. I probably would have stayed with the plan, even though my feet were cooling; however, I was finding myself seriously concerned about being out of the new field of cardiac catheterization with no real prospect of getting into it.

A spot of light brightens darkness—an invitation came from the colonel who had been my chief of medicine at Crile General Hospital, where I had first reported for the Army. He was the same steel-nail-biting, pipe-chomping man. He was now out of the Army, back at his base at the University of Kansas, and acting chairman of Medicine. Would I be interested in looking at their cardiology department? The university had never had a full-time cardiologist, but, like many medical centers before the war, had been dependent on private practitioners who volunteered their services. Now the great burst of energy in medical schools, following the return of their faculties, was coinciding with the growth of the National Health Institutes. The Institutes were funneling money into the university medical centers and, essentially every medical center was recruiting full-time faculty.

The week after I returned from a visit to Kansas City to look at the job, Paul White was speaking in Houston. I was able to get a military plane from the School of Aviation Medicine to fly me down.

The plane blew a tire on landing and ground looped, but I tried to present a composed, mature image to Dr. White. He was his delightful, effervescent, energetic self. He was full of excitement about his new task as director of the National Heart Institute. He told me of the prospects for the National Heart Institute, and the role it was going to play in funding programs at academic medical centers. He brushed off my attempt to tell him that I was not certain what to do. He had a way of not hearing all you wanted to say, simply because he had such enthusiasm about his own full life that he wanted to tell you about it. From the moment I mentioned the possibility of starting a new department at Kansas, he took over and told me how he had started the first Department of Cardiology at MGH. Dr. White's life was so full, so exciting, and so packed with personal experiences that your own small decisions became even smaller. His advice was, "Go!"

Although the Kansas job had 10,000 merits and was a path into life in academic cardiology, I had one large concern about the situation. These concerns all were based on my half-year at the Crile General Hospital. There I had benefitted from the intense discipline of Colonel Mahlon Delp, and had learned to have, as did the others of us in the medical department, a begrudging tolerance for his almost tyrannical administrative style. Such an acceptance was possible in the Army because there were no options. He was not a man at ease. Almost all conversations were cryptic, fairly wordless, but accentuated and shaped by deep breathing, sighs, smoke clouds from his pipe, coughing and rubbing of temples. His migraines were a recognized hazard.

We in the Crile medical group learned to live with his demerits, because he not only demanded discipline from us but because he equally disciplined himself. He sincerely tried to create an academic environment in an Army situation. The others found it tolerable by knowing that they were in the last months of their required Army time. The general feeling was that one could tolerate anything with demobilization in sight.

I had almost learned to enjoy him at Crile, and, through a winter of playing singles handball with him, had developed a degree of warmth. Handball, also, almost ended our relationship. He was already a conditioned, seasoned player when we first competed, and I was windless, out of shape, and had never even played the game before. He thoroughly enjoyed our first six or so games and my physical ordeal gave him pleasure. Finally, my swollen hands, blistered feet, lungs and circulation began to recover and the 15 years difference in our ages began to show. One night I ran him to the ground and won. As he sat in the dressing room, exhausted, pouring sweat, alternately gasping for air, coughing and spitting, he cursed and said, "God damn you, you have almost killed me! I think I am in pulmonary edema!" I felt it was almost a moment of affection.

Now three and a half years later, I was excited about the potential of building my own heart unit, but I knew Dr. Delp was not someone I wanted to work for the rest of my days. I wrote in my diary, "I'm going but 10 years is the limit."

My colleague, Fred Wilson, was not dismayed at my decision as he, himself, was missing much of the excitement of academic medicine. He returned to Indiana University Medical Center. Some indication that we were a group with some potential is hinted by our future jobs.

Within three years of our closing down the Austin dream, Fred was chairman of Ophthalmology at Indiana; our general surgeon was chairman of Surgery at Southwestern, Dallas; our urologist was chairman at Indiana in Urology; our radiologist had the Chair at Louisville; and I was chairman of Medicine at Kansas.

Life can only be lived as it happens, but Fred and I would wonder the rest of our lives what we might have created if we had held to our Austin goal.

Austin was and is a perfect place to live, and the "social ambiance" was a joy. Audrey and I had found friends there. Just the thought of leaving those qualities for Kansas, a place neither of us had been, was also a cloud. Our style of life still remained simple. We had been married five years, had our faithful Buick, and now a Doberman named Beau, a Siamese named Ming, and a few items of furniture, but essentially we were still footloose and mobile.

After we left Boston, Audrey did not work again. She had found an enjoyable way of life in Austin, and so as we loaded the car with clothes, cat, and dog, and headed north, we both were doing it because of that thing called a career and for no other reason. On July 1, 1950, we arrived in Kansas City. I parked Audrey, dog and cat in a motel, and hurried to the medical center. Dr. Delp had scheduled me for a series of lectures in electrocardiography to begin, essentially, at the instant of my arrival.

I was able to laugh about this. First, because I was excited about performing in my new job but also because it was so typical of his approach to another person's life. At Crile, he had always made complete rounds on Sunday morning, the only chief in the whole hospital doing so, and the entire staff of Medicine was required to be present. Dr. Delp equated suffering with responsibility and wanted everyone to have a full measure of both.

Of course, much of the preparation for these lectures came from the work at the School of Aviation Medicine. This I built on, and for the full 10 years at Kansas, I gave a personal, one-week-long, 36-hour course in electrocardiography for the physician in private practice. I placed myself on a high stool; and, with an overhead projector beside me, went on hour upon hour, taking an audience through the full range of electrocardiography. This kind of teaching, slow, thorough, complete, I found satisfying, and much of what I did as a teacher in those years used this style.

My special audience was always the man in private practice. From this teaching, came a book on the subject that went into four editions, ultimately printed by Little, Brown and Company, and another EKG book published by C. V. Mosby. In 1956, I assembled a major seminar on digitalis and this also resulted in a book. The revenue from these publications was put in a Fellows' fund which gave us discretionary money. With this money, it was possible to send essentially all of the Fellows, at some time in their training, on a visit to other cardiology programs. Usually, this was back to Indianapolis to the Eli Lilly Clinical Research Unit, run by longtime friend, Bill Martz; but often, too, it was down to Houston to observe Mike DeBakey.

Immediately, the first Sunday morning and every Sunday, Dr. Delp required all to be present for a journal club. He was able to instill a sense of personal guilt and weakness if you at all wavered under the required hairshirt ethic.

My comment about a hairshirt ethic is undoubtedly excessive. Delp presented himself as a role model who, through his every act, demonstrated and demanded intense discipline, a discipline which placed service to the patient as the primary duty. However, to my inspection, he placed discipline even ahead of service.

On balance, he left a mark for good on the students of the medical school. Every medical school would be well served to have someone as demanding and severe in the midst of their department of medicine. Now, years later, those who remember Dr. Delp are divided into those who cherish their experience with him and those who cannot forgive the meanness they saw.

Dr. Delp devoted himself to the care of the patient and made that effort into a battle with the rest of the world. A misplaced chart, delayed lab specimen or lost X-ray was cause for a full firing of all guns, which included deep breathing, prolonged sighs, massage of temples, a direct verbal assault on the opposition and dire threats. In spite of his devotion to the patient, he gave me an insight into the practice of medicine which, over the years, grew in my experience to be essentially a truth. He said, "If you practice medicine for 30 years, you become a cynic. People are no damn good." I know what he meant. A physician's privileged exposure to the inner lives of people leaves one aware of how much pettiness, meanness, cruelness, selfishness, and dumbness there is.

I end up knowing exactly what he meant, and would say that you become a cynic, yes, but you must always enjoy how much good survives in those all about you. All the qualities are in all of us. Keeping them in order, drawing them out, is the game of life.

My job was to set up the heart service of the medical center, and that was a delightful, stimulating duty. Delp never interfered in that area.

The Heart Station consisted of an Adirondack chair for the patient, an EKG machine and technician, Margie Delich. Margie stayed with the lab for the full 10 years that I was there. It would be wrong for me to pass by Margie's value without adding that she kept an atmosphere of good cheer and enthusiasm, which made the EKG lab a pleasant and welcome environment for the dozens upon dozens of students, Residents and Fellows who passed through over the years.

Nothing can undermine an education program more than a gray cloud of discontent in a key area. Margie was always able to rise above the day's problems and make us all feel better.

The medical center was in an exciting time of great growth, and we fitted into a close-knit social group made up of the chairmen and their wives. Between my work as a cardiologist and committee duties with the medical school, there was very little extra time.

The once-a-week gathering of the chairmen and their wives at our homes was not only good companionship but the basis for effective administration of the center. It was one of the happy circumstances of an academic institution that I was never quite able to capture again. Our youth and the newness of it all gave us a camaraderie. Among those that I knew and enjoyed, were the chairman of Urology, Bill Valk; the chairman of Obstetrics, Leroy Calkins; Bob Stowell, Pathology; Herb Miller, Pediatrics; Gunnar Proud, Ear, Nose, and Throat; Dave Robinson, Plastic Surgery; and Al Lemoine, Eye. Their wives were equally good company. In the very early years, Paul and Hilma Schafer were a part of the group.

The Dean was a special source of energy and imagination. His name was Franklin Murphy. He was the son of a Kansas City internist and had a socially active mother. He had been trained at Penn and he had practiced cardiology privately in Kansas City before getting the deanship.

Audrey and I liked Franklin and his wife, Judy, and, over an occasional drink, he and I would compare notes and enjoy telling each other of the irascible swings of Dr. Delp's moods. We both saw his considerable merit, but we both felt his personal masochism made it difficult for the whole institution.

It was undoubtedly a great time to be at any university medical center. All were building their full-time faculties for the first time. Half of an entire new floor was available for the heart unit, and later, we added a larger room for cardiac catheterization.

We were certainly not a carpet-and-drapes-plush facility, but we had everything then useful to work with, and there was so much new knowledge in the field that we were all fully stimulated.

Nationally, there was a new group of us who were young and in cardiology; and I soon became friends with a network of men of similar age, each building a career, and each building a heart program. Years before, when I read for Harry Baum, there had been a network of, perhaps, 10 or 15 of this breed called cardiologist. Dr. Baum and I could read all there was to report in a single journal. Those original leaders were now placing their "progeny" out over the whole country. For the first time, medical schools were expanding into huge patient-care referral centers.

Suddenly, there were more of us, but still it was a definable network. I knew exactly where each man fit the whole, what his unit's strengths were; and we all could read all the literature, meet at the annual meeting and know we were the academic framework of American cardiology.

I was 31 when we arrived in Kansas, a time of life when vigor and energy are unlimited. The entire institution was growing, and Franklin Murphy had done a good job convincing Kansas legislators to put money into the medical center. The department heads were young, excited and building their programs. We had new buildings, and the National Heart Institute provided money to develop the heart units and training programs.

There were three fundamental ways in which to develop the Kansas unit. First, to make the reputation of the unit in a field of basic research. Another path was to become a respected patient referral center. The third route was to attract postgraduate students who came to you for training. This latter ambition, obviously, was influenced by whether you had built research strengths or a patient-care reputation. One kind of a Fellow would come to work in the research lab; another entirely different individual would come for the patient-care emphasis: different in personality, in ultimate ambition, in background training.

I actually had little choice in this decision. Everything that had happened to me, from my time with Dr. Baum when I was still a medical student and Fellow; then the experience with Robert Moore; on through the Crile and Tokyo experience; Colonel Berle; and, of course, the time with Dr. White's strongly clinically oriented unit prepared me, by every design, to be a clinician's clinician.

Even if my preparation had not taken me in this direction, my own attitude towards life and people would have steered me away from the bench-investigator route. I enjoyed the human contact, the human challenge of working with complex personalities, the intellectual competition associated with bedside diagnosis, and the ambiguity of the issues which face you as you go from patient to patient. Even though I never strayed afield from a very tight personal discipline, I found satisfaction in the variables and challenges presented by erratic patient conduct.

My unit took the route towards competence in placing labels, in taking on referred cases of every complexity, and taking it as a challenge that we would make the right diagnosis. We would sort through the mix of disease and personality, define precisely what was wrong and what should be done.

Before my first month was over, I took off on a tour of heart centers. I took almost a month for my tour. I was more interested in methods of administration than in the scope of research. The kind of administration I was looking for, especially, was the organization of the electrocardiography work. In the early 1950's, the scheduling, taking, mounting, reading, coding, filing and getting reports to the staff was the major function of a "heart lab."

Paul White's unit at MGH did this well but with a certain ponderous conservatism. For example, no one in Dr. White's unit remotely would consider using that new-fangled gadget, a dictating machine. Louise Wheeler, the unit's senior secretary, was appalled at the thought of taking her instructions from a machine, and took pride in her ability to handle in shorthand the great volumes of dictation done by the physicians. One classical example of the effect of this kind of person-to-person communication was that when Dr. White was on a train returning to Boston, his secretary would go to a station 100 miles or so from Boston, there board the train and take down in person Dr. White's response to the correspondence she had carried to him. The liberation a dictaphone could have given each of them was rejected as but an example of how the machine age was eliminating human skills.

For my trip, I first went to Chicago to the Cook County heart lab, which did not take long and was so chaotic that it served me as an example of how not to run a unit. I quickly went on to Michael Reese Hospital, to Louis Katz's unit. This was a superb experience. Dr. Katz was everything a chief should be. He fought like a lion for his Fellows, stimulated them, berated them, never let up on his demands for intellectual honesty but spent little time on staff niceties. When you were trained by Katz, you were trained—and bruised.

His unit was superbly administered, and much that I instituted at Kansas, in terms of the EKG section, came directly from Louis Katz. In addition to this major benefit, my visit to the unit gave me a personal lifetime reward. Dr. Katz assigned one of his Fellows to be my guide.

This guide was a very lean, rapidly moving man of about my age who spoke in staccato explosions of sentences, and had no hesitation in blasting a burst of spleen, sarcasm, ironic wit, and intelligence at any and all. One reads of minds that are "rapier-like." This man's mind was rapier, hammer, and cutlass, all transmitted by a machine gun of words. His knowledge of cardiology was supreme; and he was the first person I had met, in my own considerable exposure to the field, who had no hesitation in giving a thorough, usually negative, opinion about the various icon-heroes of the field. He had served long, hard, and dangerously in the European Theater in the Second World War; was a bachelor; and lived and breathed cardiology. He had a large burst of very black, very curly hair, a handsome face enhanced by alert intelligence, and, in truth, was a junior model of his chief, Louis Katz. His name was Herman Hellerstein, and, then and there, in Katz's unit, we formed a friendship which never wavered, never varied, and has been a constant and repeated source of pleasure for me.

When I gave my first postgraduate course at Kansas, he was on the program, and when I gave my last, before going to California, he was there. Equally, the first and last programs in California had him on the program, and many, many times in between. We toured Nigeria, the Sudan, and India together. We were in China together and, years later, when he retired at Case Western Reserve in Cleveland, I was there to express my affection.

I watched him through the years when he was the stormy petrol of any panel in which he participated, on to the wonderfully quieting effect on him of fathering six children. During the early years of his fatherhood, he was essentially unable to comprehend what he had wrought, as he would say, "from his loins." His superb wife, Mary, the daughter of the respected cardiologist at the Crile Clinic, Harold Feil, herself trained by Spock, took over the management and growth of this huge brood while Herman covered the world, speaking, teaching, castigating.

I can remember so many meetings with Herman on one of my panels, and, after another panelist had expressed his opinion, Herman would lean forward, snatch the microphone to him, and with teeth bared in a snarl, would shoot a burst of response through his clenched teeth, usually beginning with, "That is the most idiotic remark I have ever heard. It reflects pure stupidity." With the other panelist bleeding and worried for his safety, Herman then proceeded, using a numerical system, to complete his decimation: "First, how can any man in his right mind say ..., Second, that is the most sloppy research I have ever ..., Third ...." This became the famous Hellerstein performance, and it lasted until his children came into their teens and each proved to be a exciting, creative, highly capable adult. The reality of what he had sired, the wonder of it, the intoxication of it, sweetened poor Herman; and he has become a gentle, wise, philosophical senior scholar, with hair grey, its wire-like curl softened, midriff thickened, and he and his Mary the proudest, happiest couple in the land.

From Chicago, I went up to Ann Arbor. At that time, the leadership in the entire field of electrocardiology was understood to be in Frank Wilson's group. This team had invented and defined the scientific basis of the subject, and Wilson, his associate, Franklin Johnston, Senior Fellow Francis Rosenbaum, and others were the source of the creative research. Today, the EKG is so standard, its use so routine, its vocabulary so constant, that it is difficult to remember that once all of these things were new, original, and exciting. People working in the field in those early years devoted great time and effort to arguing about what leads to use, what to call them, and even how to mount them for the record.

My gain from the visit to Wilson's unit was to learn how he coded and classified the electrocardiograms, and this system served well at Kansas.

From Ann Arbor, I went on to see Wiggers' lab in Cleveland, back to Boston and spent time at MGH and the Brigham (in Sam

Levine's unit), then to New York City to see the unit of Charles
Kossman at NYU, and to the Presbyterian Hospital, then to
Philadelphia to Charles Wolferth's unit. I kept notes and on the
long trip home summarized how to use what I had learned.

The unit I wanted to construct would be different than any I had
seen. I meant to build a clinically intense program, based upon a
large referral practice; a place for the training of Fellows from all
over the world; a unit that took a major hand in the medical student's education; that carried on research, but to subdivide the research so each unit had its own chief; and to devote major effort to
postgraduate education. The doctor in private practice would be
our overall objective. The teaching, stimulation and leadership of
this specific group would be the real agenda of my team. Parts of
this I saw in the various places I had visited, but not one of the
places had put together the full package. I came home worn down,
stimulated, and began the building of the parts.

The field of heart surgery was changing almost week by week.
Walton Lillehei at the University of Minnesota was working out a
means of using a parent's own heart and lungs, as an auxiliary
heart-lung for infants having open heart surgery. Gibbon was developing a heart-lung machine. DeBakey was experimenting with
methods of using cloth to replace blood vessels. The potential of
the cardiac catheter was an unending challenge to the cardiologist. These new opportunities attracted a new kind of cardiologist
into the field.

The cardiologist traditionally had been a conservative, gentle
physician, offering psychic and emotional support because there
was little positive intervention to be offered.

I came along at the transition, and was thoroughly trained out
as an old-style diagnostician, but I was just at the right point in my
career to get enthusiastically into invasive cardiology. One of the
great attributes of Paul White was that, although he belonged to
the era where the cardiologist's stock in trade was optimism, he
still always saw the potential of aggressive surgery, and, at every
point, was eager to try new and undefined fields.

My unit at Kansas was the first catheter team in the state. Setting up the team, training the personnel, and doing the first procedure was a large event.

From a very early time, I was convinced of the value of electrocardiograms done while the patient was exercising; my group explored and pushed this field, often to the alarm of the older physician who had been trained to believe the heart was an organ to be rested, not stressed.

One event naturally followed another. My training had prepared me to be comfortable speaking and lecturing; the State of Kansas, spread out over several hundred almost empty miles, had physicians who needed new medical information brought to them. Equally, they needed a reference route for their difficult cases. All of us at the medical center joined in the postgraduate education approach, and, both at the center in Kansas City and out in the state at a dozen locations, we were all teaching, consulting, and, at the same time, building a substantial referral practice.

Weeks after my arrival, I had my first cardiac Fellow. Not only was he the first Fellow in cardiology at Kansas, but he was my own first Fellow. He was Larry Lamb, and he initiated what became for me one of the largest satisfactions of my teaching career: the care, grooming, and stimulating of Fellows. There is nothing quite so personal in terms of the teacher's own emotions as the graduate physician who comes to him by his own free choice, and gives time and energy to the program in exchange for something he considers worthwhile: the knowledge and judgment of his chief. Before I closed out my fellowship training program many years later, I had a series of delightful men and women from all over the world who spent time with me. Larry Lamb was the first, and because we both were so young, and life so casual, I must admit that he remains a bit special in my memory. Of course, he undoubtedly remembers some of the odd variables of his time with me, such as the opportunity to help me lay sod around my new house. Today, such an imposition would have an ethics committee straining to wreck your career. Then, Larry and I thought it was fun. When he was called into the military service, we were able to get him assigned to the School of Aviation Medicine, and he built a substantial reputation there by his energetic analysis, coding, and interpreting of the electrocardiograms of thousands of young airmen. His actual call up to military service stimulated me into giving him a farewell party—then he was

deferred—another farewell party—another deferral—and all repeated again. When he finally left, everyone was exhausted.

Later, he established himself as a major influence on the public's health through his widely syndicated health column. We
maintained, throughout our lifetimes, a sassy, insulting, affectionate badinage.

Very early in the life of the Cardiac Lab, a generous gift came
from the editor of *The Kansas City Star*, Henry Haskell. I made a
decision in the use of this money which was an early clue of my
enthusiasm for international relationships and the kind of international mix which I had found stimulating at MGH. One of the first
foreign visitors to our new unit was Dr. Paulo Schlesinger from Rio
De Janeiro. Paulo was a well-informed cardiologist, and essentially
bi-cultural. His English was perfect, and his sister was married to
a teacher in Kansas. We agreed that for a 10-year period, I would
use the interest income from the Haskell money to award scholarships to young Brasilian future cardiologists, recommended by
him. This launched a Brasilian influence in my group, which remained throughout the years I offered an active training program.

From this came a natural interest in other South American
countries. In the next two decades there came Everton Santos,
Jose Martins, Sergio Cardoso, Alberto Benchimol, Rafael Luna,
Mario Anache, Alberto Guimpel, Hugo Palmero, Luis Morettin,
Luis Ortuzar, Josefina Caravaca, Carlos Velasco, Azaria Duenas,
Horacio Orejarena, Damaso Talavera, Evandro Lucena, Fernando
Carvalho, Alfredo Gomez and others—some who became Ameri-
can citizens, most of whom returned to their countries.

As is life, each was a different personality, and each brought
contributions and problems. One does not manage a training program for young people without also being involved in their worries, their finances, their hopes, their romances, their illnesses,
their future jobs, and career decisions. I found myself comfortable in this role and tried to develop a sympathetic way of listening, and yet avoid letting my own biases be too heavily weighted
in the advice given.

I have learned that the best approach to giving advice is to listen. I hope I have learned that. Eventually, the one seeking advice
gives their own answer. One never quite knows what are all the

variables weighing on the other person. Definitive, specific advice can be dangerously inadequate, or just plain wrong.

On many occasions, in fact, most, the question being asked is one which the bearer has already solved, and coming to see me was a diplomatic maneuver to shift me into saying the right thing.

I well remember when I was young, and filled with the importance of my wisdom, a Chinese colleague came to me to discuss the appropriateness of his seeing a certain young woman. Dumb as it now seems, I advised him against the liaison. Then, with quiet shifting of feet and clearing of throat, he brought me into reality—he and the young lady were already engaged—the real purpose behind the visit with me was to advise me that he was getting married; I had not yet learned that the real questions are not the apparent ones.

I also learned to be extremely tolerant of what may seem to be major faults of conduct and prudence. I include in this a considerable variety of sexual peccadilloes. Careful analysis of many activities which seem to be of a no-no nature, often proved that no one should judge the other's sin. Lest I seem to be relating these thoughts only to the behavior of the South American Fellows, be assured that my thoughts are based on global observations. Today's shadowed conduct can be tomorrow's happy marriage.

Within a year, the work of the unit had reached a point where I needed a partner. Larry Lamb was called to the service and no one was yet ready from within the Kansas program. Again, perhaps as evidence of my attitude about the world, and undoubtedly influenced by my time in the Orient, I invited a young Chinese physician, trained in the United States, to join the unit as a junior staff man. His name was Tung Kuang Lin, T.K. Lin.

T.K.'s family was from Shanghai, and with the victory of the Communists, he and a large number of siblings had dispersed into the Western world, all with Ph.D.s or M.D.s. We worked together for several years, and although he may have learned a fair amount of cardiology from me, he gave me in return my further education in understanding, perhaps a little, the differences between East and West.

The China Medical Board, originally founded to aid health care and education in China, and moving its influence out over east

Asia after the coming of Mao Zedong, noted my interest in international education, and, very early on, began placing people in my
unit. Mehru Banderawalla, Sita Ram Kapoor, and V.S. Raghunathan from India; Endot Achya from Indonesia; Mohammad
Azeem from Afghanistan; Chaveng Dechakalsaya from Thailand;
Dean Tam and Ngoc Huy Nguyen from South Vietnam; Nobuo
Ito, Toyozo Aizawa and Ichizo Fukuda from Japan; Romeo Divinigracia and Pio Poblete from the Philippines; Nong Ting, C.M.
Chen, Yen Shen, Teh-Lu Wu, Yeou Bing Li, and Liang Foo Chen
from Taiwan; all came to work in the unit.

The representative of the China Medical Board was Dr. Harold
Loucks. Years later, when I was personally involved in China, I
came to realize what a powerful force he had been in the early
years of the Peking Union Medical College. Repeatedly, I met
Chinese surgeons who spoke of him with the special reverence
the Chinese hold for a respected professor. Later, after Loucks retired, I enjoyed working with his successor, Oliver McCoy.

In the early years, given the definitely conservative mid-American location of the medical center, I am sure I seemed almost sub-
versive with this one-world flavor to our program.

The longtime chairman of the Department of Internal
Medicine, Dr. Ralph Major, had retired the year before I came to
Kansas, and Dr. Delp was the acting chief. Dean Murphy found
himself in a major dilemma. The logical successor was Dr. Delp,
especially in the minds of those physicians, out in Kansas, who
had served in the same military hospital unit with him overseas.
There were other audiences the Dean had to listen to, and these
included all of the other chairmen who, almost to a man, vetoed
the thought of working with the prickly man. Among the university's regents, there was opposition, as well as some outspoken opposition from powerful physicians in Kansas City. My own daily
contact with Dr. Delp made me keenly aware of the problem. No
one could have been more loyal to the state, to the medical center, and to dedication to the profession. In his own intense way,
the man wanted the best for the medical school and its students.
No one could have been more his own worst enemy. In long sessions with him, closeted in his darkened, smoke-filled office, he
could only slump into personal attacks on essentially everyone

with whom we worked. I soon realized that he carried the burden of inordinate hostility towards anyone who had a degree of success. He was not paranoid—he did not concern himself with what others thought of him—instead he was angry, negative, hostile and took his pleasure from downgrading most of those about him. This did not include certain men who had passed his loyalty test, I gradually learned that part of his need was to have around him individuals who were intimidated by him and willing to accept that status. Many of the issues I worked with through the years at Kansas were sharply divided along lines of those who became his devoted disciples, adopting some of the same characteristics, and those who saw him as an angry, even mean, man.

I paint an incomplete picture of this very substantial personality if I do not include more description. He wore his hair in a vigorous wire-brush cut, maintained a deep tan from his home tanning unit, and cared for the trimmed mustache with waxed tips. He dressed very well, wore a huge, several-centimeter-large Navajo turquoise ring, a gold bracelet, and always parked his sleek Corvette, complete with leopard seat covers, in a conspicuous place. He was as dour as a sin-finding minister, as disciplined as a Prussian officer, a demanding martinet, yet had these several vanities. I sometimes felt that inside all his rigid and frowning conduct, there was a man who would dearly have loved to know how to have a good time.

Murphy approached me about the Chair, and I had to tell him I had not yet even taken my Boards in internal medicine, and that I had come to Kansas prepared to work with Delp as chairman. Murphy did not enjoy this kind of problem, and I well remember his using the very phrase, "the horns of the dilemma."

The chairmen would not give, and Murphy was faced with what is the largest kind of pressure a dean can face, united chairmen. The chairman of Surgery, Paul Schafer, was not only especially adamant, but represented the most powerful department. Even more stressful, he was the Dean's closest friend among the faculty. Dr. Ralph Major, who had immense respect from all of the faculty, and from the Kansas City community, was approached by Murphy, and his help was sought in cultivating a fresh opinion from the chairmen. Dr. Major adroitly refused. He gave the Dean counsel which, in essence, was, never weaken your position by turning to retired faculty for clout. When you do, you will never again be quite in charge of the school, and the next thing you know, the old-timers will be forming a veto club over your own authority.

Murphy finally bit the bullet. He called me out of the theater at the University of Kansas City one night and said he was recommending my appointment as chairman to the Board of Regents. I reminded him that I was not even Board-certified. He said that I could be an interim chairman and associate professor until I passed the Boards. I made a gambler's suggestion. I told him that I had no desire to be an interim anything. I believed it would be best if he gave me a letter telling me I would be full chairman if I took and passed the Boards in internal medicine, *first time taken*. If I failed the Boards, the subject was forgotten. For the reader, this may not seem like too much of a gamble. Surely one can pass an examination.

The gamble comes from the fact that this particular Board had a very high failure rate, and the risk was magnified by the fact that I had never had a residency in medicine. Further, I was extremely busy in the founding, starting up, and running of the cardiac unit. I did not have time to study as one should before sitting for this notoriously difficult exam. Franklin agreed to the letter and conditions, and I launched into an exhausting chapter of life: running a very large consulting practice, teaching all over the country, and taking a test for which I had not been trained. All of this, from beginning to end, occupied a year, a painful year, and when the letter with Board results came near Christmastime, I opened it with a very empty feeling.

I had passed. I was immediately made chairman; I was 33, the youngest chairman of Medicine in the United States.

Chapter Six

As CHAIRMAN OF MEDICINE AND head of cardiology, I moved into a considerable level of busyness but, as a good physician friend, Mark Dodge, said to me, "After you pass those Boards, you finally have time to read and do what you want to. They are like a prison."

With the Boards passed and the chairmanship of Medicine and the leadership of the cardiology group in my lap, for the next decade I was out of bed at 5:30 a.m. and at the hospital before 7 a.m.

Recruitment for full-time staff in the Department of Medicine occupied an inordinate amount of time, although Dr. Delp had assembled a good nucleus of local people. All of these I kept on.

Max Allen was a special jewel. In addition to being a true clinician, he had somehow found a means of working with, and for, Mahlon, and remaining himself. I don't know at what price he accomplished this; perhaps it was mute evidence that he was a master clinician and could handle any situation.

In Neurology, Pulmonary, and Gastroenterology, I went outside to find new staff. As with Cardiology, I chose to have the department take a major clinical role. The quality of the residency program was first in my ambitions. I felt that if good Residents could be attracted, good patient care would follow or, just the obverse could be reasoned: A quality care program would attract good Residents.

In these same years, a new Veterans Administration Hospital was built in the area and another large task came with it—finding staff and fitting it into our residency program. Such opportunities are important and are not to be delegated. Although all over the country, new VA hospitals were being built on medical center campuses, the reality of the power of Harry Truman meant our new hospital was built very near his home city of Independence, miles from our base, and a problem, I am sure, down to the present. Politics and what is right are not close relatives.

During the entire 10-year period, I made bed-to-bed ward rounds in internal medicine from 1 p.m. to 5 p.m. each Friday at the Wadsworth VA Hospital, near Leavenworth, Kansas, and this broadened my experience in diagnosis. A special dividend was meeting and knowing Ed Twin, who for three of these years was my Resident in Medicine at Wadsworth.

Other users of time and, equally, an extension of the Department of Medicine's influence, were the development of an education program, both undergraduate and graduate, at the regional Menorah Jewish Hospital, and an extension of the residency training to include experiences in the Kansas psychiatric hospitals of Osawatomie, Parsons, and Winfield. I am sure there are internists from the Kansas program who well recall their tour of duty at one of these institutions. I remember the ingenuity of our Resident, Sherman Steinzeig, who when faced with the crisis of days of over 100 degrees, no air-conditioning, and dehydrated, exhausted, incapacitated, mentally deficient patients hovering on heat exhaustion, brought in a hose and watered the whole area, floor, patients and all. Bold, inventive, effective therapy.

For the 10-year period, I was on the selection committee with responsibility for selecting candidates for enrollment as medical students. This experience made me have a lifetime awareness of how little science there is in such selection, and how often a judgment is wrong, wrong both ways: good people being missed, and mistakes getting in. This 10-year period also served as a training program for me when I had the duty to set up a selection method for a new medical school.

Postgraduate teaching became a large part of my activity, with several yearly programs at the medical center in both cardiology and medicine. Twice a year, I joined two or three other members of the faculty, and spent a week or two barnstorming Kansas by station wagon. A well laid-out route took us on swings through what is truly a vast area, Kansas. Unless one has done this, it is

difficult to understand the distances, the isolation, and how a pre-
vailing wind from the southwest never eases. There is a sense of
openness, cleanness, emptiness, out in the high plains of Kansas,
which makes city life and urban problems seem to belong to another culture. One begins to think of islands in a vast sea after
driving for miles through nothing but fields of wheat, and then
coming ashore with a grain elevator serving as a lighthouse.

These teaching trips were called circuit courses, and, although
they were mixed in with tornados, heat waves, and blizzards, they
were always a welcome break. They brought a chance to get to
know not only the men in practice out in the remote areas, but
even a chance to get to know your own colleagues, in a way you
could not back at our base. No one ever made those trips who cannot offer his contribution to the folk tales and legends of a "circuit
course." It made us feel as if we had shared a wartime experience.

The quality of the people who originally settled Kansas trans-
mits down to the present, and I continue to cherish the seriousness, the civility, the durability, and ability of the Kansas citizen.
Parenthetically, they make superb physicians.

In 1955, a delightful dividend came into the medical postgraduate scene at Kansas. A slender, dark-haired, 28-year-old man became the lay staff for the medical center's postgraduate courses,
both at the home campus and for the circuit courses. I am not
speaking of a small responsibility; the teaching of the man in practice became a large endeavor, involving, ultimately, thousands of
physicians.

He was immediately appreciated because of his goodwill, energy, and intelligence. He also immediately mastered that very difficult nuance of how to get along with the prima donna conduct of
physicians. With him it was never a problem, not because he was
obsequious, but because he so radiated goodwill and enthusiasm,
strengthened by solid judgment.

Later on, as he moved into larger circles in postgraduate
medicine, he mastered a quality often overlooked for success in
such a role—he devoted almost equal time to getting to know the
wives, their names, interests, the children, and the hobbies of the
family. His good judgment, willingness to work hard, and obvious
intelligence made it impossible for even the most difficult physi-

cian personality to find friction. His name was Bill Nelligan. He was another example of the quality and talent of people bred out on the plains of Kansas. He was raised in Halstead, the little town made famous by Hertzler's book, *The Horse and Buggy Doctor.*

We worked together at Kansas until I left in 1960. Then in 1964, he went to the Medical College of Georgia. I kept him on my list of prime talent not to be forgotten. We had learned the art of post-graduate medical education together.

One small fact expresses what was done in Kansas: In a single year, 49 percent of the Kansas practicing physicians enrolled for courses at the medical center; in a three-year period, 62 percent were enrolled.

In cardiology, my unit moved to another level of sophistication, and I was able to bring up from the School of Aviation Medicine one of the Operation Paperclip research stars I had met there, Kurt Reissmann. He came along with his entire torsion ballisto-cardiograph, a medieval-looking, monster-piece of equipment, and took over the physiology research of our cardiac unit.

At about the same time, a local ear, nose, and throat physician, Dr. Sam Roberts, persuaded a sizable philanthropic gift from the McIlvaine family to be used for basic research. Sam was a good example of the kind of enthusiasm mixed with energy, naivete, and little real medical judgment, which institutional fund-raisers must not only encourage and direct but, if really successful, learn how to thoroughly enjoy and cherish. With this unexpected, several-hundred-thousand dollars, I went after Santiago Grisolia, who was deep in research at the famous enzyme institute of the University of Wisconsin. We were able to get Grisolia, and a large laboratory area in a new building. As head of the biochemical research unit of our cardiac laboratory, he quickly built a major program.

Without forethought, the internationalization of the group was continuing: Grisolia was Spanish, Reissmann, German. Within the year, Nobuo Ito, the Japanese physician who had been assigned to my EKG station in Tokyo, was in Kansas City, working under Grisolia, and he remained a number of years. Ito, Ito-san, and I re-mained, as I have described, formal, bowing, nonconversational friends throughout the rest of our lives.

My private referred practice of cardiology became huge. Paul

White advised his former patients and referring physicians in the Midwest area to turn to me for their service. The practice area included Kansas, Missouri, Oklahoma, Iowa, and Nebraska—a mid-America heart service. I held to a commitment that all patients, private or not, would be seen in full partnership with the Residents and Fellows, outpatient and inpatient, and the experience produced a substantial number of able cardiologists. These, in truth, were my finished product, and I cared about them and considered them my friends. They are the lengthened shadow about which one reads.

The medical center had a private-practice plan, and we were able to do all our own billings, collections, and reap the benefits of the reward, free from any university tax or tithing.

We had all the equipment we needed, and were able to practice world-level cardiology. Heart surgery developed rapidly, and when I was not comfortable with our ability to handle certain operations, I referred patients to Michael DeBakey, Denton Cooley, and Walton Lillehei, all who became personal friends.

One of the events of the time was that new medical centers grew up all over the country, and for the first time, there was no longer the domination of the Philadelphia-Hopkins-Boston trilogy. Of course, the trilogy did not know this, and remained comfortable, not appreciating what was happening in American medicine.

I had observed the progress of a Kansas graduate, James Crockett, and followed his career as he served time in the Navy. I wrote him and asked him to join me upon his return to civilian life. By 1956, he was a very able, promising cardiologist, and we entered into a formal practice agreement. No one could have been a better choice, and through many years of working together, not only in cardiology at Kansas, but in postgraduate teaching, in organizational work for the American College of Cardiology, in overseas teaching assignments, and in such plain hard-work projects as making medical audiotapes, Jim was always able and willing. Our personalities complemented each other and, where I might have been too quick, he provided the carefulness of detail. Marti, his wife was, equally, a personal friend. One of their sons, Brian, I could have enjoyed stealing, and when he was older, we took him off to a vacation on Capri.

These professional experiences did not occur in a family vacuum. In 1951, Audrey and I made an extended tour of the East Coast, and saw our friends in Boston, and went up to Dublin, New Hampshire to see the Thoron family, friends from Texas, at their summer place.

This visit included my first time to meet Grenville Clark. Although he was a very respected figure in law, government, and an activist in international law, I, from my limited perspective, knew him simply as a patient of Paul White's. One's view of life certainly can be small, and mine was at a limited level. At his home, I met Reinhold Niebuhr and another time, Felix Frankfurter. Over the driest of martinis, I instantly recognized their range of comments and world-affairs sophistication was at a level that I would enjoy, but was beyond my own growth. Winona and Terre Haute had prepared me for a life of honorable but limited horizons. Medical school and the Army had lifted my sights considerably, and the excitement of MGH had not been lost on me. But here I was literally being shaken and offered a sample of the ranges of a world beyond medicine. The lesson was a powerful one and never has it been forgotten.

The summer of 1952 we made an extended auto trip to San Francisco, then to the Monterey Peninsula, Carmel, the Big Sur, on down to La Jolla, into Mexico to Ensenada, and then back home, across the Southern deserts. But not without knowing I had seen two grand places for grand living: Carmel joined my list of places where one must live, and then La Jolla proved even more captivating. Of course, we saw all the points in between, from the cable cars to the Grand Canyon, but a new entry entered my list of ambitions—to raise my family in La Jolla.

In that first stay at Carmel, I found a small piece of redwood drift and, there on the beach, carved from it a wing, a free-form wing. Forty years later, this carving was cast in bronze, large-size, and placed in front of the medical school. The wing, the memory of the moment of finding the wood, the beauty and free spirit of the location—all these things made me name the piece Take Wing, and hope that it stands there as a symbol of the life I wish for each graduate.

Audrey and I built a redwood home out in the countryside of

Kansas. I rode horses, raised orchids and in 1953 our first child, Lark Grey Dimond, was born. I was 34, Audrey was 31. We had been married almost nine years. Lark was named after my mother's brother and what a perfect name it has been for her.

Major events were happening in the life of the medical center. Life is never static, and even as I recite them here, I think of ten thousand other things that seemed so very important at the time. It takes time for things to gain their right size.

The chairman of Surgery, who was a main influence because of his involvement with cardiac surgery, came onto a very difficult personal problem, and suddenly he was no longer at the medical center. My own definition of latitude of conduct did not influence the more righteous chairmen. Cardiac surgery did not suffer too much, for two able men, Creighton Hardin and Fred Kittle, pushed ahead in this field, and we developed into a cordial working team.

The largest change occurred when the university head, the Chancellor, was attracted away by Cornell, and Franklin Murphy moved up to that task, and thus moved out of our immediate lives to live in Lawrence, Kansas. He was a good choice, and the university benefitted.

We at the medical center did not, however, and for more than a year, we were somewhat adrift while a senior internist, Edward Hashinger, served as acting dean.

Dr. Hashinger was an internist in private practice in Kansas City, Missouri. For many years, in fact since the early 1920's, he had been a loyal, devoted volunteer member of Dr. Major's department, running the outpatient clinic. He had been a member of the same military unit as Dr. Delp, and the commanding officer of the unit. The two should have been good friends, but neither man had good words about the other. Privately, Dr. Delp referred to him as Skippy.

Dr. Hashinger married for the first time when he was about 60, marrying a widow of some considerable wealth who had already been a major benefactor to the university. Ed was well-meaning, inclined to posturing, eliciting puffery, and telling considerably expanded stories which were based on a proud finale of, "And so I said ..."

Ed could readily irritate one by his initial presentation of bluster, but I found I could handle it, even enjoy it, by associating his arrival with the wonderful rolling word: "fanfaronade." With the comfort of that resonant label, I was able to enjoy the performance.

He was not a man of small achievement, however. When young, he had competed in a national competition for speed in shorthand and typing, and, so the story was told, came in second to Billy Rose. More verifiable was the fact that he was a collector with some knowledge of early American glassware, was a skilled furniture craftsman, played the piano very well, and waltzed like a dream, in the grand, sweeping manner. One of the heroes of Kansas City medicine had been Logan Clendening, a famous author, columnist, and raconteur. Hashinger had entered practice as his junior partner and had co-authored a medical textbook with him. In fact, Clendening's widow and Hashinger came very close to marrying. Personally, I enjoyed Ed, and for a number of years was his personal physician.

The acting deanship of Ed Hashinger trickled along, and Franklin remained hesitant about making a permanent choice. I found all of the gossiping and polarizing painful, and got too much involved when some enthusiasts pushed my name for the job. Finally, one Sunday morning, I drove over to Lawrence, to the Chancellor's lovely residence on Lilac Lane, and while Franklin was dressing, told him the medical center had to be stabilized and that I thought he should appoint Clarke Wescoe as dean. This was not only the stimulus he needed, but it also made it clear that I was not wanting the job. Wescoe immediately was made dean.

A deanship was not exactly worth trading for my new chairmanship.

Clarke brought in as assistant dean an M.D.-pharmacologist from the University of Illinois, Vernon Wilson. Wilson had entered medical school late and had had experience in industry. He never practiced medicine. He felt comfortable in management, and with an intense loyalty to Clarke, took on many of the administrative actions which brought conflict with the department chairmen. In the late 1950's, he was recruited away to be dean at the University of Missouri in Columbia, and I was glad to see him go. However, the relationship we had had at Kansas was one made for conflict. I was defending a department's turf; he, acting for Clarke, was charged with increasing the Dean's dominion.

A few years later, under other circumstances, Vern and I became natural allies and found we had a common basic philosophy about medicine. The conflicting times in Kansas were because we were cast on the stage as opponents, we were victims of the titles we carried. In truth, we were co-conspirators and when given the right circumstances, we enjoyed each other, and ended our careers friends and allies. I have often found this to be a painful truth; a real hostility will develop between two people only because of the jobs they represent, and the place from which they speak; the arena and the audience make them gladiators.

It is easy for someone to be labeled as a stormy petrol, a troublemaker, and have this label stay with him the rest of his career, when the truth is that the person is reasonable, likable, useful, and is criticized, stigmatized, for fighting gross inadequacy. Equally, and this is an irritating reality, the individual who is grossly inadequate can go steadily up to very high levels of success with no fundamental ability, originality, or even intelligence. By being pleasant, by having minimal willingness to fight for anything, he acquires the sobriquet "nice guy," not a problem-maker, and even when he becomes the maximum prototype of Parkinson's Law, no one dares criticize him because he has had such a successful career. I only know well the world of medicine, but can say with confidence that some of medicine's honored heroes succeeded not for what they did, but for what they didn't do.

During the years I was chairman, I was frequently with the retired chairman, Ralph Major. Dr. Major had been chairman of Pathology of the school until he left for World War I and in 1921 he was brought back as the first full-time head of internal medicine. His career at the medical school went right back to its roots.

He was one of three retired men of integrity who continued their interest and dedication to the school, and were impressive by their determination, resolutely, to avoid a semblance of invading the decision process of their successors. The other two were the former chief of Surgery, Dr. Thomas Orr, and Dr. Harry Wahl, the former head of Pathology and also the dean prior to Franklin. All were trained at Hopkins, a forceful reminder of not only the greatness of that institution, but also of how limited were the sources of talent at that time in the United States.

I had many happy evenings over dinner and drinks with Dr. Major discussing famous names in medicine; he knew essentially everyone of his era who had placed his name on a disease. He was a skilled author, and one of his books, *Classic Descriptions of Disease*, had given him access to the source of almost every eponym of his time. He and his wife, Margaret, were gracious intellectuals with an enthusiasm for Germany, the Germany of his university youth; the Germany of Hitler had been a bitter time for him. The Majors toured Europe every year, and his plans always included visits with the famous names of medicine.

He was a man who loved to talk and was good at it. The word "raconteur" was created for him. He did not tell short stories, but complete, involved, often witty, lengthy ones. He enjoyed playing several parts in a scenario, changing his voice and tone as he recounted each character's words. He did not await your turn with expectation but instead, when you began to volunteer your own clever item, he would quickly find an opening, and with, "Have I ever told about the time I was in Bad Nauheim..." and you were again a listener. He wrote a history of the medical center titled *An Account of the University of Kansas School of Medicine*, and it is a delightful example of the blending of humor, fact, and embellishment of the truth in which he excelled.

We talked about everything, and I made it a rule always to keep him informed. Yet never once did he make a comment, criticism, or suggestion about the department he had founded and I had inherited. This was such an example of graciousness that it remained with me and I have held myself to such conduct when I passed on from a task. At least, I think I have. My successors can evaluate this better.

He also taught me a lesson about age and how foolish a young man can be. When he was 70, he and his wife made their first trip to Asia, and in Hong Kong he had a suit tailored. I remember how bemused I was at his optimism, when, at his advanced age, he had two pairs of pants made for the suit. My snickering thought was, how could a man of that phenomenal age waste money on two pairs of pants? Now that I am substantially beyond that age, I freely call myself, the self of that time, callow.

By the summer of 1956, I had completed a full six years at the school. I had been determined at all points to take advantage of the university option which permits a professor to have the seventh year as a break, a sabbatical leave. This was not a break in the sense of a vacation, but was available at half-pay compensation for one to go to another center to study, to do research, to write. It is one of the little elegancies which make the lessened income of an academician not quite so painful.

I was as fully engaged with the world of cardiology as one could be, and, equally there was no issue of emotional fatigue or other commonly cited justifications for a sabbatical leave. I was not tired; I wanted to see the world—and think of other places.

Anyone in an administrative position, whether it is academia or industry, has to give thought to the question of security of the position, if he or she departs for a substantial period of time. Many a chairman or dean has left happily for a sabbatical only, to find a palace revolt or a carefully timed house cleaning eliminated his power base—and his job.

I did not have an internal warning signal that this would be a problem and it was not. There were no corridor susurrations—and I am a firm believer that one must listen to all rumors. Rumors have a tendency to be either wrong or right, and you are better off to know their tenor and perhaps lean upon making them wrong or right.

Ed Hashinger, as acting dean, was very supportive, and Franklin, as chancellor, was enthusiastic about international experiences. There was, however, a considerable factor influencing me that had nothing to do with a need to refresh my knowledge of cardiology.

Over the years of my chairmanship, Dr. Delp and I had worked out a level of mutual respect and were as cordial as our different personalities would bear. Delp was never pleasant, but I had a thorough respect for his dedication and his convictions. There was a logical question one had to ask: Were the next 20 years best used in a relationship neither man enjoyed?

I was carrying other burdens, if "burden" is the appropriate word. The six years at Kansas had been very good to me and

were, in every sense, a continuity of the education that had begun
in my sophomore year when I began reading for Harry Baum; I
had been in cardiology and had stayed with it for 15 years. I had
led a cardiologist's life, if anyone ever did. The issue I was weighing was the basic one which, in a perfect world, would not be
asked. I felt no internal agitation, impending moment of crisis, instead I asked myself if I would hold to my original commitment to
10 years only in Kansas, what were the ambitions and goals I
might take on if I did turn away from the honor and power of the
Chair in Medicine? And equally, did I intend to be a cardiologist
for the rest of my career?

An outside observer could quickly have given the comfortable
answer: "Yes, of course you should stay at your task. Don't be erratic and vary your course. You are comfortable and what you are
doing is good enough."

Comfortable? At no point in life have I ever been able to say my
goal was to be comfortable. Comfort makes me uncomfortable.

University medical center chairmen are secure, more secure
than deans. To do the job adequately is not difficult; to keep on
with the task for a full 30 years, until I was 65, was certainly possible. The job of chairman, done well, is one of the best uses of
one's talent possible, and I make that evaluation thoughtfully. To
do what I had been doing as chief of Medicine was certainly not a
lost career. To not try other routes was the loss.

My basic, natural instincts made me want to try my wings. The
ultimate reach in academic medicine is the Chair. I had reached it
at 33. To not explore other horizons, to settle for the security and
prestige of the position, was simply not how I wanted to use my
time on stage.

The Fulbright program had just begun, and I entered myself
into competing for a Fulbright professorship at the University of
Utrecht in the Netherlands. Utrecht and the nearby university,
Leiden, had very good cardiology programs, and I requested a
three-month sabbatical with Professor van Ruyven at Utrecht, and
three months to visit the cardiac centers in Europe. In part, of
course, my interest had been stimulated by the yearly visits of Dr.
Major to Europe and the great stories he brought home.

A Kansas City industrialist who had been, remarkably, Paul

White's Harvard College classmate and a patient of mine, came forward and at a party at Dr. Hashinger's home announced that he wanted to honor his old classmate. He was giving me a Paul White Traveling Scholarship so Audrey and I could combine our time in Holland with a trip around the world. He felt that one of Dr. White's achievements was to have become an international citizen, and he hoped with this gift that I might follow my teacher's example. He was Parker B. Francis, the founder of Puritan Gas, the original medical oxygen company and of Puritan-Bennett, a prominent source of respirator equipment.

Obviously, July 1, 1956 was taking on a very attractive dimension and so I requested a half year of leave. Other things fell in place well: James Crockett, who had joined me in private practice on January 1, 1956, made me comfortable in turning away from my practice, and I knew the cardiac unit would be safe in his hands. I had a very competent secretary, Kathryn Calderwood, who, after five full years, knew every detail of the place; I formed a committee to handle the operation of the Department of Medicine; and little Lark, age 3, was secure, as Audrey's mother moved into our home.

When we sailed on July 1, Audrey was 34 and I was 37. It was just about 10 years since I had been out of the country. It was my first trip to Europe.

We landed in France, "did" Paris, and in every way received the education of a neophyte abroad. My education reached a peak at the Eiffel Tower restaurant when our dinner cost more than $100. Remember, it was 1956.

If being carefree means being unprepared, we were carefree. I had an appointment in Hamburg, Germany with a Volkswagen used-car agency for July 14, room reservation at the Istanbul Hilton for August 15, and had told Professor van Ruyven I would arrive at his office on September 15. I had, resolutely, no other plans, no map, no guidebook, and not a single appointment, reservation or responsibility except these three: Hamburg, July 14; Istanbul, August 15; Utrecht, September 15. My first point of contact with home was to be the American Express in Istanbul. In between, we were two birds who had flown the coop. Neither of us spoke any German, and my college credits in French were exactly that—college credits in French.

In Hamburg, I bought a VW beetle for $1,100 and we started southeast across Europe. The only map I had was provided by the German Automobile Association and it was for West Germany only. We drove South through Frankfurt, then to Heidelberg, on to Berchtesgaden, and it was so delightful, exciting, stimulating that we decided to make the rest of the trip without a map, without a reservation, and live by only the discipline of adequate gasoline and the prospect of a clean hotel room in Istanbul. As I remembered the meticulous preparations always made by Dr. Major for his European tours, with a full schedule of appointments, lunches, dinners, interviews, I felt like a gypsy, and even a gypsy would have been alarmed by our lack of plans.

My main logistical tactic was to inquire as we bought gasoline, calling out loudly, loudly so others could hear my question. I varied my query from "Istanbul!?" to "Turkey!?" with large hand gestures towards the southeast. There may be other ways to get there now, but in 1956 there was essentially one paved highway crossing Yugoslavia and therefore, once we got on it near Ljubljana, one stayed on it through Zagreb, Belgrade, Skopje, and on into Macedonia. With luck, you end up in Saloniki, Greece, and then you are ready for the considerable adventure of going east across Asia Minor, past Edirne, and at the end of an interminable drive, and with apprehension hovering on doom, squeeze out a few liters of gasoline from a military depot and get to the Istanbul Hilton at 11:30 p.m., August 15, 1956, blessing fate that the reservation had already been paid.

The next morning, with both of us regretting the need to reenter organized life, we picked up mail and money at the American Express. Only one letter had a surprise. One of the best Residents in Medicine, Roger Halliday, who finished up his residency on June 30, the day before we had left, had married my trusted secretary, Kathryn Calderwood, the very same secretary about whom I felt such confidence—had married her, and they had left immediately for California—for good.

Life is designed to not have a grand pattern. The value of a sabbatical leave was vividly demonstrated. If I had been home on the job, the loss of a superb secretary would have been a catastrophe.

With six weeks of sabbatical as an antidote, the loss gave me pause—a shrug, and a grin of happiness for them. And it gave me a lesson in the inadequacy of corridor susurrations.

Istanbul did for us what it does for all Westerners: it brought home another world. On the long trip across Europe, in spite of the marked differences, it still remained a familiar, basic, European, Western culture. At Istanbul you knew you had fallen out of the world you had known; the world I had seen in the Far East was more understandable than this. The vast reaches of Asia, which begin at Istanbul and do not end until one reaches Han China are almost missing knowledge for us, and yet, have been the basis of much of history. On that first "sampler" trip, I resolved to spend time and scholarship in learning about Asia.

We left Istanbul for Athens by ship, taking the faithful VW with us. The Turkish ship was dirty beyond belief, and it was a painful moment when I found a bronze marker in the lounge identifying it as the former S.S. Solace, a famous American hospital ship in the War. We had all seen many photographs of it, white, pristine, hygienic looking—it had come on hard times.

We "did" Athens, Thermopylae, then went by boat through the Corinth canal to the heel of Italy, landing at Brindisi, up the Appian Way to Naples, the Amalfi Drive—all in our little car. We boated to Capri and, in Capri, hurried up to Anacapri to find Casa Surya, where Paul White and Ina had stayed for six months while writing the first edition of his heart textbook (1929). In Anacapri, I was fascinated by the home and story of Axel Munthe. Then back to Sorrento, to Pompeii, up to Florence and Rome, to Venice, to Lake Como, to Geneva and Zurich, on across Germany to Denmark, to Sweden by ferry, on beyond Stockholm to the Norwegian border, changing there back to the normal side of the road, on to Oslo, then back to Denmark, south—hurrying to make the date—arriving in Utrecht on September 14, finding a hotel base, and suntanned, exhausted, skinny, stimulated, reporting—with a feeling of regret that our wild geese flight was ending—to Professor van Ruyven at 8 a.m. September 15, 1956. We had navigated a giant cross, west to east, south to north, and back to center. We felt we had a beginning knowledge of Europe.

The night before, I had produced my stethoscope from the lug-

gage and looked at it almost as a foreign object. It had been the
longest period of time, in a full 15-year period, I have ever gone
without using it, essentially daily. It took me a week to get my
"ear" back.

The Professor and I got along well. I learned quickly what a position of power "The Professor" has in Europe. An American
physician who also becomes a professor does not consider the
"professor" title to have greater distinction, or even as much, as
"Doctor." "Herr Professor" gathers a range of power and social
position we poor academics in the United States never find. I capi-
talize Professor here when discussing Van Ruyven, for as it was
used in daily communication, it was definitely "all caps."

At his invitation, I sat beside him in his office as he dealt with
administrative issues. It was soon apparent that his opinion carried weight beyond anything I would dare assume at home. One
of the first visitors was a Fellow who came to seek the Professor's
permission to marry. This alone would have been a shock at
home. My own personal secretary had married my own Resident
and no one even bothered to tell me. The Professor asked the
young man questions, many of them quite specific. Finally Van
Ruyven ended the interview with a negative answer. No, the marriage was not acceptable. The young woman was not of appropriate social position. She was not a suitable candidate! The pale
young man thanked him and backed out of the room.

Professor van Ruyven had one material possession that I immediately coveted. His home was a place of such warmth, with the
captured charm of an old Dutch painting, with delft blue tiles,
copper cauldrons, the deep reds and blues of oriental rugs, all
topped off by a huge roof of deep brown-golden thatch; it was anyone's dream house.

At the hospital, I was given an office in the garret, a bright,
freshly painted office, with not a window, but, instead, a wonderful crystal-clear skylight. Autumn rains are frequent in the
Netherlands, and I found this nest in the garret a tranquil sanctuary, with great white clouds drifting by overhead and then, suddenly, a sweep of rain coming in off the North Atlantic.

I volunteered to read the daily electrocardiograms. The heart's
electrical signal is an international language if there is any. The

Residents and Fellows were an older group than I worked with at home. In a fixed, nongrowing society such as the Netherlands, one stays in training, sometimes for years, waiting for a practice opportunity to open. This aging process gave the group a very solid level of information, and I found myself learning as often as I taught. The level of cardiology was very good, and in one area, the display of material from autopsies, the program was substantially better than my own unit. Weekly teaching sessions with the pathologist presenting his findings were an improvement over anything I had experienced.

I quickly found myself walking a very fine line between educator and insurrectionist. The men in training found it irresistible to have a young American professor in their midst, and, by ones and twos, would come to my skylighted hideaway. Their stated purpose of discussing a nuance of cardiology done, they got down to their real issues: Would a professor like theirs be tolerated in the United States? Did we have such academic dictators? What did I think about the lack of opportunity for them in the Netherlands? And then the question I knew was coming, "What could you offer me in Kansas?"

I danced, walked, ran around these attempts at palace coups and jumping ship, but when the dozen men in training kept up their campaign, I took a coward's path and suggested to the Professor that I should run over to the United Kingdom and Ireland and check on their cardiology. Two men who had been at Paul White's at the same time I was there were in Galway and Dublin, and I wanted to see the National Heart Hospital in London, the institution I had defaulted on when I had elected to go to Austin. The Professor agreed. We hurried off to a happy exposure to life and private practice in Ireland.

Timothy Counihan picked us up at Dublin, and after a time with Tim and his Mary, Sean O'Toole came and took me on a sequence of house calls as we drove back across Ireland. Each house call required a "wee drop of Irish," and by the time we reached his handsome home on The Crescent in Galway, I was intoxicated, and happy that I was, for his great stone and brick home was heated by the most diminutive of peat-burning fireplaces. We were blue cold for much of the visit.

Sean added to my list of never-again experiences when he took me out in Galway Bay in his small fishing boat. It was a lesson I already knew, but could not evade, the lesson being never let anyone get you in their boat unless it is an absolute yacht with a crew. There is a dangerous personality in someone who finds some emotional release on a small, rocking, damp, slippery boat, with the wind and the sea and gasoline fumes in his nostrils. I am not a total landlubber and have spent weeks on river boats, cruise ships, and other islands of civilization, but the small personal boat with the "skipper" is an arena that I have taught my daughters to avoid.

In London, The National Heart Hospital was more than I had expected. My visit was brief, but I saw Paul Wood perform in the clinic, and I knew that I had found a place to return to. He was a small man, not much different in body build than Dr. White, but that was the only similarity. Dr. White was always the essence of courtesy, discretion, thoughtfulness. Paul Wood was quick, abrasive, witty, articulate, knifelike in his comments to his juniors. His very laugh was a bark, a honk, painfully forced. He was so obviously intelligent and filled with huge amounts of bedside skills that he could not contain himself. Clinical pearls and sarcasm fell around the room in a burst. Strangely and satisfactorily, he and I got along immediately and well. We found a means and a level of communication which suited each of us, and began immediately a friendship that lasted until his death.

We returned to Utrecht, and my two-week absence had allowed things to settle down. A rhythm of life fell in place. Hotel living with full maid service and a well-run dining room provided the good life, and even this was improved upon as I learned that I was being paid in Dutch currency my full U.S.A. salary, and this arithmetic was multiplied by the very inexpensive cost of living. Then a directive came that none of the currency could be taken from the country when my professorship ended. I was faced with the obligation to spend a considerable amount of money or create a Dutch bank account and come again for a future visit. We did both. Our remaining time was a mix of five full days of cardiology, and weekends of galleries, museums, flower shows, theater, and superb meals. With a car and almost three months of weekends for exploration, the tininess of Holland and its sophistication makes it an ideal small, civilized book to be read, appreciated, savored. The only flaws in our experience were the repeated small insults, asides, and rudenesses expressed when the occasional Dutch noted the German license plate on the German car, and assumed we were German tourists. The War and the anger were still fresh enough that this was not always acceptable. Physically, this showed itself by fists pounding the roof or fenders and the radio antenna disappearing. The largest expression was a long sweeping scratch on the car side, made with a key, as we drove through a crowd.

Thanksgiving was made memorable with a gathering of several hundred Americans in the old church in Leiden, where the Pilgrims had worshipped before heading out on the Mayflower. After the service, we gathered for the full Thanksgiving dinner, down to pumpkin pie.

I had been to Leiden several times already, for the head of cardiology there, Dr. Herman Snellen, had a vigorous program in rehabilitation cardiology, one of the first of the efforts which have gradually built up until now there is a general acceptance of the value of reconditioning the heart, even if it had been damaged. My friend, Herman Hellerstein, first met at Louis Katz's lab, made this his life work, and was responsible for one of the earliest, large efforts involving heart patients. In Snellen's unit there was also a classic jewel of an academician named Hartmann, who worked in a minuscule area, filling it with the pungent aroma of his constant cheroot, as he enjoyed his study of the phonocardiogram, and especially the jugular venous trace. I hacked and wheezed my way through several sessions with this generous man.

I had been back in Holland but a few days when the Hungarian uprising began. Immediately, the Western world was ignited. Volunteers were called for, and I felt this was an ideal time for me to be involved: I was already in Europe, I was essentially free, Van Ruyven certainly had no real need for my service, I was young enough. I made the attempt to join expeditionary groups being dispatched to Hungary. A thoughtful bureaucrat took down my credentials and my offer of my medical skills.

After a few delicate questions, which covered the facts that I was not a surgeon, not a generalist, had not served in combat, had no experience with blood donors, and was a diagnostician, only at home in a center with sophisticated equipment, and whose knowledge was restricted to children with congenital heart disease and adults with bad hearts, he gracefully refused me and said that there was really no place for a medical cardiologist of my type in an area that was fighting for its life.

He suggested that if they were successful and regained their independence, then, perhaps at some future date, I might go as a Fulbright professor and give some lectures.

This moment of possible usefulness opened on October 23, with the students uprising; it closed on November 3 with the new massing of Soviet tanks.

It took me awhile to recover from this estimation of the value of my abilities, but as I reflected upon it—then, and often over the years—I have come to appreciate (perhaps appreciate is an inappropriate word; accept would be better) that we medical cardiologists are only useful in a nonemergency society. A society which has reached the luxury of time and money sufficient to try and salvage those who are imperfect or damaged is where we fit. In those countries in which the issues are visceral, crisis weighted, a real doctor is needed, not someone who needs several hundred thousand dollars of electronic gear and a team of Fellows in order to give his performance. The man told me in the nicest of ways that I was such a luxury and their need was for someone useful.

The lesson was not lost and it went into my collection of vital truths, and made me realize that my early opportunity with Harry Baum had at the same time closed out paths that I was never able to explore. As I came to know Paul White and Paul Wood, came to know them as men and not heart doctors, I found they, too, had moments of severe regret and murmured to me the wish that they had taken alternative paths.

In December, I drove back across the German border to Wesel and sold the car. One was obligated to sell it in the country of registry. Fifteen thousand miles together had made the Beetle a trusted companion. It had never varied in performance, never had a hiccup, a flat nor faltered. It brought $1,050. Fifteen thousand miles of driving had cost us $50.

The Utrecht group gave a farewell party on December 8, honoring both my 38th birthday and my visit. They presented me with a medieval map of the Lowlands, striking just the right note. I treasured the map and now it is with my daughters. The Fulbright sojourn ended on December 15, and that day I immediately became the Paul Dudley White Traveling Scholar. We flew from Amsterdam to New Delhi.

In New Delhi, we were met by Dr. Shreenivas Shreenivas, who had been a Fellow with me at Paul White's, and after seeing the Taj Mahal and absorbing, if but a smallest fraction, the exotic difference of India, I knew that this was not a country in which I could find a natural harmony. I have returned several times, but the despair I feel does not lessen. Shreenivas has remained as a small opening through which, by letters and visits, I have sought to gain an intellectual, if not emotional, appreciation. My Western man, practical man, nonbeliever man roots, have not given me the right capacity for this insight.

The next stop was Bangkok, and we were under the care immediately of one of my former Fellows, Dr. Chaveng Dechakalsaya. The grace and gentleness of Thailand was different than Japan, but I immediately knew I was in the Asia of the Oriental and felt at home. The Asia of Turkey, of India, is different, alien, for me. My homeyness was attenuated somewhat when we came out of a great Buddhist temple and found that my big black leather shoes, size 11-D, had been absorbed into the economy. Stolen. One entered the temple only in stocking feet. I remained in my stocking feet until we reached Hong Kong. Bangkok, in 1956, just did not have shoes large enough for a misshapened Westerner, and for our around-the-world trip, I had packed no extra shoes.

In Hong Kong, we were guests of no one and for three days could relapse into pure tourism. The excitement of Hong Kong has never grown old for me, and, in another reincarnation, I would like to have a year or two of H.K. life. We stayed at the Peninsula Hotel, and the grand service in that hotel, and high tea in its magic lobby, perhaps caught me up in the romance of foreign correspondents, espionage, and Eurasian beauties. I can sit and daydream wondrous romance in that lobby.

We flew on to Manila, and were given the complete Mariano Alimurung treatment. I use that phrase, and for all those who remember Mariano, the words will bring a smile, a thought of his hospitality, and a wave of exhaustion. Mariano was the essence of Philippines graciousness, and that graciousness, verve, and cordial encompassing a visitor to Manila receives is the grandest on this earth.

I have made five trips to the Philippines and when one arrives at the foot of the steps from the plane, all control of life is gone. First, every nuance of Western press, publicity, and propaganda has been mastered and elaborated. Cameramen are ubiquitous, reporters hover and invade, all events are an occasion. The West perhaps has mastered efficiency in its business world. The Islands have mastered the efficient social calendar. No moment is left unused. Merchants and tailors are at your hotel door. Measurements are made instantly for your native pineapple cloth shirt, the barong tagalong. Black pearl cuff links appear to give it the right touch. Gifts flow, flowers appear. Everyone met is poised, smiling, happy, friendly. When night comes, there is no rest. The pace quickens, and outdoor fests under colored lights take over. Flowers are everywhere and their scent is delightful. Reception lines are used on all occasions. After a long, superb dinner, come the very ornate speeches, and medals, awards, appear by the box. An occasion worth having is one worth its own plaque.

Bedtime is not recognized; the dazed guest, collapsing internally, is summoned to the dance floor. Attractive Philippines women, gay and lovely as butterflies in their puff-sleeved long dresses, all know how to—and expect to—rhumba, tango, cha-cha-cha. So do the men; your wife is exhilarated by the attention and forgets fatigue. The evening ends the next day.

You are advised the car will leave for Baguio at 8 a.m. Mariano and his equally energetic wife appear precisely on time (I did not expect time precision, but it was a reality in the Philippines). The two days in Baguio offer no rest. The photographer appears. It turns out that he is Mariano's own photographer and is towed about to record all events. There are cockfights to be seen, Igorot aboriginal villages to tour, art festivals, complete with receiving lines, elaborate meals continue. On Sunday, a yacht is produced and 50 of your new friends come aboard. A large basket of straw hats has everyone laughing and finding one their size; everyone has shield from the sun. Dancing, laughing, and eating out into the Bay. The photographer catching it all. Then to Corregidor. Hours spent in a painful tracing out of the ruins and a reminder of the disaster experienced there.

Perhaps all of this was but evidence of Mariano's own energy, but when I returned for other occasions, and he was not there, it was the same.

Mariano was one of the men with Dr. White at Massachusetts General Hospital when I was there. He saw himself as a bridge between the United States and his country and was an unceasing ambassador. He made the long flight several times a year, and no national heart meeting was complete without him. In the ultimate of tragedies, he was murdered in his Miami hotel room while attending an annual heart meeting.

Three former Fellows from my own unit met us in Taipeh, Taiwan, and we celebrated Christmas there. The inherent reserve and calmness of the Chinese was like a balm after the outpouring in the Philippines. One could not have a more vivid expression of the difference in national psyche. Their National Defense Medical Center occupied a good part of my time, and I was back into business, lecturing, teaching, and seeing patients. The senior man who had been sent to my department by the China Medical Board was Dr. Nong Ting, the chairman of Medicine at the National Defense Medical School. He was an impressive man with quiet dignity and a calm which masked energy and drive. The KMT escape from the mainland was only seven years old, and there was still a realistic quality to their discussions about the possibility of a return to the mainland. The power of China Medical Board money was impressive as we toured new facilities created by the board. Later, I returned to Taiwan twice more, and one of my regrets is that my later mainland involvement essentially precluded my cordial contacts with good friends and colleagues in Taiwan. With the political reality of the time, there was no logical way to be welcome in both arenas. One of the losses was the potential of working with Nong Ting. He went on to be a leader in Asian-Pacific cardiology.

In Tokyo, I had no reasons to see the 49th General Hospital. Military units have no constancy, no memory, and 10 years had passed since I was stationed there. Instead, we spent time with the Yoshio Hamada family, my best contact with what life is behind the facade in Japan. It was painful to learn that the daughter our American group had known best had died from tuberculosis. We extended a hand to their oldest and youngest daughters, and agreed to sponsor them for visits to the States. Later, this happened. My old friend, Dr. Nobuo Ito, was also with us, and he asked if he could come for training in the Kansas unit. This, too, came to pass.

The Royal Hawaiian Hotel in Hawaii re-entered us into American life, and I put in a few vigorous days trying to learn surfboarding without drowning. I neither drowned nor surfed. As in Hong Kong, I found Hawaii a place that deserved a definite period of living. For Hong Kong, I have had to be satisfied with almost yearly visits for a 20-year period. For Hawaii, I have done better, with not only frequent visits, but through the more substantial commitment of having my daughter, Lark, move there.

We landed at the Kansas City airport on New Year's Day, 1957, squeezing the last moment out of the six-month sabbatical. At the airport were Jim and Marti Crockett and T.K. Lin. We were home.

I was assured that all was well. The lesson from the whole experience (there were other lessons, of course) was one should never miss a chance to have a sabbatical leave. I held to that rule for the rest of my career.

In my skylighted garret at Utrecht, I had spent time sketching an outline, a plan for what I intended to do over the next two decades. Almost everyone does this, perhaps the experience is at a peak as one nears 40. For some, it is in writing; for most, it is in the quiet of the night, in their heads. No matter what one does, or at what level, life is a sequence of wishing, praying, hoping. The writer who said that life, for most, is a matter of quiet desperation was wrong. For most, it is a life sustained by an optimism that tomorrow will be better.

Such was not precisely my own motivation for introspection. Life was already a delight. By the rules of success, my 38 years were well used. I was moved by an internal itch, a deliberate intent to not be secured by the comfort and perquisites of the tenure that I had.

I was, as I expressed to myself, committed to being me, not a Chair.

I found my comfort in believing, undoubtedly overoptimistically, that one can, with a few breaks, control what life brings. Perhaps this desire to be analytical, to enjoy making very long-range plans, is not analytical at all, but is excessive weighing of life. I find a kind of happiness in sitting down with a blank piece of paper and drawing out a time line, putting in the branching options—then tracing the options out to their "what ifs" end. This I had done at Utrecht. I have continued this long-range chess game throughout my life.

I was back in Kansas City and my own chess game was set in motion. I had decided to be on to a new chapter of life by the end of my 10th year at Kansas. But the place to begin, was to do well the job of head of Medicine and of Cardiology.

All was indeed well at the medical center. As each section chief reported to me, I could note no real problems. The main weakness of the department had always been the lack of fundamental research. Now, the laboratories of Santiago Grisolia and Kurt Reissmann were filling well that need, and they were augmented by the research ability of a native Kansan, Robert Bolinger. Also, an unexpected chance came to recruit a major research worker in the field of atherosclerosis. George Curran was an established investigator of the American Heart Association, a very honorable recognition, and one which carried funding wherever the person chose to work. For family reasons, he wanted to live in Kansas City. He was a reserved man, not fully able to express himself, but with a hidden, droll sense of humor. His presence added quality.

The medical center's role as a referral center for the State was very successful, and the quantity and variety of patients brought the grist for our clinical teaching programs, and the income which made it possible to grow beyond the State budget.

I added a swimming pool to my home; we brought Eiko Hamada from Japan. Dr. Ito came, too, and worked in Santiago Grisolia's lab, as I did once each week, for I was determined to have some awareness of the new field of enzyme chemistry. Shreenivas came from India, and one of the Fellows from Utrecht arrived.

He arrived on a weekend; 48 hours later, a telegram came from his wife, informing him that the practice position he had been waiting for, for 12 years as a Fellow at Utrecht—yes, 12 years— had been opened by death and he should return home. He did, the next day. And thus ended my role as a listener for the Fellows at Utrecht.

Eiko Hamada came from Japan for the main task of helping Audrey when our second child was born. Lea Grey Dimond was born on March 1, 1958, and living in our home on that date were Eiko and Paul Wood from London, the impressive head of the National Heart Hospital. Paul and I had moved ahead in our friendship, and he had come as a visiting professor. Again, we found each other to be good company and we agreed that Audrey and I would come in the summer of 1959 to London.

Lea would not be Lea, at least by name, if it had not been for the presence of Eiko. We had long planned on the lovely Southern name of Drucilla, and the birth certificate went on to the State capital: Drucilla Grey. Immediately, it was apparent this was not a livable name. Eiko disliked it and we agreed with her after she spoke it a few times as Drureeyuh; the name did not survive a week. We worked our way through the bureaucracy in the State capital and got a second chance, expunging the lovely word Drucilla.

Although Lea Grey and Lark Grey have seemed good, appropriate names over the years, I have always had a bit of regret that I didn't call Lea by the good bold name of *Kansas*. She and I, in fact, share this regret. She would be a perfect *Kansas*.

Clarke Wescoe, the dean, went out to the Far East under the sponsorship of the China Medical Board, and I gave him an introduction to my Hamada family in Tokyo. He and I then acted as sponsors for the other Hamada daughter, Tomiko, who came on to our university and got her degree. She later married an American, became a citizen, and fully bridged the two cultures. My time in Tokyo at least changed one life.

Chapter Seven

I HAD A SMALL CIRCLE, during the Kansas years, of nonmedical friends, but in the main my contacts were with the medical center, and, although the Kansas Cities, one Missouri and one Kansas, were a geographic whole, it was interesting how formidable the state line was in terms of our small faculty group. We lived, worked, schooled our children and socialized in Kansas. Missouri was not a part of our daily lives. However, I did come to know well four men, not only know them well, but thoroughly enjoy them, whose careers were in Kansas City, Missouri.

The first very pleasant surprise was to find that the Linvilles lived immediately next door to us, the same Linvilles who had given me a ride back to the Purdue SAE house on an April day in 1939. They had prospered; he was now the comptroller of Kansas City Power and Light Company. They immediately enjoyed Audrey, and we began an enduring friendship. One special reward was to learn that from the stein I had sent them, he had found a hobby, and now had a substantial and valuable collection. My family's stein was a part of it, and kept in that stein was the letter I had written to express my thanks.

Among the lasting friendships formed in Kansas City were a former book salesman who founded a women's sorority, a former rabbi who ran the best restaurant in town, and a former dean of the New School of Social Research in New York City, now Executive Officer for a local private philanthropy.

Walter Ross was in his early 50's when we met and he, too, I met because of Paul White. On one of Dr. White's visits to see me, several of his local patients gave a dinner for him, and at that dinner I sat next to Walter. He was a handsome man with the most consistently benign look on his face that I have ever known. If he had really evil thoughts, I never found them.

In making conversation at that first dinner, I conveyed an enthusiasm for the history of the Santa Fe Trail, which had originated at the riverboat landing which is now Kansas City. In my remarks, I commented that it would be a wonderful experience to "do" the Trail by horseback. I, of course, was speaking in the abstract, not in the least knowing I was talking to not only an absolute authority on trail riding, but a man who kept horses, bred horses, and loved long trail rides above anything. Walter thought a day was perfect when he ambled along slowly on horseback for eight hours or more. He also was a man who could not stand to hear someone express a wish without immediately moving heaven and earth and horse flesh to get it accomplished. The next day he telephoned to tell me he was working on the details of getting supplies, adequate trailers, camping-out equipment and personnel. Could we count on taking six weeks for the trip beginning in July?

With a feeling of deep phoniness, a glib con man caught in the act, I found enough courage to tell the truth and tell him that I knew essentially nothing about a horse, had ridden a few times, had never thrown a saddle on a horse, and I made it clear that there was no way I could ride a horse from Kansas City, Missouri to Santa Fe, New Mexico. Anyone less than Walter Ross would have ended this tenderfoot relationship, telling all his friends about the big-winded cardiologist at the medical center. Not Walter. He immediately came to my home to see what facilities I had for keeping a horse. My two-stall barn and five acres of pasture passed approval, and he, with obvious joy, set about finding me a five-year-old palomino mare and handsome saddle. This was not free; he tactfully inquired first what amount of investment I was willing to make. What he really had in mind was a full-blooded Arabian stallion, such as he rode. I demurred and suggested we could call that "stage two." He was also a bit taken back when I said I didn't want a full western saddle, but preferred a plantation saddle. This nicely padded saddle had been one that I had been enamored with as a young boy when I had seen the overseers in Winona riding out to the cotton fields on their walking horses, seated on plantation saddles. Later, as I learned more, I did find it comfortable, but when we were on a ride and met Walter's friends I knew they considered my saddle as pure evidence of a tenderfoot.

Walter had begun his career as a Depression-time book salesman, going door-to-door, hoping to sell the *Book of Knowledge* and the *Encyclopedia Americana*. His territory was Kansas, and in those years there were few reasons why anyone would or could subscribe. The Depression and the Dust Bowl era were bleak competition. However, Walter found in the little farm towns something that his quick mind saw as a way to not only sell books but to very much enhance the lives of the women, who, in a real sense, were stranded in a cultural desert. There was no money for them to go to college; there were no extension courses and although many of the rural and small-town women were desperate for some intellectual stimulus to their lives, there was no convenient, affordable schooling for them. Walter invented, pure and original, logical and altruistic, emotional and practical, a women's Greek sorority. A sorority with local chapters, with rituals, ceremony, pins, prose, rites of passage, and a sorority which had regular learning sessions, planned classroom work, all based upon the very book material which he could provide. To sell books he took them the gift of the Greeks. His plan was to have the group of women share the cost of the master reference encyclopedia, and he would develop a study plan for them, a study plan with increasing levels of achievement, a plan with a jeweled pin, progressive stations, and rituals of advancement. He offered them a lifelong sisterhood of good, thinking women.

He gave them an organized way to raise themselves out of the trap of dust and Depression and called it Beta Sigma Phi. He was the original Music Man, but, instead of horns, he sold books, and because of his own innate goodness and pleasantness, there was no spirit of the huckster. By the time I knew him, the sorority had hundreds of thousands of members and had spread all over the world.

He provided for me a companionship, unrelated to cardiology, and a good reason to put on Levi's, get on a horse, and just amble down the lane. We solved no problems, but we worried a lot of them.

Walter, from his years of serving as leader for the thousands of women who joined his sorority, had useful aphorisms, originally fitted into his talks with them. These had become a part of his vocabulary and of his conduct. One remained with me, and although borrowed from Walter, served me equally well. He would place this phrase at the end of a what, at the moment, was a weighted, sensitive situation: "Never forget that it is very, very important," and then after a pause and shrug, "but really not important at all." So many things one gets involved in, actions which get enlarged out of proportion, meetings which take on aspects of confrontation, issues which polarize a group or an organization— and which later, when time has weighed and judged—are very, very important, but not important at all. It is only a phrase, but when heard by a thoughtful listener, it is a phrase which effectively can diminish, pull down, and deflate some subject which seemed so "very, very important."

Walter Ross collected friends. Once you crossed into that magic designation, "friend," in Walter's mind, you were several sizes larger than in real life and, by word or act, he devoted himself to increasing your happiness, increasing your life, and, on occasion, increasing your reputation beyond its just dues. Walter had no small friends. If he decided you were worthy of the designation, "friend," you immediately began increasing in stature; he would cluck over your problems as if they were his and embellish, exaggerate, and expand your abilities.

This had little to do with your own status or recognition in life. If your profession was that of a veterinarian, then he happily and vigorously went about seeing that all of his friends knew that you were the greatest veterinarian in the world.

If your profession was that of water diviner, he equally endorsed you as the greatest who ever handled a willow stick. South of Kansas City, there was a retired willow-stick diviner with the just right name of "Crick." Crick had built his house beside the best well he had ever found, and fresh water, out on the hot, dusty plains of Kansas, bubbled up at Crick's doorstep. Walter had decided that nothing made Crick happier than to have dusty, thirsty horsemen stop by and solicit a cool drink. Therefore, many of Walter's friends, myself included, made the 20-mile horseback round trip from Walter's farm to Crick's front door, theoretically for the pleasure of the ride, but privately, in Walter's mind, to give Crick a moment of happiness when the troop came to a stop at his front porch. Walter and Crick would go through their conversation. Walter would bring his horse to a stop, turn halfway in the saddle, and talking over his shoulder, tell the men that he wanted them to meet his old friend Crick, who "knew more about finding water than any man in the West and had the sweetest-tasting cool water of anyplace around." And Walter's smile glowed as old Crick bowed to the compliment and passed a dipper of cool water to his friend.

Walter, with equal enthusiasm, promoted the abilities and potential of a refugee European dressage expert; of Berle Berry, a local automobile salesman; and Farrell Webb, his dentist; Old Tom, his groom; Mr. Harris of the famous Chicago bank; Chesapeake retrievers; Ted Mack, the radio and TV host; Thomas L. Thomas, the singer, and on and on. Walter didn't like his friends; he loved them.

He made another contribution to my family. From the time Lark was born in September 1953, until we left Kansas in 1960, Christmas Day included the arrival of Walter and his horse groom, Tom, with Tom splendid in his Santa Claus suit. This all began by my asking Walter if he had seen a picture in the paper of some family that had this tradition. For all the Christmases we lived in Kansas, the day's highlight was the arrival of Walter and his full-suited Santa.

One had to be careful with Walter—a comment became his purpose. I acquired from him an Afghan hound and a Chesapeake retriever in just this same manner. Moving to California did not end our friendship, but it ended my days on a plantation saddle.

My translocated rabbi friend was Max Bretton. I never knew him as a rabbi, but knew him as the owner of Kansas City, Missouri's absolutely best restaurant. His restaurant served superb food, had happy, cordial employees, but the ingredient which made the whole place special was Max. Max did not run a restaurant; he simply had a place where he every day looked forward to visiting with his friends. The restaurant was his salon, and what a salon it was. Max, well-read, intellectually sophisticated, a liberal when being a liberal meant sensitivity leavened with intelligence, moved from table to table, a philosopher king, with just enough timely, politically apt stories, little jokes of a literate and possible salty nature, and when he found someone who wanted to have a really good discussion, joined them, and out came the best level of cerebral entertainment one can imagine.

His restaurant was across the street from the Kansas City theater that featured Broadway shows on tour and concert performers such as Jan Peerce, Leonard Warren, Robert Merrill, and Grace Moore. They all knew Max and his wife Mary, (a former light-opera star). After the theater, the performers came to Max's restaurant and the scene became a bit of New York. On especially grand occasions, he used his restaurant staff at his home and gave a marvelous evening of food and, one night I remember well, informal, glorious singing by Jan Peerce.

Max provided not only the stimulating joy of his own company but Wednesday lunch there for 10 years, gave me a place to meet my third special friend, Homer. We ate, talked, analyzed, criticized, and dreamed. And, of course, Max was right there, joining in.

Homer Wadsworth had come to Kansas City a year ahead of me, brought there by a local group of small philanthropies, not one of which was major money, but gathered together, had several million dollars and the promise of more. The organization was called the Kansas City Association of Trusts and Foundations. When we first met, Homer was 37, lean, handsome, with dark, wavy hair, and he moved with a quickness, almost dancing on his toes. His smile was big and beamed forth, saying he was coming forward in happiness.

Homer was recruited to Kansas City by Arthur Mag, an eminent lawyer whose firm, Stinson Mag, represented the coalition of trusts who were seeking professional help. Homer's immediately prior job, dean of the New School for Social Research in New York City, certainly suggested he would be a vigorous social activist.

From the day he arrived, he was everything the organization could have hoped for—and more. They had recruited him to come, manage the office, and give them a professional guidance in how to distribute their money. He did this, and at the same time, raised their social consciousness to a level which some found painful. To make sense out of the giving, Homer founded a staff of city planners, of social scientists, of professional data gatherers, and called the group The Institute for Community Studies.

Using this as his source of facts and by getting deep into every aspect of life in Kansas City, Homer became the most effective instrument for social change, for good social change, in the city. From parks to theater to the public schools to junior colleges to universities, Homer guided his board into planting seed money, and then, through Homer's own phenomenal skills of persuasion and a Talleyrand ability at finding progress though compromise, he shook, changed, and facilitated the right thing to happen.

Author Richard Rhodes in his book, *The Inland Ground - An Evocation of the American Middle West* (New York, Atheneum, 1970), titled his Chapter 12, "The Most Influential Man in Kansas City Has No Money and is a Native of Pittsburgh." He was speaking of Homer, of course.

I met Homer immediately upon my arrival from Texas through the guidance of Herbert Miller, chairman of Pediatrics, and, as are pediatricians almost by nature, a man seeking social justice for the young and a way around the barriers of financing when giving health care to the young. Herb's wife was the daughter of Norman Thomas, and this connection furthered the friendship of Homer and the Millers. Homer had known Thomas in New York City and was an admirer. If the reader draws the conclusion that Max Bretton, Homer Wadsworth, and Herbert Miller were liberals, and therefore I was probably associated with the left-wing gang of Kansas City, please rest. Walter Ross was pure conservative.

My friends of a lifetime have no uniformity of style or pattern. From Vic to Margie to Woody Suttle to Bill Martz to Fred Wilson, Father Lerhinan, Nobuo Ito, Colonel Berle, Paul White, Herman Hellerstein, Ed Twin, Jim Crockett, Bernie Lown, Paul Wood, Flo Mahoney, Walter Ross, Max Bretton, Homer, Nathan Stark, Edgar Snow, Henry Mitchell, Tom James, Harriet Dustan, Norman Cousins, Harrison Salisbury, Ed Cross, Bern Dryer, Ginny Calkins, Mary Ann Morris, Vern Wilson, Dottie Lansing-Penman, Jim Threatt, Wu Wei-jan, George Hatem—there is no single common thread but the pleasure of their company—and perhaps a level of intelligence and sensitivity.

Of course, there are many other men and women for whom I have fond memories and with whom I have shared work, plans, and life. But the listed ones were each a special stimulus and a source of intellect and humor. I realize my error in even making such a list, for omission of a name suggests I really did not care—which is not at all the truth.

When Homer and I met in 1950, the field of psychiatry was undergoing large changes, changes set in motion by new experiences in the War that suggested that much of mental illness could be treated in ambulatory centers. It was a time when the great bleak semi-prisons out in the countryside, the asylums, were being replaced by a more active approach to treatment in the community. A whole range of new chemical psychotherapy had begun, also.

This was almost the first area Homer got into in Kansas City. He began what was to become a pattern, a pattern of putting a little seed money into an idea, having the Institute of Community Studies look at the idea, get interested citizens involved, and form lay boards. Then make special efforts to keep the editors of the newspaper informed, thus getting some well-timed editorials, to help the general public's awareness. He essentially never had a position of authority, but was the supreme catalyst; one of the reasons he was so effective was the obvious truth that he had no financial interest in any of these things, that he sought no office, and distributed no patronage. He was that most dangerous of men, a man who did good for the sake of others. And he was intelligent, a very effective weapon.

From our conversations about the day-care psychiatric center on Hospital Hill, we evolved into discussions of medical care and medical education. It was from that beginning that, even though I went on to California, Homer and I remained in steady contact and he knew of my interest in taking on a major effort at a change in medical education. Of these three men, Homer is still alive and active. Walter and Max have passed on, but Walter's sorority continues its mission under his sons. Max's restaurant is gone, and that void is a loss to civilized life in Kansas City.

Homer also was a Kansas City loss, a major one. He outgrew the board he served, outgrew its resources and its imagination. The Cleveland Foundation took him away, and this gave him immense funds with which to use his skills. Life in Kansas City lost more of its heart and soul than many of its citizens will ever realize when Homer left.

A chairman of medicine seeks to know those who come for training as Residents and to leave some mark, small or large, upon them. Many of the Residents were Kansans, through and true, with the low-key, taciturn, quiet affect of those stoic people who, for generations have settled and survived the rigors of the Great Plains. They were not a lively, gregarious, outgoing group but, to my mind, almost the ideal material for what makes a very good doctor: stable, dependable, consistent. As one small step towards knowing them, both before and after my sabbatical, each year I took all of the third-year men and women to Chicago, to the Central Society for Clinical Research. We flew up together, stayed at the same hotel, and one evening we all had dinner at a northside restaurant-entertainment center called The Ivanhoe. A camaraderie came from this, and I thoroughly enjoyed knowing them and watching them grow.

The Central Society was, and probably still is, an exciting contact with the full range of medical-science talent in the whole central area of the country, from Minneapolis to New Orleans. The format itself made one sit on the edge of the seat and feel the excitement. Each speaker was allowed no more than 10 minutes to present his subject. At nine minutes, an orange warning light on the speakers' stand flashed on, and at 10 minutes a red light came on and your time was over, finished or not. Back home, weeks had been spent rehearsing, and getting on this program was both a thrill and an achievement. But the real adrenalin flowed in the five-minute discussion period following each paper. Then your presentation was torn apart by audience participation, and the remarks could be lethal. One of the great memories of all who attended in the 1950's was the rasping, cutting voice of Louis Katz, who placed himself directly in front of the speaker, and, when comments were invited, sprung from his seat and came to the microphone. Louie Katz was a world-level researcher (the same man

I had visited in 1950) in the field of cardiovascular disease, but equally, he was a primary force for exactness, clarity, and cleanness of research design. With stiff, wiry hair, grey-black hair full-erect, with a voice that could be heard into the balcony, a voice that tore at the speaker and left all vulnerability exposed, he used his rapier, always concluding with, "I would like to hear what the speaker has to say to that!" The Central Society was where our group saw the wider world of medical science and a look behind the scenes.

The department held a yearly picnic at Dr. Delp's home, which was a huge, festive event, complete with volleyball, baseball, and horseshoes. I was young enough and competitive enough to enjoy all. In addition, we had a yearly event at my home, by now named *Diastole*. (This home in Kansas was named *Diastole*; my canyon home in California was *Diastole-West*; the Hospital Hill home was my final *Diastole*.) At this annual event, the Residents acted as the host for some very well-known American physician. We hosted Paul White, Tinsley Harrison, and George Thorn in this manner.

The real chance I had to get to know them, and them to know me, was during their months of training in cardiology, during which time we were together daily, practicing medicine together. The majority of the men and women in training became my friends, and a pleasure of my later years has been to watch them become the medical backbone of the region.

I began putting together all of my own experiences, including the value of the very early exposure to patients through Dr. Baum, and the intensity of learning in a clinical setting as I had enjoyed it in Japan. The value of very early medical-care responsibility, not only for the knowledge acquired, but for the maturing which responsibility brings; the way of learning at MGH where we were a small team of diverse experience and age, all working in harmony in an atmosphere of goodwill. All under a chief who was loved because of his kindness, not feared because of his intimidation. A natural pattern of education began to form in my mind.

Now, as my experience with the residency program grew, I found the merit of this graduate level of training also came from these same advantages: placing individuals together, a mix of older and younger, more and less experienced; building a supportive team in a clinical setting, and not harassing them by repeated tests and grades. In fact, the ideal team was one with the complete spectrum of all those trying to learn the craft—students, Residents, staff; they all taught and they all learned. They did not learn from a textbook—they learned from life, and used the textbook to fill the information spaces.

This real schoolhouse of medicine education was to be found in small teams, charged to work to help each other, teaching each other in harmony, not in a sterile classroom, but, instead, immersed in pertinency, urgency, relevancy, because they were actively taking care of real people.

The trick, or the key, was not to have a punitive, test-loaded educational system, but to have one which was closely supervised, real-life based, with a close-by observer—a supervisor, yes, but more than that, a friend who wanted you to succeed—not someone who was threatening, with a quiz/test-based authority over you.

Chapter Eight

I WAS BEGINNING TO MOVE my own awareness from the pattern of tradition to a still-nebulous theory of how the making of a physician could be done better.

I realized as much as I enjoyed being a physician, I had become a man with convictions, and because success had come so very early, I was beginning to find myself in a position where I had the time, the understanding, the willingness, to take on campaigns for change.

I began putting articles in the literature on medical education, distinctly philosophical in nature, and taking a position contrary to what was being done, contrary to the establishment, and this was to be my pattern for the rest of my career. I wrote them, each based on my experiences, but each a deliberate step on the path I had chosen in my Utrecht retreat.

I did not pass through any religious conversion, nor see a star in the sky, but I had to smile when I remembered how many of my ancestors had been preachers and had made large investments of life in what they believed in. They would have nodded their heads and said I was just another family gene out to do good. However, removed from a religious orientation, I was beginning to think of issues and change—and not just one patient at a time.

The reader will find the following pages filled with more description of American medical education and medical care than patience will accept. Bear with me, for I need time to explain, perhaps you will say, "rationalize" the decisions I made.

In the mid-1950's, the major medical society for cardiologists, the American Heart Association (AHA), decided to expand its purpose beyond the original intent of being an educational source and forum for the heart doctors of the country. When the association had been founded in the early 1920's, Paul White had been one of the founders, and had remained a vigorous force in its policies.

The annual meeting of the AHA and its medical journal, the *American Heart Journal*, had become the main source of specialty education in the field.

In the 1950's, Dr. White, from his experience at the National Heart Institute, came to realize there was an immense untapped reservoir of private philanthropy that could not be reached by a government agency such as the NHI. He and others felt keenly that the great need in medicine was to bring both public and private dollar resources to the university medical centers and support investigators and their research. The AHA took on this new direction, and the local heart associations of the entire country were reorganized into fund-raising chapters. The purpose of the organization, nationally, remained Education, but to this purpose was added—and Research.

I immediately became involved and in the Kansas City region founded a chapter which we named after the local river: The Kaw Valley Heart Association. This was my first personal experience with a fund-raising endeavor. It was not a natural environment for me, and I soon found it was equally uncomfortable for a great number of physicians.

From my considerable exposure through postgraduate teaching to the men in private practice, I found a very real sense of loss and irritation: loss because the good fellowship which we had enjoyed from the local and national meetings of the American Heart Association that were now much lesser events in the minds of the new national staff in New York City. And irritation because we, the private physicians, were being used, cozied up to now by fund-raisers.

Not a little bit of their irritation came from the fact that a large amount of any money raised locally was sent off to the national office.

Throughout the country, a new kind of staff person for the AHA appeared, the kind that had long been active in the Christmas Seal efforts and the March of Dimes. The physicians understood this, but they equally understood that this new effort placed the companionship and education of their peer group, which they had treasured, at a much lower level of importance.

With AHA's new orientation towards raising money for research, there was not only the feeling of being left out, as expressed by the private physician but, at the same time, the AHA became the natural ally, the funding source, for the university investigator. As the role of the regional physician went down, the importance of the Association to the university investigator skyrocketed. The AHA's annual meetings became a gathering place for investigators.

The old conviviality of the AHA for the men who daily practiced cardiology and took care of people was lost. If it was not lost, they at least felt lost in this new bustle of young research talent, all full of the excitement and energy of academic creativity, an excitement and energy which left the middle-aged man from Wichita or Omaha or Evansville feeling out of date and forgotten.

This sense of loss was aggravated by the very success of the National Heart Institute and AHA in causing great new cardiac knowledge to be generated. More than at any point in medical history, new information important to the welfare of patients was pouring out, and the need for a vigorous education program for the men already in practice was what I convinced myself was the critical missing piece.

The *American Heart Journal* was abandoned by the Association and a new journal, more research oriented, was founded. Here again, the man in private practice found this replacement for his long-enjoyed journal was now not planned for him, but had become a much more research-oriented publication. Just as the journal had been, he felt abandoned.

The years of major effort on my part in postgraduate teaching had given me a nationwide friendship with men in private practice. I had talked before medical societies at city, county, and state levels, actually all over the country, and had served as a consultant for hundreds of generalists and internists.

To understand their feeling, it is necessary to understand what a national organization offers the solo practitioner. In his home region, he has hospital staff meetings, county medical society meetings, state medical society meetings. Some of the actions of these groups are educational, but, in the main, their purpose is closer to medical politics than to quality specialty education. I am speaking of the 1950's.

There is, also, when one is in his hometown setting, the reality of local jealousies within the profession, jealousies compounded by an undercurrent theme of competition. Everyone in the doctor's hometown who is taking care of heart patients in private practice is obviously a competing challenge to every other physician taking care of the same kind of patient. It is difficult to attend a local teaching meeting and enjoy the anonymity wherein the listener can ask any question. Instead, one remains quiet and avoids competitor's snide smirks. Local meetings are too personal and too close to where one makes a living.

These sensitivities were very real, and I gradually began to form a larger understanding of how the physician, no longer a medical student but, throughout his career, a student of medicine, needed his own university. It needed to be a national one. It did not need a campus. It did not need a faculty, but needed access to all the faculty of all the universities. It needed to set a standard of expectation for the teacher's performance which would bring to the listener a level of sophisticated presentation almost resolutely missing in the lecture halls of medical schools. I say "resolutely" simply because there is no other way to explain the inadequate classroom presentations given by some of the most prominent of so-called teachers.

In sharing with practicing physicians the care of their patients, I had become someone with whom they were comfortable, and much of our effort and literature from the courses offered at Kansas had stressed that they were for the practicing physician. Deliberately, I took the continuing education of the man in private practice of cardiology as my special interest.

From my School of Aviation Medicine time, and the large amount of energy I had put into postgraduate teaching at Kansas, the art of teaching had become very real to me. This national postgraduate cardiology college would need a professional staff who knew how to put a teaching meeting together, who knew how to get a room dark, to get it cool, to get the projector to work, to have slides that could be seen, microphones that could be heard, telephones and restrooms that worked. This staff needed to learn how to work with, and care for, this very special client. The private-practice physician is a quite independent, proud man with a considerable degree of cynicism, dignity and expectation— a challenging, valuable student.

Surely, you will say, those are basic, obvious truths, and surely all medical schools and their administrations knew these simple truths. But these were large issues, and in the years of which I write, these needs were well ignored by most medical schools. I remember having dinner with Carl Moore, a very prominent physician and head of the Department of Medicine at Washington University, St. Louis. I voiced the above concerns, and his adamant reply was that the teaching of the practicing physician was not the schools' responsibility. The schools should concentrate on research, Residents, and medical students, in that order.

I was irritated at the time because I certainly was leading my own Department of Medicine full-charge into postgraduate teaching. But at the same time, I took his remarks to heart and decided I would look for some nonuniversity educational organization for the private-practice cardiologist.

I was practical enough to understand that Moore's attitude reflected the judgment of a man from a well-endowed school, and my own view was shaped by the covert but real value of postgraduate teaching, in attracting patients to our medical center.

The quality of teaching, the very act of communication, for both the medical student and practitioner, was, in the 1940's and '50's, painfully lethargic. The students were a captive audience and the torpid lecturer and his torpid classroom were a part of the initiation rite the pained student had to endure. Often, the lecturer from the research lab had no great sense of mission to communicate in the classroom. Much of the teaching was a burden, a task to be dispensed with, and when that same lecturer went out on the practicing-physician teaching circuit, he took the same murky slides, the same mumbling skill, and no one gave a moment of attention to the amenities of the arena in which it happened.

Little was done about communication skill, the skill used on the stage, or by the real professional, to create a sense of belonging, an atmosphere of participation. It was bad enough for medical students, but for the thousands of men (then, few women) who did the daily task of taking care of the public's real and imagined heart disease, there was even a lesser opportunity and effort. Of course, there were islands of quality, but there was much sea between.

What was needed was a collegiality, and from that collegiality would come the harmony which would make it easy, convenient, and happy for the practitioner and the teacher to come together. The leadership of this teaching, nonuniversity group would make the teaching arena a pleasant place in which the teachers came to realize they were expected to truly teach. The man in practice would know every moment of his time was well invested, and he was being brought to the firing line of new information.

These changes in cardiology were not occurring alone, but were part of the post-World War II revolution in all university medical centers. The funds I have described as making possible the new vigor at my own Kansas University Medical Center were flowing everywhere. The new money that had helped launch my heart unit was but a token of the multiple millions of dollars that poured into the universities' science laboratories. This new money brought success in research but, also, from the importance of the new money, came the change in purpose of the medical schools. This has continued down to the present, and has been a factor in the public's lessened enthusiasm for the medical profession.

The same thing which had changed the American Heart Association was rapidly changing the medical schools—research money. The phenomenal funds available from the National Institutes of Health carried with them great good and great loss. The good came from the immense number of new full-time investigators who came to the schools and the research they did. The harm came from the entire redirection of the mission of the medical school, as perceived and carried out by this new dominant force, the basic science faculty. The brass ring became research and grants.

The political power and academic power at the medical schools moved to the side of those able to bring in the millions in grants. The clinician became, by the new rules of the game, a second-level academician.

The actual teaching of the medical student became a burden to

somehow be passed off. Where, in the past, and this is a true example, one professor had been the personality who gave the yearly lectures in biochemistry, and thus the students saw the cohesion of the subject as organized and presented by a single
intellect, 32 different biochemists, each an investigator in the department, divided the course amongst themselves and they each
gave one lecture. The students heard 32 superspecialists recite
the scope of their own research, but no one gave a correlated, all-
encompassing view of the field. This happened in various ways
and various patterns throughout the country.

The clinician could not compete with the scientist-investigator
who was able to bring in large grants of money, which carried
with it, new money for the administration.

This money, "overhead money," became the institution's reward, and the new yardstick for success became a dollar-based
one: How much external support does your institution have? In
the national pecking order for judging excellence of medical
schools, this became the standard. The question of excellence of
education of the medical student came to be judged by this same
dollar-sign figure.

The obvious fact that the quality of medical research is different than the quality of medical education was not ignored, instead
the establishment declared the former to equal the latter, and this
fallacy remained an uncontested truth.

The reader may exclaim; "Why, isn't good research the backbone of medical teaching?" Of course, it is. The issue is not one of
"know-nothing" clinicians critical of the new knowledge coming
from the research laboratories. The fault rests in the assumption
that new knowledge and the atmosphere of the laboratory is, in
any manner, related to that very human interplay between a sick,
worried person and a sympathetic, caring, listening, cautious,
compassionate physician. The fault is in this assumption.

The grant era encouraged a new reward system, fostered an
emphasis upon attracting to medical schools science-oriented students, rewarded the activities of the laboratory, and denigrated
the skills which characterize, historically and forever, the good
physician.

The objective, fact-seeking, goal-oriented life of an investigator is not training ground for the ambiguous, mix of facts and psyche, personal orientation of the doctor at the bedside. Neither side is wrong, they simply are two different cultures.

Thus, by the late 1950's, I found myself beginning to form an idea about the need for change in both undergraduate medical education and the graduate education opportunities for the practicing cardiologist.

The American Heart Association was well into its new mission, and when I spoke earnestly with Dr. Cowles Andrus, then the AHA president, he disallowed my concern and told me the real need for the public's health was research, and that the practitioner would never respond to a quasi-collegiality, and, in his experience, most men in practice were not really interested in a whole lot of lectures.

I spoke with Irving S. Wright and he assured me that the American College of Physicians (he was president of that organization), served well the exact role I was describing; there was no need for a new organization. I took the stand that specialization was occurring at a rate that required separate organizations for the individual specialty fields and that the College of Physicians was too large. The era was passing when physicians could be brought together and effectively taught all of internal medicine. This was one of my main themes, and I felt it keenly enough that I soon stopped attending its national meetings.

I then began what was to be a major commitment for 10 years. I knew there was a heart organization that had the very effective title: The American College of Cardiology. I knew it had been founded by a small group of refugee physicians from Europe who were forced to leave behind positions of prestige and revenue. This particular group had settled chiefly in New York City, and, in the recent years, had begun having national meetings with attendance by a few hesitant physicians who were not quite sure what this organization was all about.

The founders had not been able to recapture their European level of prestige and authority, perhaps due to a mixture of bigotry from the U.S. academic cardiologists and, perhaps, because the refugee group did have one or two very aggressive, even aggrandizing, members. They had begun the difficult task of trying to break into the very tight circle of academic cardiology, first in getting the level of professorships they had had in Europe, and secondly, by asking the Brahmins to join their little society.

They were quite unsuccessful on both accounts, and there was a definite unwritten resistance from the leadership and staff of the American Heart Association. There were undercurrent grumblings that this new group was trying to get in on the new fund-raising potential, and the New York City group harmed their position considerably when they did raise some money, and then used the money to fund some of their own board members' projects.

They had shown major foresight in the choice of their name, The American College of Cardiology, the exact name that I was seeking. They had foresight in incorporating in Delaware with impeccable papers, and then built into their constitution a clause which essentially made their college a permanent fixture. Article VIII, Dissolution, stated unequivocally, "The College shall not be dissolved while five percent of the Fellows in good standing dissent." The organization could not be disbanded, closed, shut down, without an agreement by vote of more than 95 percent of the membership. The only option was to create a restructuring from within.

I attended three of the College's meetings, one at the Chase Hotel in St. Louis, one in Cincinnati, and, I believe, the third in Memphis. These were strange meetings, in the main attended by peripheral figures in cardiology and (perhaps it was my own sense of guilt) the atmosphere was vaguely one of something below the table, not quite ethical, and those of us there from universities were quite sheepish and apologetic to be found among those present.

I could not remove from my mind the very good title, The American College of Cardiology, and the well-defined impossibility of eliminating the organization by a vote. This latter issue came to a head when I finally flew to Boston solely to tell Dr. White I was thinking seriously of making an attack on the organization and attempting to capture it as the practicing physicians' own national college. Dr. White was enthusiastic, but said my duty was to get on the board and then vote the organization out of business! He was unswerving in his commitment to the AHA, and his antipathy for the founders of this new college was as close to a negative expression as I ever heard him make.

Of course, none of this occurred as sequentially and logically as one makes it seem when describing it decades later. Life, duty, work, and vacations came in their sequence.

As planned, Audrey and I were in London and I was at the National Heart Hospital for the summer of 1959. In addition to being with Paul Wood, I came to know others in the London world of cardiology. Lawson McDonald, Jane Somerville, Walter Somerville, Aubrey Leatham, and Wallace Brigdon became cherished experiences. The British Cardiac Society had its annual meeting in Edinburgh and this gave us a further chance to know Paul and Betty Wood. Away from London, Paul was witty, debonair, a man with a twinkle in his eye, who enjoyed the driest of martinis, made a connoisseur's assessment of the menu and wine list, enjoyed mixed company with good-looking women present, and equally, enjoyed every dance.

In London, one could only say Wood lived an agitated, demanding life and worked beyond anyone's stress level. As we had time to have drinks together, he gradually shared with me the unseen aggravations, jealousies, and tensions which so often are masked by what seems a life of success and acclaim. As I listened, I realized the external conduct which took such a toll on those around him was one of the escapes for his own sense of entrapment. He was a one-man act, a vastly successful act, with a position achieved by merit and steely drive. He also was exhausted, but could find no way to step, even a little bit, off the merry-go-round. He, a colonial from Tasmania, had achieved his success in London in the class-conscious profession of a class-conscious society. He was proud of this, but there was just a little "to hell with the bastards" feeling, hiding beneath his surface.

The late 1950's brought many new actions at my Kansas base. A pleasant one was a gift for $100,000 from the estate of Lacey Haynes, a journalist who for many years covered the State of Kansas for *The Kansas City Star*. With this money, I built the first in a series of teaching rooms, rooms in which I have tried from every angle, to make the perfect translation of Mark Hopkins' log-teacher-student equation. My aim in each of these rooms has been to wrap the audience in and around the speaker and to make the distance between teacher and taught essentially none. Intimacy is a word for other situations, but it conveys what I sought. Later, I had such a room built at the Scripps Clinic. After that, I persuaded the Inn at Rancho Santa Fe to prepare such a room for my classes. Much later, I had the chance to have one built into the new medical school in Kansas City, and finally, at *Diastole* on Hospital Hill, I think I have taken the best from all the others and have there the environment I have sought through the years.

The Lacey Haynes Room at Kansas was very small, seating about 20, but every seat had an electronic stethoscope and everyone was within feet of a large screen displaying heart sounds. In the same manner that I tried to teach all of electrocardiography, I took on the subject of heart sounds and gave many courses on auscultation for the physician in practice. Paul Wood was a master of this field, and after my time there I felt I was versed at world level in this subject. I must add that I found the Paul Wood group a little sleepy, or perhaps I should say conservative, when it came to electrocardiology. That field was moving faster with my group and, in general, in the United States.

The Kansas City Star must always appear in any narrative about life in Kansas City simply because it was and is an all-pervading force. The medical-science writer was Conwell Carlson. Conwell was a seasoned newspaper man who held faithfully to taking notes during an interview only on the backs of old envelopes, which he would dig out of pocket of his rumpled jacket. He was always pleasant, very relaxed, and always unimpressed by whomever he was interviewing. To this somewhat jaunty, seemingly careless approach, he added the presence of a constantly lighted, redolent cigar. To see Conwell was to see a cloud of gray all-enveloping smoke.

On one of Paul White's visits to Kansas City, Conwell inserted himself at our breakfast table, and, through a choking smoke screen, began quizzing Dr. White. One always underestimated Dr. White because he projected such an innocent, almost naive pleasantness. We hacked our way through our breakfast, eyes smarting, then Dr. White hopped to his feet and with a gay smile, said to Conwell, "Come on up to my room and we can finish the interview!" Conwell crumbled his envelope in a pocket, cigar smoke all about him, and hurried to keep up. Dr. White walked him to the elevator, past the elevator to the staircase, and, taking the steps two at a time, called back to Conwell, "Come on! We will walk up. I'll be seated all day and I have got to get some exercise." Dr. White was 72 then, his room was on the 13th floor. Through the years, Conwell, when seeing me, would begin our visit, "Say! Did I ever tell you about the time Paul White and I walked up 13 stories at the Hotel President?"

On my branching list from Utrecht, I certainly had one branch which read "deanship." In these same years, I was approached by three schools and asked if I would be a candidate. One was in the deep South and the other two were on the West Coast. The two West Coast schools were prototypes of the research-based institution that I was finding wrong, and I declined to go for a visit. It was on my list to build a medical school—but it had to be a completely new one, and one free of the always impressive, and oppressive, forces of academic conservatism.

The Southern school was tempting. I felt a certain pleasure at a return to my family roots. I went for a visit (remember this is just at the time of the Eisenhower Administration's showdown in Arkansas) and the large permanent signs over the front door, over the elevators, over the drinking fountains, over the linen chutes, marked Colored or White, made me know I did not want to bring my daughters into the deep South.

There was an experience for which I can take no credit other than the fact that there had been one Kansas City, Kansas private practitioner taking my EKG course, from the beginning, named Hughes Day. This man was dedicated to somber dress, somber demeanor, and projected a lean cheerless asceticism fitting a Presbyterian preacher seeing sin. These were the years we were first learning the potential of shocking the patient through the chest wall to restart the heart, and to strap electrodes to the chest wall and rhythmically shock the patient's heart to maintain a heart beat. We were all just at the beginning of the pacing, defibrillation era, and the techniques were essentially done only in a university medical center environment.

In my lecture, I gave live demonstrations of the use of these approaches. I made the comment that a university medical center was not the right place to get experience in the use of the new monitoring and pacing techniques because we had so many exotic forms of heart disease and so little of the coronary disease seen in the private hospital. I gave the example that we had two coarctations of the aorta in our beds at the moment and not one acute coronary occlusion. The private physician should take over and provide the leadership.

Shortly after that I left Kansas and moved my unit to California. Hughes Day came to see me in La Jolla in December 1960 and said he had been thinking about my remarks in the postgraduate course, and he had a solution. He said these procedures could be put in the community hospital where he worked and that a patient with an acute coronary occlusion could be in a special room where the heart beat could be monitored on an oscilloscope, around the clock, and a standby emergency team should be on hand to use the defibrillator.

Now, with the modern hospital considered incomplete without a coronary intensive care unit, it seems improbable that there was a point at which there was none, and one day there was but one. That "but one" was Hughes Day's contribution. Lean, dour, humorous he may have appeared but he was able to conceive of such a care unit; he went to the Hartford Foundation in New York City and persuaded them to fund his experiment. To their credit, they were willing to back this essentially unknown physician from Kansas City, Kansas. His bibliography consisted of one article, not on cardiology, in a Colorado medical journal.

On May 20, 1962, the world's first CCU was opened at Hughes' Bethany Hospital: The Hartford Coronary Care Unit. He invented the phrase Code Blue to be the hospital emergency signal for a cardiac arrest. Why Blue? Because Code Red was already in use at his hospital for identifying a fire. Hughes Day was an original and probably did more for saving lives than the next 1,000 of us who spent our careers talking about it.

In 1958, Franklin began a hot political dialogue with the Governor of Kansas regarding funding for higher education, and there were encouragements for Franklin to run for the governorship; later the senate race was discussed. This period of acrimony went on for sometime and was a stimulating gossip item for all of us.

Franklin had real potential in politics, and, I am sure, was intrigued by the prospect. His given sobriquet, Franklin D., was a natural. A question of orientation, Democrat or Republican, was perhaps a hindrance. He had substantial family ties to the Democratic Party and his own slant in those days was substantially liberal, yet as life unfolded, he moved into the Republican ranks. He would have had the backing of *The Kansas City Star*, as well as the equally conservative monied class of Kansas City, certainly substantial strengths.

Wescoe had not been at the medical center for long before he moved up to dean. He had impressed all by his solid contributions in committee work. He was an M.D. but had chosen pharmacology as his arena, not the care of patients; he and his wife, Barbara, had come to Kansas from Cornell in New York City, the attraction, in part, being her family and her father's good connections as a respected judge.

Clarke was a small, dark-complexioned, very round-headed man, the roundness being accentuated by early balding and rounded glasses. He not only followed Franklin as dean, but later followed him as chancellor, an unusual circumstance of a university having two consecutive leaders from the medical profession. They both then left academic life, and the rest of their endeavors were in the business world.

Their careers therefore had a symmetry which was not matched by their talents, or at least they each brought dissimilar abilities. Franklin had a charm, a flair, an Irish charm and flair, a natural grace and an enthusiasm for culture in all of its ranges. Clarke brought a Teutonic thoroughness and hardness, a drive to dominate and a hunger to have financial reward. Franklin had great financial success but one never felt this was a primary motivation. Clarke was crafty; Franklin had imagination. They were very different, both very able, and they remained supportive of each other.

Franklin solved the state political issues by accepting the chancellorship of the University of California in Los Angeles. At the same time that he had been considering this move, Ed Hashinger and his wife, upon leaving the acting deanship, retired to La Jolla, California, and Ed became active on the Board of the Scripps Clinic. The Scripps was in the early phases of a renaissance, and

in 1959, just before our London trip, I was offered the job of director of an institute for cardiopulmonary disease at the Scripps. Just
at this same time, the American College of Cardiology offered me
the presidency of that organization.

Too much was happening. I told the College that I could not accept because I would be too busy in the next year with the move
to La Jolla. They replied by telling me the vote still was effective
for a year later. I think they chose me for their presidency because I was the first chairman of a department of medicine who
had ever attended their meeting. I was not flattered by the offer,
and thought long and hard about it. There was no single action I
could take which would be more harshly interpreted by the medical academic world. Yet, there was no other way to literally seize
the organization.

Once I decided on my plan, I felt it necessary to tell some special people. Of course, I told Paul White and he understood that I
was acting on conviction. Jim Crockett, Bill Martz and Herman
Hellerstein were the three I told individually. I did not want them
to think I was having an aberration, and I thoroughly explained
my purpose. Bill Martz and I had come through Indiana University Medical School together, sharing the days of the ASTP, and I
knew I could count on him to be with me.

The very mention of the American College of Cardiology was
one to be greeted by a negative expression. Where the American
Heart Association represented absolutely the best of academic
talent, and was rapidly becoming an honored source of research
funding, the College cast an image of something non-American,
and no hesitation was made to label the founders as the shysters
of the profession. All of this was enhanced by the very real fear
that this College would enter the fund-raising competition.

In one swoop, I was turning my back on two large icons of the
establishment. By actually walking away from a full professorship
and the Chair in Medicine, I was either breaking emotionally or I
had chosen to go to the West Coast and grow rich. This latter in-
ference was widely bruited about the Kansas center.

It is only said here for my own pleasure, but the income offered
at the Scripps Clinic was exactly what I had been given at Kansas.
(As an aside, which I owe myself, I never made any decision in

my life which was based upon making money, which is a self-serving and undoubtedly hypocritical statement.) I went to La Jolla to gain the freedom to take on the laundering and rebirth of the College, to gain time for my own exploration of other fields, to concentrate on cardiology, to place my family in what was one of the finest places to live one could imagine, and to get ready for the day I would build a medical school or an international heart institute. Those were the two branches on my Utrecht chart. Money was not part of it.

My last year at Kansas was a happy one. I had in the lab the best and largest collection of talent to date. The Fellows were a mix of young and old, American and foreign. A medical school classmate, John Phillips, came out from Indiana for training in cardiac catheterization; Ernie Crow, a prominent internist from Wichita came for training; Dave Waxman left his practice in Kansas City to come as a Fellow; Alberto Benchimol was one of the Brasil Fellows as was Rafael Luna; Raghunathan was with us from India, and the China Medical Board had sent Yen Shen from Taiwan; Americans John Carson and Thurl Andrews came as Fellows. Jim Crockett and I had invited one of our previous Fellows, Marvin Dunn, to join as a new staff physician. The group was stimulating and able.

The whole year was a full example of the pleasure of learning and teaching, where one is not sure who is learning and who is teaching.

Later, after my departure, Crockett took over my private practice and the cardiac unit; Marvin Dunn was his associate. Jim later went on from the medical school to private practice, taking what was essentially my own private practice with him and founded the very successful Mid-America Heart Institute. Dunn then inherited the cardiac unit at Kansas and later became dean of the medical school. Dave Waxman became the executive vice-chancellor of the medical center; Luna returned to Brasil and became a leading national cardiologist there; Phillips returned to Indiana and has had a career as a prominent interventionist cardiologist; and Ernie Crow was one of the prime movers in founding the new medical school in Wichita, Kansas.

When I left for La Jolla, Benchimol and Carson went with me, as did our head nurse, secretary, catheter technician and research biochemist. Grisolia stayed at Kansas and became chairman of the Department of Biochemistry and Reissmann, Chair of Physiology. One can wait a long time for compliments in this world and I have never believed in returning to a former scene to seek a bow, but, as the first academic cardiologist in Kansas, there was a certain legacy left behind.

One of those special plums of life happened in the last week of my Kansas stay. Four prominent Jewish citizens, Hyman Brand, Max Gluck, Morris Garfinkel, and Dr. L.M. Shapiro, all patients, gathered to present me with an engraved gold pocket watch. I treasured it, and years later when my godson, Dr. Steve Waxman, Dave Waxman's son, reached maturity, I took satisfaction in handing it on, with the request that at the correct point in his life he, too, would pass it on to the right person in the next generation of physicians.

There was still one other plum. The Residents in Medicine reserved Max Bretton's restaurant for an evening, and with speeches, kidding, and that mix of levity and thoughtfulness which marks a transition, we had one last good evening together. Their gift was especially touching. Although I have not mentioned it in these pages previously, there had been a bibliophile constant in my life since my Japan tour as an Army doctor. Colonel Berle, with whom I had so many evenings over caviar and drinks, one evening had told me a story, poignant, gentle, touching, about his internship and a young patient, a prostitute dying of bacterial endocarditis. She had only one possession, a *Rubaiyat* of Omar Khayyam. Near the end, she had given the small book to him. There in the old Grand Hotel in Tokyo, he had passed it on to me. This special complex of emotions, the moment, and my affection for him, had launched in me a determination to make a lifetime collection of the *Rubaiyat,* and I have done that.

In Max's restaurant, at the end of my chairmanship, the Residents presented me with one of the great copies of the *Rubaiyat,* the Crowell Folio edition. Nothing could have sent me away with a warmer feeling. They also gave me a telescope with the admonition that I was to find a house above the beach in La Jolla and develop a skill at whale-watching. Whale Watch is one of the joyful brushes with nature's mystery, coming with Southern California living. I found the home and the whales.

PART THREE

Chapter Nine

WE LEFT KANSAS AT ONE of those right times in life for a change. Audrey and I were definitely young, 38 and 41; Lark and Lea were ideal ages for change, 7 and 2. We had no debts, a large van of furniture, cars, reserves—and 10 good years of life in Kansas behind us.

When I had left Austin and made the move to Kansas, I had committed 10 years. I know there is nothing made absolute by such plans. For every plan made and completed, there are several dozen altered, forgotten, rationalized out of existence. But my comfort level has always been awry if I did not at least think I knew what I was doing, why, and for how long.

Many of us walk a certain path because it was the path we did yesterday, and its flaws we have adapted to; those little dreams all of us play with in the three-o'clock in-the-morning time, remain just dreams. It is an obvious truth that one can't quite do everything; but it is an equal truth that the trying might be worth a new risk. Whenever I have had a job with a substantial title, it has always been a discomfort to me to find myself judged by the worth of the title. Titles are certainly satisfying and necessary; they also quickly become the shield behind which inadequacy can hide. Equally, they entrap the mantle-wearer who attempts to hang onto the title, when he and everyone else knows there are more talented prospects stymied by his presence. Every institution is obstructed by talent which has plateaued. John Gardner has written of the importance of self-renewal. Taking on the stimulus, the threat of a new job, is a part of self-renewal.

The observer might say that this is all evidence of an odd personality, a social misfit, a malcontent. Of course, these, and a few

143

other units of umbrage, may well be true. I take a little assurance from the facts; I have been happy every day, have slept well, never have had a drug or drinking problem, have a wonderful blood pressure of 110/60, never been jailed, detained, celled, never visited a psyche doctor, love my daughters and they seem to find me lovable. If this is being a social misfit, it could be worse.

A basic part of happiness is to have a cherished nest. One of the unremovable fondnesses I have for La Jolla is the superb home we found on Ludington Lane. It was of sea- and wind-aged redwood; the wood had acquired a ghost-gray color. It was located just far enough above the sea to miss the dampness, perched at the center of the La Jolla Cove, so one looked out west and north from almost every room towards the Pacific, and up the north shore towards the Scripps pier, and on beyond to the Torrey Pines. The daughters walked to school; I walked to the clinic along a path, almost a trail, just above the cliffs where the cormorants nest.

The clinic had remodeled for our use a three-story building, the former nurses' residence, a carry-over from the days when a nurse was something between a medical worker and a nun, and often lived in sequestered quarters. We shared the building with Bill Vanderlaan's endocrine group. We fitted in snugly and had a catheter room, fluoroscope space, electrocardiograph station, handsome offices, exam rooms, Fellows' room, biochemical research laboratories, and a second edition of the cardiac conference room at Kansas, except this one was quite lovely and, as an amenity from the days of the nurses' home, a fireplace.

My task was not only the heart but we were expanded to include the lung, thus we were identified as The Institute for CardioPulmonary Disease. This was more of a mouthful than gave many comfort. Ed Keeney, the clinic's director, urged me to call it the Heart-Lung Unit; he extended the thought to urge the gastroenterology group to be known as the Gut Team. He probably was right, but something in my soul rebelled at this Saxon directness.

The Scripps has an interesting history. As in any true history, it was the story of a contesting ground of strong men fighting for their version of the truth. The original name had been the Scripps

Metabolic Clinic, reflecting that when insulin became first available, a whole new field of diabetic care occurred instantly. Dr. James Sherrill was the founding director, and the clinic that resulted was the result of his energy and that of a few good men who put their careers there, too. Time made it apparent that diabetes does not exist alone, and slowly, painfully, the idea of a full internal medicine diagnostic clinic evolved. Two able basic scientists, Eaton McKay and Arne Wick, did make a major contribution in their work on fatty acid metabolism; they were relegated to the basement by Sherrill and, even though they were both gone when I arrived, the institution still talked about the internecine war between McKay and Sherrill.

The place remained a group practice of conservative internists. No surgeons were on staff. San Diego and La Jolla specialists were called in when needed, but the atmosphere was low-key, conservative, slow-paced, and expensive. The clinic did things well and it made no pretense of catering to the less favored. This, of course, was before Medicare and Medicaid.

With Keeney's appointment, the place began shaking and rattling. The administrator of Peter Bent Brigham Hospital, Norbert Wilhelm, took over the administration; the retiring chairman of Biochemistry at Harvard, Baird Hastings, was persuaded to come. These events were happening just as Jonas Salk was cashing in on his vaccine honor, and the Polio Foundation offered to build him an institute in La Jolla. With Salk leaving the University of Pittsburgh, there was a willingness-to-roam atmosphere at Pitt, and Keeney was able to get their pathologist, Frank Dixon, an experimental pathologist, to come to SCRF with a considerable staff and, equally important, a considerable collection of national grants.

This was not only a coup for Ed Keeney but it brought into the clinic, for the first time, people who knew the business of getting grants. The clinic was off and running and never looked back. It parlayed a combination, with great success, of obtaining funds from national sources and generous gifts from the uniquely wealthy patients who get care at quality watering places. The other basic sciences were recruited and the Research Foundation definitely became all capital letters. The clinic was not quite the place it had been when Sherrill developed it as a center for dispensing insulin and diets.

At the very same time, the politics of higher education for the entire state finally agreed that the Scripps Institute of Oceanography would be but the first block of a whole University of California-San Diego, complete with a new medical school. It was exciting to be a part of the birth of the medical academic scene in San Diego in the early 1960's.

Keeney brought onto the Board friends who saw things as he did. He had the name changed to the Scripps Clinic and Research Foundation, a good name; but one which never quite settled the issue of what kind of a bird was the place—patient care or research, and whether there was any role for medical education.

I omitted deliberately one of the administrative experiences from the Kansas decade until this point and, at the risk of tedium, I need to pursue this issue of the twin frictions, twin cultures, which are surprisingly disruptive to a medical institution: seeking to carry on both patient care and medical research.

This marriage of two cultures is a somewhat different dilemma than discussed by C.P. Snow, but the same tensions apply. The two cultures in the medical education/research world are the clinicians on the one hand, and the basic scientists on the other.

Usually, but certainly not always, the basic scientists have Ph.D. degrees and are compensated at a lesser level and, always, the clinicians have M.D. degrees and are rewarded at a considerably higher level. The tensions are related to both income and status, two powerful, even painful forces. There are other issues, which my Scripps days convinced me are beyond status and income.

At Kansas, during my first years, there was no problem. The clinical faculty was all at Kansas City, and the basic science faculty was all at Lawrence, 30 buffering miles away. One of the criticisms of the Kansas medical school, made by national accrediting bodies for years, had been this divided faculty. Under the deanship of Wescoe, himself an M.D.-basic scientist, and with Franklin as chancellor and also a physician, the schism was ended; the basic sciences were brought to the Kansas City campus. The medical school was made whole with clinicians and basic scientists working at the single campus.

This seemed so logical that all involved were elated. The inherent tensions were lessened by the happenstance of Wescoe being a basic scientist but also a physician, and his successor in Pharmacology was a physician, as was the head of Microbiology, Tom Hamilton. Grisolia and Reissmann, who became heads of Biochemistry and Physiology, were physicians. These were unusual circumstances, and perhaps obscured the cultural difference. As I left Kansas, the gap between the two cultures seemed closed. Let us return to the La Jolla scene and, later, pick up on the longer view at Kansas.

Every possible effort was made at the Scripps to bridge any division between the scientists in the laboratories and the physicians in the clinics. The income issue was solved by a uniform salary scale, in fact, there was a very strong likelihood that the basic scientists were frequently better rewarded than the clinicians, somewhat like the star system in baseball. The trustees provided us with free lunches in a charmed patio setting, which should have been balm for any wound. We thus broke bread together daily. We walked down the buffet line together, and, immediately, separated ourselves by sitting with our colleagues, the colleagues from our side of the dividing line. This was not done out of animosity. It just is a unremitting truth that over lunch one looked forward to a good discussion with someone of like interest. In an atmosphere of creative, enthusiastic people, lunch is not for recreation, it is for talking about what you have been doing.

Further, Keeney made every effort for the weekly grand rounds to be an exercise in the correlation of clinical problems and the latest in basic research. These are two different kinds of skilled endeavors, and a very competent clinician has very little to say which is worth an hour of a very competent scientist's time.

The vocabulary of the scientist is an alien language, and, strangely enough, is not necessarily, when you are dealing at the very frontiers of basic research, related to any clinical situation that at that moment is occupying the energy of the clinician. Good basic science is truly basic, whereas the best of clinical medicine, academic or otherwise, is an applied science, an imperfect art.

One field is precise, gaining information by measured increments of defined protocols. The other, clinical medicine, is a compromise between the knowledge you seek, the patient's condition, and the ambiguous variables of the individual personality.

One is tidy, one is not. Two cultures, two reward systems, two vocabularies.

The Scripps had one other value to add to the effort to find harmony between the two cultures. This was Baird Hastings.

Hastings came to Scripps upon his retirement from Harvard Medical School. He had had a very illustrious career, often in a role where he had been a spokesman for the basic sciences. He saw himself as a bridge between science and government, between science and funding agencies, and, in our group, as the senior statesman who would ease the frictions and bring harmony.

He called himself the "great conciliator" and his career offered many examples where he had been the voice of compromise.

He failed at the Scripps to have any influence in these areas, not because he did not talk about it, speak about it, and claim he was carrying out that role. His lack of success was, in my mind, because he was not really a conciliator but, instead, hovered upon being a synchophant, playing up to the trustees, to the administration, and enjoying the perquisites and recognition that this brought his way. My analysis is overly hard; I only knew him when he was retired, perhaps made insecure by being in a new place, outside of his familiar academic security, and seeking to protect his new sources of rewards and support. I walk carefully in faulting a man who had such exceptional success through a very long career. He eventually came to retirement age under the rules of the clinic. He then had an appointment and office at the University of California San Diego (UCSD) and remained active on into his 90's.

Perhaps Baird Hastings had little impact on bringing the Scripps Clinic AND Research Foundation into a harmonious whole, simply because they are separated endeavors, should be separated, and work best when separated. At any institution which claims they are integrated, close scrutiny reveals the claimed harmony is in the mind of the administration—and the press agent.

The two cultures are just that, two cultures, and the attempts at marriage are made by well-meaning people who are enthusiastic about the nomenclature of cooperation, the claimed efficiency, transfer of knowledge, etc.

Later, when my knowledge of Kansas picked up again, I discovered that the human nature which separates the two cultures had been solved again after Wescoe had left the scene. The basic sciences were still at their transplanted site in Kansas City but, like the phoenix, they were very much alive, alive and competing, back in Lawrence. The removal to the Kansas City medical school had provoked an entire rebirth of all the basic sciences at the Lawrence campus. The Lawrence basic scientists were not above hinting that they were the true scientists, and the medical school departments were no longer quite among the elite. The culture gap had survived.

The basic scientists who had made the move into the clinician's camp were now not only estranged from the clinical faculty, but from the REAL basic scientists at the Lawrence campus.

The true wisdom is to enjoy each because of their uniqueness, and not do a window dressing for the sake of the administrative chart.

When the time came for me to build a medical school, from the drawing board out, a major part of the plan was one which would enhance complete, separate independence—a School of Medicine and a School of Basic Life Sciences.

Of course, I realize that at some unknown date in the future, an enthusiastic conciliator will come on the scene, and with great emphasis on the value of working together and building bridges, a new broom will have a try at rediscovering marriage.

Today, at the University of Missouri-Kansas City, there are two schools, each doing what it does best—and, undoubtedly, outside accrediting bodies will someday come and recommend consolidating them.

My narrative returns to the California scene. The Scripps Clinic's embargo against the surgical fields was continued. I devoted a considerable amount of energy to developing cooperation with the nearby community hospital and community cardiac surgeons. No other field of general medicine is so much a marriage of the diagnostician and the surgeon as cardiology. Within weeks of our arrival, we were doing every possible variant of cardiac catheterization at the clinic, without the backup of cardiac surgeons, including direct left ventricular puncture. Then it was considered risky; now the efforts to contain cost urge that catheterizations be done on an ambulatory basis, and the question of surgical backup is forgotten. Motor homes with mobile cardiac catheter units are now accepted.

A well-trained surgeon from the Varco-Lillehei group at the University of Minnesota, Ivan Baronofsky, took on most of our surgical needs. By October, we were deep into full cardiac care, including surgical care. I did have conversations with other heart surgeons, including Dick Varco and earlier, John Burroughs, but none felt the move to La Jolla was a sufficiently reassuring prospect.

Ivan Baronofsky's fascinating, resonating name was matched by his appearance: a handsome, rugged face, an inspired mane of vigorous hair, and a nose to be honored. I enjoyed working with him for several years, and, at all times, recognized the difficulties he faced in trying to do the full range of difficult cardiac operations from a solo, private surgeon base. There was enough of the spirit of the buccaneer and the dramatic actor in his make up— and he managed to carry it off.

The arrangement was not perfect, and I never let up on urging the clinic to drop its resistance, and get on with the full spectrum of medical and surgical care. Keeney had other problems and needs to solve and could not be persuaded. The medical field in which he had spent his career may have accounted for his judgment. He was from the generation of allergists in which the treatment of the patient had questionable scientific logic—and with essentially no relationship to the work of a surgeon, other than odd sinus drainage procedures.

The clinic under Keeney prospered. He skillfully took the weaknesses of a small private clinic, not too well endowed, and raised the place to a level of research reputation far beyond its inherent potential. He did this through gathering a board which faithfully endorsed his actions, and catering skillfully to the plethora of wealthy people who have found life delightful in this special part of Southern California, and who reason that an investment in health research may prolong their ability to enjoy such a life.

In choosing the original group of basic scientists, he chose well. They were the kind of scientific entrepreneurs who could expand their research empires through their well-established connections at the National Institutes of Health. None of this was wrong. The results must be admired. One of the clinicians of the group, Bill Vanderlaan, was also a very able investigator, and yet, he was never on what Bill referred to as "Ed's fair-haired list." This was a useful term because Keeney saw the clinicians essentially as an instrument of public relations, not as the future of the place. Vanderlaan was the epitome of quality, with a quietness that masked the toughness of his Dutch origins.

He and Ed were made in diametrically opposite molds. Ed was laughing, toothy, debonair, marginal in the accuracy of some of his statements; Bill was pleasant, very low key, precise, earnest, voice pitched at a level which made one check to see if he were speaking. One was very external; the other, very internal.

Bill and I could have enjoyed the comment attributed to Jacques Costeau: "We must believe in luck. For how else can we explain the success of those we don't like?"

In this environment, my group went on about our purposes, building a referral practice upon which we could maintain an active research and fellowship program and, through postgraduate teaching, pick up on my large concern for the continuing education of private-practice physicians.

I was especially interested in comparing the large meeting hall course to very small group instruction, one- or two-dozen men, conveying the sense of a retreat.

Alberto Benchimol grew rapidly into a skilled man at the end of a cardiac catheter, very able at setting up research protocols and accumulating publishable data. John Carson proved to be the ultimate patient-devoted physician and his natural caring way, plus his integrity and honesty, made him outgrow the kind of episodic care which a referral clinic offers. After a year, he joined a private-practice group in La Jolla and prospered.

Graduates from Kansas came and joined us for their fellowship in cardiology, and, with our nucleus of those who had come with us, we were a little western extension of Kansas. Among these were Bob Van Citters who came down from Rushmer's program at Washington, Harold Lowe, Jean Legler, Bob Voth, and Darrell Fanestil, who quickly moved into bench research with Baird Hastings.

My close friend from our medical-school days, Bill Martz, had become head of the Eli Lilly Clinical Research unit, and he sent two Indiana graduates, Phil Akre and Alan Bures, for fellowship training. Nobuo Ito returned from Japan to be in the biochemistry research unit of Josefina Caravaca, who came out from the Kansas lab of Santiago Grisolia. Van Citters teamed up with Dean Franklin, also from Rushmer's lab, and soon they were off and running with an elaborate research program measuring the blood flow in essentially every major blood vessel in the free-roaming, exercising mammal.

Their research, plus imagination, plus a love of adventure, had them in Africa studying giraffes, in Alaska studying sled dogs, out on the race track studying greyhounds, at the San Diego Zoo studying baboons and, in truth, there was no limit to their imagination nor travels. We were able to find funds, and to work out a cooperation with the Scripps Institute of Oceanography, and build for them a facility for the study of the circulation of comparative mammals up on the new University of California San Diego campus.

Franklin was a special kind of talent, the kind that can fall through the holes of an academic institution; he had no college degree and was unencumbered by a high-school diploma. What he did have was quick intelligence and a mastery of his field.

In the eight years of the program, we had a total of 52 Fellows. Just as at Kansas, we were able to practice cardiology, Fellow and staff man, side by side in the outpatient clinic and on the floors. A considerable number of them became well-known cardiologists in Southern California. Among them were Mark Roberts, Jim Lasry, Bob Urquhart, Newton Freidman, Jim Getzen, Allan Jay, Arnold Roland, Ira Monosson, Frank Trotta, Phil Akre and Alan Bures. One delightful man, John Grammer, came out from Texas and managed to resist California living, returning to practice cardiology in Dallas.

Medical students came and gave us the completion of our older-younger teams, which I considered valuable for teaching. Among them were Taylor Greenberg, Mike Singleton and Wayne

Siegel. Watching their later careers was satisfying.

My practice grew quickly, and, although we were, by definition, not a surgical institution, we quickly had a large surgical practice.

One of the quick lessons one learns upon leaving behind a Kansas practice based upon the low-key, stoic, accepting mid-American is that you have left behind exactly that kind of a practice—a calm, flat-eyebrows, untemperamental practice. The patients of Southern California, and I accept that this is not an absolute statement, have a very high level of histrionics. Their emotive capacity and willingness to express it are uninhibited. In the 1960's, the phrase, "let it all hang out," had not yet been invented. The patients did not know this, and they were enthusiastic about letting all emotions hang out. In Kansas, I could tell the farmer that he had to have a heart operation. No change in his face occurred. No change in his voice. The operation was done. At the Scripps, the slightest message of potential surgery was followed by widened eyes, a clutch at my white coat and tears. Before one could leave the room, the patient was on the long-distance line telling, even enthusiastically, the grim fate that had just been presented to him (or her). Upon my return to my office, the calls then would come in from the patient's friends. Each came in a different variation, but the message was that this patient is one of the greatest talents in the business, that the speaker on the phone wanted the best doctor to see the patient, that no cost was to be spared. I exaggerate, of course, and enjoy it. Southern Californians come in all versions and many were as ho-hum as the best from Western Kansas. Most were not.

I suspect that the very special circumstance of the Scripps, with its reputation for quality, expensive quality, its location in lovely La Jolla, all were attractive to the entertainment world. I didn't complain, in fact, once I had adjusted; I found it stimulating, even fun. Such dramatic people, creative people, are usually very intelligent. They are in a daily endeavor where the norm is hyperbole and, of course, they do not deal in science. Real illness was such a jolt to their make-believe agenda that it was hard, very hard, to accept. The response was the one which served them well in their daily life—theatrics.

The Scripps handled prominent patients well. One could come

there with a complete assurance that privacy was secure. Among those I saw in consultation were Jeanette MacDonald, Robert Taylor, John Wayne, Eddie Cantor, Mrs. Clark Gable, the President of Mexico, J. Edgar Hoover, Mark Twain's daughter—the list goes on, and it made the practice have a zest which was especially enjoyed by the Fellows.

In the field of science, a special pleasure was getting to know Per Scholander. He was always known as Pete, and had a research unit at Scripps Institute of Oceanography. We met immediately after my arrival, and he, too, had been in La Jolla only a short time. He was a genuine, first-class legend and character. His basic education was in medicine, but nothing constrained the range of his interests. A Norwegian, he could find an instant reason to study some aspect of physiology in the Arctic, but he could just as easily be off to Tahiti, or the Amazon. As skillful as Van Citters and Franklin were in their ability to justify field trips, they were first graders compared to Pete. His autobiography is titled, *Enjoying a Life in Science*—and he did.

He had more fun doing creative, original work than anyone I ever knew. In fact, he was destructive to the discipline of a physician. My physician's life was pale in comparison. Taking care of heart patients, putting tubes in patient's hearts, carrying patients through heart surgery, seemed like a restrictive burden. Why couldn't we play like Pete did?

Pete was usually dressed in cords, a thong tie, and sandals. His reputation for thinking up unusual problems and offering unusual solutions was well-known, and almost any research money he sought, he got. A high point of his career, and an achievement that could only make one whistle in admiration, was the Alpha Helix.

Pete conceived, invented, created the belief that the world of research was limited because there was no ship that could roam the seven seas, anchor at the site of some geographically distant place, and accommodate scientists from all over the world who would fly there, and an important point, a good chef could fly in, too. There, up the Amazon, for example, the ship's laboratories and the scientists would come to life and find data not possible without the Alpha Helix, and dine well.

Pete not only had the idea, but he persuaded Baird Hastings to use his good reputation in Washington to get the money.

A ship firm in Tacoma took on the building of the ship and when launch time came, the Scholanders, the Hastings, ourselves, and a few others flew to Tacoma, and sent the Alpha Helix down the ways. This is not quite accurate. We were all just arriving for the ceremony when an urgent cry came that the ship had slipped its blocks and was launching itself. The ship tumbled all the wood supports as if a bowling alley, slipped down and into water. A tug rounded her up, brought her back to the dockside, and speeches by Pete and Baird were done properly.

This was the kind of near disaster which often attended Pete's efforts, and as usual, the situation was retrieved; Susan Scholander appropriately smashed the champagne on the bow. The ship was not the end of his imagination. He also managed to find a way to have built a large circular swimming pool, large enough for dolphins, sharks, etc., and in the center was a laboratory which could house the cardiac catheter unit. Imagine a doughnut as the pool and in the middle of the ring, the research station. Pete was able to train seals, for example, to cruise the doughnut circle while being studied.

Pete was a contagious disease, and if I had met him earlier, it would have been cords and sandals for me. I made one trip with him to Guadalupe Island, off the west coast of Mexico, and had the fun of a full immersion in a Scholander adventure. We studied the circulation of the elephant seal and I did the right and left heart catheterizations on them.

Pete and Susan were warm hosts, and evenings at their home were an exposure to their cordial warmth, Norwegian food and, of course, schnapps.

Each Wednesday afternoon, we shut down the cardiac work at the Scripps, and met at the La Jolla Shores Beach for an afternoon of volleyball and picnicking. I am serious when I say, "every Wednesday." I don't believe we missed a single time in the years of the lab. Pete's group would join us, and those Wednesdays on the beach by the Pacific were an extension of academic reward almost as enjoyable as a sabbatical leave; in fact they were a mini-sabbatical.

We were not good volleyball players but, barefoot, in trunks, leaping, stretching, jumping, we enjoyed the try. Bob Elsner from Schlolander's group joined in with us on many activities and later, after Pete's death, took the leading role in getting Pete's manuscript about his life into print.

One small casualty of this athletic endeavor was that in March 1967 I had to have the medical meniscus of my left knee removed. The tear had begun in high school football; the La Jolla sands completed the task.

As the sun went down, we broke up, went home, cleaned up, and then reconvened at the institute for fruit, cheese, good bread, and wine, a prelude to our Wednesday evening journal club. If I were to list the perfect fellowship program, it would begin with that Wednesday time together. In fact, the program at the Scripps was almost "perfect." The limitations were those inherent in being based at an institution which did not want to invest in cardiovascular surgery. Such a limitation, in the world of modern invasive cardiology, was immense.

Although I was the head of the two parts of our work, heart and lung, I never ventured over into the lung work. Herman Froeb was the clinic's pulmonary specialist and I made no attempt to transgress. A Canadian-American came later, Arthur Dawson, and added solid strength to the pulmonary work. He was also an avid volleyball player. He brought a stimulating, puckish wit and intelligence to our group.

Chapter Ten

AUDREY AND I IMMEDIATELY WERE deep into the unique social structure of La Jolla and San Diego. Probably because San Diego is a "Navy town," there is an ease of acceptance into the ongoing social scene. The coming and going of the Navy due to transfers kept the area from having a rigid social caste.

I was also impressed by the lack of isolation brought by widowhood. In many parts of the United States, the active life of the couple stops for the wife with widowhood. Such was not true in San Diego. Grand dame widows were in the forefront of all gatherings. The retired military, the wealthy were attracted to La Jolla, and later the talent brought in by the University, made for a very congenial, diverse, socially sophisticated scene. One's dinner jacket was in steady use. I held the pace to a certain extent, but there was no way a hard-working clinician could match the social potential.

One of my first new friends I met through Irving Wright, the same physician who had been president of the American College of Physicians and with whom I had discussed the need for a college of cardiology. When he learned I was moving to La Jolla, he urged me to look up the retired internist who had originally taken Wright, as a young man, into his Madison Avenue practice many years earlier.

This I did, and this gave me an introduction to Rancho Santa Fe. This was a community that I quickly cherished and maintained property in for almost 30 years. The retired internist was C. William Lieb, Billie Lieb. Billie was 70 when we met, and a man of considerable intellect. If he had made one mistake, it was that he had retired too early. He had stopped his large Madison Avenue practice shortly after he was 50 and, after thorough analysis, had decided Rancho Santa Fe was the choicest physical location in the United States. A creature comfort of this kind was important to Billie and, when I later had years of living there, I knew he was an expert.

Rancho Santa Fe is the climate lotus land, cupcake land, of this country. I could not have found a place that suited me more ideally over the years. I enjoyed it for the retreats and holidays. I never tried to live there steadily.

Although Billie had retired too early, he did have one redeeming reward. When the second World War came, and there were rumors that the Japanese would bomb, and perhaps invade the Coast, the value of land fell, and Billie acquired large amounts of the precious acres of Rancho Santa Fe for almost nothing.

Early retirement may have left much of his potential untapped but one compensation was the reward of being present when others tossed away their land.

I found real pleasure in Billie's company. He was an internist, an experienced one; we talked the same language. Although the Ranch provided him with many good friends, he was hungry for medical conversation. His wife was an extra dividend, and the two of them became regular hosts for lunch.

Her name was Nadia, "Nonnie," and she was French. This bit of France made the luncheon a delight, and the generous wine made me a useless clinician for the rest of the day. Nonnie also taught me a useful lesson. Many of our homes have crusted, half-empty bottles of after-dinner liquors, liquors of all kinds, in practice, never used, but too pretty and too precious to pour out. Over a decade or two, a home can accumulate a dozen of these unfinished bottles. Nonnie used the sugary liquids to fill her humming-bird feeder. It was a perfect use. The colors were attractive and the sweet liquor brought glittering flashes all about the Lieb patio. Billie insisted the birds were inebriated; Nonnie said the alcohol was good for them.

I put a small cabin on land I acquired from Billie and this gave me a sanctuary away from the heavy social scene of La Jolla. The cabin was deep in a canyon, a real canyon, made by the San Diegito River, with a closing-in at each end. Access to the cabin was by our private gravel road, which ran one full mile from the nearest public road. When one was in the canyon, one was definitely isolated. I had a pond put at the foot of the cabin, a regular old-fashioned swimming hole. If there is any place my daughters would identify as the grand remembrance of their childhoods, I suspect it would be the canyon and the cabin.

Our friends from Austin, the Thorons, bought the other end of the canyon from Dr. Lieb and used it at Christmas and vacations. Between my own every weekend use, use for retreats with the Fellows, regular postgraduate courses, and the visits of the Thorons and their five children, the canyon became a lively place. On my 45th birthday, I evidently was carried away by enthusiasm and did something that I never did again, and now, as I think about it, I am overwhelmed with the thought. Fortunately, one's energy is just right at certain times of life to do things which later, if the challenge were similar, would fill you with fatigue. I suspect that raising children is a good example.

On this occasion, my 45th birthday, I invited 45 people to the canyon—staff, secretaries, technicians, all from the heart unit—and personally, alone, solo, cooked and served a Japanese sukiyaki dinner to all. The size of this performance requires a youth, verve, innocence that, as I said above, was possible then, and now I shake my head and roll up my eyes.

My friendship with Dr. Lieb was a constant pleasure. His long years of practice had left him mellow and graceful about people and their variations. He never expressed the cynicism which had been such a strong part of Mahlon Delp.

The death of Dr. Lieb carried a message and made me think of my friend from the Japan days, Colonel Berle.

Colonel Berle, too, had reached seniority in medicine with his joy and enthusiasm intact. He and Dr. Lieb left life by different routes. Colonel Berle was struck down by an instantaneous total stroke which left him alive, thinking, but unable to move his body or speak. This happened after he had returned to San Francisco and retired. He lived on for a number of years in this more dead-than-alive state. On many visits to see him, I would sit, hold his hand, and he would look me intently in the eye and cry.

He understood every word, and when I expressed my sorrow

at his catastrophe, he and I both remembered our thoughtful conversations at the Grand Hotel. He had told me that a precious ability one must never loose was the ability to decide when it was time to leave. Now he was caught, a prisoner within himself, no longer with the right to decide when to leave. Billie Lieb had shared similar thoughts with me. As he came into his very senior years, he chose to not run the risk of Colonel Berle's entrapment. In 1967, Billie shot himself.

Other deaths among my friends in 1967 were the famous industrial designer, Henry Dreyfuss, and his wife. The special circumstances of their passing left a considerable lesson with me.

One cannot forget the image of the devoted couple, dressed in their best evening clothes, iced champagne between them, their favorite music on the tape deck, sitting in their running auto, garage doors closed.

Lest one senses life was all morbid in those La Jolla years, I hasten to report the successful visit by two prominent English physicians, Geraint James and his wife, Sheila Sherlock; she, the great liver specialist. We placed them in a lovely seashore cottage and they found the romance of Southern California quite special. Nine months later, James wrote me, "The La Jolla ambiance works wonders. A red-haired little girl was born exactly nine months after our weekend there. Thanks!"

At a postgraduate course in the canyon, Herman Hellerstein was one of the speakers, and, after a typical Herman hell, fire, and brimstone lecture describing the benefits of regular exercise for improving one's heart, he announced he was going to have the whole group hike straight up the side of the canyon and thereby test their heart conditions.

Other guests at that same time were Dr. David Ruhe and Dr. Bern Dryer. Ruhe had skills in medicine, in flora and fauna, art, and video production. He and Dryer were out on the Coast to have discussions with me about a medical television series. Dryer was trained as a psychiatrist, but was also a novelist of considerable skill and success. I have never been with anyone who was Bern's equal as a raconteur; he was a classic spellbinder-storyteller. He put even Ralph Major to shame. Any action, small or large, would remind him of a story, and the stories were always germane, clever, often philosophical, and worth hearing. It did make for a disjointed conversation because the usual give and take was steadily intercepted by a Dryer tale, a good one, and always worthy.

As Herman led our group of inadequately fit, amused physicians across the quite wild canyon bed, he kept up a running monologue about fitness and this included regular stops at which every one had to count their heart rate. Seen from above, you can visualize this Moses leading the followers to the promised land, with periodic pulse stops. Coming behind him, strung out, were the 25 heart specialists and among them was Dryer, carrying on an entrancing story about walking across the Algerian desert, and Dave Ruhe, who gave every bush and beetle a full classification.

At about the halfway point, David Ruhe called out gleefully, "Look! Here is a rattlesnake!" This did turn the attention of the group to him, but it did not bring a falter in Herm's clinical comments. He simply used it as a pulse stop. Bern shifted into a tavern story about whiskey as a snakebite remedy.

The group gathered around Dave and the rattlesnake. Dave calmly informed all that he would now show us the technique of catching a rattlesnake by seizing it behind, where, in essence, its ears would be. He extended his hand and looked up to see if he had the group's attention. The snake accurately, immediately, bit him on the end of his thumb. Dave's first reaction was what most of us would do and that was to suggest the snake had tried to hit him but had failed. This was difficult to sell because 25 physicians had all seen it happen. The snake was forgotten and Dave, shaken, sat down on a rock in the canyon bed. Herman did not for a moment hesitate. He immediately moved his lecture into the subject of the pulse after fright and the effect of tension and stress on the heart. If left alone, he would have continued up the canyon side.

A quick inventory of the 25 cardiologists indicated that not one of them had ever treated snakebite. I found the kit I kept in the canyon for this purpose and we put a tourniquet about Dave's wrist, lanced the area, sucked it, and then walked him back up to the cabin. Dave assured us he was all right and, obviously embarrassed by the outcome of his demonstration, he stretched out on a bed.

Dryer pulled up a chair and began telling Dave about the interesting relationships between snake venom and its use in clinical medicine, and how certain snakebites were absolutely fatal. Dave, who is the ultimate man of good manners and deportment, maintained the conversation, trying to avoid looking at his sausage-size, blackening thumb.

Herman gathered the group in the living room and went right on with his lecturing. After an hour, Bern called out and suggested things were not right. The whole hand was huge. We moved the tourniquet to the forearm and the tremendous swelling moved up. Someone suggested we should call the UCLA poison control center. This was done, and we were told that antivenom might have helped if it had been given quickly, but it would be useless now.

Dave was, by now, very uncomfortable. The tourniquet was at the upper end of his arm, and the swelling filled the full hand, lower, and upper arm. He continued to try and project calmness about his problem, but was definitely developing twitches and signs of central nervous system hyperirritability. We agreed to stop the session, and several of us took him to the emergency room where nothing was possible except a clean bandage.

The day ended with Herm and Dryer in Dave's hotel room, both talking happily and vigorously about a possible television series in which the viewer would be in a submarine inside the bloodstream and see the heart on a journey through it, and Dave continuing to project pleasantness and good cheer, joining in the conversation when he could forget his pain.

In the end, he lost part of his thumb. This long story is apologized for, but it does give me a chance to tell of the kind of teaching we did, the role of the canyon and the kind of friends who made it all special. And not one word of this story is an exaggeration or expansion of what really happened. I had my little Minox with me and photographed it all.

Any physician could, if not handicapped by a personal hesitation to talk about his patients, write stories just as touching, as humorous, as entertaining as those told by James Herriott about his animal practice. One could do that if one had his skill.

I have, as does every physician, a treasure-house of vignettes.

The Scripps was a special collection of interesting patients. Kansas had patients who were just as complex, but a doctor's storytelling is enhanced if the patient is prominent. My inhibition comes from a lifetime unwillingness to ever discuss a patient's story, and the sense that this present narrative must stick to my own experiences and not take off into another subject, "Interesting Patients I Have Known." As I said earlier, a lifetime of taking care of patients does remove most illusions about the innate goodness of people; perhaps, as with Delp, most of us end up cynics. But I think we become optimistic cynics, aware of the bad, yes, but convinced that if you expect good from people, you often provoke them into doing good.

The care of a patient becomes extremely complicated when the patient is someone of great prominence. The Scripps was a good place for such patients to come for care because of the private nature of the organization, its smallness, and its uniquely tucked-away location on the La Jolla peninsula. We were able to control publicity and a shield of privacy could be offered.

In addition to the patients who came from the United States and Mexico, I had many patients who were from the local area. Many of these became good friends and, more than had happened at Kansas, I became for them a kind of general medical advisor. This is an enjoyable role and gave me a hint of how satisfying a full private practice could be. However, I was traveling so much, both in the United States and abroad, that I could not accept much responsibility for continuing care. Dr. White had told me this had been true throughout his career. One had to accept this flaw in this way of practice, it was a price paid. John Carson, who had come from Kansas with me, saw this, and chose to go into full private practice.

A few patients became very close friends. Among them were Herb York; Armistead Carter; Billie Lieb, whom I have already mentioned; a retired newspaper man, John Kennedy; and Aida Rodriguez.

Herb York is a physicist and had been director of the Livermore Laboratory and the head of the military research program under Eisenhower. He came to La Jolla to be the first chancellor of the new University of California-San Diego. Herb was, and probably still is, the perfect example of superb intellect and unending innocence. He knew every detail of rocketry, throwweight, and atomic weapons. He had been in on the ground floor of their development, and knew this country's plans for their use. In fact, he knew so much and had such candor that he became a prominent spokesman against atomic weapons. He wrote substantial books advocating major changes in American military strategy. I first met him as my patient, and then he and I became inveterate walkers, taking Sunday hikes of considerable duration.

If Walter Ross was a trail-riding expert, Herb was equally committed to doing the same on foot. When I wasn't walking him, he had his poor wife, Sybil, up in the mountains, under pack, using her feet. My walks with him were both a pleasure and a problem. The walking I enjoyed, but Herb was the ultimate talker and he simply wore down my listening capacity. He did not tell stories with any particular cogent ending, they were never off-color nor humorous. They just never stopped.

He was chancellor of UCSD at the time of the launching of its new medical school and when Dave Bonner, the original leader brought in to start the school, died of lymphoma, Herb's search committee brought in Joe Stokes to be dean. This new medical school could not have been more at a right angle to what I thought a medical school should be. The founders chose the full route of the research establishment, and set out to collect a research-oriented staff, to seek students who were research oriented, and to measure success by size of grants achieved.

I was not in on the basic planning, but made it clear that I would not build a new school in that mode. This attitude was essentially a private one which I expressed only to Herb and never publicly. I did meet on several occasions with York's successor, John Galbraith, and with Galbraith's vice-chancellor responsible for planning the medical school, Bob Tschirgi. Although I knew the new school probably would be in the mode of the rest of the campus—strongly research-oriented—I put a considerable amount of energy into telling them that I thought the flaw in American medical education was its emphasis on research, to the detriment of expressions of concern for humanism, ethics, and personal dedication. This has been the basic theme of my commitment to medical education.

My last year in California coincided with the beginnings of the federal program, the Regional Medical Program (RMP). It is difficult now to understand the unusual enthusiasm and excitement brought over the entire country by what is now a forgotten effort.

In the Johnson Administration, and particularly while Wilbur Cohen was head of HEW, the Mary Lasker and Mike DeBakey lobbying group put intense energy into getting national funding for several—a dozen or more—large patient-care and research centers dedicated to heart disease and strokes. These were to be regional medical centers. Perhaps the initial impetus came because DeBakey had a keen need for funds for such a center at his Houston base. The original use of the word "regional" was limited to this concept. These blood-vessel and heart total-care centers were to be new facilities. There was no explanation as to how they were to fit into the ongoing system. Whose patients were to be taken over to fill these new facilities? What was to happen to local hospitals and existing routes for referring patients? The answers to these vital questions were missing in the original bill. The lobbying efforts of hospitals, surgical specialists, and the AMA were stimulated, and fought this original plan into a compromise. The final bill never quite figured out what it had compromised.

DeBakey lost his centers but was spared the embarrassment of losing the bill. They kept the name but the purpose of the bill changed in its intent. It became an attractive source of unexpected money, often dispensed through the dean's office, but, for him, freed of the entanglement of his chairman and their wishes.

Wilbur Cohen, as head of HEW, gave his impression of what RMP was to accomplish. In a speech, he said: "[Its] essential purpose is to speed up the diffusion of knowledge." With those words, he did express the tenor of the day. That thought was popular at the time. I never believed there was a communication problem.

So much progress was being made in the intensive care of the cardiac patient that there undoubtedly was a catching-up to be done by the man in practice. I had no concern. I worked full time in this arena, and knew that the continuing education of physicians was going on at a very high level. Very rapidly, new information and techniques were put into practice. It was the exact reason for the American College of Cardiology, and the College carried out its education duty superbly.

Too often, the disbelievers, and unfortunately, some of them were authorities on education, maintained that there were no measurable differences whether a doctor participated in continuing education or not. Of course, the problem was not the doctor or the teaching. It was the educator. He knew only how to use stereotyped examinations typical of a classroom. He had no comprehension of the rate that new medical information is absorbed and put into practice. The educator did not know how to measure an applied science, as is medicine.

In RMP's original years, it attracted to its administration some outstanding talent, and the whole country, in terms of marginal academic medicine, was involved. I say "marginal" because those who got involved were not the first-line power structure of the schools but those on the periphery. These, often, were those who had wished the schools were more involved in their communities and more interested in "community" care. They were not the research-oriented, nor the mainline academicians.

The word "regional" came to mean this: regional in terms of cooperative planning, but, resolutely, no new buildings for patient care. RMP gave these people, these community-oriented planners, a place at the planning table. For a grand five-year period, RMP gave them money with which to work. By the fifth year, the Nixon Administration was in, and the attenuation of the budget began. The death of RMP was complete in 1974.

Here again, I visited with Galbraith and Tschirgi to explain how this new bill could be used to help them build a network that would make their new medical center have a patient-care support system. My urgings were premature; they had too many other things to think about.

The American College of Cardiology, speaking for America's practicing cardiologist, obviously had a major interest in this new law, and I was made chairman of the college's RMP Committee and spokesman for them in Washington.

When the first chairman of medicine of the UCSD School of Medicine was selected, they chose Eugene Braunwald, a very successful investigator at the National Heart Institute.

Gene and I were friends, and when he told me he was coming, I offered him an opinion, something one should seldom do (is this true?). I told him that he would not find La Jolla his cup of tea. A few years later when he left to go on to the Brigham in Boston to take the Chair there, he chatted with me and said he had not quite understood what I meant when I had made my negative remark—but now he did. What I was expressing was the hedonist environment of a Southern California beach town, which is what La Jolla truly is.

I knew the kind of driving, high-achieving person Gene represented, and I knew he would never quite enjoy the tuxedo/dinner/dance social pattern which would inevitably seek to gather him up. I knew this because I had already found this to be both the pleasure and the problem of life there.

Joe Stokes, the first dean, did not have the durability to be a dean. He was a pleasant, somewhat inept person, and it was painful to see the tremendous resources made available to the new school and the fuzziness of his leadership.

Braunwald gave me the title of professor-in-residence and Scripps Oceanography made me a research physiologist on Scholander's staff.

A very special friend of the La Jolla years was Armistead Carter. Although I met him first as a patient with occasional bouts of atrial fibrillation, essentially he was a very healthy bundle of animation. I met him when he was about 65 and we remained friends until the moment of his death, years later. He was retired, wealthy, and had the capacity to enjoy the constant whirl of the city's society. Armie was a Democrat and a liberal from the time the concept was discovered, yet all of his friends were wealthy Republicans. In the abstract, he detested Republicans; in practical daily life, they were his closest friends.

Armie was an enthusiast. He bubbled about San Diego; he chortled about the new university; he boosted the zoo; extolled the theater, which was named after his father; he loved the food and wine society; he loved his golf buddies; he loved people. Being generous was his way of life, and this included being generous about the achievements of his friends. His day consisted of passing from one friend to the next, lavishing praise, and boasting their talents and the career of everyone he called friend.

In the last year of Pat Brown's governorship, when he was running against Reagan, Armie decided I should be a University regent. He bombarded the Governor by mail and phone, twisted the arm of everyone who owed him a favor, and for several weeks did nothing else but lobby on my behalf. He extracted from Brown the promise that as soon as the election was over, he would take up my appointment. Reagan won the election.

Years later, upon his death, his will had a small paragraph, designating a gift of $50,000 for his friend, E. Grey Dimond, to be used on Hospital Hill in Kansas City "in any way which will further his efforts." We built a handsome courtyard at the entrance to the Medical School, the Armistead Carter Courtyard. My only regret is that those who walk through that courtyard in Kansas City never knew the wonderful, buoyant man who made it possible.

For some years, I was physician to the former President of Mexico, Abelardo Rodriguez. The title he used was The General, and he is credited with having ended revolutions in Mexico. At least, it is said that after his presidency there has not been a coup and each president has served his term. His wife was very devoted to him and spoke with pride of his career. She had one phrase which perhaps carried a different message when said in Spanish. In English, it was, "My husband has no living enemies." She said this with pride, and still, I felt a certain chill when this message was expressed.

A pacemaker was placed in The General and several years later, when his pacemaker continued effectively to drive his heart, yet a bleeding stomach lesion kept exsanguinating him, a very delicate, final decision had to be made. He, his wife, and I all shared the same philosophy. We did it.

The volume of people remaining at or near the hospital during this final illness, made clear the fact that this was a man of vast power and respect—and wealth. His widow remained a close friend of my family, and up until the time of her death would come to Kansas City to celebrate Thanksgiving with our gathered clan. My daughter, Lark, was especially close to her, and they spent holidays together in Mexico City, on the Caribbean, and on a cruise to the Fiords. Aida Rodriguez was an impressive woman.

Another patient of that last California year was Dr. Ward Darley. Darley had been the longtime head of the Association of American Medical Colleges (AAMC) and, before that, the president of the University of Colorado. In earlier years, he had been an internist and chairman of Medicine at the University of Colorado. During his years as leader of the AAMC, he had been an outspoken critic of the overemphasis on research, and he had advocated that the medical schools should concentrate on educating primary-care physicians. His message, succinctly, was that Americans should have one basic doctor who is their family physician, who takes care of them, and, as Ward said, protects them. By "protects them" he meant seeing to it that they had good medical care, but also were protected from the excessive enthusiasms of the specialists.

He and his wife were delightful, graceful people, and I enjoyed the responsibility of going up to his retirement community to see him. From that contact, he became my ally and coplanner. Much of what I intended to do in a new medical school, he wholeheartedly endorsed. All through the founding years of the new school, he and I had long, leisurely talks by phone. He was the closest reality I had to a counselor from 1967 until his death, shortly after the dedication of the medical school building.

When we dedicated our new medical school building in Kansas City, Ward was the keynote speaker. Prophetically, he had warned me of the inevitability of a showdown with the entrenched old-timers in the AAMC. He knew them all and enjoyed the satisfaction of venting old memories. He told me of the conflicts he, himself, had experienced and was sure that somehow they would strike at my education plan.

Another patient brought a completion of my childhood. Mom's only brother had been her beloved Lark. He was her trusted confidant through her bleak years. When I took her from Muncie to Terre Haute for burial, he came to be with me. When my daughter was born, I named her Lark. He now lived in California, and was ill and failing. I took care of him, tried to comfort him. He died July 19, 1968, just 25 years after his sister.

I have omitted comments about the American College of Cardiology in order to relate a considerable amount of my other experience, uninterrupted. Life was not that way, and, in real life, there were an enormous number of phone calls, letters, air trips, meetings: breakfast meetings, lunch meetings, dinner meetings, late-night meetings, all-day meetings. The ACC was a large part of my life at that time.

Chapter Eleven

IMMEDIATELY UPON ARRIVING ON THE Coast, I began a working relationship with two Los Angeles cardiologists, George Griffith and Eliot Corday. Both men were in very successful private practices, George using the Good Samaritan Hospital, and Eliot, the Cedars of Lebanon (later, the combined Cedars-Sinai). They were not only important to the future of the American College of Cardiology, but they also taught me a new definition of energy. Somehow they not only took care of very large, demanding practices, but from the beginning of their commitment to the concept of the College as a national force in the world of cardiology, they gave generously of their time to the College, often absorbing the cost of their travel, hotel, etc. Because there were two of them and one of me, we always met in Los Angeles, and they were fundamental to the giant change which took place in the decade of the 1960's in the College. Each man undoubtedly had some level of irritation which showed itself at some point, but I never found it. They were so unremittingly pleasant that I was at first certain I was in the presence of two confidence men. No matter how long, how late, how tense the session, they never lost their pleasant, almost sanctimonious voices, facial expressions, and demeanors.

George was Pennsylvania Dutch and at one point had either been, or hovered on being, a minister; he found it difficult to squeeze out a word of mildest profanity.

Eliot was from Canada. He was a mix of unique pleasantness and energy. The College's success with its International Circuit Courses is a monument to his endeavor and persistence. In the years we worked together, he always had the enthusiasm of a new bridegroom and, with a slight lisp, maintained a courteous dialogue through thick and thin. I worked with them only on shared College projects, and, back home, in competitive private practice they may have been ogres, I never saw it.

I told Jim Crockett that I was working with two hair-oil salesmen from Los Angeles; he warned me that I was just a country boy among the wolves. After years of knowing them, I never met the wolf.

I became president of the College in 1961 at its annual meeting in New York City and served until the annual meeting in Denver in June 1962.

As president, I was entitled to have a convocation guest speaker. I invited Paul Wood to come from London, first for several days to our home in La Jolla. I showed him our institute and group, then the three of us, Audrey, Paul, and myself, flew on to Denver where, as a perquisite of the office, we had the grand suite on top of the hotel. We had more than a week together, and it was a sharing, harmonizing time.

Paul was wound tight upon his arrival. He was jumpy, his mood swinging from harsh, jolting laugh, to a sullen, sarcastic depression. He smoked incessantly, spoke in staccato sentences. The three days in La Jolla with tie off, camera in hand, beach strolling, tourist-style, began to put him back together. The three of us had now seven years of exposure and friendship, and when we moved on to Denver and began to enjoy our elegant shared apartment, we could put on our robes as the day wound down, open a bottle of the best champagne and expand our friendship and trust.

He unburdened himself and talked about the trap he was in at age 55 and how he had to find some way out. We reviewed the possible ways to go, including a candid analysis by himself of his younger colleagues in London and why each one, at least to him, had a drawback. By the time we said farewell, we had agreed that I should bring the whole family to London the next summer, join him, and see what the potential might be for our making a permanent move.

We said goodbye in mid-June; he flew down to Atlanta to give a talk for Willis Hurst's group at Emory, before going back to London.

I picked up the *New York Times* on an early July morning and on an inside page read of his death. He had left us just three weeks before. Paul's death was an immense loss to the world of cardiology and, in a real sense, it ended the era of English international leadership which had begun with MacKenzie, then to Thomas Lewis, Parkinson, McMichael, and to Wood.

Of course, very good men and women carry on now, but with Paul's death, the challenge to American dominance in the field was over. His death was my loss, too. I enjoyed his company more than anyone I had known in cardiology. We were good for each other, and we each found a release in telling of our burdens and frustrations, which we did not do with others. With his going, the potential of a move for myself ended, of course, but the message of the long, emotional conversations we had in our week, remained with me. He so clearly expressed his reservations about his future. How could he handle the next advances in cardiology? Were the personal prices he had paid worth it? He spoke about his fatigue, and his unwillingness to either sacrifice what he had, or try to continue to compete. He talked of the other aspects of life one had to forego, about the shaky foundations upon which his own authority rested, about the energy it took, and the sense of entrapment.

One of the reasons this was a substantial remembrance for me, was that on one occasion, one only, when Paul White had asked my help for a major problem involving one of his adopted children, he, too, exposed painful depths of unhappinesses, and said things that sounded almost like the words of Paul Wood. I well know that inside of each of us, there is a suppressed listing of all the hurts, the prices paid, the slights felt, the wish to have a clean slate, the paths that could have been taken—one's inner list of hurts. This I well knew but equally, I paid attention to these cries from within and never forgot. Cries from within, made by two victims of their ambitions.

Eliot Corday took on the very large project of getting the American College of Cardiology into the international scene. This was a closed field, pre-empted by the American Heart Association. How to have a presence on the world scene was high on our list of the plans for the College.

The American Heart Association considered itself the official organization representing American cardiologists at international meetings. A meeting of all the heart associations of North, Central and South America: the Inter-American Society of Cardiology, held every four years, recognized only the AHA, as did the European Heart Society. When Dr. White led in the formation of an International Heart Society as a gathering of each nation's heart society, the AHA was the American-designated group. This was logical, even understandable, but an issue too large to be allowed to be permanent. Too large an issue if there was to be any acceptance of the organization which I had chosen to back.

The American College of Cardiology took a path that could not be blocked. This was the single most effective initial move we made. We took the idea of the circuit course as done in Kansas and expanded it as a method of entering into the field of international education in cardiology.

We founded the ACC International Circuit Courses, and Eliot carried the idea through the corridors of the State Department, a lonely task, for he was acting as the spokesman for a group with little reputation, in fact a considerable nonreputation. Eliot persevered; his energy and tenacity were formidable. He discovered a program titled: "American Specialists Abroad." This was an ongoing effort by the State Department to facilitate this country's international policies through the altruistic efforts of actors, singers, musicians, scientists, etc., as representatives of our country. When one reads of rock-and-roll bands in Poland, for example, it is usually under the sponsorship of this program.

The effort is a relatively hands-off apolitical effort, and Eliot got there just when no one had made a proposal similar to ours. I don't believe anyone could have done the job but Eliot and, even now, after 20 years, and several dozen international circuit courses, this cooperative effort of the State Department and ACC continues, with Eliot carrying the physical, negotiating, planning effort, down to the present.

There was another benefit from this program for our master plan of making the ACC palatable to the American academician, who, at that time, was fully committed to the AHA. By offering a fully funded, State Department-sponsored overseas experience, we were able to overcome the resistance of the "hard-liners" and capture them, one by one, into a position of recognition of the ACC, by the very real act of their going overseas under our banner.

We planned for five cardiologists to go abroad for two to three weeks, and work with each country's universities; to go and give a well-planned series of formal lectures, case presentations, panel discussions. We did not propose going in as specialists who would do surgery, procedures, etc., but held to our commitment of being an educational organization only. We avoided that well-used trap of volunteering one's surgical skills overseas, with the anticipation of harvesting referred cases back home.

One of the men who had been at MGH with me, Mariano Alimurung from the Philippines, had remained a close friend and had, several times, been a visitor to my unit in Kansas and California. I had been his guest in Manila in 1956. We corresponded with him, and asked him to be the host for the first circuit course. He proved to be a powerhouse of an organizer, local politician, and expediter.

On October 26, 1961, in the midst of my presidency, Eliot; Simon Dack, the very skilled editor of the college's journal; George Burch, chairman of Medicine at Tulane; Walt Lillehei, cardiovascular surgeon from the University of Minnesota; and myself met in Los Angeles, prior to taking off for Manila, and immediately had a happy harmony.

Getting Burch involved was a major break because there were few more conservative, establishment cardiologists in the country. Getting Lillehei involved meant the absolute frontier, at that time, of American heart surgery was with us. Evidence that we were on the right path came later as Corday, Burch, and Lillehei each became president of the ACC. Simon Dack had already been the president of the College, the sixth president, and has been perhaps the only bridge from the original New York City group to remain a major effective force in the College. Few medical journals have had an editor with his quality and durability.

We flew off to Manila for the First International Circuit Course. Mariano had organized a program at Santa Tomas Catholic University, which included the presence of the Rector Magnificus, a fantastic title; he gave us a Church blessing, honorary Santa Tomas Professorships, and produced an audience of more than 1,200.

We were exhilarated and amazed. Our first speaker got up on the stage, and there, before this Catholic audience, faculty and administration, gave our opening talk. His subject was, "When should a pregnancy be interrupted because of heart disease?" It was the right paper in the wrong place.

It was only because of the promise of better to come, of Mariano's diplomacy, and the tolerance of the Rector Magnificus, that we were not immediately escorted to the airport. After that moment, the program was a great success, and although the teaching and social schedules were overwhelming, we were excited, and knew we had a format for the international scene.

We flew on to Taipeh and there Nong Ting hosted us. He had been one of the students sponsored by the China Medical Board to come to our Kansas unit, and now, with himself as chairman of Medicine at the National Defense Medical Center (NDMC), all doors were open. This was made especially true because the three cardiologists at the Taiwan National University had also been sent to my unit at Kansas by the CMB. Thus we were able to walk the fine line between the tensions of those who were from the mainland (NDMC), and the native Taiwanese who were from the national university.

Our team disbanded as we left Taiwan, and I went on to Tokyo especially to visit the Hamadas and Nobuo Ito. Eiko, who had been with us in Kansas when Lea Grey was born, was a special pleasure.

From her American "liberation" experience, she had blossomed into a career woman, marketing rare gems. The change in the Tokyo I had known in 1946 to this exciting international city, was matched by the change in Eiko, who, in 1946, was in full kimono at all times, and remained kneeling, head bowed, during the visits to the Hamada home by physicians from the 49th General Hospital. Now in only Western clothes, colorful clothes, hair waved, with make-up, jewelry, she was the new Japan.

Among the personal benefits from this first circuit course was getting an exposure to Walt Lillehei. At the professional level, he was impressive. He had seen so many congenital heart problems at the operating table and had had such a vast experience with all of the associated electrocardiograms, heart sounds, X-rays, etc., that he could cover any aspect of congenital heart disease. Few surgeons have this breadth of surgical experience as well as diagnostic information. Lillehei was the best I ever saw.

At the personal level, he was a formidable socializer. No matter how late the hour, or how early was our next day schedule, Walt was ready to dance, drink, go. I took on the task of getting him to bed and getting him up, both major projects. His social agenda was exhausting but livable, or at least entertaining, and subsequently, he and I did a circuit course to Colombia and Chile, South America, which was my postgraduate course in how to harness the variety of talents hiding inside Walt.

One experience on our South American trip can help the innocent reader understand the kind of hazards associated with keeping up with Walt in his young, salad days. He had heard of a rather well-known night spot in Santiago which featured absolutely no light. You knocked on the door, a hand reached out, took your hand, lifted a curtain and then you were led, through absolute darkness, to a spot, and, in a whisper, told to be seated. You were at your booth. From nowhere a female voice asked for your order. From nowhere your drink appeared.

After awhile, you noted the glow of cigarettes around the room; there was no other lighting. You became aware of the soft shuffling of feet in time to the music, and you realized people were dancing. You and your partner eased onto the dance floor, murmuring apologies to bumped, unseen bodies.

As you began to focus your hearing, you became aware of the giggles, the occasional ooooh and once in awhile a small cry, even a masculine curse. You began to realize that there were various stages of love being made, but at the same time, there was a considerable amount of surreptitious pinching, and not all pinching was between partners. You and your dance partner were under attack from all sides. The novice retreated to the booth for safety. Walt defeated me by disappearing into the darkness. I did not see him again until I pounded on his door the next morning.

George Burch, on the Philippines trip, was a welcome balance to the nighttime energies of Walt. George was a mannered, soft-spoken, quite rigid, no-drinking, no-dancing, colleague. On the evening the Manila hosts gave a Fiesta Filipino grand event for us, Walt was in on every native dance, including Tiki-Tiki, where one leaps in and out between two large bamboo poles rhythmically smacked together, ankle high. I was able to escape by claiming

I had to keep George company.

In those initial years of the circuit courses, I made a major commitment and was not only leader of the first one in 1961, but, subsequently, leader of a team in 1963 which took me to Colombia, Chile, Argentina, and Brasil; in 1964, a team which went to Czechoslovakia, Sri Lanka, Indonesia, and Vietnam; and in 1966, a team to Nigeria, The Sudan, and India.

Each of these gave me a further chance to catch significant American cardiology teachers into our network by inviting them to join the overseas faculty. Among these were Ernie Craige from Chapel Hill, who had been trained by Paul White, and thus his association with the College was of significance; Travis Winsor, who along with Burch had co-authored the most successful EKG book of that time; Charles Hufnagel, the heart surgeon who had made an exciting advance in the treatment of leaky heart valves; Forrest Adams, a very well-known pediatric cardiologist, which gave us a credibility in that special field; and then the real coup, the addition of Helen Taussig herself, the grand doyenne of pediatric cardiology, for our big trip from Prague to Saigon in 1964.

Evidence that we were making progress with the College's reputation, came when the European Cardiological Society, at its meeting in Prague, asked me to represent both the AHA and the ACC.

The African trip in 1966 was a special pleasure because on the team were my two old buddies, Jim Crockett and Herm Hellerstein.

In 1972, when the door opened in China, I was there with an ACC circuit team: Eliot Corday, Jeremy Swan, Suzanne Knoebel, Abraham Rudolph, Bernie Lown, and Don Effler.

Of course, there are dozens of individual remembrances from the circuit courses, and hardly a day goes by but what I recall some completely irreplaceable experience in some far-off country. We were always there, carrying the flag for both the United States and the ACC; the evidence that we were definitely related to the foreign policy of this country, was in the countries and experiences selected for our visits. Nigeria was rich with oil, but deep in revolution, and sending American specialists there was a means of expressing this country's commitment to the existing government.

The nature of the problem came to us quickly. As our plane

landed in Lagos, an explosion blew off the front of the hotel where we were to stay. When we were in Saigon in 1964, and feeling very responsible for the welfare of quite senior Helen Taussig, our briefing officer, calmly gave us two units of advice: "As you exit the hotel to get in the waiting car, do not go out as a group, but scoot out one at a time. You will make less of a target. And if an explosion occurs while you are lecturing, remember to throw yourself away from the direction of the explosion. This will protect your head."

In Chile, from our hotel room we looked out on large demonstrations and police activity, demonstrations which were the forerunner of the era of Allende.

There were definite dividends in terms of my knowledge of cardiology. Each country had some unusual version of a heart problem that I had not seen. In Nigeria, a cavitation of the heart muscle, almost like a cluster of grapes, was new for me; in South America, Chagas Disease was an addition to my experience; in China in 1972, a rare form of cardiomyopathy, Keshan Disease, was a distinct new increment.

Of course, there were the reverse lessons. In Saigon, I spoke for an hour at the Saigon University Medical School on angina pectoris. When my grand performance was done, the professor of Medicine got up to make the host's response and quietly said that they had never seen a case of angina pectoris. Yes, I had a hollow feeling.

This was the same professor who, after we had made the trip all the way to his country, had gotten ourselves through the barricaded streets and into his lecture hall, leaned across his tea cup, just 30 seconds before we were to speak, and suggested that we all lecture in French, that the audience was more comfortable in that language. One-upmanship, Viet style.

One other example of the history lessons such travels give, came on the Saigon afternoon we were escorted though the very substantial national museum by its senior curator. All the complex layers of the country's history were represented, laid out by sequence. One large area told the story of the thousand-year suzerainty of China, another substantial area covered the century of French dominance. I asked the curator how the American's role would be told. Without hesitation, he responded, "Perhaps a small room."

The circuit courses were a major success. At the same time, the campaign to bring the ACC into a peer position with the AHA continued on other fronts. George Griffith, with the help of a Los Angeles cardiologist, Clifford Cherry, took on the task of giving the investment ceremony of the College style and significance. The question of academic gowns, of the mace, of the entire annual ceremony, was worked out. We were making the point that we were not an association but a college.

Dwight Harken of Peter Bent Brigham came in early and immediately became a strength. He suggested a "blue-ribbon" list of significant cardiologists whom we should go after, and working through friends who knew them, get them into the College. This was pushed forward on every front, and the fundamental strength of the College, dues-paying members, began to fall in place.

The AHA had made research their special interest and, through the considerable amount of money they were distributing, they earned this right. However, we were building for the future and young physicians doing research needed recognition. During my presidency, we began a program, The Young Investigators' Award. This is a cash award made by a scholarly jury, for excellence; the choice is made during the annual meeting. You, the candidate, and four or more other candidates, present your paper before the jury. There is spirit of real competition, which certainly facilitates one's performance. With the award now almost 30 years old, it is reaching an age where one can begin to enjoy seeing the mature careers of the talent picked out from the field when young.

The College continued to be based in the Empire State Building in a two-room suite. The location was further diminished by being on the floor used by the hosiery industry. A group of us began a determined campaign to move the College from the hosiery department. This was not easy because the move would represent the break with its past and all vestige of influence from the founders. It also meant we had to solve the influence of their founding executive director, who with the help of one assistant, literally *was* the College in 1960 when our take-over effort began.

All of these events were, of course, events involving people, personalities, ambitions, hidden agendas, and hidden hostilities. Eliot and George remained strengths and at every point were helpful. Dwight Harken was an absolute backer for the move to Washington. Bill Likoff threw in with us. George Burch became both helpful and, because of his natural conservatism, someone to be persuaded. Bill Martz and Jim Crockett were on the board, and gave loyal, vigorous help. Donald Dupler in Philadelphia was a positive contributor. Bill Sodeman, well-known as the author of a popular textbook of medicine, joined in with the weight of his reputation, and, through important committee work, gave mature guidance.

We came down to the point of optimum possibility. The executive director, Phil Reichert, was at a possible retirement point. The American Heart Association opted to move its headquarters from New York City to Dallas. This was the grand mistake which opened up the Washington, D.C. area as the logical terrain for our organization. The Heart Association, to use a cliche, gave us a window of opportunity. We moved into the window.

The major talent I had observed and worked with at Kansas, Bill Nelligan, had moved on to Augusta, Georgia in 1964. He and I had remained in contact; he was ready for a move. George Griffith was head of our search committee. We, all working together, pulled together the package which made the College into the international presence which it now has become. We retired Phil, with courtesy and honor, and during the presidency of Eliot Corday, produced Bill Nelligan for interview at the ACC annual meeting in Boston. The officers were impressed and offered him the executive directorship.

He played his part perfectly and said he would be very interested in the task if the College was not in New York. We moved the College, overcame the resistance of some who thought we were being extravagant beyond our means, bought land in Bethesda, Maryland, commissioned an architect, and built Heart House. And had Bill Nelligan as the executive director for the rest of his career.

All of this took time. From Bill becoming executive director in 1965, until the college moved into the finished Heart House, in May 1977, took 12 years. A great deal of the success in raising the money for Heart House was due to the hard-hitting, sustained fund drive led by Dwight Harken.

No story is all clear victory, although the story of creating today's ACC is as much a victory as one gets. At each step there was always some impediment, most of them people-invented. At the same time, much of the success was due to the cheerful, volunteer efforts of a handful of men, and after 1965, aided by the steady competence of Bill Nelligan.

With the move to Washington, and with the purchase of the Bethesda land and commitment to build Heart House, there was nothing more I needed to do or could do. The College was launched.

New talent and new leadership poured in from everywhere. From what had been a small gathering of hesitant men at the Chase Hotel in St. Louis in 1959, the College now has the largest physician education annual meeting in the world.

The roster of applicants for membership now includes everyone who entertains any possibility of being recognized as a cardiologist. The College is the voice listened to on Capitol Hill; the education commitment and energy of the College expresses itself not only Capitol Hill, but at the National Institutes of Health.

For the practicing physician, that person whose need was my original stimulus, the College's journal has the largest subscription of any heart journal; the College audiotape journal reaches thousands; the College is a source of educational videotapes; and is a sponsor of a nationally televised medical television program. Courses for men and women in practice are given across the country, and Heart House itself is the site of major in-house teaching programs.

One of my own pleasures was to give the new facility my collection of stethoscopes. When I entered medical school, a Terre Haute doctor had not only lent me money but gave me my first stethoscope. I kept adding stethoscopes and my friend from Japan, Col. Berle, gave me several he had collected. When I became head of the institute in La Jolla, Dr. White gave me an impressive gold-plated stethoscope, which I used with pride and a little embarrassment. It was definitely glamorous. During a visit to his office in 1967, he gave me his own collection, which, of course, went back into the very early years of the founding of cardiology as a specialty. A Kansas City artisan mounted all of these in a handsome display, on blue velvet, and the hundred or so bits

My first photograph.
With Mom.

(Top left) My first suit. Age 6.
(Top right) On Dolly, my pony, in Terre Haute. Age 6.
(Above) Dad, Mom and Runt.
(Above right) With Mom. Age 7.
(Right) At Sarah Scott Jr. High, Spring 1934, with Jack Roach, in suit, and Vic Aldridge.

(Top left) End on the Wiley High football team, 1936, with Jerry Lentz.
(Top right) With the Wiley High School track team in Terre Haute, 1936. Maury Grey and Woody Suttle are on my left.
(Above left) Walking with Mom in Terre Haute. 1939.
(Above) Age 18.
(Left) At the Sigma Alpha Epsilon house at Purdue, Fall 1938.

(Top left) At the 42nd General Hospital. Tokyo, 1946.
(Top right) On Spring leave, 1947, at Mount Fujiyama.
(Above left) At Kansas University. Age 40.
(Above right) With Paul Dudley White on his visit to Kansas University.
(Right) Ward rounds at Scripps Clinic, 1962.

(Top) With other past presidents of the ACC in the White House in 1966 to testify for the RMP bill.
(Above left) With Paul Wood at the ACC meeting in Denver in 1962.
(Above) At the State Department in Washington D. C. with Jim Crockett, center, and Herm Hellerstein in 1963.
(Left) At Scripps. 1961. (L. to r.) Jim Snodgrass, me, Darrel Fanestil, Ray Gilmore, Paul White, Baird Hastings, Pete Scholander.

(Top) Groundbreaking ceremonies at the University of Missouri-Kansas City. January 1972.
(Above left) At the lectern.
(Above right) On my right, Dick Noback, the first dean, and on my left, Bill Steinhardt, the University publicist, Homer Wadsworth and Nate Stark.
(Right) Digging the first shovelful.

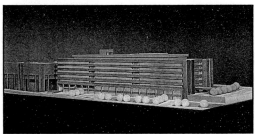

(Top left) With U.S. Senators Stuart Symington and Ted Kennedy at the Truman Medical Center groundbreaking ceremony in 1973. *(Top right)* Local, regional and national dignitaries fill the dedication ceremony rostrum. *(Above)* At the dedication lectern. *(Left)* The design of the future hospital complemented the medical education plan.

THE MEDICAL SCHOOL PLAYERS (CIRCA 1970'S)

Homer Wadsworth

Nathan Stark

Carl Migliazzo

Richardson K. Noback

Edward J. Twin

Edward B. Cross

Maxwell G. Berry

Henry A. Mitchell

Robert L. Brown

THE MEDICAL SCHOOL PLAYERS (CIRCA 1970's)

Robert S. Mosser

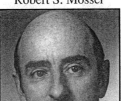

Marjorie S. Sirridge

William T. Sirridge

Andrew McCanse

Charles B.Wilkinson

Ned W. Smull

Lee Langley

Harry S. Jonas

Virginia Calkins

SCHOOL OF MEDICINE DEDICATION, OCTOBER 27, 1974

(Top left) The symbolic key presentation.
(Top right) The ceremony tent was full that Sunday.
(Above) The new School was now ready.
(Right) Ward Darley, seated on my right, an early friend of the School, delivered the dedicatory address. At the lectern is William J. Randall, U.S. congressman from Missouri.

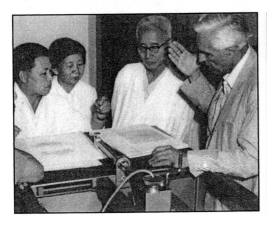

(Top left) September 1971. En route to the Ming tombs, northwest of Peking. Mary D. on my left.
(Top right) 1972. Mary D. and I on the Great Wall of China with George Hatem, "Dr. Horse of China."
(Above) February 1976. The UMKC School of Medicine travel party on the steps of the Great Hall Of The People.
(Left) 1977. Ward rounds at Fu Wai Hospital in Peking.

(Top) The 1971 city skyline and the future site *(lower right)* of the medical school and the new hospital.
(Above left) An aerial view of the completed school and the hospital.
(Above right) A recent photo of the medical school.
(Right) The hospital today.

THE STETHOSCOPE DISPLAY
AT THE AMERICAN COLLEGE OF CARDIOLOGY'S HEART HOUSE

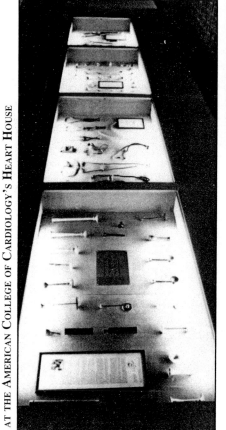

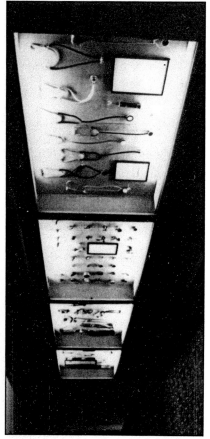

My lifetime collection of stethoscopes found a good home at Heart House in Bethesda, Maryland.

DIASTOLE: THE MARY CLARK AND E. GREY DIMOND SCHOLARS' CENTER

(Top left) Diastole's backyard provides a commanding view of the medical school. Formerly the home of the Dimonds, *Diastole* now serves as a University meeting place.
(Top right) The solarium portion of the Scholar's Center.
(Above left) The *Kiva*, a theater-in-the-round that seats 75.
(Above right) The entryway.
(Right) The interior courtyard.

(Top) My wonderful women. From the left, my daughter Sherri Grey, granddaughter Becky, granddaughter Kelly Grey, daughter Lark Grey, stepdaughter Claire Pyle, daughter Lea Grey, me, stepdaughter Louisa Thoron, adopted daughter Joan Wu.
(Above left) My favorite dog, MaMa HuHu, a giant schnauzer.
(Above) My favorite snapshot of Mary D.
(Left) Mary D. and I at a reception at the Nelson–Atkins Museum of Art in 1969.

(Top) Nate and Homer. 1971.
(Bottom) Three friends two decades later.

of history are now on permanent display at Heart House.

There is some irony represented by the collection. My own breed of cardiologist was active at the time that the full range of usefulness of auscultation was reached. We who used it became able to correlate what we heard with true anatomy and physiology. Just as I left the field, better ways of doing these things, with more precision, became medicine's standard.

My collection, in a sense, celebrates the high point of bedside cardiology and the use of the stethoscope.

By the end of the 1960's, there was no way to stop the College. I held to the rule I had made for myself of leaving a scene when the job is done. I left the College's central administration, and, at the same time, I continued organizing and presiding over, twice a year, in April and November, a limited-enrollment postgraduate course, the Course for the Consultant, at the Inn at Rancho Santa Fe. This continued, sometimes modified, for 20 years. I offered this course 47 times. The course took on a life of its own, and, with eight to 10 speakers for each course, gave me a quite private and personal means of continuing my own cardiology education. I planned, engaged the speakers, moderated, and sat through all sessions. The course also convinced me that, for that time and circumstance in the United States, this was the real way to carry on the education of the man in practice. The fellowship we felt to each other, the joining in of wives, the coming back year after year, the affection we all developed for the group, was the closest to what I believe a professional brotherhood could become. Those couples who came once and twice a year for more than 20 years, were a profound experience—for all of us.

Also, for 10 years, I took on the launching of the College's audiotape, Access and Accel. At one point, I even had to fight the College trustees to be certain that the profit from my taping efforts went to create a maintenance fund to protect the College against the unpredictable new expense of having Heart House.

My longtime friend, Bill Martz, was the person who got me into this taping project, and although producing a one-hour tape once a month for 10 years was a burden, it also was a stimulus. I not only learned how to use audiotapes for a physician's education, but because I was aware of the large, critical listener group, it made me have a focus to my medical reading, and a need to be certain my own thoughts were cohesive and defensible. Also, because I used dozens of physician guest narrators, I acquired exposure to the whole academic world of cardiology, and felt I knew who was "who" and who was producing what research. Doing the tape was a decade-long project which gave me a way to teach the physician in practice but it also was an education for me.

In 1974, on the occasion of the 25th year of the founding of the College, I contacted that host of friends I had made in American cardiology and had each man and woman, each in their own voice, tell of their career and of their contribution. This packet of tapes will never be done again because many of the participants had been a part of the spectacular growth of the field, were founding fathers, and were near the end of their careers. Thus, the 25th anniversary volume, catches a profile of the originals of American cardiology, many of whom now are gone. The contributors are a listing of my professional friends and those who were active in the years I was on the scene, essentially from 1942, when I began reading for Harry Baum, until 1977, a span of 35 years. As I assembled the taped voices of 50 American cardiologists, I thought of those evenings with Harry Baum and how he had taught me to understand and evaluate the literature.

With the 1974 anniversary tape, I understood, privately and alone, that I was now ready to close down my days as a cardiologist. From the beginning, I had enjoyed the sense of competition, the feeling that I was in a race to become the best there was as a bedside clinician, a diagnostician. In the late 1950's and early 1960's, I felt comfortable, deep inside where one admits the real truth, that I was among the handful who could claim mastery of this skill. When other responsibilities made that no longer a truth, a fact which I did not enjoy, but understood, I decided I would stop being a cardiologist. The game had been played. I had won a certain number of battles, and it made me uncomfortable to not be at the very front edge of the competition. Life is a series of races. Each race has a finish line. Nothing in my soul could let me finish out my career as a less-than-the-best. I chose to walk away.

Chapter Twelve

IN CHARLES CHAPLIN'S AUTOBIOGRAPHY (*My Autobiography,* Simon and Schuster, 1964), he tells of a meeting with the prominent biographer, Emil Ludwig (Napoleon, Bismarck, Balzac), and their conversation about the accuracy of biography. Ludwig commented, "Sixty-five percent of the story is never told because it involves other people." The percentage would be variable, but the truth is there. If one is describing one's life, and is not trying to be sensational nor capture the attention of the media and gain instant dirty-linen fame, some governing attitude does prevail. Telling your story just cannot justify a tour of someone else's private life.

"Autobiographies" frequently are on the *New York Times* Best Seller List, but to gain that mark seems to require tactics which most of us must forego. Strangely, to have a best-seller autobiography, it appears it is necessary *not* to write it yourself. In an honorable world, this is an oxymoron comment (I have winced at the popularity of that term and only use it here to show I am involved in the modern scene). But if the truth were known, amanuensis has probably served a major number of claimed autobiographies since the beginning of writing, so one cannot fault ghostwriting as modern moral decline. Ghostwriting does dilute one's view of the subject, however.

The special quality which puts a book on the Best Seller List is the vigor with which the teller tells all. This means details of sexual exploits, the more names and details the better. Selling well today, also, is the ability to tell of the beatings of your childhood, and carnal assault by a parent; in fact, any data one can give proving how mean, cruel, and sadistic a parent is, the better. If your parent was famous, and, in life, had been judged to be a major success, and you have been an insignificant failure, then you have a real coup. Your failure is entirely your parent's fault. Also, with major cachet for best-sellerism, is a lengthy narration of your own depth of alcoholism, narcotic addiction, moral depravity, and then succor from the Lord. Full-blown psychosis, with complete details of the foulness of your behavior, can be strengthened by episodes of reincarnation and examples of psychic communication and extrasensory perception. These do not in the least make the reader suspect you are unbalanced, but, instead, enhance the sales.

A major reason why I cannot tell of my experience with most of these areas is that they just did not happen to me. It is true that one of my parents was an alcoholic and his problems were a burden. But I don't think any harm was done to me; it is probable that the hell that my parents went through, just as I entered manhood, made me do just that, enter manhood, and not arrest at some stage of excuse-making.

If someone had interviewed me, then assembled it into a clever whole, this book would cover the same areas, but the wording would inevitably be not mine, but mine as heard by someone who processed me through his or her own vocabulary and interpretation. Areas which I, through discretion, elect to pass over, would be handled differently by the hired writer who inevitably would be seeking to increase the salability of the story. I would not enjoy that.

Life left me unexposed to being reborn or a recycled anything. I have no evidence that I am receiving messages from someone departed, nor am I able to give evidence of psychic strength. Perhaps this is why a ghostwriter is a good idea. His input excuses you from the embarrassment of saying such things yourself and you can always blame the excessive remarks on the ghost.

Still, Ludwig was probably right; 65 percent does not get told.

PART FOUR

Chapter Thirteen

THESE PAGES SEEM TO BE a constant recitation of travel. For what purpose? Was it for fun? Or, as is often the truth, were the problems at the job something to run from? I don't believe I ever traveled for that reason, although it is certainly a relief to get away from the daily schedule.

An issue often heard in discussing the kind of education a physician should have, before getting the medical degree, relates to liberal arts. The enthusiast endorses the great value of a four-year exposure to the great Western literature, to the great thoughts of the Judeo-Christian origins of our society, to the philosophical and sociological truths.

All those things may happen in a perfect elysian setting; they do not happen often. The image of what is described cannot be faulted. Reality is simply different. This is true not only for pre-medical students, but for all who pass through this area defined as "liberal arts."

By these remarks, I am not endorsing the present attempts in many universities to throw out courses dealing with the culture of the Western world. False and phony attacks on academic traditions are but a means of rebelling against academic standards. They are frequently but cover-up for a lack of discipline and scholarship.

This discursive detour, with my venting about claims that liberal education must be gained in college, is prelude to my purpose. My definitive message is that life's liberal education comes from travel, travel augmented by reading. My objective in educating myself has been to learn to understand others and to understand myself. A closing circle. Travel and reading, over a lifetime, gains in that direction. It is forever an incomplete journey.

189

Most of my travel has not been a holiday, except for the wonderful sabbatical leave of 1956. Usually, the agenda has been packed, and the whole thing an exhausting circus. Churchill once made the observation that the way to recover from your fatigue is to turn from what you are doing and do something else just as energetically.

Logic of that sort has served me well, and I have avoided for most of my life a lying-in-the-hammock-let-me-snooze vacation. Two days of that and I am feeling ill, ache, grow dim-witted, and know I must get active, if I am to feel well.

Without an objective other than the desire to see the world, almost all of us start out. Few of us when young have a philosophy or purpose. It takes aging to make one feel his actions need an explanation.

My childhood was not one for opening one's vision. My parents were patriotic, loyal Americans, a definition which includes the fullest possible collection of bias. They were not biased because they had any cause to be; neither had they suffered because of their race or religion. They were biased because White Anglo-Saxon Protestants were what had founded this country. WASPs they were, and they were comfortable with the thought.

The principles of the Constitution were not analyzed by them but they knew in their bones that being their kind of an American was right. Being something else was not only suspicious, but probably undermining. If you were not what they were, you were alien. Both parents carried this conviction into the family daily conversation, and discussions of newspaper articles included their comments about fish eaters, kikes, jigs, polacks, jigaboos. They believed the Roman Catholics were agents of the Pope and not at all American. They believed there was a great Jewish conspiracy. There was never an analysis of these attitudes; their feelings were pure—pure bigotry. They moved our place of residence when I was in the seventh grade because Negroes were accepted into the school, and later, Dad was bitter when I played high school football and competed in track with Negroes. Yet I cannot fault him. He was normal for the time and background.

What I label as their bias, was for them evidence of their patriotism. I cannot recall any word or comment about Asians or Arabs.

They were too rare to enter their thinking. In today's world of instant television news from every remote part of the world, have these feelings now been removed? We tell ourselves that we are now more universal. But, who knows?

Without knowing it, and without a moment of conversion, I came out of my childhood convinced that my parents were wrong. I had no grand quarrel with them and attribute no singular event that opened my eyes. Their bias was so complete, so basic to their conception of the truth, that it was an area to avoid.

Perhaps my attitude is evidence of the democratization that occurs in the American public school system. I accept this in part, and credit my 12 years in the Terre Haute schools with no great success in my book education, but in providing a good, stable microcosm of life. There were enough classmates with money, enough who were poor, enough Blacks, Jews, Roman Catholics who were all just like the rest of us, in terms of desires and insecurities. The public school as I experienced it prepared one to live in this diverse society. It was a good place, a good support system, for growing up.

I certainly did not come forth as a rabid reformer, out to solve the race issues. My first racial or religious engagement was in college. There, I did take on considerable established resistance when I persisted until successful in getting a friend and Jew into my fraternity. Medical school did not test one's strength in these areas, except some of the classmates I enjoyed were Jewish. Life in the Army and in Japan was a considerable process in teaching acceptance, and my friendship with Father Lerhinan was but one of many friendships with Catholics, Roman and Greek Orthodox, Buddhists, Muslims. The real education came at MGH where I found myself, side by side, equally educated, competing intellectually, with all races and religions and liking them, one and all. In terms of my personal acceptance of anyone's sex, race, color, religion, I don't believe it has been a factor I have weighed since that time.

It would be accurate to say I have led a fully integrated professional life. Yet, at the same time, my private life has remained segregated. I suspect this is how many of us would evaluate ourselves.

The constant sequence of Fellows in cardiology from all over the world to my Kansas and La Jolla units was certainly an education in the diversity, and the sameness, of human beings.

I admit I am prejudiced as to whom I call friend. I certainly find myself "segregating" in my willingness to work with a person or to spend an evening with someone, but that segregation is based upon my own personal pleasure of cerebral stimulation. If the individual, man or woman, is talented, productive, able, knowledgeable, then all the bias, so thoroughly delivered by my parents, is lost.

My exposure to ideas of world order and thus, ideas of world peace, was by chance, not by my seeking. I was exposed to two men who made these issues a fundamental part of their careers, Paul White and Grenville Clark. When I was under Dr. White at MGH, he was just beginning to move into that phase of his career.

To a great extent, he was influenced by Grenville Clark, an American of integrity and capacity to influence, who devoted the last 20 years of his life to seeking a world order based upon adherence to international law.

Later in this book, as I explain how my relationship with China came about, I will repeat some of what I detail here.

Clark saw the flaws in the charter of the United Nations immediately upon its founding, and put a major effort into defining how the U.N. charter should be rewritten to give it the necessary strength to implement world law. He also helped found an action group, the United World Federalists, which was dedicated to a method of protecting each nation's individuality, safeguarding the small nations from the larger ones, and creating a world in which conflict would be resolved by law, not by arms.

Dr. White was his physician and close friend. They became allies in this cause.

Clark was a respected world figure in law and had access to many heads of government, and he knew personally Roosevelt, who had been his classmate at Harvard, as well as Truman, Eisenhower, Kennedy, and abroad, Attlee and Nehru, among many others.

White, as a consulting physician, also had access to many powerful figures. He considered "the privilege of the bedside" a physician's special opening, and used this position vigorously to state the cause of a world peace system. Through such a circumstance, he spoke to Eisenhower, following the President's coronary occlusion, on behalf of Clark's efforts.

The two of them, Clark and White, were activists in this arena, and, when they felt it was essential to have the involvement of China, even if their own government refused to recognize the People's Republic of China, they decided personally to carry their message to Mao Tse-tung.

They expended great effort in trying to get American visas, using Clark's special access to the then Secretary of State, John Foster Dulles. They also reached out and made contact with Edgar Snow, soliciting his help in getting an invitation from the Chinese side, and planned to slip in to Beijing, visa or no visa. The plan fell through. Their correspondence of the time shows what tenacious, skillful "schemers" were these two.

Clark was a man of great influence with resources of money and friends, multiplied by his own reputation for integrity.

I also have had a long friendship with Bernard Lown, who later went on to found an organization using the voiced consciousness of the physicians of the world to protest against nuclear war. This group became vocal and influential, especially in Europe, and was awarded the Nobel Prize for efforts on behalf of peace.

His considerable achievement in the international scene has brought him well-deserved recognition everywhere—except by his own country. When younger, he chose a political course contrary to what was accepted as the patriot path for Americans. His entire career, a career of major achievement and success, has been shadowed by his earlier deliberate persuasion.

Lown and I first met in Kansas when he came to speak at one of my postgraduate courses, and, later, he was in La Jolla on more than one occasion for the same reason. We have traveled to China together, also. I very much enjoy his quick mind and concern for world affairs. We found time at the national meetings to get together, and I enjoyed good visits to his laboratory and to his home in Brookline, Massachusetts. Our talk was never about cardiology but about social issues, politics, and world affairs.

When I became president of the College and the circuit courses became reality, I deliberately committed a major amount of time to these travels. I wanted to understand the politics, religion, customs, history, geography of the world. In the midst of these came the stimulation of meeting Ed Snow.

At the same time, I was walking and talking with my La Jolla friend, Herb York, who had a completely different background than White or Lown in medicine, Snow as a journalist, and Clark as a lawyer. As a physicist who had headed up the Livermore Radiation Laboratory, and had been in the Defense Department under Eisenhower, he knew the full story about atomic weapons, the rocketry involved, the fallacy of there being any victor in their use in war. Much of his discussions with me later appeared in his excellent book: *Race to Oblivion: A Participant's View of the Arms Race* (Simon and Schuster, 1970).

The five men could not be more different in their educations and their approaches to international issues, yet they were all working at the same challenge: how to have a safe world.

The circuit course sponsorship by the State Department gave me, as a participant, a wider view of the world although my military service in Japan and the sabbatical-leave travels had well begun my education. I was in the Philippines, Taiwan, Japan, Colombia, Chile, Argentina, Brasil, Czechoslovakia, Sri Lanka, Indonesia, Vietnam, Nigeria, the Sudan, India, all in a four-year period. For each of these trips and in most of the countries, the State Department gave us its "briefing," explaining why the country was important and where it fitted our government's view of the world. One of my realizations was that I found I had a much larger view of the true world relationships than the State Department briefer, who was essentially limited to the "party line" of the current American diplomacy.

In these same years, I was in Mexico often, not only Mexico City, but I also saw much of Baja California, the Yucatan peninsula, the west coast at Acapulco, and, out in the Mexican islands off the West Coast, I was involved in research on whales and elephant seals. Much of my exposure to Mexico was facilitated by my relationship as physician to Albelardo and Aida Rodriguez. Some of this travel was for adventure but often the trips were for consultation, or to lecture, or to attend a Pan-American heart meeting.

Although the dedication of Clark and White was to universal disarmament and a world government empowered by enforceable world law, either through the United Nations or by a new organization, I never found myself comfortable with the full concept.

Universal and total disarmament replaced by an adequate peace-keeping force under the control of a single world order, offers too readily a means for a new totalitarian risk. If all nations are disarmed and world peace is to be maintained by a military force under the direction of a world government, then there is no means of protecting the rights of those who may be opposed to the legislated actions of the world authority. Where would the sanctuary role played by the United States be placed? If the United States had not had the arms to defend this concept of sanctuary, what would be the fate of those millions who have escaped, fled, run to get here?

If there is but a single, all-powerful police force for the whole world, then the whole world is always at risk, for nothing can assure against seizure or misuse of that force. There would be no balance of power; there would be no sanctuary.

If a world legislative body existed which had the military power to enforce its will, how could any revolution succeed? For it would be logical that the world order would be a defender of *status quo*. *Status quo* is peace, if you are among the happy ones. Retrospectively, if there had been a world government in 1776, there would have been no United States—and most of the nations of the U.N. would not exist.

If the entire world was policed by a single military force, then one coup would place the world in dictatorship.

The risk in having a single world-order mechanism seemed to me so great that it was first, a mistake in placing trust, and second, a mistake by those who assumed that the rest of the world wanted peace as defined by the Western democracies. The State Department, by sending me to a dozen countries in the world, had given me an education, perhaps different than the one intended. I saw too many examples of the diversity of cultures, the power of religious differences, the high-handed mistakes of European colonial conquests, the barely hidden anger felt by much of the world towards the West and, an issue not well-received and not often heard, the many ways in which our government or its representatives, conducted themselves embarrassingly, overseas.

I became convinced about, and to believe in, balances of power, of treaties, of economic agreements, of international corporations. And in efforts at homogenizing, softening conflict through education and shared communication, and the vital strength gained by getting people to know each other. I felt that the largest mistake in my country's foreign policy was in Asia, where we had attempted military solutions but had declared direct, personal contact with the largest potential power on earth, China, to be taboo.

Our efforts, militarily, in Korea and in Vietnam, were hardly good examples of peace-keeping. After essentially a state of war with the Chinese government from 1949 to 1971, most people would think an example of a better solution was the 1972 agreement signed in Shanghai when China and the United States "agreed to disagree." Such an agreement, which changed nothing about communism, was still a more powerful weapon than bombs. Even now, after the Chinese government's put-down of the 1989 uprising, it is obvious that our ability to influence China is enhanced, compared to our Korea and Vietnam military solution.

I decided to devote no more time to the minor players of the world scene, but concentrate on how to bring China into its fair place in a stabilized world.

I optioned for world peace through regions of harmony, not through a supra-government which held the world's weapons. I decided that it was China that had to be brought into world decision-making, and, knowing there was little I could do as an individual, it was still better than not trying at all. By the beginning of the 1970's, I concentrated on China, and was there once or twice a year for the next 20 years.

Chapter Fourteen

As 1966 ENDED, I BEGAN to concentrate on that dividend of the seventh year, the sabbatical leave. The Scripps was not an academic institution in the full sense, but I had included in my original negotiations the intent to have a free seventh year, or part of it.

July 1967 was just the right timing for a sabbatical; I had thought through how I would try to change medical education and I needed time to get the thoughts organized and on paper. In La Jolla, the new and potentially very good medical school of UCSD was exciting, and, between my appointments at the Scripps Clinic, Scripps Institute of Oceanography, and UCSD Medical School, I had an adequate base in cardiology, if I wanted to continue that career. The refusal of the clinic to open a full general hospital with heart surgery made the Scripps Clinic an attenuated option, however.

Keeney's effort to build basic-science research was succeeding. It was obvious that the clinic board could not be persuaded, against his resistance, to get on with creating a full general hospital.

The medical school would have offered an alternative base for me, but it was pursuing a course exactly opposite to what I felt was the fundamental purpose of a medical school: to prepare physicians to practice medicine. It would have been wonderful to have the full backing of the Regents of the University of California. Their generous concept of budget, and the willingness of the State to experiment, would have made that an attractive base, but that battle had already been resolved when Roger Revelle chose David Bonner, a basic scientist from Yale, to lead the planning for the new school. For that time and place, and with the research orientation of the new university, the right kind of medical school was launched. I simply was not interested in that version of a school, even though I knew it would be an outstanding one.

Dr. Roger Revelle had carried the lobbying effort and the sustained attack to get a university in San Diego. His dedication to research excellence as the prime purpose of the whole university, including the medical school, prevailed. One of the grand ironies, and evidence of how real can be the pain within the ivory tower of academe, was that this very able man, dreamer and doer, was denied the privilege of being the founding chancellor. The new university has prospered, but the first two decades saw a procession of chancellors pass through. The very beginning of the conservative movement, the Reagan era, and its origin in California, brought the sacrifice of Revelle.

Homer Wadsworth and I had remained in steady contact after my move West. In 1962, Paul White and I had met in Kansas City to participate as speakers in the dedication of a new research building at Menorah Hospital. At that time Homer and his close ally, accomplice, and co-conspirator, Nathan Stark, had asked me to sit down on Nathan's screened porch while they told me what they were trying to do about medical care for the poor in Kansas City.

They had persuaded the City to give up its patronage hold on the old General Hospital. They had founded a lay board which contracted to have an arm's-length relationship with City Hall and to take full responsibility for the hospital. These activities had been the natural next step from Homer's early involvement with an ambulatory psychiatric center on Hospital Hill in Kansas City, Missouri. They thought they had the beginning base for a medical school, and they had been working with the dean of the medical school of the University of Missouri in Columbia to put a branch campus at their general hospital.

The words "Hospital Hill" go back into the history of Kansas City. The Santa Fe Trail and Oregon Trail take their origin at the bend in the Missouri River where it turns from north-south to east-west, before crossing the state to St. Louis. Here grew the Town of Kansas and inland a bit was Westport Landing. Steamboats brought the immigrants to this landing. Then began their over-land toil. Those who had come down sick on the river trip and those who got the fevers in the river bottoms needed a sanctuary, a quarantine sanctuary. A high hill with adequate fresh air and distance from the settlement became the site. It was called Pest Hill. It was visible to the immigrants as they worked their way up from the riverbanks on to the high land at Westport. When Kansas town, later the City of Kansas, later Kansas City, was founded, the Hill was the logical place for the first public hospital, which through the decades, grew, was rebuilt, enlarged, and became a series of Kansas City General Hospitals, the last one built in 1905. As many German settlers came to the area, they founded their German Hospital on the same hill and the name evolved into Hospital Hill. The adjacent hill became Dutch Hill.

Wadsworth and Stark found a natural ally in Vernon Wilson, the dean of the University of Missouri School of Medicine in Columbia. This was the same man who had been Wescoe's assistant at Kansas. He was willing to extend the activities of the clinical departments in Columbia to the staffing of Kansas City General Hospital, and, from 1962 through 1967, much energy was expended in this attempt to get an academic atmosphere into the General Hospital.

The board formed by Homer and Nathan to take over the old hospital from the City was a creation of the two of them, using the skills they had acquired in the art of bringing private and public enterprises into a productive partnership. Stark was a lawyer who had come to Kansas City as legal representative for a manufacturing firm, but had later joined Hallmark Cards as a vice-president for Community Relations. He had taken on important volunteer tasks in the community, many of them in the health field. Homer had spotted him as real talent in the difficult skill of getting people to work together. They developed a plan which would include representatives from a wide spectrum of the real forces which move a community: private citizens, carefully balanced to cover labor and management, religion and race, wealthy and poor; representatives from the elected process of the city and the county; and university representatives.

This board negotiated with the City, and it was given the complete responsibility for the old, tattered, under-budgeted charity hospital. It was easy to suggest that they were naive and were taking on the worst kind of albatross a modern city can offer. This was a complicated process. Everyone looking at it from the outside claimed nothing could be managed by such a group. Now, almost 30 years later, with a record of immense accomplishment and not one shadow on its integrity, the Wadsworth plan stands as an example of how to apply the concepts of democracy to the melding of the public, private and academic worlds.

Nineteen sixty-two was not only the year of the founding of the Board of General Hospital, but an even larger event in the life of the city was begun, again with a great deal of input from Homer. This was the beginning of talks concerning the taking over the University of Kansas City (UKC) by the Curators of the University of Missouri.

In the very bottom of the Depression, a private university had been launched in Kansas City, the University of Kansas City. The saga of its founding, its antecedents, its successes and troubles, must have its own book. Here, I identify the fact that by 1962 it was a near-bankrupt university, and its salvation was in getting the state university to add it to its responsibilities.

Missouri politics are basic: If Kansas City is getting State help, there must be something equal and adequate for St. Louis. And the reverse. In this case, the fact that UKC was a worthy investment by the taxpayer was not the logic which prevailed. The bargain could be struck when the curators also agreed to put a matching campus in St. Louis. This idea took a great deal of salesmanship. Homer was deeply involved and critical to the final negotiation. By 1963, there was a UMSL (University of Missouri-St. Louis); a UMR (University of Missouri-Rolla); a UMKC, (University of Missouri-Kansas City) and the senior, original campus, UMC (University of Missouri-Columbia).

The truth is that even after that, for a number of years, there was the real campus where the real football team was located, and the real fraternities were housed. All of the curators were graduates of that real school, and the three minor units were not at all considered equal partners. But the foundation had been laid and it was this foundation that led Homer and Nathan on their long sustained campaign to get a new medical school in Kansas City. They wanted a freestanding new school, not a branch of the medical school in Columbia.

This was a very large idea to sell to the curators, who already had an expensive medical campus in Columbia, and were led by a president who had very little interest in these peripheral campuses. He certainly did not want the headache of a new medical school. Again, the real ally within the university system was Vern Wilson. He was at the peak of his success as dean of the Columbia medical school, and he had well-mended political fences in the state. His first suggestion was to have the Kansas City medical group be a part of his school, but essentially a freestanding clinical teaching unit. This would be a two-year unit, where Columbia students in their last two years could get their clinical training, benefitting from the huge pool of patients at the City hospital.

From my California base, I had become a sounding board for Homer, and it was my feeling that this would be an unsatisfactory way to go.

The Board of Kansas City General Hospital then made its major play, the play which would make it very difficult for the curators to object to placing a full medical school in Kansas City. They took on the campaign of getting a bond issue before the public for voting to rebuild the charity hospital by issuing Jackson County bonds. The Byzantine potential of Homer's mind vividly is displayed when one looks at this proposal.

Essentially, the proposal was that the people of the County would bond themselves to build a new hospital; the people of Kansas City would support the daily cost of the hospital through their tax money; a lay board, unpaid, would run the hospital and, this was the turning over of their hole card, the curators, with State tax money, will fund the operation of a new medical school using this free, new, teaching hospital.

The curators and President of the University began a dance, a dance suggesting they were barefoot and on hot coals. A dozen excuses were invented. The Governor, the State legislators (other than the Kansas City members) were equally negative. However, at this same time there was a major outcry that the State was suffering from a major shortage of physicians. That useful technique for gaining time was called for—a consultant's report.

The State's Commission on Higher Education asked Dr. Stan-

ley Olson to give them a written report: What was the best way to
add one hundred new graduates to the medical pool in Missouri
each year? Essentially, their definition of best was based upon the
issue of "least expensive."

The possible ways for creating 100 additional students were
first, to expand the medical school in Columbia, second, to give
funds to the two private medical schools in St. Louis, Washington,
and St. Louis universities, for their expansion or, third, to build a
new medical school on Hospital Hill.

Stan Olson had been dean at the University of Illinois Medical
School, later the dean at Baylor, and was, at the time of his report,
at Vanderbilt. All knew him to be a prudent, careful, step-by-step
man, and that his report would carry weight.

A very heavy shoe fell when the voters of Jackson County
voted to bond themselves for the new hospital and the vote was
the largest plurality in the history of the County. Five out of every
six voters endorsed the hospital bond issue.

The Hospital Hill Gang, as some malcontents enjoyed labeling
Homer, Nathan and their allies, then made the issue even sharper
by successfully negotiating to have the largest children's hospital
in the region rebuild its hospital and place it on Hospital Hill,
without cost to the University. This was announced almost at the
same time as the oldest dental school in the middle of the country
announced it was joining the new University and was building its
new School of Dentistry on Hospital Hill, and would raise the
money for it from its alumni.

Homer's first efforts on Hospital Hill, the small ambulatory psychiatric day-care center, had earlier been made a part of the State
psychiatric system, and this included major new buildings, again
on Hospital Hill. Finally, a lay Catholic order, Brothers of Mercy,
declared its intent to build an extended care facility there, also.

The voting, the agreements, the contracts for all of these actions had already been accomplished by 1967, but University leadership and State legislators were not in the least able to hear the
logic of the need to build a four-year medical school in Kansas
City. Homer and Nathan played their cards carefully, knowing
that the only power they really had was the logic of being right—
and the political strength of Kansas City, which included *The*

Kansas City Star.

From the beginning the *Star*, through its medicine reporter, Pat Doyle; its editorial writers, Al Bohling and Jim Scott; and others, carried, loud and clear, the argument of why the medical school was needed.

In 1967, a sudden change in the administration of the University in Columbia, Missouri occurred. At first this seemed to be a disaster, but was really a victory. Vern Wilson gave up the deanship of the medical school to become the whole university's vice president for academic affairs. Thus, it looked as if the main help at the Columbia medical school had been lost. Vern quickly made it clear that in his new position, and with a weak president, he could make sure the University became committed to a four-year medical school at Kansas City.

He placed his protege, Bill Mayer, in the Columbia deanship. With Homer's subtle input, they approached me about an endowed Chair in Columbia, the Middlebush Chair. Homer thought this would get me into the scene and from there the Hospital Hill project could get backing.

I had already told Homer I was planning on a sabbatical in Washington for the summer and he had suggested joining John Gardner, then secretary of HEW. I elected to do neither, the Chair or HEW, but instead obtained an appointment as scholar-in-residence at the National Library of Medicine in Bethesda, with absolutely no duty other than to write out a plan for a new medical school.

I took my daughters to Washington and spent three months of delightful weekends seeing everything from Williamsburg to Boston and, during the week, wrote out the details of an Academic Plan for a major change in medical education.

The Boston trip was an especially nice time; I wanted my daughters to meet Dr. and Mrs. Paul White. We planned ahead for picnicking with them and, on the day of our gathering, it was raining. Nothing stopped their intent; Dr. White spread a blanket on the floor of his office. Ina White opened up her wicker picnic basket, and we sat there are the floor, happily chattering. My girls were a little daunted by the menu; Mrs. White had decided Russian borscht was the ideal item, and my girls, having never seen it, having no preparation for its vivid red color, and blob of thick, white cream, were convinced they were under torture. Nothing is more recalcitrant than an unsophisticated palate.

The librarian of the National Library was Martin Cummings. He was trained in microbiology, as I remember, and after an academic career at Oklahoma, had gotten into the bureaucracy of musical chairs on the Washington scene and snagged for himself this very good position. The librarian, by definition, suggests a bookish, scholarly pedant. This was not Cummings. He was a somewhat overweight, balding man, with a clumsy bear gait, egregious at times, sunkenly impassive at times. A man with large swings in mood, bullying to those "bulliable," and with no known library talents. He became a superb librarian.

He advanced the range of usefulness of the library immensely. He was successful because he comprehended what computers would mean to the library business, something that true, book-steeped librarians ran from. In addition to this, he understood the Washington scene.

What he understood about the Washington scene is that much of what really does happen in government happens because the civil-service bureaucracy makes it happen—and this bureaucracy will not let much happen that it does not want to happen. Cummings knew how to trade within the system, to give support to others, pass along useful gossip, scratch the right back, always advancing his own budget needs. He understood how to glamorize what had been an essentially musty business.

His major hobby, the thing he would do when his cyclothymic mood needed care, was to take his powerboat out into the Chesapeake Bay and play at being a sailor. One time only did I violate my rule of avoiding small boats captained by the owner. Cummings knew my daughters were with me. One Saturday, Lark, Lea, and I made the large error of letting him bobble, sway, and buck us around the bay, inhaling the fumes of the engine and watching his glee as a major storm moved in. He stood, nobly, Viking-like, at the wheel, cresting wave after wave, as the three of us huddled, wet, cold, and nauseated, in the open cockpit.

It was, forever, my last experience in a small boat. I believe the day was also useful to my two girls; I think they learned the wisdom in father's rule about small boats and their owner's enthusiasm.

My office at the National Library of Medicine was in the basement, room B-13, among the stacks. It consisted of a chair, a desk, and a lamp. No phone. It was the ideal place to concentrate on what I wanted to do. I could surface when I needed air, but, hour upon hour, I could just sit and think. Thinking purposefully, deliberately, and carrying on a debate with myself, carrying both sides of the argument. What had I learned about medical education? What had been the high points of my own education? What did I really believe versus what had custom declared was the norm? In addition to the actual education content, what were the best learning strategies? How would you administer such a plan? What would it cost? Was research the primary purpose of a medical school or was the preparation of a physician the true mission?

How do you go against the tide of the medical-education establishment, which had bought, whole cloth, the dogma that research is the basis of a medical education? This acceptance was so absolute that it determined who got accepted for medical school, and, by the test system, determined who could get through to graduation.

To make a physician an absolute first-class, lifetime physician, is the research requirement perhaps a detriment? What does a physician absolutely need to know, not just in book-acquired facts, but in dexterity? Are knowledge and dexterity inadequate? Is not major attention needed to get caring students into the school— and to shape them by an unceasing exposure to the sick and the worried?

What was the right way to use the period called premedical education? How should you test a student? What were ways of testing which were not punitive, but could even be considered educational? How would you reward the teacher-physicians and how would you manage their practice plan?

I had arrived in the Library of Medicine straight from a very vigorous, active physician's life and the first education for myself was to not get too comfortable. The greatest impediment to thinking is any hint of distraction, which includes a lounge chair. The difference between thinking and dozing is about 30 seconds.

The leap from a life with a full, committed schedule dealing with people, one after another, to one of entering a small cell, sit-

ting on a hard, straight chair, concentrating on nothing but abstract reasoning, is considerable. The greatest handicap is any
possible distraction, entertainment, conversation, coffee break,
gossip, television, magazine, or newspaper. Thinking is just plain
hard work, and sustained thinking is both exhausting and exciting. Yet a distraction is so pleasant. My monk's cell, deep in the
stacks, surrounded by the muffling of sound and the odor of old
books, gradually became a delight for me. It was the largest period of time of my whole life, not just adult life, in which I essentially withdrew from people contact. Before it ended, I found myself
enjoying it, humming cheerily as I trotted down the metal steps
into the stacks, and definitely irritated when the librarian of the
place occasionally felt moved to see if his scholar-in-residence
was surviving. When the sabbatical ended, I had a complete master academic plan and was in the market for a medical school.

I also used my evening time to begin to understand Capitol Hill,
the legislative process, and how power moves in Washington. I
met the most skillful lady in Washington, Florence Mahoney, a
latter-day "hostess with the mostest," and enjoyed the pleasure of
many evenings at her Georgetown home, where the guests were
a spectrum of the movers and doers of Washington.

Her tactic was simple: a small group, informal, drinks before,
and six or eight at the table—and good enthusiastic talk; men and
women, all, engaged in it. I stress men and women because Flo
has a special ability to be admired and liked and trusted by both
sexes, in itself an infrequent talent. Flo has honed her skills,
which began as the daughter-in-law of Governor Cox of Ohio (the
Cox of the Cox newspaper empire), then a lifetime on the Washington scene, beginning with the Truman era. With no weapon
other than herself and her skill at picking an objective, for example, a new health bill, then "educating" Capitol Hill and the White
House, she became the one-person, extraordinary lobby. "Educating" was one of her favorite words.

Sometimes she raised money for a cause or for a certain congressman's campaign chest, but in the main, she used the phone
and her home, to talk, explain, and cajole. Low-key, gentle-lady approaches, never with the slightest personal gain involved, which,
of course, was a major part of her effectiveness.

Health was her special field and she kept up an unremitting attack on obtaining legislation and funding for solving "aging." Flo did not encumber herself with trying to understand the basic science involved. This was not her special skill. She did work hard at knowing the people in the research labs and knowing what they needed. Her accuracy in separating real science from charlatan science was not precise; she occasionally backed a rejuvenation expert who had mastered promotion and mystique.

No evening was without a purpose. Yet no evening was a drudge. Flo had access to everyone on the Washington scene, from politicians to the press to lobbyists to wealthy onlookers, and one of her special skills was to spot young, coming talent. She always had a stable of new, bright potential stars. She enjoyed bringing them along, showing them off, opening doors for them.

This included not only the political field, but painters and writers as well. She used the walls of her elegant Georgetown home, perched high above the bend in the Potomac, to display the paintings of her proteges. She was the ideal patron, offering wall space seen by those who had the immediate potential of buying and whose own walls would be well seen.

On one evening, her dinner table included Hubert Humphrey, John Gardner, and James Reston, just as an example of why I found this an exciting time. There was no doubt Flo was presiding, and there was no doubt she had an agenda, as she pulled forth from each at the table their participation. I give the wrong impression if this seems to be an evening of guile or manipulation or arm-twisting. Flo would be busy with her food and then sweetly and cheerfully turn to Gardner and say, "John, tell Hubert about that wonderful paragraph in your book on how much talent is being wasted by forcing people to retire at 65!" With that done, she serenely and enthusiastically returned to her meal. The evening was off with the thinker, Gardner, stimulating the politician, Humphrey, and the powerful columnist, Reston, getting the material for several columns, columns which would expand the informed public.

All this was carried out with a single woman in the kitchen, handling the cooking and serving. The hostess' good taste in every aspect of cloth, china, candles, and food made it more elegant than a dinner costing 10 times as much. Because the kitchen help was from Central America, the menu was often Mexican and simple. When the meal ended, that useful interlude, too often forgotten, when the women are escorted upstairs and the men gather with an after-dinner drink, gave moments for those mixes of gossip and hints, which more accurately tell the truth than do the published facts.

Lister Hill, John Fogarty and Mary Lasker get proper credit for their influence on legislation and budgeting for health in the United States, but an unseen spinner of the finest web of them all, was Flo Mahoney.

Flo was closely allied to Mary Lasker, but where Mrs. Lasker sought all the kudos she could acquire, Flo was resolutely low-profile. Her skills were at their highest when a Democratic President was in the White House, but in Republican years her reach into friends in the Senate and House was a delight to observe.

In writing this, one moves in and out of present and past tense. Her efforts have spanned so many administrations and so many players on the scene that it is, in reality, past, present, and future time.

Among my own circle of friends, friends in the medical field, friends who had the privilege of knowing Flo and seeing her work her magic, nothing gives us more pleasure than telling of our time on her stage, a stage which remained active for more than 50 years. One of our favorite topics is to attempt to assign an age, even approximate, for her. With her enthusiasm for solving the problem of aging, she has been adamant in insisting that one's chronological years have no relationship to anything. Making a reasoned guess about someone's age is usually not too difficult. But if the subject is Flo Mahoney, there are considerable complications. She has maintained or kept a youthful demeanor, a grace in movement, and her full head of hair has a youthful sheen, undoubtedly assisted by the weekly visit to the salon near the Mayflower Hotel. But salon or not, guesses about her age vary over a 25-year range, good evidence that her campaign against aging has, for her, some merit. Any attempt to discuss the year of a graduation, a wedding, the age of her sons, or any vital statistic which could be used as a measurement of her own time scale is rebuffed. This taboo is carried to the lives of others, and Flo can assume the most blank, uncomprehending expression if an untrained guest asks, for example, how old is a certain senator. Age is not even a condition in Flo's vocabulary, but a disease to be eliminated.

After a full three months in Washington and the completion of a thorough plan for a medical school, I returned to La Jolla, via Missouri, and laid plans with Vernon Wilson, Homer Wadsworth, and Nathan Stark. We all agreed the time was still premature. My time in Washington had made it clear to me that any big project in the health field would need a large amount of federal funding. Although my three partners knew the world of university, city, and county government inside and out, it was now obvious to me that I needed a substantial amount of time in Washington, in order to understand the congressional process and federal programs. I had had careful training to be a cardiologist; now I needed a training program in government.

I returned to La Jolla to begin the groundwork for this. No small part of my concern was that I understood I was crossing a personal river, a professional river. To take on a task in Washington and to build a complete medical school and teaching hospital, following the academic plan I had drawn up as a scholar-in-residence at the National Library of Medicine was not compatible with running a major, graduate care-and-education program in cardiology.

I was at the point of leaving the life that completely had used my energies since my sophomore year in medical school when I became the reader for the blind cardiologist at Indiana University.

Chapter Fifteen

As I RETURNED TO LA JOLLA after the summer in Washington, I settled down to the work to be done in practicing cardiology, and running the fellowship program. This program had expanded into an additional effort, a full nine-month-long postgraduate course for individuals who wanted a thorough review in the field. This course brought some new personalities, men who were older, had been in practice, and now wanted to develop new, more specialized skills, especially in electrocardiography. They brought to our group seasoned perspectives on what life is like in the trenches of solo private practice, and added to my own understanding of that special student I considered as my real audience: the man in private practice (I note my steady use of the male gender; during the years of which I write, cardiologists were males, 98 percent).

I had begun this nine-month program earlier and Alberto Benchimol had been an able course coordinator. In the years since coming from Brasil as one of the Haskell Fellows to our Kansas unit, steadily he had grown and matured. We worked together for many years, and then he was stolen, as good personnel should be, to head a program in Phoenix. I lost him in January 1967. Harold Lowe and Phil Akre had come through our program and became well-appreciated staff (they, too, moved on later to become prominent California cardiologists). To head up the pulmonary section, an area in which I had neither interest nor skill, a delightful Canadian, Arthur Dawson, came. He was a special blend of intelligence, wry wit, diffidence, and gentle scoffer.

In what was to be my last year in full private practice, I had several patient-care experiences, each characterized by my own personal involvement in an unusual amount of medical care. Each of these patients essentially took over my full time, night and day, including sleeping in the hospital, not as a gesture of attentiveness, but in moment-to-moment decisions, especially about fluid and electrolyte care. These were rare experiences for a cardiologist where one truly felt that his attention had saved a life. More than we physicians would care to admit, much of what we do is in giving comfort and aid—and without us, the patient would still have recovered or died. Even in the highly technical field of cardiology, where the cardiologist does, intervenes, manipulates, tests, medicates, it is a painful truth to admit that the data proving the absolute value of much that is done are still questionable. The progress is great, the addition of years of good living real—but to know you, personally, saved someone's life is not a frequent reward for the medical cardiologist. Having said that, I know physician readers of this will, not in the least, all agree with me.

But in the circumstances of this year of which I write, I found myself in the full flower of my professional skills and enjoying a large referral practice. Just as at the end of 10 years at Kansas, I had a delightful team. I have mentioned Arthur Dawson and Phil Akre, and, in addition at staff level, we had Dean Franklin in biomedical research, and Josefina Caravaca and Carlos Velasco in enzyme chemistry research. Three of the staff who had come from Kansas with me were still in the unit, Rosemary Chapman, Dorothy Thomas, and Herbie Clark. As Fellows in the final group we had Al Bures and Alan Jay from the United States; two men from the Philippines, Pio Poblete and Romeo Divinigracia; Raold Rode from Norway; Newton Freidman, who was taking a special interest in echocardiography; from South America came Hugo Palmero, Azaria Duenas, Horacio Orejarena, Fernando Carvalho, Evandro Lucena, and Alfredo Gomez (some of these men from South America had come earlier). Enrolled in the final nine-month program were Charles Mims, Robert Manley, George Bascom, John Morgan, Damaso Talavera, and Langdon Hooper.

Americans James Lasry, Frank Trotta, Harold Lowe, Phil Akre, Alan Bures, Robert Urquhart, Mark Roberts, John Grammer, James Getzen, Joe Ellis, Manohar Singh, Phillip Geller, Sherman Rosove, Ira Monosson, Robert Busiek, Arnold Roland, Harvey Tippit, Jean Legler, David Cross, and Robert Voth, were in the clinical fellowship group over the eight-year period, and all went on to clinical careers. Good men who had been good companions.

In the fall, as I had done for several years, I gave a major week-long postgraduate course in cardiology, using Sherwood Hall at the La Jolla Museum of Modern Art. This course attracted several hundred physicians and required elaborate planning and staging. In the spring of that year, I gave my small-group course in cardiology, ten days long, with a personally selected group of attendees. I used my canyon property for the location. This course was a delight and gave me ideas for the future.

From a grateful patient I had attended came a substantial gift, and with it, I formed a partnership with Pete Scholander's group and had built in a canyon on Scripps Institute of Oceanography land a large facility for studying the cardiac system of free-roaming mammals.

As I have described earlier, this took our group into studying greyhounds, giraffes, baboons, sled dogs and seals, and led to research expeditions to Africa and to the Arctic. Dean Franklin and a former Fellow, Robert Van Citters of the University of Washington, headed up this program. These two men and their colleagues were expert in bioinstrumentation and, at the same time, had more fun in carrying out their research work than any team I ever met. It was impossible to not be envious of their expeditions. They were of the school of tieless, Hush Puppies, corduroy pants, let's-have-a-beer research, whose role model was Pete Scholander.

Bob Van Citters went on to become the dean of the University of Washington School of Medicine and has had a very successful career in not only investigation and medical-school administration, but as a wide-ranging consultant in medical science.

One does not shut down a major laboratory without careful attention to those in the unit and the programs under way. The part of all of these years that I had found most personally satisfying was the fellowship program. Talent coming from all over the world to learn with you is a powerful stimulant and heady flattery.

First, I sent out a letter announcing I was closing my fellowship program. For 18 years, this had been a large part of my pleasure. Stopping it was painful and it signaled the end of my personal role as a teacher of cardiology. At the same time, I advised the China

Medical Board that I could take no more Fellows from them. The training-grant division at the National Institutes of Health was advised by me to cancel my grant. Eli Lilly and Company, with whom we had been doing enzyme and trace-metal research, had to be advised. This relationship had been especially satisfying, for the president of Eli Lilly had been a friend and colleague of Dad's and had known me since I was 10 years old. For me to be working with them in the research area was completion of a circle that gave me satisfaction.

In leaving a profession in which I had been unusually active and had made friends with essentially every cardiologist and cardiac surgeon on the scene, I automatically removed myself from their orbit. My very closest friends knew I was primarily interested in medical education, but most of them, even the closest, would have assumed I would try my hand at medical education and continue at the same time in cardiology. I made no attempt to do this. I had seen so many very good men who did this and were neither fish nor fowl; they almost always ended up stranded someplace in an administrative job, still claiming they were a clinician, to the embarrassment of everyone. My quite clear approach was to be the best diagnostician I knew how to be—and then stop, cold, clean, and forever.

Of course, I took away with me an entire library of memories, inside stories, gossip hovering on slander, behind-the-scene vignettes: who said what about whom; who was trying what in his lab or surgery; and what disastrous thing had recently occurred in such-and-such lab and surgery. Those were the years of the invention of dynamic intervention, with direct attack on the problems of heart disease, and all cardiac surgeons and cardiologists were daily walking a fine line between care and experiment.

An example of how new was the territory can be given by telling briefly of the question of entering the left ventricle. A folklore of warning about the left heart had existed for decades. To touch it was an immediate step towards the patient's death. Surgeons knew this as an absolute rule. Dwight Harken, through his unique wartime experience in Europe, where he frequently and safely invaded the left heart subsequent to penetrating wounds, had finally made it clear that there was no reason for a surgical taboo.

But in medical cardiology, a new alert came when a well-known cardiologist reported he had attempted to slip a cardiac catheter down from the aorta into the left ventricle in conscious patients and a rash of deaths occurred. Harken's experience with trauma evidently did not include the awake, tense human, and it was postulated that the catheter set off fatal arrhythmias. Therefore, those of us who were cautiously feeling our way into techniques for recording blood pressure inside the left ventricle, in the awake human, knew we were walking a precarious line. I was one of those. On those several occasions where I slipped a needle between the ribs of the awake patient, directly into the heart wall, and then, with a pop, into the left ventricle—those were moments of high tension. There was some skill involved, some knowledge of anatomy, but there was also a large factor of luck. And I am not too far removed to forget that it was the patient that had the luck, not the physician. The entire procedure was done blind, and there was no way to be certain the rather large bore needle would not neatly, cleanly, disastrously, slice a coronary artery.

A prominent physiologist, Julius Comroe, wrote about this entire era (*Retrospectroscope*, Julius H. Comroe, Jr., Van Gehr Press, Menlo Park, Calif. 1977) in which physicians and surgeons were risking their reputations daily, doing dangerous things not done before. The news media were inclined to speak of the surgeons' courage in doing these unproved practices.

Comroe wrote very effectively about this very simple question of courage in medicine. Whose courage? Is it not the patient who is courageous? Is he or she not the one who may not live through the surgical moment? Why label the surgeon courageous? Did any surgeon ever give his life in the operating room? Of course, Comroe was right, and he went on, in his book, to speak of the degrees of courage. "Courage, Size 1," is what the patient shows when he or she is put to sleep, knowing there may be no awakening. Comroe was hesitant to award surgeons the Courage Award, even Size 4. He did suggest that some of them could qualify for his Perseverance Award, which came in several sizes.

In this field of aggressive cardiac surgery, surgery which was actually carrying out the missing research, directly on the sick human, there were perhaps a dozen real pioneers, a dozen plus.

Lillehei, at Minnesota, I have mentioned; DeBakey and Cooley, the Houston tigers, each strengthened by his hostility for the other; Harken at the Brigham; Kirklin, McGoon at Mayo; Hufnagel in Washington; Gerbode, in San Francisco; Swan in Denver; Potts in Chicago; Blalock, at Hopkins; Lam in Detroit; Beck in Cleveland; Bailey in Philadelphia; all in the United States. Abroad there were Craaford and Bjork in Sweden; Brock in the United Kingdom; Bigelow and Vineberg in Canada—19 men—all larger than life. I leave out Gibbons. In spite of his essential work on the heart-lung pump, he just was not of a similar cut as these men; perhaps he was too caring and cautious? All were exceptional personalities, all, in spite of Comroe's definition, had some kind of courage, courage to be wrong, to risk a reputation, courage to carry on, even when the death rate was horrible.

In November 1945, Bailey tried the first mitral valvulotomy, the patient died on the table. Patient #2 died 60 hours after surgery. Patient #3 died in three days. Patient #4 died on the table. Patient #5 survived. In the next nine months, he operated on 10 more, a total of 15. Ten died. What kind of faith sustained him?

Years later, at a national meeting, Bailey and Harken were on the podium together. A member of the audience asked Bailey if the appalling number of surgical deaths had not been a terrible emotional burden for him to carry. Bailey, who always wore a somewhat devout expression, similar to the mien now seen on television ministers, replied in serious, sacerdotal tones, "Yes, it is an awful burden. It never leaves one. I awaken at night and I can see their faces all about me." Dwight Harken, interrupted, grabbed the microphone, and exclaimed, "Charlie must sleep in a large room!"

In the above quote, I am guilty of paraphrasing, but the general relationship of Bailey and Harken is well expressed. They were two bantam roosters, each full of confidence and assurance, each in deadly (excuse the word) competition for the mantle of who-did-what-procedure first.

I well remember an Atlantic City heart meeting, where both men had exhibits, one across the aisle from the other, and each man manning his booth, calling out to the sauntering physicians, "Come over here and let me show you what we have done with a bottle baffle to cure mitral regurgitation!" The similarity of their performance and that of the hawkers out on the boardwalk, selling their special vegetable cutters, was striking. It was impossible to not laugh and think of them as two early American medicine men. Perhaps they were.

These were also times in which the very first efforts were being made to treat coronary disease by surgery. An operation had become extremely popular, literally being done by the hundreds of cases, and with an impressive gold mine of surgical reward. I could not see a reasonable logic for the surgery. It was justified by very slender physiological evidence, and yet, the patients were enthusiastically reporting how they felt well immediately after the operation. My faith in the human being is considerable, and part of that faith is that almost any of us who has a very serious health problem, and we then live through a highly charged moment of surgical treatment, accompanied by the surgeon enthusiastically telling you that you are much better—that most of us will be better—at least for awhile.

When my friend, Norman Cousins, carried this power of joy and positive thought to a level of almost spiritual healing, I understood well what Norman was fostering and always agreed with him that the inner will to live has a place in the equation. However, equally, I never forgot that one is dealing with a very tenuous truth when the yardstick is the patient's personal testimony.

Testimonials wherein the patient declares himself healed are a dangerous minefield. In a certain sense, they are what one might expect from an inoculation of Norman Cousins' positive thinking.

Of course, the issue well antedates Norman; it is as old as the human race. All the temples, grottos, Delphic arenas of history, and of course, the religions, document the value of positive thought. Norman did not discover it; he said it well for our era and, with his journalistic skills, knew how to spin the lovely tales that gathered followers.

In a way, Norman was similar to the surgeon who was, so very successfully, carrying on his coronary surgical procedure which the patients hailed. Norman said it with words, parables, and laughter; the surgeon was doing it by ligating the internal mammary arteries and filling the literature with positive reports. Both honorable men were making patients feel better because the patients were told they would feel better, which is certainly better medicine than being told you have no future.

Working with our surgeon, I set up a protocol which required unusual patient cooperation. Specifically, the patient was told that we would make an incision in his chest, would dissect out the internal mammary arteries, and in half of the patients we would tie the vessels, exactly as the famous surgeon was doing. But in the other half, there would be no tying of the vessels. The surgeon would do all the motions, but not tie the vessels. The surgeon would then back out, and close the wound. We were not obligated to tell the patient which category he was in, tied or not tied—for several months.

To make the research even more free of bias, the surgeon sealed his surgery records and did not reveal them to me.

In today's circumstances, such straightforward human research would be difficult to do. Then, we were able to have 18 patients participate. All announced they were improved, almost all of them greatly. The objective studies I carried out, using mainly the exercise electrocardiogram and patients' diaries detailing their nitroglycerin use, before and after the surgery, showed no improvement in any of them. The operations were done under local anesthesia; one patient was ecstatic in his enthusiasm, heralding loudly that the tightness in his chest stopped the instant the surgery was done. However, when the surgeon's records were ultimately seen, this patient was one of those who had not had the vessels tied.

Comparing those who had the vessels tied to those who did not, revealed a simple truth; essentially all of them said they were improved. Even their use of nitroglycerin frequently decreased; yet their electrocardiograms continued to deteriorate. Perhaps this was but proof of Norman's message, the value of a positive attitude. It certainly was no proof the surgery was effective. Surgery is a powerful placebo. Throughout the world, the operation died after we gave our report.

Another area in which I put a lot of effort was in developing a means of transmitting the electrocardiogram by telephone. A very able engineer, Fred Berry, came up with the idea of converting the electrocardiogram into an FM signal at the sending end, then demodulating it down to an electrocardiogram at the receiving end. This we did, and, as one does with such a media-attractive idea, we got carried away and did it across the country, then to Hawaii and back. It made a good show. This was a very straightforward solution; it became the basis of a multimillion-dollar industry. Telephone transmission of EKGs is a normal, daily event throughout the world today.

It was a satisfaction to be at the beginning. In leaving cardiology, it was as if one left a large family and moved into a new, unknown environment.

It was not a role in which one simply folds the tent and fades. Hundreds of letters went out to patients advising them of the close of my practice; doctors who were good friends through the years were similarly advised. It was not at all easy, and even now as I write, decades later, I cannot handle serenely this loss. Stopping the practice and stopping the Fellows were losses not replaced.

Was it the right thing to do? Who can be objective? Who can be fair? I am, on balance, everything considered, glad that I took on the building of a medical school. The end result is perhaps the lasting answer; the careers of every graduate of the school are, in a symbolic sense, an extension of your own career. Yet, I cannot deny that many nights I recall the satisfactions and pleasures of those years as a very vigorous cardiologist. They are painful losses.

Sometimes I am asked if it was not very difficult to leave the beauty of the sea and the beaches of Southern California. Of course, such an environment is almost a miracle, and for a land-based man who had spent years in Mississippi, Indiana, and Kansas, life in La Jolla and Rancho Santa Fe is a treasure not denied. However, when one is in the career-building years, the years when work, projects, and people pour in, the physical world about you becomes obscured. I recall the end of one summer in La Jolla when it dawned on me I had not been to the beach once that year, and even more telling, I had not even looked out the window at the sea for some time! It takes breathing room to take time to smell the flowers.

My move away from California was not quite a complete break; I kept the hideaway in the canyon at Rancho Santa Fe, with a good bit of land around the cabin. This I held and expanded through the years. With the luck of chance, and the booming California real estate market, this was an unplanned bonanza in later years. Also to keep my hold on the place, I stored there my 1959 Ford hard-top convertible, so I could be assured proper Southern California transportation when I slipped out there.

My time in Washington and the contacts there bore fruit, and the Assistant Secretary for Health and Scientific Affairs and I began a negotiation for an observation post for me in his office. I, above all, did not want a daily schedule or a paper-processing job. We danced around for several months on where I could be fit in, and finally we invented just the right title, Consultant on Medical Education. Not only was the title right, but the job specifications included an office, access to a secretary, a place at the table at this high level—and no duties.

The Secretaries of HEW, while I was there, were John Gardner and Wilbur Cohen. The highest-ranking physician in government, the Assistant Secretary for Health and Scientific Affairs, was Phillip Lee. Assisting Lee were Phil Silvers, Ed Rosinski, and Ed Cross, all well-meaning, good people. The Surgeon General was Bill Stewart. Richard McGraw also came in, on occasion.

The people in responsible positions, responsible for health care policy, during my time in Washington, men with whom I worked, included Phil Lee, Ivan Bennett, Irv Lewis, Jim Cavanaugh, Robert Marston, Joe English, Hal Engle and a knowledgeable woman, Ruth Hanft.

I did not get to know Wilbur Cohen well, but on one trip to Los Angeles we flew out together. He asked my purpose and I told him about the Rancho course. I asked him his destination and he told me he was flying out for a business mens' group as speaker. I commented that he had done this for a lifetime and I asked if it was still worthwhile; did he think he was educating anyone? His answer was straightforward. He said that he only did this for the big fees. With the kind of money he got from this, he could afford to do other things he cared about (he meant caring things, not fishing). He went on to say that John Gardner did not agree with him. Gardner thought "speaking" was useless. Gardner had told Cohen, "If you really have a message, put it in a book. Then you

will begin changing people." Cohen laughed and said, "He probably is right but that takes patience and time. I don't have that."

It was a Democratic administration and the orientation of all of
them was liberal, towards increased entitlements, and increased
government involvement in health benefits.

Phil Lee is the son of Russell Lee, a founder of the Palo Alto
Clinic. The senior Lee was a substantial figure and had earned a
major role in California medical and political circles. The removal
of Stanford Medical School from San Francisco to Palo Alto was facilitated by his involvement. The senior Lee was a longtime friend
of Flo Mahoney's, and there is little doubt that a behind-the-scenes
effort to get Russell's son in the HEW job had included some of
Flo's unique skills. Phil and I had not known each other before;
Flo was an active agent in explaining us to each other.

Vern Wilson and I maintained steady contact, and he saw the
value of my being in Washington. He and I felt my position in
Washington would have just the right status if I also had an academic base at the University of Missouri. He arranged for me to
have a professorship at the medical school in Columbia. This was
first the Middlebush Professorship, named after the retired president of the University, offered to me in November 1967. Vern ran
into some complaints from Middlebush himself, who wanted a
visible professor carrying the dignity of his Chair, not some unseen expatriate.

Vern then offered me a choice career title, the University of
Missouri Distinguished Professor of Medicine, and this seemed
just right. This title was an all-university appointment made by the
curators, themselves, and Vern made the point that with this level
of appointment, I was directly responsible to the President, not
the campuses. The telegram telling me of this came on March 30,
1968, and substantially cleared the way for me to have an adequate academic base while in Washington.

In September 1968, Chancellor Olson at the Kansas City campus appointed me Consultant to the Chancellor, and this gave me
an appropriate connection to his office.

The professorship title lasted the rest of my career. I must
admit that I was a professor-in-absentia. I was only in Columbia
for one or two days, served no function for them and, to assure

those looking for misuse of public money, received no compensation from the University while in Washington.

The constant campaign I had kept up at the Scripps Clinic since the day of my arrival, urging expansion into a full-fledged clinical institution with all fields of medicine and surgery, continued to be unwelcome. Both of us, Ed Keeney and myself, knew we could not resolve our personal animus; parting company was good for both of us.

Victory and reward come in clever disguises. Within a very short time after my move to Washington, the clinic expanded into a full, all-services clinic and hospital.

Halfway through my last year at the Scripps, family differences became apparent and with no other comment offered in this book, a summary must do. It was agreed that I would take Lark and Lea with me—Audrey would remain in La Jolla. When we parted, Audrey left for Nevada to take up residency while awaiting divorce.

Chapter Sixteen

HOUSING IN WASHINGTON IS A notorious hazard. I accepted the risks involved and went to the best agency in town and told them I wanted a furnished, real house, not an apartment, not something in the suburbs, and something very convenient to the city's center. To add to the imperialism approach, I asked to have it within a week.

Such foolishness has its merits. First, it eliminates all the dragging through people's homes, invading their privacy, burdening yourself for days. Immediately, the agency, apologizing at the thought, but wanting me to know there was one "impossibility" that was available. The Malagasy Embassy had come on bad times and had had to sacrifice its ambassador's dwelling. It was on the rental market, completely furnished, in the embassy area, and just one block from the sunken parkway drive which funnels traffic into the city. I had to go to an atlas to identify Malagasy.

I toured the house and found a quite handsome three-story stone house, plenty of bedrooms, a grand living room, a commercial-sized kitchen capable of turning whole sheep on the spit, and, suggesting the ambassador had lived fully, a master bedroom, spacious, elegant in its French furniture and powder-blue carpet, and—completely lined, all walls and ceiling, in silver-blue mirrors. So was the bathroom suite. I showed it all to Flo Mahoney, and when I threw open the bedroom door and the blue grotto shimmered at her, she paused, almost speechless, and finally brought out, "Well! One could certainly make history in that room."

The convenience of its location and its availability, furnished, prevailed, and I leased it for a year. I found two Jamaicans, Teresa and John, to run the place and a governess to help me with the daughters. It all worked out very well, and the extravagance of it was compensated for by the fun of the place. I entertained often, and the blue-bedroom tour was always included, just after dessert and coffee. Wives were never quite sure what to say.

We added two black Chihuahuas, sisters, Honey and Jet, a hamster named Mr. Wiggles, a canary bird, and two dime-store turtles. The latter proved to be formidable survivors, and one was with me 17 years later. The two dogs, (and the wonderful dogs before and after them), remind me of that poignant phrase, "The trouble with loving is that pets don't last long enough and people last too long."

We settled into a vigorous time in Washington. For me, it was all new, a new field of experience and with no real responsibility. I had, both from my work and from Flo, a ringside seat on the Washington scene, especially a view of the health-legislation field.

Washington life is a heady experience. I have enjoyed time in two other national capitals, Beijing and London, and even if you are at the outermost fringe of the show, it is still exciting theater. The stage setting itself is always impressive, for it is in the capital that one looks out on the great public buildings, whether it is The Great Hall of the People or Parliament or the U.S. Capitol building.

And the stage is filled with those who occupy the morning newspaper and the evening television, filled with visiting dignitaries, with delegations, some very important, some trivial, all calling loudly for attention, all excited because they are having their moment to be heard.

In Washington, it is one theater with two stages, the White House and the Capitol building. The White House commands its own special place in the competition; however, Congress knows it not only has a role, but that its members must play every moment to the folks back home, and to be really heard, the congressmen must loudly and daily be in disagreement with the President.

These main actors all swell up and gather a personal opinion of their size and importance; they stop being people, private citizens, and only rarely can a participant remain himself. Most, from both the White House and from Congress, become actors, and their voices deepen, their conversation becomes a series of clevernesses, each thought clipped out to make it newsworthy.

But the real work in Washington is that being carried on by the bureaucracy, the civil servants, who at a certain high level, have very definite agendas of their own, have programs which they want to implement (and have funded, of course).

Hurrying between the White House cast, the elected on Capitol Hill, and the upper-level bureaucrats, is the real energy of the system. These are the lobbyists. Americans, of course, know of the lobbyists and their activities. Few of us could possibly expect such universal representation of essentially every piece of American life—and foreign. Lobbying is the voice, the way the democracy is heard, and although it is easy to resent giant lobbies of the medical association, or of oil, or of education, they do keep the legislative system stimulated, provoked and on balance, educated. My intent is not to disparage any of the characters. The system works because they are all there.

But they are all changed by being there at the center of power. Even if few have power, it is the rumor of it, the possibility of it, the hint of it, which stimulates all—and, in a true sense, actually creates power. Another way of saying it, is that one need not have power, what one needs is to have others perceive that you have it.

One gets an overwhelming lesson in civics from living in Washington. Things which seemed clear when you looked in from the periphery stop being clear. I have always had a hostility to the lobbyist. The very word, for me, was a castigation, an indication of a person with no conscience. The lobbyist was someone who was paid to get his clients' wishes made legal, though legal or not in the first place, and, usually, funded, whether it was for the good of the people or not.

My Washington time confirmed much of this, but it also convinced me that the lobbyist was, equally often, very well-informed, and regardless of the possible funds being contributed to the politician, the lobbyist was often a real source of information and education. With enough lobby activity, the congressman could hear enough about an issue and form a reasoned opinion. After all, each elected person on the Hill has one, and an equal vote on every subject. No one of them can possibly be informed on the full range of the legislative agenda. Someone needs to educate.

The observer also learns that this informed opinion of a congressman is not his opinion, but is from his own staff, which has it own agenda; the congressman does not form his own opinion, but it is formed for him by his staff. One learns that the quality of the congressman is directly a measure of the quality of his staff. When a congressman retires or is beaten, it is the staff which is his legacy and which is vigorously recruited by the remaining or incoming congressmen.

The secret about Washington is that there is a network of continuity provided by the Capitol Hill staff people, the upper-ranking civil servants who administer the government agencies, and the great permanent colonies of lobbyists.

In years past, it seemed clear to me that the elected officials should not be allowed to be reelected forever. A fixed period of service seemed a needed way to bring fresh talent on the scene, and an effective way to break up the cartels formed by having a person in power too long. I still believe that, but now know well that the real activists are those of this second level: the staff, the bureaucracy, the lobbyists, and, if all congressmen are changed every eight or 12 years, there would be fewer results than expected. In fact, what one might lose is the strength knowledgeable congressmen acquire on how to make the system work, and how to get this hidden, but powerful group harnessed. Forcing the elected officials to shortened terms might only increase the power of those not facing election, the bureaucrats and the lobbyists.

But it was when day was done and evening came to Georgetown that so much of the real work began. The elegant homes, the homes of the Flo Mahoneys, became the demi-stage for the cast. A handful, men and their spouses (now, women and their spouses), with the list very carefully selected: just the right person from the White House staff, the right senator, the right lobbyist from the highest level, the right visiting dignitary or expert to give the gathering a purpose, a respected journalist to keep the group on stage. Long black cars bringing those nesting in power, the tone of the evening one of informality, quality, quiet, and animated conversation. Drinks, dinner, after-dinner time, and no need to guide the conversation because all present had the same interests.

I floated in and out at several levels, serving usefully as someone fresh from the real life of medicine, someone who had an ear at the upper level of health administration, someone who was not exactly labeled. Not exactly labeled because I was not elected, was not lobbying for anything, had no real authority, and had no hidden agenda. I was simply going to school at Potomac College.

By fall, when school started, I tried to practice integration with my daughters, but this was a dangerous failure. Within days, both girls had been harassed and one physically attacked by classmates. This brought me a rapid education about the private-school opportunities, and, for the rest of our time, both girls had lengthy busing to their private schools. That ended any thought of, or willingness on my part, for the blessings of integration.

While still in La Jolla, and when in Washington the previous year, I had gotten considerably involved in the potential of television, compact discs, and computer software. Martin Cummings' deputy, Ruth Davis, was trained in the technology disciplines; I learned a great deal from her. Old friends, including Bern Dryer, David Ruhe, Herman Hellerstein and I, took on a project for the AMA with the purpose of developing a demonstration teaching package on the care of coronary disease that pulled all these media together.

Dryer had written a book, *A University Without Walls*, which was a skillful, vivid look into the televison-computer future. We were charged with implementing a demonstration of his message. We worked hard at this, all to no end. The AMA did not have the attention span such a project needed.

On the West Coast, these same allies worked with me to make a demonstration televison package on coronary care. An able physician who worked in the margin between medicine, television, and Hollywood, Richard Scott, helped us. Cy Wexler, a skillful production man took part. I was back and forth between the VA, NLM, and commercial prospects, such as McGraw Hill, working, talking, planning, about a National Postgraduate Medical Center. The fall-out of all this work, and certainly not solely due to my input, is now expressed in the Lister Hill National Center for Biomedical Communication and, separately, Heart House.

Bern Dryer, David Ruhe, Cy Wexler, Dick Scott, Ruth Davis,

and Herm Hellerstein were an example of able talent, ready and willing to take on a new field. But we were premature, the whole area needed time to develop, and time for sources of capital to take the risk. Twenty years later, the time has come. Twenty years is a wisp of time in terms of this large field, but for those of us who are mortal, 20 years is sufficient time to leave us behind. It would be wonderful to have that collection of energy and talent available today and to be involved.

During the summer and early fall, I was finding myself in the attractive position of being a sought-after odd man at dinner parties, and this gave me access to delightful evenings in the arena of those who made the system work.

Mary Clark Thoron, now divorced, came down frequently from New York City and, after careful conversation with our varied children, I asked her for her hand in marriage.

The lives of our families had been intertwining for 20 years. Both families had had the blow of a divorce; we were both 50 and time was flying. We gathered our respective clans in New York City and had a proper and dignified wedding. We flew the entire group back to Washington to my house and, perhaps because of the vast blue-mirrored horror, Mary D. insisted that our wedding night be spent at a hotel. All during this hectic day, the bride had been coming down with the flu, and, by the time we reached the hotel, she tottered into bed with hot toddy, hot-water bottle, nose drops, and Kleenex. I was banished to the couch in the next room. Such was the wedding night.

Our life together was a joy. Mary Clark Dimond was just the companion to suit me. We had 15 years of enthusiastic, shared endeavor. We brought to the Washington home her youngest son, Tommy, and with my Lark and Lea, we used the weekends to do the special family things which make Washington one large university: the Smithsonian; the Lincoln, Washington and Jefferson monuments; Roosevelt Island; the Botanical garden; and the great art galleries were a steady delight. We took on a persevering, continuing tour by which we attempted to see all the statues we could find in the Washington area, and make an effort to learn why the individual was worthy of the statue—not as simple as it may seem. We went sightseeing along the Potomac; picnicking on its shores; to Williamsburg and the grand old-tidewater mansions: We did it all.

In addition to educating myself about the federal programs related to medical schools, I turned my personal interest in audiovisual teaching to working to get for the National Library of Medicine a major audiovisual-computer unit. This was promoted under the title, "The Lister Hill Center," certainly a demonstration of one of the arts of Washington. Pick some illustrious person to honor, especially among the senators or representatives, and define a program which essentially no one could resent, such as medicine, and a library. Then build a very quiet, persistent, education campaign, making the rounds on Capitol Hill and the White House. Of course, first, make sure that your parent organization knows about the program. However, when one is very skillful, it is possible to escape from under the rein of your own administrative unit and still build your claque of support. The Lister Hill Center was of this nature. HEW had many other things it needed money for; the needs of the National Library were of a low priority. Cummings' request was given the various kinds of red-tape treatment, with no one wanting to be guilty of saying "No," but with the HEW senior staff determined to ignore the request. Martin Cummings, the librarian, quietly began an end run around HEW, and based his campaign on the Senate, where he sought to persuade senators that such an inexpensive program, resulting in such a beautiful building, was a very nice way to recognize their former colleague. Senator Lister Hill had been a major force for the federal launching and funding of new health-care programs, and there was ample support and feeling about honoring him. With my position at HEW, I was able to defend, lobby, cajole, and keep the project from the death wanted at the HEW level.

The Lister Hill Center was, in essence, a graceful pillar of a building, to be built adjacent to the very artful National Library itself, with the roundness and fluted roof of the library accentuated and complemented by the beacon, lighthouse-like reach of the Lister Hill Center. Its price tag was small in Washington terms, in the range of $15 million (in the beginning). There was one point at which $1 million was needed to keep the project alive, and I made this money my special project.

I appeared at a Senate hearing to speak on behalf of the center. Arrayed about the room were charts with the budget requests for all of HEW for the year under consideration. One of the senators kept asking where this center was on the charts. No one could find it, and I was getting just a little nervous with the thought that the senior HEW staff had conveniently forgotten to put it into the planning process. Then a person slipped up behind the chairman and explained: The charts gave no space to anything below the hundred-million-dollar mark. All the figures on the charts were "rounded off," not rounded off into 100's or 1,000's or 1,000,000's, but to the closest 100,000,000. The program which we were all fighting so hard for, didn't even make a blip on the charts. It was beyond the decimal points. Getting the center was one of the major achievements of Cummings' tenure, and working for it gave me exactly the kind of experience I needed. The Lister Hill Center bill was signed into law in September 1968.

I also became involved at the Veterans Administration, again as a diplomat without portfolio, and took part in a considerable range of discussions there. Again, I testified on Capitol Hill, this time on what I considered the merits for creating a national VA continuing-education center. Again, the experience was good, but the idea did not catch on; my efforts taught me why you cannot produce real change if there is an intermarried staff and lobbyists. The VA was, and is, such a complete mating of the permanent Washington staff and the various veteran representative groups that there is no margin of tolerance for new ideas.

Working in and about the central administration of the VA was a magnificent lesson in what entrenched bureaucracy, working hand-in-hand with the vested lobbyist, can create in terms of dug-in positions.

This locked-in system for the VA extends to the Senate and House, where the chairmen of the VA committees enjoy great support during their elections from the veterans' organizations, and where the only agenda is how to extend the benefits and increase the VA budget.

The system of VA medical care is one of those nontouchables which make any discussion of budget balancing futile. As the concept gradually builds around the country that some better plan for the whole country's health-care system is needed, it is impressive how no one is willing to factor in the possible cost savings of transferring the entire VA medical care program to the private sector. I make this remark with no suggestion that service-connected problems should not be served—but with the question of why this should not be put into the national health-care system and budget. One of my lessons from the Washington time was to learn that certain programs, certain entitlements, are essentially beyond logical attack.

The national medical director of the VA was Hal Engle, and I found him an enjoyable, knowledgeable physician. He was open to suggestions, an articulate bright man, but also a career VA physician who knew the precise margin between fighting to improve the care of the veteran, versus fighting to improve the system. They are not one and the same. Career VA physicians are survivors. At the VA, I also enjoyed working with Harold Schoolman and Lionel Bernstein, both able physicians, trying to do useful work, and not get too deep into the slough of despond. Many able men try; the VA is indeed a testing ground.

I also saw how well-meaning people, for example, the lay lobbyist, Mary Lasker, and her star system of those willing to testify for her favorite programs (DeBakey, Ravdin, Farber, etc.), went about their objectives. And did so honestly, within the system. With no great distribution of financial patronage, they could pull Congress in behind their programs and create entire new legislation and funding. Time after time, I saw this. Many of the results were excellent, and the country benefitted.

Occasionally, the programs were soft in concept, wistful dreams which should never have been tried, and which were loose cannons on the American medical ship. Not all such efforts were Mrs. Lasker's; there were other prime movers. Examples of how, on occasion, the plans were ill thought out, and sought utopias beyond reach, were the Regional Medical Program, the Comprehensive Health Planning Program, and the Area Health Education Centers Program.

All of these were efforts to improve health care by adding quilt patches to the system, patches which often had no rationale or means for relating to the reality of medical life in the United States. They were the misplaced efforts of those who wanted to change the system, and, instead, wasted money and a great deal of the medical profession's energy. I was as guilty as all others and when I got into building the Kansas City medical school; I, with enthusiasm, used the RMP, CHP, and AHEC money. I used them legally, usefully, but not in the least with any misconception that we were carrying out the original legislation's intent.

Did I acquire Potomac Fever? I can report immunity. Mary D., on the other hand, fitted Washington well, understood and enjoyed the system, and was a natural for the same kind of role played by Flo. Mary D. would have been delighted for us to remain there. I had seen far too many physicians and politicians who became so enamored with the game, the Washington game, that when their legitimate reason for being in Washington ended, they began a scramble for any kind of a foothold which would keep them, even slightly, connected to the scene: true Washington Fever. The pain of losing an election—losing an election when you truly believe you are doing important, good work and have much to offer—is visceral. I saw this happen many times. I especially remember Fred Harris from Oklahoma, who just could not believe he had lost his Senate race and therefore no longer had the power, the attractiveness, and the attention he had become accustomed to.

Similarly, I remember Bill Roy from Kansas, who was very involved in the whole health field, and was a primary spokesman for Capitol Hill. Suddenly, after an election, he was back to zero, back to Topeka, suffering from incurable Potomac Fever. It is painful to admit, not only did Roy lose, but so did the country, because his good attributes and knowledge were lost to the legislative process.

So many physicians get called to high-level jobs in a new administration, serve well, enjoy the sense of purpose and importance, and with a change of administration, just cannot tolerate the thought of returning home to Arizona or Washington State or North Carolina. The whole Washington area is rich with special institutes where those out of power, but unwilling to go home, have cubicles. There they write papers, form fund-raising organizations, become lobbyists, and scramble to be expert witnesses. To have a title, any kind of a title which will justify an office, a phone, and a calling card, becomes the objective.

Although I resisted the disease, it was not because I did not see the delights and satisfactions. I was self-assured enough to believe I could have prospered as a medical administrator in Washington, but the kind of prospering one does is really cosmetic and not permanent. One can be useful within government, but I knew I would not fit that role; my kind of style or bias would not thrive in civil service. Equally, I had no desire to earn my way into a legitimate role by running successfully for office. This, too, was clear, honest (hopefully) self-evaluation. The third possibility, that of being an activist by the social route was a very real possibility. I have already commented that the perception of power is as real as power itself (almost).

Those who are powerful in Washington may have absolutely no title or position. Among the most influential are those individuals. They accomplish their ends through a kind of salon persuasion. The more I observed and learned, I understood that there is this cluster of society's committed dilettantes, if one can use those two words together. Again, I had to hold a close analysis of myself; I knew I would not be happy without real goals, real projects, real challenges which required full involvement.

Although I had made the decision to stop my fellowship program and essentially stop my consulting practice during this Washington time, I traveled a great deal in consultation and in teaching. I was too well launched into cardiology to suddenly become anonymous.

My good friend from medical-school days, Bill Martz, was enthusiastic about the future of medical audiotapes, and he tried to convince me that I should take on the task of building a nationally distributed, quality audiotape in cardiology, sponsored by the American College of Cardiology. I personally could never learn from an audiotape and had had very little experience or enthusiasm for the medium.

Bill was convincing, and I finally, almost reluctantly, took on the project. A one hour-long, audiotape each month, year after year, is a much larger task than one might think. As I got into it, learned

how to do it, learned how to not kill time while speaking by saying "uh" or "ah," learned how to not hiss my "s" or explode my
"p" and "b" into the microphone, it became satisfying.

We launched it under the name ACCESS, for American College
Cardiology Extended Study Services. We quickly were advised
that someone had this name registered as theirs, so we changed
over to ACCEL, American College Cardiology Extended Learning. The tape was a success, almost uniformly listened to by the
physician while he was in his automobile. A group of medical colleagues helped me, among them Jim Crockett, Bill Martz, Jim
Getzen, Bob Oblath, Al Soffer, and Murray Hoffman; they did
tape interviewing at medical meetings. I first did the tape assem-
bly in New York City, and, after coming to Kansas City, had a special dividend by working with a true old-timer jewel of the recording business.

His name was Ed Roche; he was a man of more than 70 when
we started, and we did 120 hour-long tapes together—one a
month for 10 years. When we finished he was much more than 80
and still going strong.

His company was Crown Recording. He was his own company,
the solo employee, and when you worked with him it was a social
function, often requiring a generous amount of sherry before we
started. He presided over a large tape-cutting machine, and, by a
lifetime of accumulated skills, could take the worst of tape record-
ings and bring it up to a level of excellence.

The art of using tape was brought home to me at one of my visits to the New York studio. Awaiting my turn in the studio, I was
able to learn how a single final high note was "purified" by a well-
known soprano. Evidently an earlier taping had produced this single, final, voiced note—but slightly less than ideal. On this day,
the original tape was played. The soprano stood by the microphone, silently mouthing her own words, then at the final note,
she took a deep breath and came forth, bell-like and pure, with
just the right sound. A moment of slicing and splicing and all
leaned forward to hear the new result. It was perfect, all smiled,
shook hands—and a great recording of the soprano's voice was
born.

During the Washington time, I also decided to not end my 10

years of teaching in Southern California, but instead to go right ahead with a major 10-day program for the consulting cardiologist. I planned to give it twice a year at The Inn at Rancho Santa Fe, California, where I had kept my home. Twice, while in Washington, we hurried out to California for this, and twice a year for the next 16 years. By then, I was completely overextended and dropped the program to once a year. I continued it on up to the mid-1980's, at which time I turned the program over to the actual participants themselves and it continued on into the 1990's.

Two stalwart helpers pitched in and made this possible. First, my original partner in practice, Jim Crockett, helped to plan and run the Rancho Santa Fe program, as well as giving major help with the audiotape.

The other major ally was the wife of a former Resident in medicine at Kansas. He was J. Harold Morris and she was Mary Ann Morris. She was one of those unplanned dividends, a lovely, elegant jewel that occasionally comes one's way. Year after year, without compensation, she set up shop at The Inn and acted as house mother, lady-in-residence, manager, and general goodwill angel. Mary Ann was always cheerful and gave real leadership in this endeavor. Giving the program was a satisfaction; working with Jim and Mary Ann made it possible.

I planned for these programs to never have more than 30 participants, and the program drew upon the best new talent in the field of cardiology. Each program brought 10 new speakers and each speaker had the whole day for his subject (five times there were women cardiologists: Joanne Coggin of Loma Linda, Jane Somerville of London, Suzanne Knoebel of Indianapolis, Nanette Wenger of Atlanta, Mary Allen Engle of Cornell). And, of course, Herman Hellerstein was one of the few who came to speak more than once.

It became known as the Cadillac of postgraduate courses, possibly partially because it was the best program I knew how to assemble, with no corners cut, and secondly, because air travel to California for two (90 percent of the men brought their wives), plus 10 days at the quite elegant Inn, plus a very steep tuition, put an impressive price tag on it.

The theme was one of a retreat for the consultant in private practice AND his wife. From the beginning, the importance of the medical couple was stressed, and Mary Ann planned attractive schedules for the wives. The program, over the years, became more than a course, more than a retreat, it became a continuing club of good fellowship, good fellowship in the highest reaches of consulting cardiology.

The large majority of the participants returned every year, some for 20 or 30 times. Some who were present at the first program in 1968, were present for the last one in 1990. Much of what I believe in about professional education was learned and proved at that course. Some of the finest physicians I can imagine were there, year after year.

The things I saw were an independence of character, each man unique, and each man carrying lightly, but thoughtfully, his dignity and pride. Each man was self-regulated, no one was there for the reason of passing tests, making money, or meeting education rules of an outside agency. They were there out of respect for themselves; for better knowledge, and better patient care. There was a wonderful *bonhomie* and sense of good cheer and respect.

They personified what I thought the profession was all about.

I planned the programs, moderated them, sat through all of it and—my only evidences of dictatorship—was that it was run on time, the speakers began and ended on time, good slides were used, every member of the audience was in his seat on time—or he was not invited back—and I kept the room just above the goose-pimple level. Alertness and brisk air go well together.

From 1968 through 1974, at each of these courses, Dr. Jack Morgan, the cardiologist at the U.S. Naval Hospital in San Diego, did the heroic project of bringing six to eight patients and naval corpsmen to the Inn at Rancho Santa Fe. Jack was a delightful man with whom to work and he found great joy in gathering the most unusual, intricate cardiac problems, collecting them for our course.

The U.S. Naval Hospital was the final care hospital for every sailor and dependent, from California to the Orient, including Japan, Okinawa, Guam, and all parts between. The range of exotic cardiac problems was formidable.

The plan for using these patients for teaching the consultants in the course was simple, direct, and potentially embarrassing—to me.

Jack hid the patients' records, placed each patient in a hotel room, and then the physicians, with their stethoscopes only, tried to make a diagnosis from the physical examination alone. Their only tools were their eyes, hands, and ears. Questions were unfair.

After two hours, we all assembled back at our teaching room and then it was my turn to be a hero or a fool. In front of the entire group, I carried out a physical examination, and at each step defined what I saw, felt, heard, then when done, wrote my diagnosis on the blackboard.

Jack then had his moment. Barely able to hide his joy when I was wrong and wryly complimentary when I was right, he took us through the full story of each patient, showing us the EKGs, X-rays, cardiac catheterization data, etc. It was the most intricate challenge to bedside diagnosis one could create—but it also was what I had begun training for when I first went to work for Dr. Harry Baum, 30 years earlier.

The event certainly always quickened my pulse, but it was also a time for a performance, somewhat like an actor who knows he has mastered the part and enjoys giving the show.

We maintained this patient presentation aspect of the course for several years but then, as the American era of litigious medicine became overwhelming, we realized the invitations to legal problems we were creating. Not the least of which was moving these patients on the California freeway from the Naval Hospital to Rancho Santa Fe and back—for the education of physicians—not for the benefit of the patients. We lost our courage and stopped the live hands-on cardiology. With that ending, I knew I was ending my own versatility in this bedside art.

The course was expensive, but had no margin of profit. Near the end of the program, we always had a quite elegant banquet. If there was any extra money, the banquet was more elegant. No course made a profit. One of the reasons I finally moved the course away from the sponsorship of the American College of Cardiology was the beginning pressure from the College for me to find pharmaceutical industry support. Such an idea was, and is, not something I believe in. The independence of the physician should not be shadowed by patronage.

We sold the tape for an honest fee, none of us took any compensation, and the profit was considerable. When it came time to get the College's officers to approve the building of Heart House, we had enough accumulated funds from the tape that we were able to place a large sum of money in an escrow account, earmarked to be used for the expense of maintaining Heart House, if the facility proved to be a more than expected cost to the College. The money was never needed for that purpose.

I extended the audiotape project into making videotapes as well, and this was also a considerable education. It was quickly obvious that the videotape was a superb learning device. Nothing came of it, but Bern Dryer, Herm Hellerstein, and I spent a lot of time making plans for a shared endeavor in this area. We were in New York and Los Angeles, meeting with promoters; we enjoyed our time together, but still, nothing came of it.

During the whole Washington time, Vern Wilson came to see me often, and we worked on the project of how to get a medical school in Kansas City. My hidden agenda in Washington at all times continued to be to sort out the ways of finding federal support for a new medical school.

It was at dinner in my home on October 1, 1968, that Homer and I made our firm plans, and I assured him that at the right time I would come to Hospital Hill.

Our friends in Kansas City, Homer and Nathan, were almost desperate in their need to deliver proof that the claims they had made could be delivered on. These claims began in 1961, when they convinced the mayor, Roe Bartle, that if he would remove the city hospital from the patronage system, there were able lay people who could run it, taking full responsibility, with no compensation, and by developing a medical school, they could upgrade the professional staff, bring in research money, and remove the embarrassment of the old charity-hospital image. The war cry became one that Hospital Hill must have its own medical school.

The lay board was carefully chosen by Homer and Nathan to represent the broadest possible engagement of the civic scene. No one was chosen because of a lace-stocking status; instead, a bold, honest attempt was made to give all strata a voice. The City Council had representatives; the Jackson County Legislature, the University, the patients, the unions, all religious denominations, both sexes, all races were represented. The original plan for the organization and for the make-up of the Board was superb. Even now, almost 30 years later, the original Board and its successors, down to the present, have been free of even a taint of corruption, of chauvinism, of bias. The planning was done to a great extent by Homer and was lasting evidence of his talent.

In 1962, the first step was done and the City did give the hospital, lock, stock, barrel and problems, to the nonprofit Board. With that move, there did not automatically come success. Initially, an arrangement was made with the State's medical school in Columbia to give the Kansas City charity-hospital's doctors University of Missouri appointments. Research programs were begun, and favorable press in *The Kansas City Star* did help. But the government of Kansas City expected an immediate result from transferring the hospital to the Board, and would not give sufficient funds to run the place. Wards were closed, rumors were wholesale, staff turnover was alarming, and patient census dropped.

As their efforts stumbled on the medical-school question, they came at it a different way. They succeeded, using urban-renewal legislation, to get a considerable amount of land declared available for the development of Hospital Hill. Some land they bought for a dollar. Then, with the kind of energy which only rarely strikes in a community, they were able to persuade the University's dental school to rebuild on Hospital Hill, to persuade the very respected Children's Mercy Hospital to move and build there. Then, as the tempo built up, and the University Curators continued to flee from the idea of authorizing a medical school in Kansas City, they succeeded, as I have described, in getting a bond issue before the whole county. By a positive vote of more than 80 percent, the people of Jackson County committed themselves to build a new county hospital, to be used by the City for indigent patients, to be managed by the lay Board, and to be made available to the University as a free teaching hospital for a new medical school. It was a masterpiece of planning, a web spun most skillfully.

The total amount of real money committed to all the new facilities on Hospital Hill was $100 million (remember, 1968 money), and the Crown Center Redevelopment Plan was budgeted at $700 million. Crown Center was an elaborate project, designed to upgrade the neighborhood of the national headquarters of Hallmark Cards. Nathan Stark was made head of that project.

Now the issue was a race against time. The old General Hospital was literally dying. Census was down, wards closing, the academic connection, as an extension of the University's medical school in Columbia, was not sufficient to carry the project to its goal.

The State's Commission on Higher Education employed Dr. Stanley Olson, a respected national figure. They asked him: Did the State need more medical school graduates? Olson reported: more medical graduates; another medical school.

This is when the final "game" began. The need was to get both the University Curators' approval and State Legislature approval for a new medical school. These two bodies skillfully played hardcourt Catch-22. Each said they could not go forward until the other agency had made the first commitment. Kansas City would vigorously lobby the Curators, using the press and all polite forms of coercion, and then at the last moment, the Curators would vote 5 to 4, or some other defeating number, to not take on the responsibility for a new medical school, unless the State first authorized the money.

The legislators, with a rural preponderance and an enthusiasm for the medical school in Columbia, would render pious compliments about the efforts in Kansas City but would not even bring the funding bill to the floor, unless the University appeared before them and pledged themselves to open the new school. The University, always under-funded, and the faculty, always underpaid, had no interest in acquiring the most costly of academic programs—a medical school.

Even the faculty at the Kansas City campus was opposed to adding a medical school to the agenda. One could only attempt to assure them that the medical school and hospital would not take money away from their always anemic budget, but would bring money to the campus.

To put in balance the reality about the Kansas City campus, it is useful to remember again that, for years, the School had been the University of Kansas City, not a state responsibility, and this local effort at maintaining a university gradually dwindled down, until in 1962 its salvation was to convince the Curators and the State to take the near-bankrupt school into the University system.

Now, non-University activists in Kansas City were trying to load on top of this precarious arrangement an entire medical center?

The county bond money for the hospital was essentially frozen until there was evidence that a new teaching hospital would have a medical school base.

Vernon Wilson, reaching out from Columbia, trying to be helpful, had a study done which concluded that with the unique facilities pledged on Hospital Hill, a new medical school there could be operated on a budget only 22.7 percent as expensive as adding 100 new students to the school in Columbia. Still, the impasse continued.

Homer, Nathan, and their allies urged me to move to a Kansas City base and take on the local, state, and national drive to get the problem resolved. I danced carefully away from that quicksand. The chancellor of the University of Missouri in Kansas City, James Olson, and I met in Kansas City, and he urged me to throw my hat in the ring. Still, it was not my hat, but my head I would be throwing, unless the impasse was broken, and one side of the equation made some firm commitment. I was comfortable with Olson and he remained a friend and support during his chancellorship and later, when he moved up to the presidency of the whole University. He was helpful in a benign, not definitive way. Often, I suspect, he wondered what he had unleashed when the School finally became reality.

In the history of the State and the University, the one initial act which puts an academic program on the State's financial agenda, and thus identifies the program as backed by taxation, is when the University asks for a building and the legislators authorize the "planning money." The amount of the planning money is not too significant; what is important is to get a program on the State's official agenda.

Much of the horse trading and maneuvering going on behind the scenes at a state capital can be discerned by noting where planning money is allocated. A new building in St. Louis? Then you are certain to see one on the docket for Kansas City—and the other political pieces of the State; The Bootheel, Springfield, the rural areas, will have their fair share. One at first has an urge to cry out "politics"—but then, is there a better way to run a state?

And when the plans are drawn, one will note a certain amount of work needs brick masons, satisfying that union, and a certain amount of stone work will assure the Carthage quarries part of the work. The steam fitters union is assured its share. The results of lobbying are all made visible when the planning money is allotted. But to even reach that place, it was still necessary to have the curators take a deep breath and authorize the medical school.

My own adamancy made this even a greater hurdle. I told Homer and Nathan that I had no desire to build a traditional medical school. I walked them through the kind of new, different, essentially revolutionary, school that I would be willing to cast my lot behind.

They are good listeners, shrewd men, and both, as laymen long active in the health field, immediately understanding of the reasons why I wanted to make changes in medical education. From sitting on Nathan's sun porch one afternoon, at which point they took in what I was after, they never wavered. They were with me all the way.

The two of them, Vernon Wilson, and I, began a happy, enthusiastic endeavor, within which we never had a single harsh word, nor a moment of hurt vanity. They were not Machiavellian, but committed to public service, and each of more than usual intelligence and social skills. They made the ideal cabal, team, clan, partners, to not only carry it off—but to have a delightful time doing it.

Nathan Stark was not a Kansas City native (none of us were: Homer, Nathan, Vernon, myself). We all came to Missouri for a part of our lives, and each working from a different approach, happened to come together on this single shared project: the rebuilding of Hospital Hill—a restored city hospital and a new medical school. We all had other things we did with our careers but the only area in which we all were together was this one. For me, because I took on the full-time task of doing it, it became the rest of my career. For each of them, it was something they were involved in with full energy, but then they each went on to larger endeavors.

Homer was taken away by the Cleveland Foundation, one of the nation's best foundations in terms of not only resources, but accomplishment. Nathan went on to become a medical administrator himself as vice chancellor for Health Affairs at Pitt, then on to be Under Secretary for Health in Washington, and then into the practice of law in Washington. Vernon left the vice-presidency at the University of Missouri in November 1974 to become head of HSMHA (Health Services and Mental Health Administration), a major unit of the government's Health and Human Services, then to being head of Vanderbilt University Medical Center.

All were, obviously, men of real talent, and only by chance and circumstance did we come together on the Hospital Hill project. As they each left the Kansas City scene, I realized that one of us had to remain to see it through, and that I did.

In the spring of 1969, Nathan was the president of the General Hospital Board and he was very ably aided by Carl Migliazzo, who would succeed him.

Nathan was a lawyer by training; he had come to Kansas City as legal advisor to a manufacturing firm. He was attracted away to the huge local organization, Hallmark Cards, and became a vice-president; one of his major efforts was to guide the planning and launching of the substantial redevelopment program, Crown Center, adjacent to Hallmark's headquarters. This huge development occurred on the western edge of Hospital Hill and brought a deteriorated area up to an elegant level. The rebuilding of Hospital Hill, of course, secured their eastern neighborhood.

Nathan is one of those unusual people who does not have the capacity to alienate anyone. I have seen him, so many times, come into a board meeting with a very difficult agenda to offer the diverse board, and through the smoothest of process, with no hammering of the table, no bombast, bring the board into a shared, cooperative "yes" vote. This does not mean that in the process he compromised; the final result was exactly what he sought in the beginning. I often thought of Homer as the anvil and Nathan, not as the hammer, but as a feather. Somehow, he tickled out the exact result needed. He is a handsome man, of good posture and physique, with brilliant blue eyes, and aquiline handsomeness. He is a man of such obvious goodwill and integrity that most opposition is overcome by simply knowing this. His wife, Lucile, is a special personality herself; Nathan's abilities have certainly been enhanced by his efforts to keep up with the free-ranging intelligence of his wife. My introduction to Lucile was when I came to their home for the first time. I was met at the door by her and promptly ordered to take off my shoes. This was not a passing fancy—no one wears shoes in Lucile's lair.

Nathan took up his interest in the health field essentially as *pro bono* extension of his community interest. Perhaps he was fostered in this direction because Lucile was the daughter of a physician.

Chapter Seventeen

IN THE SPRING OF 1968, I flew back to appear before the Curators and lay out the full details of the academic plan I was interested in building. Vernon, as the vice-president for academic affairs, had done his preparation work well, and the nine curators fully endorsed the plan and authorized the School. From that moment to now, the curators have never hesitated, never challenged the program, and, although they never remotely generated the amount of money the program needed, at the same time they never second-guessed the effort and never interfered in any way. In many respects, that kind of support was worth more than money.

Essentially, they called my hand. If I was serious, I had to shut down my life in Washington and move the family to Kansas City. It was time to get in the trenches—or get out of the act.

Mary D. made her judgments in life based on the quality of the people involved. She completely approved of Homer and Nathan, just as she did of Jim Crockett and Mary Ann Morris. She enjoyed being in their company. Still, the idea of moving to Kansas City seemed a considerable adventure into the wilderness. I remember one day when she returned from shopping, prior to our leaving Washington, and she had purchased 100 tubes of Meltonian shoe cream, in all colors. She was certain that once she stepped off into the unknown, there would be no more shoe cream.

To make the move palatable, we agreed to keep a small apartment at Dupont Plaza, near the Potomac, so we would have a base for retreat.

Finally, Homer and Vernon telephoned me to say that the State Legislature's appropriation committee had agreed to approve a planning money bill and that the bill was to go to the floor of the legislature at once. It was not much money, only $200,000, but it was a final, firm action. Neither man could see anything that could derail this commitment.

We all met again, Homer, Nathan, Vernon, and the chancellor, Jim Olson. The time had come to get specific, very specific, about authority. My terms were simple. I expected to have complete responsibility and authority over every aspect of the health schools' academic programs run by the University in Kansas City and also equal authority over the hospital. I asked for none, and expected no authority over Children's Mercy Hospital, except as it related to the undergraduate medical education program.

Getting along with the very independent Board of Mercy would not be gained by fiat, but by a demonstration, over time, that they were better off because of the new medical school.

My relationship to the General Hospital Board would be smoothed by Homer, Nathan, and Carl Migliazzo, but essentially the Board was so delighted to get the hospital on someone's back, that they would have wrapped it in ribbons if necessary.

Vernon was keenly concerned that I have the right title. His style of administration gave this more importance than Homer, Nathan, or myself considered it worth, but Vernon had been deep within the University system and understood all the nuances of title. My own need was more discrete—I wanted to be in charge, the title could come along as it was needed. To make the commitment they were asking, I intended to have absolute authority—at least as absolute as anyone gets in such a situation. And I knew well that the lifetime of such authority is indeed short.

For institutional reasons, related to the newness of the four-campuswide University system, and the reluctance of the curators to expose themselves to the criticism that they were immediately becoming top-heavy with administrators, there was no title such as "vice chancellor" within the whole system. Such fiddling with a table of organization is characteristic of government and quasi-government systems. The work is obviously being done by someone, but don't give it a title which can catch the eye of the press or the politicians.

That was true then—and now there are vice chancellors, associate vice chancellors, assistants to the associate vice chancellors, assistant vice chancellors, deputy vice chancellors, *ad infinitum*. Administrative systems tend to proliferate.

We came up with the title Provost for Health Sciences. None of us knew exactly what it meant, and we felt comfortable that no one in the State Legislature would know, either. From the dictionary, we learned that it meant the highest academic officer, which by its omission of the word "administrative," made it a perfect euphemism. The important word was the modifier "highest."

We therefore agreed that I would be the University's highest authority in Kansas City of the health-science schools: medicine, pharmacy, dentistry, and the University's authority on Hospital Hill. This University agreement came from Vernon and Jim Olson.

Homer and Nathan agreed that I would be the person in charge of old General Hospital and the building of the new hospital all under the Board. This authority included all aspects, from administration to planning to budget, to the residency program. Homer laughed when this agreement was made and said, "Old Buddy! You are welcome to the whole place. We will meet you at the City limits and present you with the biggest bag of worms you have ever seen!"

Somehow, as I flew back to Washington, I had the feeling they all sat down and had a drink and laughed about what they had done to me.

Nevertheless, with this assurance, we loaded the family in the station wagon and began the trip from Washington to Kansas City. The two dogs left us and went on to live with the governess, who returned to her apartment in New York City. With us, we had Tommy, Molly, Mary D.'s youngest daughter; Lark, Lea, the canary bird, and the two turtles. It was a happy journey, and in Terre Haute, Indiana, I telephoned Homer to tell him we were safely on our way.

He hesitated and then began a verbal circumlocution, a tactic in which he is skilled. Gradually, he came around to his message. The state senator responsible for the State appropriation committee, and therefore responsible for our planning-money bill, had suddenly, without warning, fled the state of Missouri, and, it was rumored, had decamped with his secretary to Las Vegas or Reno!

No one knew why; there was no evidence he would return. The appropriation committee was in shambles and our planning bill a part of the shambles!

My fine new title and complete authority given with it was suddenly as useful as being emperor of a deserted island.

It was so awful that it was funny. Our first instinct was to just drive on through to Rancho Santa Fe, California, where at least we had a base, and forget about the birth of a medical school. Mary D.'s good New England sense of rectitude had real trouble comprehending a representative of the people with this character.

The performance of the whole Jefferson City process could always anger her and bring out a desire to have the whole system impeached. Her father's concept of a private citizen's duty to rectify the wrongs of society was one she equally believed.

I assured her that changing the political system of Missouri was an arena I would leave alone, and that the reason we were making this move was to launch a change in medical education. The game we had to play was one of getting done what we wanted to do, in spite of the system in which we had to work. And that system was both political and medical.

She instantly saw that, in its own way, this was what her father had always done—getting something done in spite of the system.

I told her that I thought the only way I was going to succeed in pulling a medical school through the system of Missouri politics, University resistance, local medical politics, and national medical accrediting groups, was to take whomever we found, and work with their strengths, wasting no time on their faults.

I said I planned to work with the people who were there, those whose lives were there, and only later would I try to recruit outside. I urged her to think of it as a mission, not a conversion, as an immersion, not an invasion. She understood, and with a laugh, said, "O.K. Let's do it. Let's do it, and let us see if we can't make everyone better for doing it!"

We spent the evening in Terre Haute with my oldest friends, Vic, of course, Woody Suttle, and Jerry Lentz. Mary D. and my lifelong friends immediately hit it off well, and they enjoyed telling her details of our boyhood years, details which I carefully had neglected to tell her.

In Kansas City, we settled into a motel and began house finding. One home which I still regret not getting was a large farm
property south of the city, but the owner was involved in a divorce
problem and when we thought we had it, it suddenly was tied up
in a court complexity.

With children still at home, we needed six bedrooms, which restricted the choice of houses. Finally, in a sinking moment of exhaustion from looking at real estate, we bought a handsome brick
home, well-located, and with more bedrooms than we thought we
could ever need. To our surprise, all 11 were often occupied.

The house was not exactly a place free of town-talk. It was a bit
as if one lived in a haunted house. The place had been built by the
whole area's most well-known name—after Harry Truman—Boss
Pendergast. We, of course, knew his story, yet he had been dead
for years, so it did not seem too important to us that this had been
his home. We lived there for seven years and from the day we
bought it, until we sold it, no one ever spoke of it as our home. It
was always "The Pendergast House." And these words were always said with a little lifting of the voice, as if the speaker was re-
vealing a choice bit of gossip, somewhat as one will say, "Oh, yes,
she dresses well—but, you know—she drinks!"

Earlier, I mentioned that Mary D. very much enjoyed Homer
and Nathan. As soon as we got in town, we met the next member
of their inner team, Carl Migliazzo. Carl was as Sicilian as one can
be. Great, large, dark eyes, deep-set under heavy brows, with
dewlaps of wrinkles and sags beneath. His hands were like thick
spades and one could never quite get a complete grasp in a handshake. Members of his family were rumored to have considerable
relationships with the regional godfather, and this thought always
hung as an aura of excitement as one dealt with him.

However, Carl lived a good citizen's life, took part in many public duties, had a wonderful wife and children, and was fundamental in getting Hospital Hill rebuilt. His style of dress was good but
colorful: silk suits, some shot through with gold thread, and
striped shirts with purple ties. He was a joy to work with, always
enthusiastic, innovative, and cooperative. He was absolutely
straightforward in conduct; brusqueness and iron when needed,
gentle and considerate otherwise. He and Mary D. immediately

enjoyed each other, and, throughout her years in Kansas City, she always looked forward to seeing him. I suspect, secretly, she hoped he was the godfather.

Through statewide speaking, through encouraging physicians to speak to their legislators, through cooperative agreements with St. Louis politicians and labor unions' leaders, through interviews with the State's chief newspapers, through very careful discussions with the City's hospitals and neighborhood clinics, but especially through the network of physician friends who had been students or Residents in Medicine or Fellows in Cardiology at Kansas, we began building the needed base for getting action out of the State Legislature.

When the planning money had been promised (before the flight of the state senator to Nevada), the amount was $200,000. When we finally got it back on track, it was $60,000. We were all so traumatized by this time that we actually felt grateful.

To get this $60,000 required urgent trips by all of us—Homer, Nathan, Carl, Vernon, myself—to Jefferson City. On several occasions we produced busloads of influential Kansas Citians in Jefferson City, and they gave grand lobbying performances.

Life offers lessons in all these experiences. I well remember when we took a large group down, took over a dining room at a hotel, and invited the legislators to come and have dinner with us, and let us tell them why we needed their support for this new school.

Our error was in having an open bar. Like thirsty locusts, they swarmed in on us, and any hopes of telling our story quickly turned liquid. Wiser, more experienced lobbyists told me that this is a natural hazard for which one must prepare. The elected officials, away from home, relaxing, stretching their small allowances as they can, should never be given the libation before the lesson.

All of this was for just the planning money.

There had been medical-school building money available from the federal government for a number of years. Remember, this was the era when it was declared that there was going to be a shortage of 50,000 doctors in the United States, and, therefore, new medical schools were a national emergency.

Richard Nixon was elected President shortly before we

reached the point of seeking such money. Among his first actions was to terminate the program giving money to build medical schools. Our crisis-oriented, perils-of-Pauline psyche was again traumatized. Again it looked as if we had been "cut off at the pass," as Carl declared.

A considerable amount of effort, with trips to Washington, corridor walks, seeing our Senators and Congressman, finally resulted in one of those quick moments which occur in government. The door to funding was opened one single additional time. We got the last building money under the legislation.

At about this same time, Vernon had taken a very active role in getting a major Regional Health Programs grant for the Columbia, Missouri medical school. It was a large, several-million-dollar award. Vernon tried conscientiously to carry out the regionalizing that was the doctrine of RMP. One of the requests he made of us in Kansas City was that we make major efforts to have real, continuous cooperative programs with the faculty in Columbia.

Equally, perhaps because he and I both had happy roots in Kansas, he wanted our new medical school to share resources with the University of Kansas. In neither of these areas were we ever successful. A large amount of time went into planning sessions, but the reality of the state line is a political reality that goodwill from Washington does not overcome.

Cooperation with Columbia was another effort in futility. The Columbia campus, from the beginning, considered us an upstart new endeavor, and worse, one competing for resources. When Hospital Hill was considered a satellite of the Columbia campus, tensions were livable; the prospect of a full-fledged separate medical school was not well received.

A major area in which Vernon and I had complete harmony was in our shared belief that the happiest arrangement for the marriage of clinicians and basic scientists (the same old question) was to divorce them.

We agreed that each deserved a full school: a medical school emphasizing the special skills *and attitude* used by a Doctor of Medicine; a basic-science school concentrating on basic research done by Ph.D.'s. This science faculty would be obligated to carry on science education for the health science schools.

The schools of Pharmacy, Dentistry, Medicine, and Nursing would all turn to the faculty of the School of Basic Life Sciences for their science teaching. Each of these schools would not maintain its own separate basic-science departments.

That is what we did, although it took years to get the final approval for the School of Basic Life Sciences. It was a radical concept, and Vernon and I knew we were asking for the wrath of the basic scientists from the traditional medical schools. We were separating them from the medical school, and the medical school had long been their primary base in the United States.

The history of the School must record the fact that our concern for clinical ability and commitment to patient care was real. In 1973, we were sued by a former student, charging us with acting without due process in removing the student from the School. The removal was on the basis of inadequate performance in the clinical areas. The case came to the Supreme Court. Publicity in national newspapers attempted to hang us on charges of sexual and racial discrimination. Dick Noback and I held to a very special theme, specifically, the adequacy of our evaluation process. There were other major issues that we chose to not make a part of the School's defense. The lawsuit against us was filed in December 1973; the Supreme Court validated our stand in March 1978. How many other very neophyte medical schools would have stood behind the commitment to the clinical competence of its graduates? It would have been easier, and some of the faculty urged it, to have given the degree and get the issue behind us. It was not pleasant but it perhaps confirmed the School's dedication. The case, and the Supreme Court's decision, is now an often-cited precept as universities attempt to protect their ability and right to require a standard of academic performance. Perhaps that is the greatest lasting benefit from our tenacity.

Chapter Eighteen

WITH THIS MUCH DESCRIPTION OF the considerable amount of energy being invested by my colleagues, and the large career investment of myself, I need to explain what kind of a medical-education program it was that I was not only willing to sacrifice a cardiology career for, but by insisting upon it, burden those who were striving for a medical school in Kansas City. I am sure they would have been happier if we were simply starting a traditional four-year school. Not Homer, Nathan, and Vernon, but the local physicians, the Chancellor, the faculty, and the Curators.

My concept for changing how one became a doctor certainly did not come late in my career, nor did it come as a sudden light of revelation.

It is true that the summer I spent in the stacks at the National Library of Medicine gave me, in fact, forced me, to put down on paper what I wanted to do. A clean piece of paper and a hard chair can be ignored, and a thousand distractions can come between the promise and the act. But the force which cannot be hidden from, is the expectation one places on oneself.

I went to the Library to do the task, took off a solid period of time to do it, and told the authorities at the Library I was writing an academic plan—I had no place to hide, either from myself or from those who had given me the "scholar-in-residence" appointment at the Library. To come out of the stacks at the end of the summer empty-handed was an embarrassment I did not care to face.

However, what I wrote was not a result of any original thinking during that summer. I had begun planning a rebellion in medical education from the first day of my premedical education experience in 1938.

I knew the justifications for the four-year premedical requirement were wrong. I knew of the harm it did to many, I knew of
the talent that was lost because of the four-year detour in time
and subject matter. I certainly knew of the inordinate financial
blow. I had watched so many good friends forced out of the race
for medical school, and had only made it myself by a last grasp.

Grade performance determines whether one will be allowed to
study medicine. For the premedical student it is not a graced
time. It is not a tranquil period of browsing the Great Books.

These four years are indeed serious.

Down to the present, these flaws have not changed. The justification is practically always based upon a book about American medical schools written more than 70 years ago, the Flexner Report.
This report certainly was useful for its time and circumstance, but
there is little in the seven-decade-old document which remotely reflects life in the current United States. It is a convenient testament
that has gained mystical proportions, especially because it is the
justification for the four-year liberal-arts requirement.

I knew the science requirements act as a filter to keep out of
medical school the humanistic talent. The entire orientation was
based upon grade achievement and aptitude test scores in science
subjects, which was, painfully, unrelated to a career as a caring
physician. The truth is that the system persists because it fosters
the financial durability of the liberal arts colleges, which to a
great extent benefit from the tuitions paid by the large numbers
of premedical students who have to go over their hurdle, even to
get to the threshold of the medical school.

Today, Harvard gains great attention over its New Pathway program. Little comment is made about the fact that this is but a
small remnant of what they had hoped to accomplish. Even with
the full backing of the Harvard president, Derek Bok, and the
medical school dean, Daniel Tosteston, their original plan for
shortening the curriculum, getting away from the four-year period locked up by the arts and science faculty, and gaining very
early patient exposure, had to be abandoned. The resistance from
the powerful arts and science fiefdoms could not be breached.

The New Pathway is the Compromise Pathway, and one well-
ventilated by enemy fire.

Every medical-student hopeful can tell tales, not in the least apocryphal, of harassment by the biology or physiology or chemistry premed faculty.

I am now at a point in my career where such truths can be said; when you are younger, or when you are in a circumstance where you need to "go along to get along," it is not possible always accurately to report.

Still, I did. As we launched the School, there was no way to avoid these issues. Of course, one does not get away unscathed. Just as the building of the American College of Cardiology left hostile feelings among the leadership of the American Heart Association and the Establishment, so did the basic-science leaders of the medical education system await their moment of attack.

But my motivation was not in the least solely because of the basic-science teaching.

Yes, I thought the content of this kind of science was over-emphasized, weighted, in the selection process. Yes, the teachers were not well oriented to the true needs of those preparing for a lifetime in Medicine. Yes, the scope of the curriculum was far removed from the needs of a physician-to-be's preparation.

Even when in medical school, the artificial division between the basic sciences and clinical sciences persists. Because it is a livable, political expedient, not because it facilitates learning, the four years of medical school are tidily divided with the basic scientists having the first two years of the student's time, and then the clinicians getting the last two years. No real attempt is made to interleaf these two libraries of knowledge.

Certainly it would be more useful to the student to see patients and their problems, and, at the same time, be exposed to the sciences basic to understanding the disease process.

Key words in a good system of education are "relevancy" and "repetition." The system I envisioned made these two experiences the core of the plan.

Another change I sought was to eliminate the strange cadence of university life in the United States, at least as it related to medical education. Much of it is a carryover from the early agrarian roots of the country. The long spring break was a time for the students to get home and help with the spring planting; the full summer break was when the farm family needed all the able-bodied help it could get; the Christmas break originated in the days of slow travel and the desire of the basically Christian society to gather at home at this time.

I felt that these reasons were no longer rational, and equally, these long interruptions added to the cost of the education, spreading the additional time out by more than a full extra calendar year. It also added to the cost of the whole academic calendar to maintain faculty and buildings, even when unused.

The experience of the thousands of us who were brought through medical school in the 1940's, on an around-the-clock calendar because of the exigencies of war, was vivid proof that an accelerated calendar is possible.

It was not only possible; we were fortunate to experience it. Very talented men came from that experience. We were not fortunate in our loss of faculty to the services, in the burden of the other wartime shortages, but the quickened calendar fully was livable.

But, more important than these valid reasons, I believed that there was real harm done by such breaks in the scholarly discipline. One of the powerful ingredients in a physician's life, if he is to remain self-educating and current in information over a lifetime, is the resolute obligation to duty; DUTY, in capital letters. It is not a life of holidays and breaks. One does not follow the calendar of "normal" life. Weekend duty, "call," emergencies, are the physician's norm. Learning that early is a valuable lesson.

My concern for a sabbatical plan in a physician's life is a reflection of the unique social commitment made by a physician. A time for recharging and rebuilding will still be needed. Now with HMO's and many women physicians, some of this will change. But not as much as some would think. The able physician, man or woman, privately employed or by an organization, will need recharging time.

Why expose very bright, enthusiastic young persons, at the height of their powers of absorption, to a campus culture which is often based upon the marvels of "Thank God it's Friday," of the somewhat childish enthusiasm for the school's teams, and the happy, but, again, remote from real life, activities of fraternities and sororities?

The supporters of these things are legion, and usually their enthusiasm is based upon the nostalgia that it was how life was when they were that age, and, "Oh, I want him to have all the fun he can; real life begins all too soon." This latter I hear still today, and I can only comment that life is real, life is earnest—and living it is not at all that bad.

Working hard and enthusiastically, at mastering the very career which you intend to devote your life to, seems more logical than sending Johnny and Mary down to State U. to have a four-year lengthening of their childhood.

I commented above that life is real and life is earnest. For a physician, this is vitally true. It is not a trade to be learned, nor a body of knowledge—it is a serious, committed way of life. To understand this commitment and the way of life involved, is one of the great events in the preparation of a physician. From my long, long experience, I believe this sense of duty, of purpose, of personal responsibility, is more important than all of the knowledge, painfully transitory knowledge, with which faculties saturate the student.

The earlier the candidate for this career learns about the pathos of life, the burdens people carry, the solace which can be given them, the dignity which must be protected, the value of hope, of warmth, of sustaining—the greater will be one's value to the patient—and the greater the physician.

The powerful urging, "Physician, heal thyself," must begin with "Physician, know thyself." That kind of knowledge comes not from a book, not from the abstract classroom discussion, but from experience at the immediate side of the stricken person.

Robert Louis Stevenson wrote: "Quiet minds cannot be perplexed or frightened, but go on in fortune or misfortune at their own private pace, like a clock in a thunderstorm."

Fontanelle gave the same advice: "The great secret of happiness is to be at ease with yourself; it is well to have in yourself a pleasant refuge."

My experiences of living had brought to me the value of knowing well yourself.

It is that quality the future physician must accomplish while in medical school. Call it, "being comfortable within." Early, prolonged, carefully regulated, carefully escorted exposure to humankind's travail is the schoolhouse.

No novel, no movie, no video, no panel, nothing can convey the rush of the moment when you are there—healthy, strong, sustaining—and the sight, odor, and sound of a human crisis is not just your environment, but your responsibility.

The unusual medical education I had under Harry Baum had taught me this as a fundamental, undeniable truth.

Medicine requires, to practice it, a great deal of knowledge, a great deal of renewing that knowledge, but over, beyond, and before, comes the personal discipline to carry on the role of healer, listener, sustainer. It is there, at the bedside, that one becomes the physician, not in a classroom—and not down at Old Siwash U., enjoying the rites of spring.

Do I make it sound too serious? Well, it is serious. In this highly scientific age, the minister certainly has his role and the lawyer his role—but there is one profession only that is directly allowed to apply the range of scientific potential, to save lives, or by error, cause harm. That is the physician.

Four years of premedical education is too precious a period of time to allow a talented, hopeful candidate to remain suspended as a juvenile.

The critic will say, often and repeatedly, "But, to be this wise and competent person you describe, the physician must have the full liberal education in the arts, social sciences, philosophy, the great Judeo-Christian culture, the exposure to the great minds and ethics, the music, the poetry, the wisdom of the Greek scholars, be able to understand the great writings, to speak a foreign language, to..." and on and on—with modifications depending upon the individual's own special interests.

All of them express the absolute: that this can only be learned in a college of arts, and, of course, the other side of the equation, the scientists crying out that one cannot safely attend the sick without knowing solid-state physics, geometry, calculus, relativity; and cannot safely read articles without studying statistics; cannot understand medications without an immense array of laboratory chemistry; cannot use prosthetic equipment and biomechanical devices without understanding physics and metallurgy—

and the list is never-ending.

The first observation is that four years of premedical college cannot remotely accomplish all of this. No one in any faculty has ever accomplished all of this.

Education is a life event. One never stops learning; from books, from all the media, from courses, from personal contacts, but, above all, from the patient. Knowledge of man is found in man.

The physician, by the very nature of his work, seeks information, asks questions, probes. These are the skills that characterize the profession. To suggest that the physician's vessel of knowledge is empty because he did not pass through a certain college experience, is to deny the unique nature of the daily life he or she will lead. It is humanism that distinguishes the great healer. The preparation for this service begins at the bedside—and ends there.

It would be very difficult to find evidence that university graduates, not just physicians, were made better, more tolerant, more dedicated, more honest, more effective citizens, by some particular panoply of course content at the university. Perhaps college does a bit of this, but, even more possible, is that it is the benefit which comes from a better income and a higher standard of living.

By none of this, do I want to indicate a belief in a know-nothing conduct. To become a physician is very hard work, to remain a good one is even harder. To suggest that the quality of the professional life you lead is lessened or diminished, because one did not have a certain credit-course exposure between 18 and 22, is just not a valid truth.

Serious, planned, repetitive travel is one great step towards being educated, towards a true liberal education. Solid, sustained reading; planned, thoughtful reading, is the other route to a real education.

Putting these medical-education thoughts into a plan had been strengthened by my time abroad. In the larger part of western Europe, including the United Kingdom; in Australia and New Zealand; medical school has long been a six-year experience, and it begins directly from high school. The skeptic could say (and did) that the high school student in those countries has a superior education compared to the American student of similar age. I was well aware of this criticism of the American education system. But my conviction was that although all American high school students definitely might not be scholastically at the level of a West German gymnasium graduate, that our best graduates were comparable to any, in terms of knowledge, willingness, and that incomparable value, energy.

And it was the very best talent that I was interested in. My ambition at no time was to democratize medical education, to make it easier for the academically disadvantaged to qualify. I had no commitment to create a lower standard of physician. If there is one characteristic I have, it is a belief in elitism, elitism of intellect and of conduct.

Nor was I interested in a process that would generate general practitioners. From the beginning, I was interested only in finding the best talent to study medicine, expose that talent to the most humanistically-oriented program possible, to maintain every proper standard of excellence, and to have the finished product be dedicated to caring for people.

Throughout the United States, during the same years in which we were launching our school, there was a major push for primary care physicians. The steady message from opinion-givers was that the American public would be best served if every citizen had a single responsible physician. This was, of course, a major objective of the Family Practice group. Equally, the Internists declared this their arena. Not to be left out, the Pediatricians declared they were the child's primary physician. The Ob/Gyn specialists declared it apparent that they were the woman's primary-care physician. I have capitalized each special field, deliberately.

Ward Darley was the academic leader in this pursuit. Charles Odegaard, a respected university president, became a vocal supporter of this primary-physician need; the Carnegie Foundation sponsored his major report.

Because we were launching a new school at the same time this campaign was underway, practically everyone thought primary care was our major objective. Nothing I said ever deterred them. Through speaking and writing, I sought through all the years to make the point that I was interested in preparing caring, disciplined, dedicated, humane physicians; in no manner did I limit our intent to primary care.

I frequently said that I did not care if the graduate was a general practitioner, an ENT specialist, or a master surgeon, the distinguishing characteristic of this school would be that the physician was kind, caring, and honest.

I sometimes said that in a form of shorthand: We wanted to graduate a "safe physician."

My implication was an encompassing one. By "safe," I meant that when you, the patient, gave your care to our graduate, you knew that from knowledge to judgment to caring, you were in safe hands. Sometimes, I simply said, "...the kind of doctor you would send your mother to."

Nothing can be left alone, however. When I used my phrase, "a safe physician," Norman Cousins promptly interrupted, "Oh, you must add, "A safe, *civilized* physician." I let that rest. It seemed clear to me that I was not describing an uncivilized physician.

Not completely separate from the intent of preparing safe physicians, was another quite immodest intent. I voiced it often and, when the School was newborn and struggling, my message certainly seemed overly ambitious. I declared that we were preparing our graduates to be "Leaders."

My purpose was not exactly "whistling in the graveyard," to keep up our courage during those difficult years.

My instincts told me that we were getting superb talent in from high school and the students were characterized by their ability and drive. Nothing would keep them from being leaders.

By putting them into a new, shortened school system, they were certainly going to be challenged by skeptics when they went out into their careers. I calculated that their responses would be those of proving their worth. They would seize leadership positions.

In a previous paragraph, I spoke of my belief in intellectual elitism. This is obviously a part of leadership. We now have more than a thousand graduates and far too many have passed through the School for me to have kept track of each one. However, I think, I guess, I hope, I believe that each of the graduates knows that back there on Hospital Hill, there is this old man who watches and enjoys each achievement, and chuckles.

I, therefore, crafted a plan which would be open to the absolute top students coming out of high school, a plan which would bring them directly into a six-year A.B.-M.D. program, continued year-round, with a month-a-year of vacation, with a blended, interlayered curriculum of the liberal arts, of science, and of medicine.

I intended for the students to see patients on the first day they entered our system. Specifically, they would graduate in June from high school, and they would see their first patient on September 1, their first day in medical school. They would be 17 or 18 years old.

From my years of running a fellowship program, I knew that one of the happiest, most productive patterns of education comes when there is a small group and a leader. This leader is a role model who sets the level of quality, excellence, and expectation. In this small group, the students are at all levels of maturity. When the learners are of all levels of maturity, they naturally teach each other. Although the role-model leader sets the pace and sense of quality, the real learning in a good fellowship program goes on among the participants. When well done, even the leader learns from the group. The more diverse the participants, the more backgrounds they bring, and the greater their range of difference, the more the learning.

This form of small-group teaching, one leader, diverse students, is what makes every fellowship program, whether it is at the bedside or at the research bench. And, as a truth, it is how great artists work with their disciples, how ballet is transmitted, and, essentially, how Mark Hopkins sat on his log and had a student on the other end.

This was firmly in my mind, and this I made the basic cell block of our new school. Not only in the curriculum, but as we planned the physical building for the School and the hospital, we had this small-group, mixed-level, single-leader role model expressed in the bricks and mortar of both buildings, the School and the Teaching Hospital.

The right number was clear to me. About 10 or 12 was the maximum size that would have the cohesion and group identity which brought teamwork, anything much smaller was too small and the dynamics needed could not be generated.

There was no suitable title in academic life for these group leaders. It seemed ponderous to call them "Professor." "Physician" was equally stiff. At first, I wanted to call these units simply "Clinical Teams" and the leader "The Clinician." Others did not feel this had quite enough distinction. We tried various terms: "Scholar's Units," "Firms," and "Health Care Learning Teams" was one awful suggestion. I even came up with the word "Propae-duetist," and this received its warranted burial.

To get on with the planning, we agreed to give each team a color recognition. With this we could provide identity and a sense of belonging. Thus, we divided the whole student body into the four colors, Blue, Red, Green, Gold, subdivided, for example, into Blue, One, Gold One, Blue Three, etc. For a few weeks, the colors were Blue, Red, Green, and Yellow; then someone rejected the designation Yellow, as being a contaminated word. Thus, we turned to Gold. Now, with our national hubris for yellow ribbons, perhaps we dropped a winning color.

To give each student an awareness of belonging, a sense of ter-ritory, we had 400 individual offices planned. It is strange to note that practically no medical school has a "belonging place" for the individual student. A small metal locker is the standard. I meant for all to have places of their own, a home base, within which these very young students could begin forming their own sense of responsibility, of being, of territorial preserve.

This gave us a way to plan, to organize, and to get on with the buildings. But still we needed a noun, an appellation. While work-ing with the architects in Chicago, one of the architects, leaning across the blueprints, said, "Now here is our design on these do-cent units." And that is the moment the Docent was invented.

Earlier, I defined two qualities fostering learning: Relevancy and Repetition. There is a third quality and this we put in the edu-cation plan. The quality is Continuity. We did this in several ways but our main emphasis was in the Docent Teams.

A student joins her or his permanent Docent Team in Year Three and remains with that Team for the next four years, until graduation. This Year Three student is paired with an older stu-dent of the same team. These "older-younger" pairings become a fundamental education unit. These pairs meet weekly in the out-patient clinic over the full four years and maintain a continuity of care for the same "practice" of patients. The students, the Docent and the patients remain together, a Continuity. We named this the Continuing Care Clinic.

Each year, all members of the Docent Team return to the same in-patient service and with their same patients, the Doctor of Pharmacy, Clinical Librarian, Social workers, Dieticians, all practice in-patient medicine for a two full months. This annual docent experience therefore is carried out for a total of eight months over a four-year period. This augmented by the same Docent and students gathering in the outpatient clinic weekly. This is Continuity.

It has often been difficult to convince the new Docent that this eight-month period is not for teaching the discipline of internal medicine. To teach a way of life is more difficult, but it is the merit we have sought.

This is what we planned and this is perhaps the distinguishing characteristic of this medical school education plan. As I write about it, you will note I have moved my tense from future to present tense. I do this to celebrate the fact that we planned it and it happened. It is easy to have plans; the fulfillment is the challenge.

Circumstances change. Although great discussion goes on about the importance of "primary care," the technical nature of high-quality medicine does not foster primary care physicians. The philosophy is sound, reality is the variable. We have tried to maintain outpatient, continuing-care clinics, with the same students and docents in attendance. Physicians, not only docents, no longer have an interest or an ability in continuing, general medicine care. Even someone as devoted as myself to continuing ambulatory care, under the same physician, must face the reality that few physicians will practice this kind of medicine. I don't condone this change—it is simply a painful truth.

As in all systems, a vocabulary is created by the participants. This annual two month inpatient docent rotation quickly became the "Do-Ro."

It is apparent that one of the critical issues in committing a medical school to admit a student fresh out of high school is the student selection process. It is the moment of success or failure.

During my time in Washington, I had been exposed to a great deal of the logic of administration. HEW, under John Gardner, sought expert advice on possible administrative reorganization.

One of the teachings stayed with me. The speaker stated that an academic unit cannot be run "top-down," but must be administered by the participants.

As with most quotations one likes, it was not the original quality of what he said that attracted me, but the fact that what he said exactly matched what I believed. I knew nothing about the management of an industry, but I did know how different is an academic organization. One can be very authoritative in the military and in the business world, but such does not work in university life.

I recognized that my own authority had a limited time frame. Getting the place launched needed a fairly high-handed autocrat. Getting out of the way quickly once the system was launched was an exercise in fine timing and discretion. At the same time, to leave too soon would cause it all to tumble down.

These thoughts were with me, and I put down on my planning list that I must remain fully responsible for eight years. This turned out about right, I moved myself out of direct administration in the tenth year. It was also clear to me that after taking my hand off the running of the place that I should remain around, if only to influence by my presence. Those following me would be less likely to toss everything out, if they knew I was brooding nearby. At that same time, I assured Mary D. that we would always summer in California and on my 65th birthday, we would head West.

I formed an administrative system for the medical school which gave everyone involved a voice. Such is not easy to do unless there is a firm set of game rules.

In the academic plan that I had set down while in the Library of Medicine, I had defined, very tightly, these administrative units, giving them unusually definitive rules. I used the phrase, "a game without rules is no fun," and that was a homily which all could understand.

The business of a medical school can be divided into three very simple questions: Who gets in? What do you expect them to learn? Who has quality control? These are the basic pieces of an education system, and how to make them very democratic, very free of politics, very free of favoritism, very free of ambiguity, and, hopefully, free of red tape, are all the issues upon which the reputation of the place depends.

These naturally fall under the terms Selection, Curriculum, and Evaluation. These groups were organized immediately and have been effective units ever since.

Knowing we were dealing with unusually young adults, all finding themselves at the same time they were fitting our rules, it was important that the game rules had broad latitude. There had to be built-in ways to handle exceptions. A petition system gave this latitude.

Among the players on Hospital Hill, there were three primary health-care organizations. I felt it was important to give each of them a hand in the new school. The director of Children's Mercy Hospital was Ned Smull, again an old student from Kansas. He took on Evaluation. Western Missouri Mental Health was led by Charles Wilkinson, and he headed Curriculum. The chairman of Surgery at the General Hospital was Andrew McCanse; he became head of the Selection group. Thus, the three primary organizations were involved, but, also, the heads of the Councils, the assistant deans, represented the three primary disciplines: pediatrics, psychiatry, and surgery, a useful balance against the Docents who, in the main, would be internists.

I say "in the main" because in the formative years, when we were trying to define what we intended by the term Docent, a family-medicine physician, a dermatologist, a pathologist, a psychiatrist, and three surgeons filled the role. Later, as the School matured and the new hospital came to life, the logical internal medicine nature of the Docent became reality.

One conviction I had then and do now, is that the Faculty attempts to teach too much. Contesting for curriculum time never eases. Steadily, subject material crowds into the calendar. In business one speaks of "zero-base budget." A wise dean would zero-base his curriculum on a regular cycle. "Curriculum-packing" is a chronic infestation.

A special value, which was planned in at that point, was that these three committees (we called them Councils) would have across-the-board authority. By this, for example, the Council on Curriculum has control over the entire curriculum, and, thus, this major issue of what is taught, was not allowed to become turf to be fought over by the various departments. Such may seem perfectly logical to an outsider, but I could not have put this in place if we were not building a completely new school. I have already described the lost battle at Harvard. The Harvard experience is not an exception.

The method of "running" most American medical schools is simple. The program is four years long; split the four years evenly into two years for teaching the basic sciences and two for the clinical experience. Let the basic scientists divide up their two years and the clinicians their two years. What the Department of Biochemistry teaches, for example, is their business. The whole school has no input. Let the Department of Surgery have three months of the last two years and let them teach what they wish. No one has an oversight.

I would not be honest if I did not identify that, over time, my effort to maintain an oversight group which had real authority over curriculum, was brought down in influence. Through the inevitable changing of people, both on the Council and in the chairmanships, and through the changing of deans, each with a varying concern for the specifics of what was done, there was a gradual reversion to turfdom. We won a little of the battle; time wore down some of the winnings.

My years at Kansas continued having their reward. The Resident at the Wadsworth VA, with whom I had made rounds for three years, was now the head of medical education at the local Baptist Hospital. Ed Twin was exactly what I needed to go into the Aegean stable of old General Hospital, and, with a sense of raw joy and exuberance, carry out the small, large; tidy, bloody; basic, general; personal, impersonal surgery which needed to be done. Ed was canny enough, guileful enough, skillful enough, confident enough, honest enough, compassionate enough, and trusted by me enough, to take on this immense project.

He also had that powerful extra ingredient of maintaining a sense of humor through it all.

When Homer had assured me that they would gladly hand me this "bag of worms," he well knew what had to be done. And with Ed Twin, I had the right man. Even now, 20 years later, with the job done and with Ed passed on, there was no one involved in the whole project who had quite as difficult and, at times, miserable, and at most times, unappreciated task, as Ed Twin.

With Ed inside Old General and with Carl Migliazzo as the Board's representative responsible for hospital operation, I had a powerful pair of warriors.

One of the important chairmen at Kansas had been Leroy Calkins, the head of OB/GYN. I had enjoyed both Roy and his wife, Ginny. During my time in California, he had died. Ginny, a Wellesley graduate, a very intelligent, education-oriented woman, had raised three unusually able children by herself. She was in the administration of the Kansas RMP program. I recruited her.

Ginny is the personification of integrity, and with an important mix of scholar's approach and sensitivity, was exactly the person to control and moderate the selection process. She understood the age group from which our selection came. By understanding them, I mean she had a special ability to see through the 17-year-old unfinished veneer with which they presented themselves for interview, and see clearly the potential.

Essentially, for the first 1,000 students we admitted, Ginny Calkins' opinion was the one that carried weight.

A school's quality is often judged by the equipment it has, the number of books in the library, the grant money, and the publications of the staff. I respect those classic thoughts, but I believe the fundamental unit of measure is the quality of the student brought into the school. Our new medical school had a secret weapon. From the beginning, we attracted very bright, very ambitious young men and women who, very early, knew they wanted to be physicians. Other schools have more of the hardware of education, but we have had an exuberant supply of prime software, the student.

On one occasion, the dean of our somewhat competing medical school in Columbia, Mo., was being challenged as to why his school needed so much of the State budget, yet our school did so very well on national testing and placement of our graduates. His reply was, although not meant to be, a delight. He said, "Well, it isn't fair to compare us. They get much better students than we do!" I am not sure that even now he quite understood what he conveyed. Much of that "flaw" in our school is due to Ginny

Calkins. We are a public, tax-supported school, with a student body comparable to the best private school, a rare combination. The new academic job we were inventing, the Docent, was not one to be filled by the typical research-oriented university medical school professor. The first occupants of this position, in fact, would be defining it, and actually creating the job description.

Our initial need would be for three Docents, and then as the School grew, ultimately, there would be 32 full-time men and women carrying on this critical task. Again, I went back to people I knew from my Kansas days. First, there was an unusually able husband-and-wife team in practice in Kansas City, Kansas. Both of them were native Kansans, that special breed which I knew was unusually honest, tough, and with a sense of mission about education.

On December 7, 1970, I went to their office in Kansas City, Kansas, and gave them the logic of why they should leave their comfortable practice and join me on Hospital Hill.

Perhaps it is the raw physical demands of the high prairie, the vengeful weather with its unpredictable blasts of heat and blizzard, and it may be the high quality of the immigrant stock that peopled the place. But for some reason, Kansans are a good breed. It may even be the result of the selectivity. Essentially, there has been no great movement of immigrants in since the influx of abolitionists around the Civil War, and, later, those who came seeking religious freedom. The selectivity had been concentrated through the decades. Those who could not, or would not, tolerate the emptiness, the wind, the weather, have moved on West. Those who remained were the best of the tough, the stoic, the doers. Kansas had been settled by people with a cause. Marge and Bill Sirridge epitomized that stock.

After Bill Sirridge became a Docent, Docent Number One, he had a memo pad printed with his message, "Dammit. Dewit." He was a true Kansan.

For the third docent, I again went to my deposit account of Kansas former Residents. Bob Mosser had finished his training and opened a private practice in Independence, Missouri. He was a square-chinned, shiningly bald, bundle of mesomorphic energy, a natural team leader, and a wonderful competitor. In fact, all three of the first Docents enjoyed each day if there was a good dose of competition. Bob became the first Docent of the Red Team and from that day forward, sported a bright-red bow tie.

The Sirridges remained with the School for the rest of their careers. I wish Bob had, also, but he had so much spirit of competition, and desire to expand, that we could not contain him. He also was an expert at institutional gossip and could activate rumors at a greater rate than we could trace them. Still, I miss him and wish he had stayed.

Although we did not have a medical school, had no students, had no permission to have them, still we needed to get on with the planning. Ed Twin's predecessor at the directorship of the Old General took on the task of interim dean for the School. This was, of course, Richardson K. Noback. Dick, a Cornell man, had come out to General from Kentucky, where he had worked with Ed Pellegrino in setting up that new school.

The General Hospital Board had given him the job of trying to pull the dying hospital through. I knew he was exhausted and frustrated from that almost futile attempt, and, although I did not yet know him well, I profoundly was struck by the sense of integrity that he projected. I knew this new school of ours, with its absolute new approach to medical education, was going to be the cynosure of many eyes. My judgment told me that our dean should be as traditional, as conservative, as old school, as possible. Yet, he must be willing, with whole heart, to take on the responsibility of administering our new model. The place would need his kind of steadying hand, and for external visitors, coming in to see what kind of a rabid school this new place was, we would be well served by having a traditionalist as dean.

At the same time, I had to have someone in this critical role who saw the flaws in medical education, and who, in his very soul, understood we were making a sincere effort to cause change. In a military sense, Dick was a master of the tactics of an American medical school, charged with applying them to a new strategy. Also, in the military sense, Dick was, and is, a superb example of the dedicated team man, who lives by a code of obligation to authority and orders. Patriotism, loyalty, respect, duty, discipline, sacrifice, are all in his basic makeup. In the more than two decades together, there is not a single incident where I felt he had misled me or deliberately misinformed me. We were a strange match and our relationship never became one of "put your feet up, have a drink" companionship. We have maintained a formal, cordial, mannerly respect for each other.

If I did Dick any one favor, it was in the area of his being a physician. When he and I met, he had been immersed in trying to save old General Hospital. Then in the initial years of the medical school, he was deep in that administrative project. His skills as a physician, skills he had had, were put aside. I saw this, and recognized that it was critical to his future, both in terms of self-respect and usefulness, to get him back into patient care. I take credit for that, but he can take credit for doing it, doing it even when carrying a very heavy load of administration. When his tenure as dean ended, he moved competently and, importantly, happily, back into a life as a clinician. He was the successful founding dean and then, a rare accomplishment, he went on to be the docent role model for the School he had founded.

One of the men with whom I had worked at HEW in Washington was a physician in the Public Health Service. He was the highest-ranking black physician in the Service. His name was Ed Cross. He came with us in August 1970. Ed came from a good quality professional family in Arkansas. He was able to walk that very difficult line between being a white man's black, a black man's black, and not be a whitey. In writing those words, I mean to be complimentary, yet I recognize the risk in making a remark.

Ed asked no favors because of color; he thought in the broad sense about people of all colors. He never sought to deny color nor use it to further himself. At HEW, I had enjoyed his daily projection of joy. When he walked in a room, he brought no troubles; he made the room a happy place. Yet, he was substantial and caring. His commitment to social justice was deep, and he wanted to put his career towards finding solutions.

Ed remained until August 1974, then he went on to Africa as head of the AID program. In leaving, Ed reminded me that he had been with us exactly four years and that is all the time the President of the United States is given, also.

In Kansas City, Ed was my associate provost. He took on much of the work relating to the neighborhood health clinics, which were begun under the Johnson administration. He handled much of the office staff work and, as we moved into bringing in funds from several federal programs, he participated in administering them. These included the Regional Medical Programs, Comprehensive Health Planning, and the Area Health Education Center program. I had had no direct involvement with these latter two programs in Washington, and as they became law, I never quite understood what was their intention. All three programs were classic examples of the policy often followed in government. That is the tactic of throwing money at problems, but avoid the hard decisions which might actually help the problems.

The Regional Medical Program (RMP) was the only one that I had followed all the way through its Capitol Hill life. As I have indicated, the program, as originally intended, had no relationship to what came out as law. Only the name remained the same. I did what every medical administrator in the country did with all three of these programs. I studied them to find out what were the guidelines, submitted a plan that fitted the guidelines, celebrated when we won the grant, and then spent the money with enthusiasm on our real needs. Each of our needs was carefully repackaged to meet the guidelines.

Still, a considerable amount of the money could not be spent this way, and one had to go through an immense number of staff hours and committee sessions, trying to salvage something that remotely would fit the rules. All three programs left essentially no mark on the American health scene. This is too harsh an evaluation, of course. Some programs were excellent; some of the staff that was developed was excellent. In the end, the main reward was in the considerable number of these younger staff people who were kept alive by using these monies. For me, all of these programs were like stones in the river—a means of crossing over.

I was determined to work closely with the physicians and hospitals of Kansas City. I had, through the years of my experience, taught myself that all good medical teaching did not have to be done at the medical school nor by the full-time staff of the medical school. Repeatedly, I had found that the kind of teacher remembered by the graduate as inspirational, was one who came from private practice. Also, the growth in the university medical centers after the WWII had been matched by growth of the community hospitals. Often, in fact, the university medical center had diminished its interest in referral practice, because the staff was playing to the yardstick of research. In community after community, the private hospitals had prospered, and were able to offer their physicians the finest equipment and resources. These hospitals had attracted the best of the new generation of physicians.

This I knew and, therefore, my major task in the first year was to go to every hospital, tell the administrator and physicians what we were doing, and then negotiate a contract to give access of our students to their hospital and staff. This was successful and no hospital asked for money. All of them were cooperative and our undergraduates and Residents had available to them the medical resources of the entire city.

I had a thoughtful helper in these negotiations. Bob Brown had been in the Mayor's Office of Kansas City for a number of years and knew the "chemistry" of the community well. He was a natural politician and a first-class staff person. We worked well together, and had many good moments after our visits out in the community, regaling each other and filling each other in on the undercurrents and backgrounds of the people we had met. Bob would have been an ideal staff man on Capitol Hill.

Other critical staff people were Al Mauro, Larry Hagerson, and Al Pasini. Mauro had also come out of City Hall and knew the fiber and sinew of the town. He helped Homer and Nathan when they first acquired the old hospital from the City, and even managed the place for awhile. He was talented and took on increasingly larger projects. When we finally had all the money in place for the new hospital, he had the task of working with Alex Bacci, our architect, and Carl Migliazzo, representing the hospital Board. Of course, there was good-natured ribbing about the fact that the largest amount of money we had was in the hands of three men, all with their name ending in a vowel. We spoke of them, with some caution, as "our Mafia."

Al continued to grow and now has become a prominent community businessman and a civic activist.

Hagerson wore several hats for us, and as each of the federal programs came into life, he moved among them, helping to interpret their rules and apply their money. Eventually, he headed up the Academy of Health Professions. He left our arena, shortly thereafter.

Al Pasini was the youngest of the group, and because of my continuing activity in the American College of Cardiology, he staffed those areas for me. We were producing and mailing the audiotape to several hundred physicians, putting on the course twice a year in Rancho Santa Fe, and several times organized cardiac postgraduate courses in Kansas City. Al was the link to the College, and was back and forth to Washington, to Heart House. Another name ending in a vowel.

In addition to the hospitals of Kansas City, I was well aware of the importance of the Kansas City Southwest Clinical Society to private physicians. The Clinical Society had been active for decades, going back to the early days when there were few places for physicians to update their knowledge. It was, and is, one of the oldest societies dedicated to the practicing physician's continuing education in the United States.

I had worked with them in my years at Kansas but, there, had been in direct competition with them. Now, with this new medical school, I was determined to not compete with them, but let them be the postgraduate arm of the new school. I had two allegiances which made this possible. The Society's very capable executive secretary, Alta Bingham, saw immediately that such an arrangement would be to everyone's advantage, and Dr. J. Harold Morris, "Jay," a private practitioner who was active in the Society, had been a student and Resident in Medicine at Kansas. The two of them agreed to be the new medical school's postgraduate arm.

As mentioned earlier, Jay's very able wife, Mary Ann, was the administrator for my course at Rancho Santa Fe. One of the interesting efforts the Morrises organized for a number of years were "Long Weekends," programs that they planned mutually and which were for the physician and spouse.

Jay Morris increasingly was interested in the life and times of the internist and later became Governor of the American College of Physicians for Missouri. Then, as a distinct recognition of his work, he came on the national Board of Trustees of the College.

There was still one more bit of reaching back to the Kansas

days. One of the visiting staff men in those earlier years, a very good friend of Mahlon Delp, was Max Berry.

Max was an internist with a thriving practice. He was also a considerable activist in internal medicine politics, and for years was heavily involved with the American College of Physicians and the Society of Internists. Not only was he a maximum talent in terms of political medical "savvy," but he was a great story teller, a witty public speaker, and a prototype of what I have commented on before, the Kansan. Max was from the Flint Hills, and not only knew every flint rock there, but knew every doctor in Kansas. Equally, he knew every internist in the country who was involved in organizational medicine.

Earlier I commented that one area that I wanted to change was to end the isolation of the internal medicine Residents at our own charity hospital. We were able there to give them an exposure to the problems that come to a large-city charity hospital. But such an exposure is only a part of medicine, and I wanted to get them, also, into the very good, private community hospitals.

Max and I wanted to form a consortium of all the hospitals and have the entire community of Kansas City share the program. This idea sounds logical and desirable, but there are not only the local medical politics that get in the way, but the national accrediting bodies are resistant to such a shared endeavor. (That has now begun to change, 20 years later.) Max was the ideal person for selling and leading this program, and he did just that. More than 20 years ago, we launched such a consortium, just at the time we opened the medical school. Larry Hagerson became the staff man, and to manage the program at a neutral place, we formed an Academy of Health Professions. For these programs we used well some of the Area Health Education Center money.

I leave an inadequate portrait of a substantial man with these too few remarks about Max Berry. He was one of those men who, by the simple act of losing their hair when about age 30, never pass through the natural aging process. He just never grew older. His hair never grayed, it never thinned. His shining head was eternal. His square shoulders, square jaw, quick grin, a sideways look, and a salty, witty remark are the same in 1991 as they were in 1950.

He developed an interest in wild flowers and in photographing wild flowers. Not just any wild flower, not any giant Kansas sunflower; instead, he made himself into an authority on the miniature flowers of the wild, especially of the prairie. He mastered their names, their locations, and how to get down on his stomach and catch their color and life on film. This was more than a hobby. He became an encyclopedia, had exhibits, and wrote about the subject. My home has three of his photographs and I treasure them.

As I have commented, Max is very witty. Several years ago, he spoke on aging, and, in summary, commented on himself. He said, "Well, with age everything doesn't work the way it used to, and what works, hurts." I have now moved into that age group; Max's wisdom is profound.

With many of these things we did, time dealt with them differently. Some prospered and lasted, some gradually evolved and changed, not only because the cast of actors changed, but because the time and need changed.

The lesson is that change is continuous; by definition, it must be. The society in which one works is in motion. What we did in Kansas City then, fitted the needs of the community. This year, and next year, and on, the needs change and the solutions change.

The permanence of something as different as what we did in Kansas City depends not only on the question of whether it was right or even if it was well done. Painfully, it also depends upon the vigor with which its survival is defended by those who later inherit it.

We planned, we did it, it worked. But unless those who come later and who are a part of it, the Administration, and above all, the Graduates, remain vigilant and defensive, the conservative forces of the Establishment, plus the natural academic infighting of a university, will bite off pieces until it is no longer recognizable.

There were others who were there at the very beginning of the School. An area in which we put major emphasis was the whole arena of medical illustration, art, publications, slide making, television, and audiotapes, all those techniques that are basic to teaching and communication but somehow get lost in a medical center.

For the head of this program, we found James Soward. Jim is

still the head of this area, which we chose to call the Office of Educational Resources. Jim is a trained journalist and writes and thinks creatively. He has mastered the technique of combining sound and multiple-screen images into major productions. Much of what has characterized this new medical school has been the very high standards of the audiovisual staff, all set by Soward.

We were also fortunate in finding, at the beginning, Betty Steinman, artist, illustrator, and purveyor of taste in all areas of publication. Betty was with us for the rest of her career, and she was another one of those especially cheerful people who bring to work every day a smile, a cheerfulness, and make being near them a pleasure. I write this thoughtfully. All of us can cite the colleague whose daily conduct swings from euphoria to a dark pall, pulling down on everyone. A daily steadiness of behavior, a constant pleasantness, an evenness, is not only a blessing to a marriage, but a godsend in an office.

With the awareness that we were taking on an experiment in medical education, I was interested in creating a unit within the medical school that would analyze and publish data about the experiment. I had been at Kansas when the original research had been done for *Boys in White* by Becker of the University of Chicago group under Dr. Hughes. It was this kind of long-term look I hoped to launch for our school. Louise Arnold, social scientist, began this work early for us. Later she was joined by Virginia Calkins. Much of the published analyses of the UMKC effort has been done by them. They were helped by Lee Willoughby, who supplied computer knowledge. Lee also was involved in the computer-driven testing system. This was the basis of the Quarterly Profile Examination (QPE).

In addition to finding support from RMP, CHP, and AHEC, we were successful in getting funds from the Robert Wood Johnson, Kellogg, and Commonwealth foundations. These all were useful and served to bridge the continuing low order of funding from the University.

The two largest dollar battles were in obtaining money for the medical school building and adding money to the County bond issue for the new hospital. For the hospital, we needed money to build the extra space that medical student teaching would require: conference rooms, pathology space, desk space in the nurses' stations, etc.

For the medical school building, we needed all the money. The State provided the planning money for "planning," but nothing for a building. We had to find the money for the actual building. As I have said, we got the last national grant under the existing legislation. With the federal money, we were able to go back to the State and get some money.

The medical school's place of birth was an office on the third floor, in the northwest corner of the campus administration building, Scofield Hall. The medical school at that time consisted of my office, one file cabinet, and a secretary. For the first half year, I had brought my secretary from California. This was useful because she knew all the cardiology friends with whom I corresponded, knew medical terminology, knew how to help in the planning for the courses at Rancho Santa Fe, and understood the logistics behind the monthly tape.

As the planning for the medical school actually began to happen, Jan Campbell took over as secretary and was with me a number of years. I mention Jan because she was one of those special experiences which occur in an academic life. From the beginning, she was obviously underused as a secretary. She was going to college but could not get her head above water enough to get free of the typewriter. I get ahead of my story a bit, but within a short time after the opening of the medical school, she applied for admission, was admitted, and is now a successful psychiatrist and the principal investigator for a large research program.

By my second year in Kansas City, we were well on our way with the planning. We took a floor in an office building at the corner of Armour and Gillham, and days, weeks, months went into the planning of the two buildings: the hospital and the school. By now we were a large group, with Dick Noback, Al Mauro, Bob Brown, Ed Twin, Carl Migliazzo, Max Berry, and the large number of architects, leaning over drawings, making the brick and mortar plans.

Twin and I were also very involved in trying to clear out the long-entrenched factions at the Old General. These issues were diverse and often obscured from view.

Systems of patronage, of sharing the spoils, kickbacks, and areas of special privilege were all about. Some of the issues were small, even trivial. But they were issues. For example, the house-officer quarters, used by the Residents on call, had a beer-dispensing machine. The beer machine went. A small issue, but one which brought Ed Twin into a confrontation with a rebellious housestaff.

The housestaff was especially hostile because the message bruited about the corridors of the old hospital was that this new relationship with a medical school was going to ruin a longstanding tradition of the hospital. This tradition was the absolute freedom of the housestaff in terms of patient-care decisions. This independence had long been considered one of the special merits of the training program at the old hospital. That was not the end of the problems; Ed and I had several sit-downs in our offices by inflamed house officers.

Not all problems were with the Residents. There were several longtime department heads who felt threatened by the idea that the hospital was to become a university teaching hospital. Ed took these on, one by one.

He found that the budget included a $40,000-a-year bonus to the Residents in Orthopedics for their services in reading the X-rays relating to fractures. No one could find when this rule had entered the books of the institution. It was simply accepted as reality. Stopping this caused another showdown.

From the outpatient clinic, to the laundry, to the kitchen, to purchasing, Ed and his broom went about setting the new standards that needed to be in place before we moved across the street to the new hospital. The superb public image the new hospital, the Truman Medical Center, has enjoyed, is to a great extent the result of the patient-care policies set in motion by Ed Twin.

At the end of the second year, we found money to remodel the old Research Hospital nurses' home. This handsome old building had fallen into our hands through one of those unplanned opportunities that render careful planning immediately obsolete. With the problems already before us, the last thing needed was more old real estate.

In its heyday, Hospital Hill had been the City's gathering place for health facilities. Not only had the General Hospital been there, in several editions, since the 19th century, but also two of the city's largest nursing schools, one or more proprietary medical schools, and a very substantial community hospital. This hospital had been built at the high tide of the German migration to the region and carried the name The German Hospital.

World War I made that name unattractive and a new name appeared over the door: Research Hospital. This hospital continued to thrive until the middle of the present century. Then the familiar urban flight and freeway-born suburbs took away the people served by the hospital. Their board bought new land in the right place, rebuilt, and have enjoyed a renaissance since. This rebuilding was the reason we suddenly acquired a complete hospital and nurses home. They were anxious to get rid of the old facilities and we did not want it, therefore the sale price was better than a bargain. They wanted $2 million dollars. Homer and Nate offered them $800,000, with but $10,000 down. They accepted with alacrity. Our new Board now had a nurses' home—a very large, multiple-storied, brick building, with more than a hundred rooms, and the several-hundred-bed hospital building, a bargain to be respected. With the mortgage in hand, it was used as security to get the land for Children's Mercy Hospital. The corporate raiders of the 1980's could have taken lessons.

Later, when this hospital building was razed, we took the name "Research Hospital" down from above the hospital entrance. There, carved in stone, was: "The German Hospital." We were seeing a part of the area's history.

We agreed to go ahead and get the School opened with a handful of students, before the school and new hospital were built. I kept hammering a theme: "The planning is the doing, the doing is the planning." Let us get on with what we are trying to do right now, with Docent teams in old Research Hospital, and use this old nurses' home as the new medical school.

Our bargain is made even more apparent if we look into the future. We used the nurses' home for several years to house our medical school; then it became the University of Missouri-Kansas City School of Nursing. It is still in use.

Where the old hospital stood, we now have an elegant modern

eye institute. The new Truman Medical Center sits on land that
had been the site of the heating plant for Research Hospital. Our
unsought-for acquisition has served well. We even used the property on occasion, as collateral to borrow money.

My sense of timing told me that getting a medical school had
been an issue so long in Kansas City, and the resistances were still
so strong in many areas in the University, that the wisest thing to
do was to make the School a reality. Get it launched, and then
those who were opposed would have lost a critical battle. It
seemed to me that so many years had gone into the fight, so many
near failures, that now what everyone needed was a real, live medical student. That would be a bit of reality that said everything.

Almost as a messenger of goodwill, a lawyer telephoned one
day to tell me that a client of his had just passed away, and in the
will, written years before, it stated that he was leaving his money
to be used, "if a medical school ever did come to Hospital Hill."
This benefactor had made this commitment almost 20 years earlier, and thus nothing we had done, or any of the present publicity
and effort had caused him to make this gift. It was just one of
those acts of luck, of chance, of fate.

Carved above the entrance to General Hospital was a quotation
from Shakespeare's *Merchant of Venice*, "The quality of mercy is
not strain'd / it droppeth as the gentle rain from heaven / upon
the place beneath: it is twice blessed / it blesseth him that gives
and him that takes."

When we first took over responsibility for the reorganization of
the hospital, the "t" had fallen from the marquee and it read: "...
and him that akes." Undoubtedly, this was an effective version,
but with this first gift, we repaired Shakespeare.

Our first benefactor was named Clear. With his gift, we put the
"t" back on Shakespeare's words, and then we remodeled the
area that had for decades been used for the student nurses and
their graduation capping ceremony. We made the area into the
handsome, well-used Clear Auditorium. We never learned why
this man had made this gift; there was no trace of a connection to
medicine or medical schools. No relative ever appeared. It was
just "one of those things."

We found more money and thoroughly remodeled the nurses'

home. There were individual offices for each medical student, just as there would be in the ultimate building. All the Councils were housed. Jim Soward's Office of Educational Resources moved in. There was space for Dean Noback and myself. The old building featured a large entrance lobby with stained glass, skylights, and a handsome fountain. We added paint, large numbers of green plants, air conditioning, modern plumbing, created a functioning fountain, and, suddenly, we had a very handsome building. It was more than handsome; it had charm and grace.

A major part of our education plan was to have the student earn both a bachelor of arts degree and medical degree in a six-calendar-year period. Now we were at a point where it was critical to meet with the College of Arts and Sciences, and see how this intertwined, shared curriculum could be accomplished.

You could ask: Why we did not do this at once; it was such a large piece of the plan, how could you go ahead without knowing if such a double curriculum could be packaged?

My approach was a calculated gamble. I reasoned that if I waited until we had legislative backing, had Curator backing, had found a large amount of financial support and the media were saying positive things, that my lever under the Arts and Sciences faculty might be greater. Greater than what? Well, every instinct I had, and all the signals, made it very clear that if I had gone to the Arts and Sciences faculty at the beginning, as tidy theory of administration would have said to do, the Arts and Sciences faculty would have spun a maze of committees, the issues would have drug on for years, and the end result would not have been livable. I played chess and saved the critical move until the board was on my side.

Luck held. The dean of Arts and Sciences, Ed Westerman, was close enough to retirement that the last thing he wanted was an internecine battle; with a touch of real wisdom, he delegated the question to one man, not a committee. Luck held and expanded.

The man he chose was a young biologist in his 30's who immediately saw the project as something to be enjoyed, not fought. This was Henry A. Mitchell, whose initials suggest his mother either had a peculiar but good sense of humor—or was unaware of acronyms. Henry is a twin and he and his twin are both bat specialists. I had never met a bat authority before.

Dean Westerman's office was in the old home that housed University administration. As is the fate of great homes which have become elephants and end up as gifts to a university, this superb building had been cribbed, chopped, and partitioned. The dean's segment of the original splendid library included the huge hearth with a limestone mantel. If one entered the office briskly, one almost entered the fireplace.

As I talked with him and noted how this formerly grand old home had been diminished into rabbit warrens of space, and the former elegance of the dining room was now a barricaded secretarial pool, it was apparent that the millions of dollars we were spending on Hospital Hill were not likely to be celebrated here.

As the dean and I talked, Henry stood in front of the fireplace, with an expression and movements I have come to enjoy. He stands very upright, dressed quite carefully (with a degree of color blindness); tilts his head from side to side; lifts the knot on his tie; and purses his lips. He looks like a bird who has delivered an exceptional egg and is very proud of the effort. This expression and movements usually precede a witticism, one that is uniquely inappropriate to the occasion. Often, the remark will relate to a daughter, a grandchild, or his Chihuahua, FiFi.

On this particular day, with the Dean and I handling each other very gingerly, and my awareness that the medical education plan depended on a successful outcome of this negotiation, Ed said, "Henry Mitchell will work with you; he will do his best." Henry tweaked his tie, puckered his lips, tilted his head right, left, and said, "Have you noticed how lovely the crocuses are this year?"

Henry took on the project and he was a jewel. No one else could have handled the problem. He knew how to read the University catalogue covering matriculation, something no one knows how to do. Catalogues are not written to be informative; they were conceived as an academic impediment. Henry read through and between the various rules, requirements, and modifying clauses. He knew how to not only interpret the stated rules, but he knew where the exceptions and the alternative routes were hidden. Within a very few days, he had laid out a large chart, defining logically, clearly, and exactly what we needed.

Henry led us through the labyrinth and defined how to get the course content we needed; how to make the calendars of the two schools fit; how to give the student reasonable latitude of course content; and end up with a Liberal Arts degree on the same day he (or she, of course) received the medical degree.

We had found a treasure in HAM.

All of these efforts were important, but none of these activities had any future if we did not work our way through the national agencies that have the final control over medical education. Campus approval, University approval, and State legislative approval are giant stepping stones that only bring you so far. One finally must earn national blessing.

These imprimaturs came in all sizes. They fitted so closely that it was difficult to find an opening. To get the money from the federal government to add to the County bond money to make the hospital suitable for teaching, one had to have evidence that you had money for the medical-school building. To get the federal approval for the money for the medical school, you had to have evidence you had permission to have medical students and award a degree. To get evidence you had this approval, you had to have an interim approval from a national accrediting body, charged with approving new medical schools. BUT to get that approval, you had to have evidence that you had—yes—the money to get the teaching hospital, money to build the medical school, etc.

Each of the steps required a national site-visit team to come to Kansas City for several days, and, often unpleasantly, attack the evidence that one had the claimed pieces. I use the phrase "attack the evidence" because each such visit opened up the opportunity for any local malcontent to ventilate. It was good to have Dean Westerman's endorsement, but when the site-visit teams came, they shook hands with the dean and then penetrated into the faculty. Suddenly, a professor of psychology had his moment to pour out his long lament and hostility about this new medical school, and why its existence would be destructive to his budget. Or the professor of chemistry would declare that there was no way he could teach medical students on his budget.

These were not minor disturbances. Each of the site-visit teams had basic-science members, and their unwritten agenda was to

document that the academic plan we were developing was flawed.
The particular flaw was not important. Any area of discontent, faculty unhappiness, or other logical problem in any area was
earnestly sought out. The fact that there certainly was faculty unhappiness about the coming of a medical school, I have already
described. Dick Noback, Ed Cross, and all of us who were committed to getting the medical school up and running became
skilled at recognizing these "hot spots" and we all worked as fire-
men, trying to cool the fires. Dick and I developed a quickened
means of expressing these sudden new problems. We referred to
them as "the sky is falling syndrome."

With us as staff, we had two examples of the University's bureaucracy who were special. Special in the sense that they were
the exception. From the University business office, I brought Bill
Berry to run my own books. This was not a simple matter of line-
item detail. We had so many and such varied sources of revenue,
so many hats to keep them under, and so many partnerships that
I personally never knew exactly how we were staying afloat. I had
asked Bill Berry absolutely to be scrupulous and at no point were
we to have any shady finances. His job was to protect and keep us
honest. He did that completely.

From Columbia, we brought Larry Harkness from the University's personnel department. He became the manager of the
dean's office, and, as with Bill Berry, Larry provided us a way to
read the University fine print, to make the red tape work for us,
and, as with Berry, to keep us honest. These two men moved on
to much bigger jobs. Perhaps we helped train them, but it is certain that they were one of the main reasons, along with Henry
Mitchell, that we were able to survive and thrive within an inherently hostile University system.

We had negotiated contracts with all of the hospitals, and had
arrangements for our students to have access to their clinics and
wards. But when the site-visit teams came, they thanked the hospital administrator for his time, and went directly to individual
physicians. Their opinions about this new school were sought.
The physician, a product of an eight-year school, often a graduate
of Kansas or Missouri, enjoyed his opportunity to lance this irritating boil which claimed it would graduate a comparable physi-

cian in six years—and without dissecting a cadaver. Each visit opened up a pathway for all contrarians to have their moment.

The members of the site-visit teams were chosen from the basic sciences and clinical fields. From the beginning, one could say "from the opening gun," the clinicians were on our side. Almost all of them knew me from my work in cardiology, and they were cordial, respectful, and often, old friends. The basic-science site visitors entered Kansas City with all guns blazing. This mad cardiologist was not even going to have departments of basic science? He claimed that he was in some way going to stop four years of premed and its precious physics, comparative anatomy, dogfish sharks, turtle-pithing, and dog experiments? There was to be no cadaver dissection? And the great blocks of basic-science teaching which occupied the first two full years of medical school would now be spread out over a six-year period? Heresy! Light the stake!

These show-and-tell visits went on and on. Dick Noback was superb in his gathering of the voluminous paper data needed. Each visit had its emergency: some fire that needed to be put out, some dike leak to be spiked, some new piece of the sky falling, some new source of resistance. Dick and I learned to laugh. Our bouquet of problems was only matched by the size of the vase. We fitted it all in.

Each approval was gained, each precious piece of paper came, but the time it took was spreading us out and our intended opening of the School in the fall of 1970 could not be met. We still did not have the interim certificate of approval for a medical school by the national accrediting body. We had done the work; the site visits had been made; we had the verbal assurances. However, the actual meeting that would give us a green light was to be delayed by several months.

This delay, interpreted as evidence of impending failure, was manna for the balky and negative, and there was no way to quiet the unrest except by action.

Equally, those who had been assembled to open the School and were excited about it, were similar to a team that had reached a level of readiness, and then—there was no game. It was apparent that we needed some positive action.

We had an agreement prepared that a parent and student could sign. It was an "understanding." The understanding was that the student was admitted to the University of Missouri-Kansas City at the first-year level, would be taught the courses required by the liberal-arts and medical-school curriculums, would be given the earned credits—and if there was a school approved the next year—they would be one year on the way. If the approval was denied, the University had no liability.

Obviously, such an idea would not be valid in any usual circumstance. The circumstances were not usual. The local, State, and all-University support was built on quicksand. A year's delay would expose every vulnerability. Getting all the faculty to share the teaching and caring for real, live medical students was the needed therapy. We chose 18 "interim" medical students; they signed the agreement, and we got under way. It was similar to jumping from a plane at 10,000 feet, with the promise a parachute would be handed to you at 5,000 feet.

When classes began on the last day of August, 1970, we had no approval to run a medical school but we had 18 candidates in the system. Ralph Hall at St. Luke's Hospital and Nate Winer at Menorah Hospital were the first Year-One Docents.

Chapter Nineteen

WE WHO WERE THERE AT the founding of the School enjoy a certain calm repose, similar to a small fleet of ships that have come through untold storms and finally slipped behind the breakwater. All who came after mid-1971 were participants in the life of the School; and many made major contributions. They enjoyed a few of the rain clouds, but the tornado days were before mid-1971.

However, I refer here to those who did the actual planning, fighting, fund-getting, getting-it-to-happen. Those who were here in 1969 and 1970 were, as Ed Twin expressed vividly, "up to our hips in the swamp with the alligators, and no time to play the violin."

What makes those years different? What kind of work goes on in the planning stage? This story is about a medical school and its teaching hospital. Similar energy and tactics would go into the launching of a large business enterprise, I assume. The similarity would be considerable if there was also a genuine shortage of money and a considerable resistance to the whole effort.

Perhaps a medical school and hospital are different. As you look through the following list, ask yourself what other enterprises would have a similar variety of partners.

In reading the following tabulation, visualize the man-hours and coordination. And think of the amount of secretarial talent involved—in the days before the word processor.

Here is the calendar for 1970.

1970

January - Conferences with all deans and all department head chairmen, UMKC, individually, approximately 40 meetings, to discuss School of Medicine education plan and its relationship to ongoing academic programs.

January 13 - Visit by Hospital Hill team to University of Vermont to study Problem Oriented Medical Record.

January 22-23 - Site visit to Hospital Hill of the Division of Health Manpower, Department of HEW, to review application for funds to replace hospital.

February - Visit to each hospital administrator and neighborhood health clinic of entire Kansas City Metropolitan area, to negotiate individual contracts for medical student access to their facilities. This included contracting 10 sites for the Year-One Docent Teams and for the Year-One summer hospital employment.

February 2-3 - Visit by Hospital Hill team to Columbia, Md. to study medical care outreach plans of Johns Hopkins University.

February 11 - First planning meeting of the Interim Council on Curriculum.

February 12-18 - Visit to Washington, D.C. for conference with all Regional Medical Programs' administrative staffs.

March 1 - National Advisory Council on Education for the Health Professions, Department of HEW, recommends approval of funding for the medical school building and the teaching hospital.

March 1 - Formal dedication of the School of Dentistry.

March 2 - Health Resources Institute is incorporated.

March 25 - Initial meeting of Advisory Committee to study management of the Department of Internal Medicine at General Hospital and how to prepare for the Docent Teams.

April 28-29 - Site visit to Hospital Hill by representatives of Lister Hill National Center for Biomedical Communication, to consider new-medical-school hook-up to national medical computer communication.

April 28 - Full-page ad in *The Kansas City Star* signed by 85 health organizations urging support of the Medical School by the State Legislature.

May 1 - Cooperation agreement entered into between Jackson County, Kansas City, Missouri, and General Hospital Board, agreeing to construction and operation of new teaching hospital.

June 18-20 - Visit by Hospital Hill team to Los Angeles to study Watts Neighborhood Health Center.

June 23 - Governor Hearnes signs appropriation bill for $4,026,100 as State's share of medical school building.

June 26 - Initial meeting of Twin Committee to plan for initiation of "Docent Team-Comprehensive Care Unit."

June 27 - Proposal for areawide continuing medical education program approved by RMP.

July 1 - First Docent Unit formed at General Hospital.

July 1 - Jackson County Medical Society approves concept of areawide continuing medical education program.

July 1 - Hospital Hill contracts with Metropolitan Area Council of Governments and Department. HEW to coordinate care program of Hospital Hill institutions and neighborhood health centers.

July 1 - Regional Medical Programs makes $100,000 grant to Wayne Minor Neighborhood Health Center for treatment of high blood pressure.

July 17 - Twin Committee recommends implementing continuing care clinics as part of Docent Teams.

July 28 - Kansas City Southwest Clinical Society agrees to be the continuing medical education arm of the Medical School.

August 12 - Initial meeting of Communitywide Residency in Internal Medicine Committee.

August 15 - Edward Cross appointed vice provost.

August 18 - Department of HEW approves federal funding of $8,856,643 for new medical school building.

August 26 - A Peer Review proposal submitted by RMP to Missouri State Medical Association.

September 1 - Edward Twin appointed executive director of General Hospital.

September 4 - Sen. Thomas Eagleton, chairman of Senate Subcommittee of Health, holds congressional hearing on Hospital Hill.

September 8 - Application submitted to Carnegie Foundation for funding of coordinating education and care programs.

September 14 - Visit to Kellogg Foundation by Hospital Hill

team requesting funding for continuing education.

September 14 - Eighteen students begin training as Year Ones. Ultimately this was the charter class of 1976, but they were "provisional students" at this time.

September 23-24 - Dr. Martin Cummings, Librarian, National Library Medicine, visits Hospital Hill to discuss medical school library resources.

September 26 - Curators formally accept federal grant for construction of medical school.

October 1 - Communitywide Residency in Medicine concept formally submitted to AMA Residency Review Committee.

October 8 - Application from Hospital Hill submitted to HEW for institutional grant for teaching and training.

October 26 - Jackson County Medical Society endorses concept of Academy of Health Professions.

November 2 - The Executive Director of General Hospital decentralizes the outpatient service and assigns outpatient responsibilities to each individual 20-bed general-medicine unit.

November 2 - Problem Oriented Medical Record formally installed at General Hospital.

November 7 - Kansas City Association of Trusts and Foundations and the Trustees of the University of Kansas City each pledge $100,000 to underwrite the first two years of the curriculum.

November 16 - Visit by Hospital Hill team to University of Colorado to view their multimedia learning center.

November 24 - Visit by Hospital Hill team to Massachusetts General Hospital to view their two-way television network.

December 3 - Joint System Committee installed to coordinate procedures of hospitalization for neighborhood health center patients at the General Hospital.

December 17 - Children's Mercy Hospital moves into its new building on Hospital Hill.

December 29 - Curators approve final location of medical school building.

The calendar for 1971 has 105 items of similarly complicated nature listed. If we were not busy, we thought we were.

In early March 1971, another site-visit team came from the Liaison Committee and gave "provisional accreditation of the UMKC School of Medicine." This was the official green light. We were a School of Medicine. This was the delayed approval that had led to our 18 "provisional students" in the fall of 1970.

In that same month, the Missouri State Legislature authorized an appropriation of $65,000 so this new medical school could begin employing staff. I have always treasured this as the ultimate example of legislative enthusiasm.

Even if it was token support, it was the commitment needed and on April 1, Dick Noback was finally officially designated Dean. That same month we moved our planning group from 301 East Armour Boulevard to the old nurses' home, now the Health Sciences Building.

On May 27, 1971, we began a series of "countdown" meetings. In these sessions, we worked our way through the entire academic plan. These were careful, personal sessions in which I attempted to explain in detail why and what we were trying to do in this new school. We all knew we were beginning something new, different, exciting, and these sessions were taped. If anyone would ever want to know what I personally thought was the academic plan of this medical school, those tapes are the witness.

On June 23, the Curators authorized the expenditure of $610,000 as part of the new school's first-year budget. This was the first "serious" money the University had committed to faculty and staff.

On June 28, we held an "appreciation" luncheon for 120 State legislators, County and City officials, and civic leaders to express our thanks for their support.

A useful question is to ask what elected officials, i.e., what politicians, were important in the success of the Hospital Hill endeavor? Early, when the bonds for the new hospital were the critical issue, the Jackson County administration, especially Charles Curry and Charles Wheeler, were solid backers. Later, when the County administration was reorganized, Harry Jonas, as the County executive, was a substantial help. The Lieutenant Governor of the state, Bill Morris, was our main Jefferson City ally. Elected officials at the State legislature, who carried our message included Lucky Cantrell, Alex Presta, Norman Merrill, Bill Webster and especially Don Manford. Tom Eagleton, as U.S. Senator, opened doors in Washington.

Kansas City's mayor, Ilus Davis, was a strong support. Roe Bartle, of course, was critical for it was under his mayorship that the City agreed to give the hospital management to a lay board. Hugh Dywer was the city health officer under Bartle and his backing was crucial at that early time.

Unelected, but from the political process, was the HEW head for the region, Jim Doarn. He was sympathetic to our plans and later, upon retirement, joined us in administering federal grants. At City Hall, the city managers, John Taylor and Bob Kipp, were cautious but, on balance, helpful.

A loyal friend at City Hall, someone who knows the obscure paths for getting from here to there, is always an essential need. Jim Threatt was this man. Jim is a wise, sensitive man and has the special ability to detach himself from the scene and see it in a reasoned perspective.

At a very delicate point in the whole effort, we came down to where we had no real State of Missouri dollar-support but we were able to construct a letter, signed by the important member of the State legislature, hinting, suggesting, very murkily, that the State did intend to fund us at some point. Nathan Stark took this gem of ambiguity to Washington, to HEW. Fate's well-known fickle finger was with us.

The HEW administration, under Robert Finch and John Veneman, would not accept this letter as adequate evidence of Missouri State backing. Therefore they would not release federal funds to us. As Nathan was walking down the hall, rejected, dejected, he glanced into a room. A gray-haired man was sitting at a desk filling out a form, his back to the door. Nathan recognized the bristly, burr haircut. It was Vernon Wilson, who was being recruited, with vigor, by HEW to take over a major administration post. Nathan and Vernon sat down together, rewrote the official letter, undoubtedly improving the state senator's grammar and sense of commitment. They got it "signed" immediately. Nathan returned down the hall and the new letter brought the release of several missing millions. That moment was "watershed."

We were able to rest the stress of those who had come at Year One in 1970, gambling their futures with us. They were now in an official medical school. We announced we were ready to accept applications for the fall of 1971. With the letter from the Liaison Committee of the American Medical Association and the Association of American Medical Colleges, we were an official, legal, real medical school. All the other efforts were but prelude. All would have been unrequited, if we did not have that one piece of paper.

Were there things that should have been done differently? Were there shortcuts we did not try? Had we invented red tape and bureaucracy and impeded our own efforts?

Quickly, my answer is no.

Understanding a society begins with understanding its history. What we had done in founding a medical school could only be done by knowing the antecedents: the kind of people who founded the State; the kind of legislators they elect; the rural suspicion of the cities; the racial facts; the cities unable to balance the rural political strength because the largest two cities of the State, St. Louis and Kansas City, are logically incompatible.

One city is very old, antedating the country itself, with solid, generation-old wealth, with major traditions of higher education, with strong corporate headquarters, a city whose thinking and self-image is towards the eastern United States.

The other city: parvenu, one-generation money, regional offices, not corporate, a city built precisely on the border of Kansas, and a city whose resources, both money and brains, live in Kansas, vote in Kansas, and school their children there, a city that belongs to Kansas, as is so well said in its very name. A city looking West.

The dissimilarities of the two cities are so many that infrequently can they find a common issue; it requires a common issue to coordinate their strength at the State capital. A new medical school for Kansas City? What does this mean for our new University of Missouri-St. Louis? What buildings are we speaking of? Because buildings mean work, work for unions, unions that can bring their representatives from the two cities to Jefferson City and control the attention of the legislators.

Decades earlier when the power structure of Kansas City want-

ed a medical school, they got one. It was 100 yards into Kansas—
the University of Kansas School of Medicine.

When Missourians wanted a medical school, they put it at their
state university, dead center in the center of the State, remote
from any source of patients. It was so remote from patients that
the students could have only two years of their studies there, and
then left to find hospital training.

In 1905, Kansas City built an impressive General Hospital, a
logical learning place for medical students; in 1907, intense lobbying to move the State's medical school to Kansas City failed. In
the 1950's, the isolated nature of the mid-state school was apparent; consultants advised putting the clinical years in Kansas City.
The rural reality of the system perversely expressed itself and
began a massive hospital-building program in Columbia. To this
day, the State's money goes generously to expand those hospital
resources, pay their deficits, even though there still are no adequate patient resources.

No, I don't think we missed any shortcuts, nor, as they say at
the casino, "made our number the hard way." Kansas City, Missouri finally got a medical school because of the unusual group-
ing of a physician in the top administration of the University, Vernon Wilson; a civic-minded lawyer with freedom to work in the
health field, Nathan Stark; the rare civic and social-science skills
of a representative of local foundations, Homer Wadsworth; and a
physician, myself, who had a backlog of goodwill from a large
number of physicians and former patients.

There was another reservoir of goodwill. I have probably spoken too harshly about the reputation of the old Kansas City General Hospital. There was not a great fondness for the hospital
among the poor and especially among the blacks. Decades of division into Hospital No. 1 for whites and Hospital No. 2 for blacks
had left bad memories. Even if this policy was finally rectified.

The goodwill and loyalty was among those who had been Residents at the old hospital, especially in surgery. This was real loyalty, different from that seen in men trained at some well-known
citadel or by a famous chief. These men (all were men), treasured
the difficulty of the training, the difficulty of working in an institution always in financial crisis, and the complex social issues sur-

rounding every patient. I knew several of these men well. They had an endless series of "war stories" about life in the trenches of Old General. They cared about the place and they were a source of support.

When Truman Medical Center and the Medical School were reality, the first endowed chair came from Dr. Ralph Coffey. He had been one of the volunteer surgical chiefs at the old hospital. Dr. Coffey was one of the original investors in the pharmaceutical firm Marion Laboratories, and when it went on to make millions, his stock did the same for him. One of our group, Ray Snider, was a surgery Resident under Dr. Coffey in the old place. Under Ray's guidance, Dr. Coffey gave our first endowed chair—in surgery, of course. Our second chair was also in a surgical field. This gift, the Rex Diveley Chair in Orthopedic Surgery, was skillfully brought into being by its first recipient, Dr. James Hamilton. Rex Diveley was a prominent local orthopedist.

In the listing of activities above, there appear the names of two organizations that have not survived. One of these was the Health Resources Institute. The purpose of HRI was to give us a vehicle for what today has become the HMO's, the Health Maintenance Organizations. In 1970, we were premature.

Even more reason for our lack of success, is that the charity base of the patients attended on Hospital Hill was not a viable patient base for an HMO. Painfully true, such a population base drives away, or keeps away the private patient. If we had had more energy and a physician staff oriented towards private practice, we might have succeeded. However, such a staff probably would not have made the sacrifice needed to carry the physician duty of old General Hospital and its successor.

In the late 1960's, at the peak of the War on Poverty, there was a new health-care entity struggling into being; I speak of the neighborhood health centers. How to coordinate the care given there which is ambulatory, with the care given at a hospital, each institution under separate boards, was the first item on the agenda of HRI. Some of the coordination, we accomplished. Some of it could not be done because the neighborhood clinics quickly developed a territoriality and fearsome independence. Few of them wanted "coordination." We put energy and resources into HRI and most of it was wasted.

The other organization that did not survive was the Academy of Health Professions.

The Academy of Health Professions had more usefulness and lasted almost two decades. My purpose in creating it was to set up a separate organization, outside of the Medical School, controlled by practicing physicians and regional hospitals. The reason for putting it outside the Medical School is the inherent conflict between private physicians, their hospitals, and a medical school.

All readers know the term "town-and-gown syndrome." It was this reality that I sought to avoid. The objective was to provide a central, cooperative organization for planning and delivering continuing education for the region's nurses, pharmacists, allied health workers and physicians. It was also the administrative base for the areawide residencies.

This plan succeeded. Max Berry put real effort into it. The demise of AHP came in about 1990. It died in the war of competition involving hospitals, HMO's, and the marketing of patients as if they were real estate. As the fight for patients became intense, cooperation and coordination became unwanted. The health care marketplace spelled the end of an idea based on the fellowship of an "academy."

As a part of this change in continuing education, and undercutting the usefulness of Academy of Health Professions, came the invasion by the pharmaceutical firms. What had been a worthy responsibility for both teacher and taught, became but another way to sell a product. Do I sound a bit hostile? I hope so.

There is a fine line between using the correct medication because it is the best medication, and using a product because, even unconsciously, you have been favored by the maker. I recognize the risk in faulting something that has now become accepted conduct. To criticize the trend of the present makes it easy for others to shrug and say; "Oh, he is just over the hill and unable to accept change." Could it be that what is now accepted is wrong? Will not the inherent need for the honesty of Caesar's wife prevail?

The other programs in which we invested ourselves with no permanent results were RMP, CHP, and AHEC. These programs were national; throughout the country good people tried to make sense out of bad legislation. I have indicated that there were some definite successes, among them the training and nourishing of young health professionals and administrators. If you examined the employment record of many in the health field today, you would find one or more of those entities in their background.

Evidence of the all-out attack that we mounted on funding was the fact that our neophyte school competed for and got one of the original 11 national AHEC awards. We were able to maintain this award for 10 years.

One contribution we made was to invent the best or worst acronym of them all, "WMAHEC," Western Missouri Area Health Education Center, pronounced "WHAM-A-HECK." A program can't be all bad that has such a label.

As an example of the things made possible by WMAHEC money, we were able, in 1976, five years into the program, to send a caravan of motor homes into southwest Missouri for the full month of October, to visit physicians, clinics, and hospitals. The entire effort was to show our students what is meant by primary care and what life is like on the firing line. The leader of this group was good friend, ally, and enthusiast, Ed Twin, by then retired as executive director, and now a Docent. Mary D. and I, in our motor home, joined the group for part of the trip, and Twin's rapport with the students and with the doctors out in the State was a delight to see.

We no longer have such money available and therefore such very useful effort stops. Even if we had the money, it would be difficult to create the kind of infectious goodwill and concern which came naturally from Ed.

The Area Health Education programs have had a protracted demise. Enough good was done, especially in rural areas, to give the program continuing support in some states. The annual federal funding is now down to $18 million, for all programs. Of course, state and local money has, in some areas, been stimulated and therefore this small figure is not a full definition of the vitality of the effort.

Still, it is far less than expected by the original Carnegie sponsors.

Our own Academy of Health Professions was a direct extension of this program and therefore we had a 20-year result.

An interesting decision was reached concerning the name for our new teaching hospital. For almost a century there had been a Kansas City General Hospital. With it, came many memories; not all were good. For much of its life it had existed as two hospitals, segregated by race. The old hospital had come through the years with not a completely happy reputation among the people it served.

We met with George Lehr, head of the Jackson County Legislature. We agreed a new hospital, seeking a new image, and the teaching hospital of a new medical school, warranted a new name. I took on the responsibility of visiting President Truman's widow and soliciting permission for the name: The Truman Medical Center. This seemed appropriate for several reasons: he was the only President from our region; he had begun his career in the Jackson County Legislature, the government group that was building our hospital, and he had signed into law Medicare and Medicaid, two actions which often benefitted the very people we served. Mrs. Truman's response was quick, one might say cautious, "Well, I don't think that would embarrass him."

One sensitive area in which Vern Wilson and I had to carefully tend our friendship was in the mundane area of how to organize the collection for physician's services. Vern had been through this in the Columbia medical-school hospital, and had refined a medical practice plan, in essence run from the dean's office, that he felt was ideal. Perhaps because I came from private practice and knew the satisfaction of controlling my billing and collecting, I was not enthusiastic about the Columbia plan. I voted for autonomy for our physicians.

Finally, the reality of the Kansas City hospital made clear that there was only one way to go. The University was not funding the hospital; it was not the University's hospital; Columbia rules did not apply. Vern and I remained at ease with each other, and I put in place a separate corporation on Hospital Hill, the Hospital Hill Health Services Corporation, for the purpose of handing the collections and compensation of the physicians. To keep it just, we used the same balancing act we had used in all of the endeavors: a shared Board, with a careful proportion of physician members, University members, and Hospital Board members. We found a young man, Jerry Stolov, to run it, and, 20 years later, it is a very viable piece of the original planning. Stolov is another of those original jewels that have carried the place forward.

In June 1972, I bought a GMC motor home, my first such experience. We bought it on a Friday; it was delivered that evening, and the next morning we began driving it to California. Any reader who has had any experience with a motor home knows that inherent in their soul is a devilish streak. Nothing works the way it should. I should have had some premonition. When the salesman brought it to the house on Friday and handed over the keys, he cleared his throat, hesitated, and said, "You know these things are not perfect." What an honest man.

For the next 11 years, Mary D. and I had wonderful interludes with our various motor homes. We never stayed in a formal camp, never rendezvoused with other motor-homers, and made it a point to stop at night in the most isolated place we could find. We had four of them before the end of our motor-homing, and enjoyed much of the vast western beauty of this country. For two city dwellers, no longer young, and with no camping skills, this was a delightful way to go roughing—smoothly.

Motor-homing in wild places leads logically to another nonmedical pleasure of those years. We always traveled with a very large dog, either a German Shepherd or a Giant Schnauzer. They were always loved, petted, spoiled, and would harm no one—but "no one" did not know that. They were the insurance program.

PART FIVE

Chapter Twenty

EARLIER IN THIS BOOK, I have told of my orientation to the cause of world peace. I return, in a somewhat different approach, in order to explain the large amount of my life that went into China, the Chinese people, and China and its relationship to the United States.

In 1964, I had been a participant in the Second Dublin Conference. This stimulating experience had been brought forth and presided over by Grenville Clark.

The participants of the First Dublin Conference had gathered in 1945, at Dublin, New Hampshire, on the slopes of the old hunched-down Mount Monadnock. Monadnock is not towering nor an inspiring mass, but a great stone uprising that seems to express persistence and durability. Mr. Clark had this same massive ruggedness and the same stabilizing, calming effect.

One feels good just sitting on a porch and looking at Monadnock. No great inhalation or gasp of awe comes, but there is an awareness that a major uprising of nature is before you, a physical presence anchored completely down into the earth. So was it when you were with Mr. Clark.

Mr. Clark had been in Washington, in the War Department, during WWII. At the end of the war, he had been a participant, in San Francisco, when the United Nations was founded. The nuclear bomb's destructiveness at Hiroshima and Nagasaki brought new reality, the reality that humankind could destroy itself.

His 1945 Dublin Conference was stimulated by this belief. Just two months and six days after the bombing of Hiroshima, he brought to the isolated serenity of Monadnock a powerful and

303

diverse group. Norman Cousins kept notes and later wrote (*Memoirs of a Man*) about Clark's opening remarks, "Despite published assurances to the contrary by the U.S. government spokesmen, he anticipated the development within a few years of nuclear weapons by the Russians and by other countries within a generation. He said it would be difficult to keep the atomic holocaust from leading to world holocaust unless strong measures were taken to create a world authority with law-enacting and law-enforcing powers." (Remember, this was 1945.)

"He believed the moment in history had come for creating the instruments of workable law. He spoke of the need for world government which would have "limited, but adequate powers."

In the years after the First Dublin Conference, the wartime alliance of the Soviets and the West was replaced by the Iron Curtain. The initial calmness of the West was shattered when it became apparent that both sides had this weapon, not just us. Mr. Clark withdrew from government and committed himself towards defining a means that could resolve this new war risk, a risk of annihilation.

Still, this was not enough; he felt a world constituency was needed, a constituency of people who believed in a world government. This organization was the United World Federalists, and he traveled widely, seeking to create a developing a world awareness. The UWF was launched in 1947.

At the same time, he knew (remembering the disaster facing President Wilson when Congress rejected his League of Nations) it was important to get sympathetic attention in the U.S. Congress. He spoke there and, from his testimony, printed in 1950 a small handbook: *A Plan for Peace*. This superb book is almost unavailable today. Its concluding words were:

"We ought to always remember that there are only two ways for the West and the East to be brought into cooperation. One way is an enforced cooperation, following the conquest of one by the other.

"The only other way is that of cooperation by the free consent of both sides, to be achieved, slowly perhaps but steadily, by mutual toleration and without requiring either to sacrifice honor or principle. That can be done and when it is achieved, the basis will exist to create the world federation by fundamental adjustment of the United Nations Charter."

From its origin, he had been critical of the charter of the United Nations, and had been outspoken in his criticism of its inadequacies. He rewrote the U.N. Charter, a major task. In this book, he described in detail how the world government would function; how it would have a parliament; how all nations would be members; and how popular vote would be used. He called for a world police force, world taxation, and world vote. His ultimate book on the large arena of a world governed by law appeared in 1958. *World Peace Through World Law* went through several printings and was translated into a variety of languages.

Clark was 76 when this book appeared. He had already been sick for several years with lymphoma. When he assembled the Second Dublin Conference in 1964, he was 82, and the reward of the week for me was not in the group's conclusions. It was in seeing, hearing a great human being rising up and beyond the day's limits.

Time had passed. The Cold War was real; the United Nations was not a popular forum and the World Federalists had not become a significant force; much of Clark's message did not seem based upon reality. But that was perhaps the weakness of many of us who were there.

Our thoughts were lessened, were circumscribed, by the realities of the day, and most of us could not see horizons still beyond. After four days, he came down with a written summation of our work and defined the needs: world order, world taxation, world police force, world representation, etc.

Although very old and long ill, he pulled forth strength and skill and none of us felt we were seeing a dying man, struggling to stay on stage. Instead, he was not of any age, but of all time. He was seeking to show us how the questions were unchanged, and reasoning people could only conclude the answers rested in moving on to another level of government.

We met in an artist's large studio; it was very cold and the vast, barn-like room was heated by a single wood stove. Mr. Clark, as did most of us, wore his topcoat at all times. He stood at the left front of the room, and a clear north light gave a soft glow to his face. The dark wood paneling behind framed him in a portrait. He was bareheaded, tall and erect, speaking with all the skills of a thousand public appearances. If there is a perfection in this thing called civilization and a man rising up to its ultimate expectation —it was there in Grenville Clark.

Paul Dudley White, Kingman Brewster, and Norman Cousins were there; my roommate was Edgar Snow. Snow brought the unexpected to the meeting. He was the one person who was not from the traditional establishment of academic, or legislative, or corporate elitism. Almost everyone else in the room had heard previously the contributions of the others and all were of like sympathy.

Snow was different.

Reaching back to his 14 years in China, to his years abroad as a foreign correspondent, to the years when he had left the United States and lived in Europe, Snow had gained an awareness of another world.

On the last day, he stood at the front of the room and told the sincere, caring group that their desires for a system of world peace through world law were premature. What they wanted did not leave room for the many people on earth who had no desire for world peace, but above all, wanted revolution.

Snow carefully, logically, explained that for many, the existing governments were but an extension of the imperialism of the last century. That rebelling world was not ready for some distant, rich, comfortable nation to declare all could be secure under a rule of law. Any attempt to proclaim the world was ready for a peaceful, legal resolution of mankind's affairs must realize that there was a large "third world" out there. This Third World did not intend to settle for the existing governments. Ed said there were many revolutions yet to come.

He made it clear that he thought these were deserving revolutions.

Most of us had never heard the term "Third World" before. Snow brought us up short.

When the final document was signed, Snow wrote an opposing minority report, identifying that our well-meaning group was too far afield from the reality of the awful life of many people and the political oppression of much of the world.

Ed and I spent hours together during those days and then went on down to Boston together. We found immediate rapport. Part of it was from his surprise in learning that I had known John Powell when I was in the Pacific. Powell had been Ed's first employer when Ed arrived in China. It was those few Dublin days together that later opened my own way into China.

Ed also was stimulated to learn that I had been trained by Paul White. He went on to tell me how Clark and White had tried hard to get to China five years earlier. Ed had written directly to Mao on their behalf, with no success. When he himself was in China in 1960, he had brought up the issue again with Zhou Enlai and had been told, "The time is not yet right for us to open contacts. We will tell you when it is."

The main lasting result of the Dublin Conference for me was a personal conviction that I would make my goal that of somehow being a facilitator in opening a path between the two countries.

Clark had already defined the urgency of a rapport. When President Kennedy was elected in 1960, Mr. Clark wrote him a long letter, freely offering a considerable range of advice about Kennedy's presidency. He began the letter by citing that he had done the same when his Harvard classmate, Franklin Roosevelt, had been elected. To appreciate the significance of such letters, one must understand the unique private-citizen role of Grenville Clark.

In this detailed letter to President Kennedy, he came down hard on urging a reality, a reality that he had acquired from Snow. He wrote: "As to China, everyone knows that no worthwhile disarmament plan can come into force without the participation of that nation...it is no more than common sense to bring China into the new negotiations from the start. For when one knows in advance that the agreement sought in a difficult negotiation can never become effective unless assented to by a certain important interest, it is elementary in my view that this interest should be asked to participate in the negotiation from the outset...In such case it is almost inevitable that the excluded party will say: 'If you want my assent and knew it to be essential, why didn't you invite me to participate instead of asking me now to sign on the dotted line? You can go to the devil.'" A great part of Clark's skill was in his definitive, no-nonsense style of communication.

Snow and I talked about this letter to Kennedy and Ed repeatedly said that he knew there was a desire on the part of those in power in China to somehow, without losing face, have a friendly rapport with the Americans. He said that our constant efforts to keep China out of the United Nations was a prime example of excluding from the world's bargaining table the very participant whose vote was needed. We talked about the efforts of Mr. Clark and Dr. White to get invited to China during Eisenhower's presidency. All efforts had been unsuccessful.

Snow said that the way to work with the Chinese was to not have an agenda, to not approach them directly for the purpose in hand, but to count on spending years just getting their trust. He laughed and said, "Nothing gets done in China, unless you pass the test of 'Old Friend.'" Ed said Americans always want to sign contracts and have formal documents. With the Chinese there first comes trust. He laughed and said most Americans cannot last through all the tea drinking that is needed.

Even Ed had difficulty getting into China. The American passport specifically excluded "Mainland China." The question of "face" was very much an issue to the Communist government and even if Ed was trusted by them, he was not welcome as a journalist. Delicate efforts by his friends in China, including George Hatem and Rewi Alley, could not elicit the needed invitation. He had been invited in 1960 by being declared a historian. Finally, he was allowed back in 1965 and was able to report the changes he saw. He was then blocked by the Cultural Revolution until 1970, when he was able to take Lois, his wife, for a five-month-long visit.

When he returned to Switzerland after the 1970 visit, he placed three articles in Norman Cousin's *Saturday Review of Literature*. In these reports, he wrote about witnessing successful limb reimplantation, surgery done under acupuncture analgesia, and about China's vigorous birth-control efforts. These were good articles and even when read today are free of cant and propaganda. They were simply accurate information about a fascinating world, a world obscured by the Bamboo Curtain maintained by the two governments.

After Dublin, I had visited Ed in Switzerland. Mary D. and I were there in 1969. As I traveled widely for the State Department in those years, I kept him informed of my adventures. When I lived in Washington in 1967 and 1968, he warned me that I was camping with the Philistines, and teased me. In our visit to Switzerland in 1969, I told him that all of this was just getting ready for my "invasion" of China. When he was there in 1970, he told the Chinese side of my willingness to ignore the injunction of the American passport.

Criticism of Ed's three articles in the *Saturday Review* stung him deeply. They were good, definitive articles, all related to aspects of medicine. Critics were unable to believe that Chinese surgeons were sewing severed toes and fingers back with success. This was not yet being done in the West, or, if it was, not with the results Snow reported. How could the Chinese be ahead? Everyone knew they were backward. Snow's report on birth control could not be true. Everyone knows that the Chinese demand big families and nothing could overcome these teachings, coming down from the time of Confucius. And this laughable report on brain surgery being done with the patient awake and only a needle wiggled in the skin?

The conclusion of the reviewers was that Ed had long been a communist sympathizer; obviously, his judgment had been distorted by brainwashing. Anyhow, how could a reporter understand the technical aspects of medicine?

If there was one part of Ed that was sensitive, it was to have his accuracy and reliability as a journalist criticized. These "brainwashing" comments were the kind of unfair, unwarranted criticism that pained him deeply.

In February 1971, he asked me if I would go to China and verify what he had written. I had no hesitation and said I would come at any time. He said he would "put out a feeler."

I had no way to anticipate the calendar. Every moment of 1971 was devoted to getting approval to have a medical school, to getting the drawings done and funds for the school building and the hospital, to interviewing and hiring the critical long-term nucleus of faculty and staff, to setting up the administrative plan for the School, to choosing the first official class of medical students.

I was making ward rounds with housestaff in the old Research Hospital that we had bought and renamed the Holmes Street Annex, certainly not a very grand name. It was August 14, our opening of the long-fought-for medical school was to occur in just two weeks. A nurse interrupted my rounds with the message that I had a long-distance call from Canada. The caller said it was important.

I excused myself and went to the phone. Coming in over the line was a very faint, quite precise voice which identified itself as the Embassy of the Peoples' Republic of China in Ottawa, Canada. The message was very characteristic of the unrelated to reality kind of message that comes in from China. I now have learned to understand and accept these unexpected, unannounced voices which can come at any hour, unaware of time zones, international time differences, day of the week, weather, or other factors important in most lives.

"You and Mrs. Dimond have been invited to China by Premier Zhou Enlai. Can you pick up your visa here tomorrow? You are to enter China on September 14."

There were no other details, no explanations, no modifying clauses. There had been no alert from Snow.

I went back to ward rounds, forcing myself to listen to the patients' histories, concentrating on hearing murmurs, and asking germane questions.

At noon I called Mary D. and quickly asked her if we had anything in the morning mail from Ed Snow. She shuffled through the mail and said no. I took a deep breath and told her about the call from Ottawa. She gave a long, low "Wowwwww."

I told her that this could not have come at a worse time. The entire Kansas City effort was coming to a grand launch on September 1 and I had serious commitments for every day between now and then.

We called Snow that evening. He was absolutely surprised to know that his efforts had had a result. I told him of my dilemma about the School's opening, and I was thinking about asking for a three-month delay. Ed's response was quick, "Don't play with a major event. Grab the visa and be there at the border on time."

Pressure is a great facilitator of decisions. Mary D. protested less than 10 seconds and agreed to take our passports to Canada the next day.

I cabled the Embassy this information and then made an important gamble. Paul White's efforts to get to China had been one of his few major failures. He was now 85 years old. I asked the Chinese for two more visas so Paul and Ina White could accompany us.

The Chinese were concerned about this very senior man's welfare in China, and were keenly aware of the international publicity which would attend his collapse while on Chinese soil. I went one step further and assured the Chinese that I would take personal responsibility for his health and welfare, and that I would accompany him at all times, take all meals with him, and we would have adjoining hotel rooms.

My purpose in asking for Dr. White to accompany me was both altruistic and practical. For Mary D. to go, was, in its way, a completion of her father's efforts. For me to go without Dr. White just did not seem right; he and Grenville Clark had tried so long and so futilely to get into China. While I had the door open, I wanted to get him through with me.

My practical reason was simple. I was going to write and speak about what I saw and experienced. What better validation could I have than to have one of the most respected voices in American medicine with me? Either of us alone could be criticized; Dr. White would be vulnerable simply because of his age. Those who wished to criticize him for going into the infamous Red China, would do so by a shake of the head, and a murmur of what a shame it was to see the old man slipping. Those who would fault me would declare me some kind of a pinko, a popular term in those years, and, using another contaminating label, would say I had been brainwashed. The fact that our trip was immediately followed by the grandest pinko-finder of them all, President Nixon, made it somewhat difficult to fault Dr. White or me.

Not only was there the complication of the opening of the new school, but I was to be a speaker at the Paavo Nurmi Symposium in Helsinki, Finland on September 6. This symposium was named after the famous Olympic distance runner. He had later become a very prosperous industrialist in Finland and gave money for this international symposium, devoted to the recognition of coronary disease.

We fit together a calendar: Get the School opened, to Helsinki September 5-10, then to Geneva to see Ed Snow and get his briefing, on to Hong Kong and meet Ina and Paul White there on September 13, cross the border into China September 15.

The Chinese added another "suggestion." Please tell no one about the visit until it is over. Previous attempts to have American guests had stimulated the guests into so much anticipation and publicity that the American government had intercepted the invitation and stopped it. If we would quietly get to Hong Kong, they would see to it that we were properly escorted through the barriers.

This, of course, gave the trip a distinctly clandestine quality. It also made a great lump gather in our chest; we were quite normal in our enthusiasm for wanting to talk about the invitation. We agreed to tell no one, and Paul White immediately saw the wisdom in this. We did not tell our children; I did not advise the University. I did quietly update my Will and wrote my daughters letters to be handed out "in case."

With unexpected suddenness, I found myself committed to be on a secret journey to China, instead of enjoying happily the first days of the University of Missouri-Kansas City School of Medicine.

The students that had been chosen for this first official medical-school class were a true spectrum of talent. Among them were Ph.D.'s, dentists, pharmacists, transfers from other medical schools, and youths directly from high school. With the 18 students admitted as "provisional" the year before (16 had survived), and this charter class, there would be 94 University of Missouri-Kansas City School of Medicine students. We, instantly, would be a full-fledged six-year medical school, with students in Years One through Five. Those in Year Five were graduate students with degrees in dentistry and microbiology, for example. With their considerable background in basic sciences, we anticipated their acquiring clinical skills in one or two years with us.

The dream of a medical school on Hospital Hill was reality. After the years of effort, I found, to use a Chinese phrase, Double Happiness.

Mary D. and I made the Finland trip. The symposium was held in an elegant lakeside resort hotel. One of the other participants was Walter Somerville, one of my friends from London. He had been Paul Wood's physician in the final illness.

The Finnish hosts took a special pleasure in initiating Walter and me to the full exuberance of a Finnish sauna. This was complete with birch-leaf whipping, competition to see who could raise the moist heat to maximum tolerance, and great whoops of victory as lesser men burst out of the choking chamber, crying out for air, cool air. When one did get out, the "pleasure" was not over. With full virility, you ran to the pool and leaped in—and then surprised by your own survival, you were expected to submit to massage rendered by very muscular senior women. The only real pleasure came from the cold beer one needed to replenish lost body water.

Walter and I, both definitely older than our hosts, tried to be cooperative guests. We went through this complete cycle several times. It was difficult not to pause and ask just why we were doing this to ourselves. This torture disguised as pleasure needs a lifetime of preparation; neither of us had had the slightest previous "training." As Mary D. and I left Helsinki and flew on to Geneva, I felt I had adequate assurance that my coronary arteries were up to the China trip.

Ed and Lois Snow lived in a farmhouse in Eysins, a home rich with charm. There were many evidences of Ed's China years, and one photograph we took of him showed him seated before a large poster of Mao Zedong. The original picture had been taken by Ed when he was at Paoan on his trip to the communist headquarters. Just before the picture was to be taken, Ed had felt the bare-headed Mao needed some of evidence of the military nature of his life. Ed had taken off his own green cloth cap, the kind worn by the Chinese troops, and put it on Mao's head. The resulting picture had become a widely displayed poster throughout China, used for years to extol Mao and Communism.

In our own picture, with Ed in the foreground, his hand is just out of the picture. In it, Ed was holding a small liquor glass, filled with mao-tai. We had spent the entire day being briefed by Ed about cultural revolutions, great leaps forward, and the makeup of the Politburo. At the end of evening, Ed, with a flourish, had broken the red wax seal on the white ceramic mao-tai bottle and poured us each an ounce.

With small claims to braveness, it has been my "duty" to have drunk in each country the native alcoholic beverage. In all societies, the offering of an alcoholic drink is a demonstration of friendship. This has included the drink made in the upper regions of the Amazon where the native women chew grain to mix it with the enzymes of their saliva, spit the mix back into a calabash, and allow it to ferment. Still, I was not prepared for mao-tai. Perhaps one of my hindrances was a remembrance of a paragraph I had read about the Chinese Communist Army and the Long March. It was stated that when the foot-weary soldiers had reached Kweizhou, the site of the creation of mao-tai, that they had thrust their feet in the vats and just sat there soaking.

The thought of any possible problem with hygiene and mao-tai is a false issue. One small sip burned that worry from me. No organism could survive. The Chinese describe the drink as a wine, but that is an apparent lack of communication. Now, 20 years later, and a hundred or more toasts later, I have reached a level of mature judgment, a maturity I did not have that night at Ed's home. My seasoned opinion is that it is the most serious form of alcoholic drink on earth. Vodka, schnapps, and corn whiskey are all docile; mao-tai is the king.

Ed had spent five months in 1970 in China and was deep into writing about it. He was a complete encyclopedia of information and had all of the facts at his fingertips, as well as knowing the personalities of the players.

He had not been feeling well. Sitting at his typewriter aggravated a back pain that he had first noticed near the end of the China trip. He found pleasure from our visit, and he took it as a good omen that we were invited as a direct result of his efforts.

None of us knew that negotiations were under way for the President of the United States to visit China.

None of us knew that Lin Biao, Mao's second-in-command,

would launch an attempted coup within the next 72 hours.

None of us knew when we said good-bye on September 11, that within 60 days Ed would learn he had an inoperable pancreatic carcinoma. And that he would die on February 15, 1972, while Richard Nixon was in flight over the Pacific on his way to make peace with Communist China.

No Greek tragedy could be more complete than Ed's life. When he was 30, he had written the definitive book alerting the West that a Communist China was about to be reality. He had been honored, then pilloried, because of this honest reporting. To find work, he was forced to leave his own country. The cruelness and blindness of the McCarthy era made even those who wrote the truth about Communist China suspect.

A prime player in that era had been the anti-communist congressman from California. As Snow died, the former congressman, now President, made the largest positive move of his presidency. No one in the American travel party could know a fraction as much about the Chinese as the man who was not invited.

Ina and Paul White flew from Boston to Hong Kong. He had mowed the grass at his home on September 11, visited a hospital patient, had his "shots" and flew off to China. As soon as he was in the hotel lobby, he called our room and asked us to meet them for tea. Any concern any of us may have had for his physical ability was turned into a concern for our ability to keep up with him. No jet lag. No naps. He was in top form.

We had learned that two other physician couples were to enter China at the same time. Dr. Victor Sidel was a well-known social activist, and he and his wife had been recommended by Galston and Singer, the two Americans who had been first to visit China. Vic was delayed in his travel plans and had to catch up with us in Beijing.

The other couple, Helen and Sam Rosen, had long been sympathizers of the Communist party and had been invited by the Chinese several years earlier. The U.S. Department of State had heard about their enthusiastic announcement of their invitation to Red China, and blocked their trip. This time they took no chances and got up on September 15, 1971, and left the hotel without us in an effort to gain the elusive prize of being the first to cross the Chinese border. Sam's professional reputation was based on his early work with stapes mobilization surgery for deafness.

The major blight on their happiness at this time was twofold. First, they had not known we were also entering at the same time, thus their uniqueness was diluted. Second, they quickly found that the Chinese reverence for age was absolute.

Dr. White was the senior person in our party and he was first in every auto procession, first received at every visit, first to be seated, first to be toasted. Each of these moments of respect was bitter tea for the Rosens, and almost a lethal injection for Helen Rosen.

Although the Rosens hurried to cross the border, they were held at the Chinese side to await us. The six of us, on September 15, were met at the border and advised that because of a tremendous storm in the Beijing area that our flight to Beijing had been canceled. We were held in Guangzhou (Canton) for three days.

During our 12 days in China, we found this was evidently a very severe storm. For example, in Beijing we were told we could not go see the Great Wall because the bad storm had wiped out the road.

We completed our trip, carried out a considerable number of negotiations, and the Whites and ourselves headed back to Hong Kong. As the train slowed at the border, just entering the New Territories, a wave of reporters descended upon us. Some climbed through the windows of the train. The aisles were packed, note books, cameras, radios were all about us.

We had been pressed while still in Beijing by Western newspapers calling us at all hours. Because Dr. White and I were cardiologists, the rumor or theory was developed that we had slipped into China because Mao had had a coronary attack. Now as we crossed the border, the journalistic world was galvanized into action to dig the truth out of us.

For Dr. White, nothing could have been more stimulating. Although 85 years old, he was still an enthusiast for media coverage. His experience in taking care of President Eisenhower during Ike's coronary occlusion had given my perfectly proper Bostonian mentor a taste for the fun and value of news media. From the moment we crossed the border, he was in a happy media heaven. We could not spend as much time as he wanted to because the Whites flew out directly to Rome, where he was to have an audience the next day with the Pope. The purpose of the audience was to present the Pope with an English translation of a Latin text from the 1500's. Dr. White had found in it the first autopsy confirming a coronary artery occlusion.

Paul White was a small, wiry man who was blessed with a body destined for longevity. It happened that he enjoyed physical activity such as walking and bicycling. He had had a metabolism that permitted him to eat anything and remain not slender, but skinny. He drew the conclusion that the secret to his degree of physical fitness and longevity was exercise and leanness. Perhaps, in part, he was right, but the even larger factor was the fact that he was born to live a long time, and he had a personal level of energy that, while sustaining him, exhausted those around him.

I had, at one time, complimented Dr. White on the tremendous success of his career. He smiled, shrugged, and said, "Well, the truth is that I am not really very smart. I just worked three times as hard as my colleagues. While they played, I plowed ahead. In 10 years, they did 10 years' work; in 10 years, I did 30 years' work." From my 25 years with him, I would judge that exactly right.

After I saw Paul White off on his plane, I telephoned Ed Snow. His first question burst out, "What is going on?! What happened to Lin Biao?" We learned for the first time, that the immense storm that had grounded us for three days in Canton, and had even blocked access to the Great Wall, was in fact a major attempt by Mao Zedong's highest-level ally to overthrow Mao. The head ringleader was Lin Biao, and when his attempt to kill Mao failed, he had fled by plane to Mongolia. His plane crashed and all were killed. The central government, in order to narrow the number of possible problems, had simply grounded every plane in China. The storm was man-made. I learned a lesson, never forgotten: The truth is subject to diplomatic improvement.

As we left China, I recognized that my short-term reward w
in seeing the honest joy this exposure to China had given Pa
White.

At the same time, I knew that the long-term reward was the
waiting: how to bring about a major relationship between t
people of the two countries. I already knew the Orient a little; no
I had to find out how to swing open this door I had gotte
through, and get colleagues and other Americans involved.

The purpose for which Grenville Clark and Paul White h
fought, World Peace Through World Law, was not how I believ
the best result would be obtained. There was not a place for
single organization or umbrella. There was no place for individu
personalities; what was needed were thousands of exchanges.

There was a China world which would not be much changed
the West. It was a much larger world than we could comprehen
From my experiences in Japan, I realized that a totally bombe
out, occupied nation could take from the West all those thin
that are called success and become a world power. Yet, such
nation would remain itself. Japan learned how to function in t
Western world. But Japan remained Japan. So would it be 1
China.

But China was of a dimension, of such a population mass, th
few people could comprehend its potential. It was easier to p
them aside as "backward." The kind of talent found in t
Chinese cannot be labeled "backward." Bamboo Curtains
dictatorships will eventually give way.

I had also learned enough about the Orient to know that tir
frames are different. The kind of change that should occur
China would not occur in my lifetime. What I could do is fii
ways of getting the talent of the two countries, the United Stat
and China, in communication. If we could find a means of mutu
benefit through trade, trade of talent and materials, the wor
buys time. My goal was no larger than that.

We had nothing to do with it, but evidence that times we
changing occurred in October 1971. After being excluded fro
the United Nations since the founding of their government, t
People's Republic of China was admitted in October 1971.

In the very good biography about Paul White, *Take Hea*

written by Oglesby Paul (Distributed by the Harvard University Press for the Francis A. Countway Library of Medicine, Boston, 1986), Paul wrote: "This was the last major journey Paul White took. Not that he just stayed home in Boston and Belmont. He continued to take short trips within the United States, often to speak enthusiastically about his experiences in China. In the spring of 1972 he visited Paris and Milan briefly, and in the fall flew to Madrid for one more medical meeting. However, the trip to China was really the happy finale to his world travels; he died two years later."

Shortly after our return from China, the "Today" show invited both of us to New York to appear. After the early morning appearance with Frank McKee, the two of us were walking back to our hotel. We came to a curb and Dr. White, caught up in talking, stepped out, almost in to the path of rushing taxi. I grabbed his arm and pulled him back. He looked up at me quickly and gave a fleeting smile. He said, "Thanks, but that would not have been a bad way to go. The time has come, you know."

Chapter Twenty-one

THE REMAINDER OF 1971 AND all of 1972 was a blend of medical school and China. My travel schedule for a two-month period in 1972, gives a hint of the "velocity" of life at that time.

April 1 - Kansas City
April 2-11 - Rancho Santa Fe Course
April 12-14 - Phoenix, speak
April 15-17 - Kansas City
April 18 - Columbia, Missouri, Curators
April 20, 21 - Jackson, Mississippi, speak
April 22, 23 - Waco, Texas, speak
April 25-28 - Wausau, Wisconsin, consultation
May 1-5 - Kansas City
May 6-9 - New York City, speak, board meeting
May 10-16 - Ann Arbor, Michigan, consultation
May 19-20 - Phoenix, consultation, speak
May 21-22 - Kansas City
May 22 - Houston, speak
May 23-24 - Dartmouth, board meeting
May 26-30 - Kansas City

What caused such extensive traveling? The agenda, looked at now in retrospect, looks almost agitated. There were several things happening, all in the same time frame, not all related. The majority of my travels during 1972 related to speaking on China and persuading others to go there and see for themselves. There was a national excitement about China just after the Nixon trip, and several of my trips related to advising national committees on how to open contact with China.

Some of the travel was strictly related to cardiology, either in straightforward patient-care consultation or, as at Wausau, taking a full look at the question of building a cardiac-care and research center there. Homer had been asked to look at this from the financial side and he wanted my opinion from the professional view.

We had children in boarding schools and whenever a trip took us near, we were with a child. On the May trip to Phoenix, I had a special treat. Lark was graduating from Judson School and I gave the commencement address. Lark gave me a dividend; she made National Honor Society.

Mary D. and I always made these trips together. She was not simply a traveling companion. Mary D. was very much her own person, with an energy, a vitality. She was a "doing" woman.

Although Paul Wood had died in 1962, I never quite adjusted to the thought that he was gone. He had been so much alive, so vital, and we had such harmony, that I carried an unfilled sense of loss. I went about writing a memorial, a tribute, to him. I wrote a lot of it on planes. Although very adequate obituaries had signaled his death, there were still many of us who had more we wanted to say. I collected from over the world material about Paul and, in July 1972, the American College of Cardiology published my *Paul Wood Revisited*. If someone would want to catch in words the essence of Paul Wood, it would perhaps be found in this small memoir.

(In 1965, I had, while Dr. White was still alive, written a small volume about him, *Paul Dudley White: A Portrait*. These two books were my venture into biography.)

By February 1972, we had evidence that word about our new medical school was reaching the important audience. We received 2,200 applications. The caliber of the applicants was high, very high; this was the important signal.

Our definitely different medical school was reaching a definitely different applicant pool. We had opened a door to first level, high-achieving, goal-dedicated talent. It was the first evidence we had that this School would make its mark, not because of buildings or research, but because the student talent would drive the place to a level of quality that could not be denied. We had planned the school to be student-friendly; one commentator said, "[I] would love to be a student at our place, the student really counts."

As the plan unfolded, it proved to be student-friendly but also student-driven. We opened the door to the top performers in high school: They poured in. We were in the position of a coach who had first choice on the draft pick, year after year.

From the beginning, the other distinguishing characteristic of the School was defined. Women wanted to come to our school. The number and quality of women was impressive and, from 1972 on, we have had one of the largest, if not the largest, number of women of any medical school.

On October 18, 1971, we had had a gala banquet at the campus to celebrate and honor the "Charter Class." Our guests were all those who had helped, those who were participating in the curriculum, and, of course, the special stars of the occasion, our 94 medical students. The Institute of Medicine, in Washington, D.C., was just in its beginning years and we asked its president, John Hogness, to be our speaker.

The evening was a success, but an extra dividend came from it. Dr. Hogness stayed at our home and we had a good visit. He was very interested in hearing about our China adventure. I put out a feeler to him, raising the possibility that he and the Institute might join me in sending an invitation to China for a delegation of Chinese physicians to be our guests. Hogness was enthusiastic. He said he would take a major role in finding the money if I could produce a delegation.

I immediately followed this up by a several-pronged attack. I visited the American Medical Association in Chicago and they agreed to be equal sponsors. From there I went to Washington, where, by good fortune, I knew fairly well both the White House physician, Walter Tkach, and the Physician to Congress, Freeman Cary.

I knew Walter through my work for the American College of Cardiology, and Freeman through my weekly consultation visits to the U.S. Naval Hospital while I was at the Scripps Clinic. Freeman was a Naval physician. From both of them came warm endorsements of the idea of a delegation from China. Dr. Tkach assured me that he would make the right contacts for all needed security arrangements.

A new group had been formed under semi-government auspices to further scientific and academic exchanges with China. This was the Committee on Scholarly Communication with the People's Republic of China. As a result of the sudden new evidence of possibilities, its staff contacted me, through Ann Keatley, and they agreed to take a major role, helping with travel arrangements and interpreters. Ann was wispy-voiced, deceptive in hiding her talent. One's first judgment would have been inadequacy; she was very able.

With all of these partners willing to participate, I felt prepared, and gathered all of them to prepare a letter to the Chinese Minister of Health. He had received us in September. His name was Hsieh Hua. He was a regular Army officer, and I had been intrigued to learn he had received his medical training "in the field." He had not had formal medical education, but was considered to be a surgeon. He was head of the Chinese Medical Association and the Ministry of Health. When Mao's Cultural Revolution had broken into an uncontained violence, peace, measured peace, had been established by turning over the control and leadership of all organizations, not just medicine, to the Army.

With all partners in place and with Paul White, Sam Rosen, and Victor Sidel in agreement, our formal letter of invitation to the Chinese Ministry of Health, inviting the Chinese to send a physician delegation as our guests, was put in the mail. The immediate hosts would be the Institute of Medicine and the American Medical Association. The letter was sent May 19, 1972.

Six weeks passed before we had an answer. The Chinese Ambassador to the United Nations, Huang Hua, wrote me in July and said the invitation had been received favorably and "perhaps a delegation would come after September 1." This was indefinite enough that Mary D. and I decided to take a two-week vacation and make a motor tour around Switzerland and the northern Lake Country of Italy. We also would drop in on Lois Snow. We had been in Switzerland for three days, earlier in the year, when memorial services were held for Snow in Geneva. We had then agreed we wanted a longer visit.

After a wonderful week in the Swiss mountains, we surfaced in Zurich on August 28 and telephoned home. Within moments of telling the office where we were, our hotel phone rang and there on the line was the familiar quiet voice from an empty space, unconnected to reality. It was some nameless, faceless person calling from the Chinese Embassy in New York City. Would it be possible for us to go to Peking? Could we pick up our visa in New York City tomorrow? Could we be in Peking on September 1? The Minister of Health had questions about the physician delegation and the trip to the United States. He would welcome us to Peking.

There was no acknowledgement of the obvious fact that we were in Europe, not the United States, and that an unplanned trip of this magnitude should have a little preparation. I remembered Snow's original advice about getting through the door when it is open. We negotiated the fact that we could pick up our visas in Bern, not New York City. For the rest of it, we agreed.

We were in Peking on September 1. Our leisurely Swiss vacation was hardly a memory.

The day after our arrival, the Minister of Health came to our hotel; we immediately got down to business. His questions were direct; direct, but through an interpreter.

Was this John Hogness a "friend of China?" Again I remembered Ed Snow's words about the importance of this "trusted" list. Was this Institute of Medicine an appropriate host? What was it? The next question was special. How do you pronounce "Hogness?" I had come halfway around the world for this query? Was the American Medical Association a reactionary organization? I was tempted to tell him "yes," but I knew he meant something else, so I gave the AMA an endorsement. When we finished, he asked if I could give them an outline of what I proposed. Where, who, what would they see? And his greatest concern. Will the delegation be safe?

This latter question was a good one. The Chinese Ping-Pong team, the most benign of endeavors, during their United States trip, had been harassed, picketed, and given cat-calls by right wing groups, agitated by Mr. Nixon's visit to China. I assured him of full safety, although I had no idea how thorough this would be.

We flew on home, arriving there just when we would have if the phone call had not come to Zurich. It was an unusual auto tour of Switzerland, including a 20,000-mile detour.

Life on Hospital Hill picked up immediately with no evidence we had been away. It is always a steadying reminder of the importance of things to find how they go on, with or without you.

With a new hospital underway and a concept of teaching medical education through team care, there was still a piece to be accomplished. Our Docent Teams would include the medical students, Residents, a Doctor of Pharmacy to teach therapeutics, a social worker, a liaison psychiatrist, and even a medical librarian. These parts we had in hand and factored into our budget.

The missing team player was the nurse. The old General Hospital had long had a nurse-training program, but the new look in nursing education faulted such hospital-based nurse training. I worked out a transfer of that program to the nearby Penn Valley Junior College. We then went to work on the University to authorize a School of Nursing.

It required rash braveness to even bring this up, after the trauma of extracting a medical school from the University. With the RMP and AHEC money, and the good help of Irma Lou Hirsh, Edith Hellerstein, and Bob Fairchild, we got well into the needed planning and discussions with the accrediting bodies. Chancellor Olson, always somewhat hesitant about expansion, held back. Finally, Homer and I worked out a commitment of initial support from Homer's local foundations. We went to the chancellor's home one Saturday evening—literally bearded him in his den—and extracted the commitment for a master of science program in nursing from him. He agreed and the degree was approved, December 16, 1972.

Note carefully that it was the degree that was authorized, not the School of Nursing. First, we had a Division of Nursing and upgrading this to a School was a long, painful task.

The path included nursing faculty rejection of their director, resignation in total of the nursing faculty, national rejection of the request for school status, the resignation of more than one nursing administrator, and various confrontations, sit-downs, petitions, and depressed, weeping participants.

From extracting the agreement for this nursing degree from Jim Olson in late 1972, six years passed before a School of Nursing was official. None of the efforts to build the hospital and medical school were as painful and just plain unpleasant. When the School was established, it was so changed from that which all had fought for, that it no longer was relevant to Hospital Hill.

The idea of nurses working together with physicians was becoming unpopular just about the time we founded the Nursing Division.

After a period of working together towards a common goal, building physician-nurse cooperative docent teams, changes in our nursing administration brought in new thinking. The new thinking moved the purposes of the nurse education program completely away from sharing anything with the Medical School. A very good ally of mine, nurse-educator Luisita Archer, brought the program right up to the point of approval and then corridor whispering and other skilled tactics made it difficult to give her the deanship she deserved.

Our original objective was lost. The politics of the time would not tolerate a cooperative education package. Team care, as we envisioned it, was not on the agenda of nursing education. Nursing was in rebellion. The University had an excellent academic vice chancellor at that time, Gene Trani. He was very good, but his agenda did not include the important need to have a cooperative nurse-physician team, nor did it include strengthening TMC by making it the main base of the Nursing School. A loss occurred, probably irretrievable.

Often, I am identified as the founder of our medical school. It is a reminder of the strength of psychic barriers that although I did "found" the nursing school, that kind of founding does not include appreciation. More than appreciation, I needed therapy when it was finally accomplished.

In 1970, a commission headed by Odegaard under the sponsorship of the Carnegie Foundation came up with another attack on how to get medical care into rural areas. The report loosely defined extensions of university medical centers which would be placed in rural areas. These would bring to the rural doctor, dentist, or nurse a support system. This would alleviate the isolation of practice in these areas and thus increase the attractiveness of rural life for the health worker. This support system first included consultation and care programs but this, as had the RMP program, quickly ran into the reality of how medicine is practiced. Interference with lines of referral was not lightly tolerated by the AMA. The purposes began to shift and, in fact, never quite held still.

Although an absolutely neophyte school, we competed. We were awarded one of the 11 programs funded nationally. This was the AHEC program, described earlier.

This support helped us immensely and gave us planning and staffing money otherwise missing. This was the support we used to plan the new School of Nursing.

The high point of 1972 came with the arrival of the Chinese physician delegation on October 12. Their visit was flawless. Two memories stay with me. The first was the security. It was total. Streets were closed as our cars moved from place to place. In Washington, a military helicopter hovered over our motorcade. At any hotel we were given an entire floor and the Secret Service commandeered one elevator for our use. A suggestion that the group would like to see a shopping mall resulted in the closing off of the mall. I quietly reflected to myself that our guests were seeing a special view of the "land of the free."

The second memory was an article in a medical news magazine in which the reporter wrote of the tour by the Chinese. "Dr. Dimond somehow wangled a visit to Kansas City out of them." Poor Kansas City. Poor Dr. Dimond. How could any important delegation come to the Land of Oz?

I told the story of this experience and of travels to China in a book, *More Than Herbs and Acupuncture,* published by W.W. Norton in 1975. The title was an error. Bookstore browsers saw the word "acupuncture" and thought it was a source book on alternative treatment. My intent had been to emphasize the title word "More." Buyers ignored this hint that I thought there was more to China than acupuncture. They bought the book to learn about acupuncture, something I know nothing about. Nevertheless, it was well received and made a best-seller list.

Each student increment required a new addition of Docents.

No other medical school had such a position. We were defining a new medical-education task.

Not only was the role of a Docent new, but, deliberately, we had removed the clinical positions all from the University's tenure system. The curators continued to be so cautious about the new medical school that they really did not want to commit themselves to offering the security of tenure to a whole new group of professors. The fact that they had gotten a new medical school without taking on the cost of the primary teaching hospital had not made them willing to spend money on faculty.

They continued to be penurious. My words are not meant to be critical of the Curators. Much of the difficulty does not rest with them, but instead, with the State Legislature. And, it is fair to assume, the legislators represent the people of Missouri. The legislators pride themselves on Missouri's 48th or 49th position, from the top, in supporting higher education. I believe only my own ancestral home of Mississippi wins out over their frugality.

I have now watched dozens of University of Missouri curators come and go, and strive as they may, there is no increased State commitment to higher education. Equally, University of Missouri presidents come and go, and each new man carries out a new study, some version of "role and scope," and sounds his tocsin that the need is more money. Then after a few years, he, too, folds his tent, and a new champion of a new version of "role and scope" comes on the scene. Nothing changes.

We turned this to our advantage—major advantage. When it was apparent that the issue of tenureship would be destructive, we made this the reason why we had to form our own doctors' corporation. There had to be some way to offer the clinical faculty safety in terms of health care and disability benefits, malpractice insurance, and retirement assurance. These are all areas for which any other university logically accepts responsibility. The clinicians at the Columbia medical school have this protection. At this medical school, there are no such benefits for the clinicians.

We therefore formed, as I described earlier, the Hospital Hill Health Services Corporation for the sole purpose of serving the medical-school faculty of the University of Missouri-Kansas City. And at the same time, we removed the professional income from the reach of the University system.

This move gained us an independence of action. We could do what is best for the school and the hospital, based upon the conditions locally, and not be second-guessed—nor red-taped—by a Statewide bureaucracy. We gave up tenureship; we gained an independence, an independence of special value. We created a contracting system whereby the Medical School purchases from the doctors' corporation the "teaching time" needed for undergraduate education. Similarly, teaching time is purchased from the staff of Children's Mercy Hospital. This plan has stood 20 years of testing.

In 1972, with the next increment of Docents needed, old friends responded. Three colleagues moved their lives to Kansas City and took on the new task of docenting.

Bill Martz, the same man who had been in Indiana University Medical School with me, who had helped in the rebuilding of the College of Cardiology, and who had persuaded me to take on the audiotape came.

Carl Schmock, a private-practice internist from La Jolla, a faithful participant in the La Jolla cardiology courses came.

Don Santschi, a private practice cardiologist from Rockford, Illinois, who had attended the small, personal retreats at Rancho Santa Fe came. They came with wives, children and vans of furniture. We suddenly were a large family. I may be wrong by two or three children but I think, in total, they brought 13 children. Bill Martz even arrived with a hearse. His sons enjoyed drag racing and their racer fitted in the hearse.

An endorsement like this by old friends touches one. It also increases one's sense of responsibility and commitment. With the Sirridges, Bob Mosser and my three friends, we were ready for the next demonstration in "how to be a Docent."

It is painful to remember how very overworked these first Docents were. They were the entire staff of the Department of Medicine at the hospital and therefore had to carry not only the clinical and teaching load, but all of the committee work for which hospitals are infamous. At the same time, they were involved in the multitude of planning sessions for the Medical School. They were overstretched.

At about this same time, I had an official visit from Oral Roberts. He was planning to launch a new medical school and came to ask me about my own experience. He was dressed in a soft-gray three-piece suit, wore a purple tie, and a fluffy but controlled hair arrangement. We talked for an hour, and my main message was that it was very difficult to fund a medical school. I told of the Hershey gift of $50 million to launch a new school, and how within a short time it was essential to get the State of Pennsylvania to add the school to the tax-supported rolls. He listened carefully and told me that God would provide. I did not try to tell him that God sometimes overlooked medical schools. As he left, we stood and I was prepared to shake hands in farewell. Instead, his hand rose to my forehead, rested there. He said, "May God bless you and your noble work."

Chapter Twenty-two

NEW YEAR'S DAY 1973 KICKED off with one of those well-known "offers you cannot refuse." From the preceding chapters, it is apparent, or to use a phrase later made popular by our third Medical School dean, "our plate was full." We had all the opportunities we needed.

The Jackson County Legislators, as their last act of 1972, voted enthusiastically, without consultation, to turn over to our hospital board and Medical School full responsibility for running their Jackson County Hospital and their Mission East Nursing Home. This hospital was a full 20 miles from our base. Their reasoning was straightforward. Jackson County citizens had enthusiastically voted to bond themselves to build the new teaching hospital. Surely the nonprofit, volunteer Board that was destined to inherit this gift of the voters would take on another public duty?

This generosity was not exactly what we needed. The Mission East Nursing Home had been created by the County during the critical times following the riots of 1968 as an evidence of the concern of the Legislators for the inner-city poor—the elderly poor. The anticipated federal funding was not coming from the Nixon Administration. The facility was in a crisis. A quick cosmetic solution? Show responsibility and take it out of politics. Give it instantly to us.

The Jackson County Hospital had originally been the county poor farm. Upgrading it had been one of the administrative responsibilities of Harry Truman when he had held his first elected county office. This County hospital, miles from anything, had struggled for years to maintain a staff, to avoid occasional newspaper exposes of neglect, to spend as little money as possible, but keep viable. At election time, it made good press as evidence of the legislators' caring.

In recent years, two community hospitals had agreed to watch over its staffing if, in return, they could send their Residents, especially in surgery, for a part of their clinical experience. As usually happens, the County hospital, being at least 20 miles away from either of these community hospitals, had little of their senior staff supervision. The hospital had become a source of "useful clinical material" for the Residents.

Unfortunately, these two community hospitals were two of the important partners in my attempt to send our students out into the city for their education. This unilateral decision by the County was not only alienating to the hospitals because it badly damaged their residency programs but it provoked in them a deep suspicion that we on Hospital Hill had orchestrated this. It was the kind of turmoil we did not need.

This was not all of the New Year's bounty from the County. We first learned about the two medical facilities. Later, they hesitantly told us that their generosity included the medical-care system at the County Jail. Hereafter, we would have full health care for all prisoners of the County as another responsibility.

This sudden New Year's gift was only livable because of the willingness of our hospital's executive director to take it on.

Ed Twin again proved his unusual worth. The County Jail? O.K. We will do it. We will make it the best jail care possible. A County hospital? No problem, we will just call it Truman Medical Center-East and we will run it at the same high level that we will the new Truman Medical Center. An old-folks home? What an opportunity!

Ed quickly realized that there was a way to look at these "problems" as opportunities. In running the General Hospital (the future Truman Medical Center), we were receiving our operating money from the City of Kansas City. This new responsibility meant we would have a second budget source: Jackson County. We would divide the cost of administration, of the laboratories, of X-ray, etc., between these two budget sources. Ed, and with Carl Migliazzo representing the Board, saw this through and we not only survived the unexpected gift, but improved all the parts.

In April, immediately following the Rancho Santa Fe course, I took an American College of Cardiology Circuit Course team to China. My colleagues were my old friend, Eliot Corday; Suzanne Knoebel from Indiana University; Donald Effler, cardiac surgeon, from the Cleveland Clinic; Abraham Rudolph, pediatric cardiologist, from the University of California-San Francisco; old friend Bernard Lown from Boston; Jeremy Swan, of Swan-Ganz catheter fame, from Los Angeles; and Arnold Katz from the University of Connecticut. The latter is the son of the famous Louis Katz I had visited before setting up the Kansas heart lab, evidence of how the years were passing.

The team represented well just about every facet of world-level cardiology and the Chinese opened their institutions to us. Remember, the year was 1973 and the Cultural Revolution was still a part of their vocabulary. Therefore, it was a "friendly" visit, but also a tightly controlled one. Significant friendships were made, and dozens of Chinese cardiologists had subsequent training in the United States because of the contacts made.

On May 12, our new medical school gave its first degrees. The nine very advanced students we had admitted with Ph.D.'s and D.D.S.'s graduated.

In September we made an addition to the faculty. This time I went to my circle of friends in Washington and in the National Heart Institute. This man had been in charge of the heart institute's training grants; we had met several times during his visits to La Jolla. While I was in Washington, I had been a guest at his home often, and enjoyed his considerable skill as a cook. He was trained as a physiologist and had made a considerable reputation as a textbook author. This, of course, is Lee Langley.

Lee proved to all that he was an exceptional teacher. He established a considerable reputation for his unique interest in the welfare of our students. He continued teaching, giving special consultations, and taking a considerable role in the administration, until his retirement.

On September 11, 1976, the students held their third annual roasting of the faculty. This had begun as the First Annual Provost's Award Night (FAPAN) in 1973. In those early years, Ed Twin and Henry Mitchell served as masters of ceremony. The drink of the evening was beer. It was only after the two of them became obviously tipsy and inarticulate, on stage, that I discovered their beer cans were filled with scotch. They worked hard and inventively to think of ways to embarrass me. Dead fish, dead fowls, and toilet seats were among the treasures they flung at me.

The students give the faculty and staff their full roasting on this night. The Education Assistants (EA's) were always well worked over.

The second year it became SAPAN (Second Annual...), the third year, TAPAN, etc. When I resigned in 1979, it became the Final Annual Provost Award Night. FAPAN, again.

This continued for a number of years, but the natural evanescent memory of the always-changing student body finally decided FAPAN meant Faculty and Peer Appreciation Night. I could better appreciate Faults and Peculiarities Ad Nauseam. However, I long ago lost my vote.

Regardless of FAPAN's meaning, it remains a delightful part of the medical school's life. It is not only the night in which the students singe and sear the faculty, it is also an index of the faculty's personalities. To be insulted at FAPAN proves the students care about you—one way or another.

Two members of my family, each intensely loyal, just could not handle the burning wit, innuendo, and liberal libeling given me each year. Mary D. and Lea Grey were prepared to declare war on the attackers, and agreed to stay home, and grind their teeth, while I went off to enjoy what I chose to call the affectionate insults.

By the fall of 1973, I was hearing enough rumbles from friends at the national level to alert me that the basic scientists within the Association of American Medical Colleges, and especially those who were involved in the medical-school accrediting process, were angry about the ability of our school to change the rules of tradition (and bias) that controlled American medical education.

An area in which I knew we were both vulnerable but right (a complex position and one that requires both stubbornness and conviction) had to do with National Boards. This is a national test, not required by all schools, but widely used as a standard. How well a school does on the Boards (their "score") was, for several decades, a national yardstick. Schools developed very strict rules about this examination. If one could not pass in three tries, one was out of school, for example.

Among many areas in which Vern Wilson and I were in complete harmony about medical education was our attitude about this particular examination. We considered it an artifice, an ornamentation developed primarily by the basic scientists. A low score in biochemistry? Obviously, there was a need for more time for teaching the subject, more staff, more budget. No one challenged this. No one asked if it was possible that the subject was being overtested, a rather critical question. We believed success on the test was unrelated to competence as a physician. We did not "believe" this in absence of data. Excellent studies had proved the lack of any relationship between success as a physician to one's score on this test. For example, a critical index, the opinion of one's peers, physician judging physician, had cleanly shown the Part-1 score was unrelated to that kind of critical opinion.

In this special medical school of ours, with our deliberate attempt to spread basic-science learning and clinical learning out over a full six years, we recognized our students were at a major disadvantage. Traditional schools put their students through two crammed years of basic-science classes; the test is given just as this period ends. The pump has been primed. In our school, there is no point at which the pump has been primed—except the moment of graduation. We have fed the basic sciences to the student along with the clinical information over a full six years. When, in Year Four, plus or minus, our students take Part-1 of the national test, our student may not in the least be ready. We don't care. Our internal checking is excellent, and if the student passes the test the first time—good. If he or she does not, relax—learn from the experience and take it again. In other words, we did, and do, use the test as a thermometer to allow the student to keep measuring his achievement of facts. We did not use it as a "make-or-break" moment. We tried to express this by repeating the analogy that all people do not run the 100-yard dash in 10 seconds. Some take longer, but they get there. This is a bad analogy if the purpose is to award a single winner's ribbon.

However, medical school is not a race. There is no "winning," the end point is professional competence and integrity, the overriding qualities not touched by the Part-1 test. All the runners (the class) must run the distance. Some may get there later—but surely. One does not raise his head from the operating table and ask, "Did you pass Part 1 the first time you took it?"

I realize that is a puerile analogy. However, many complete competent students, future honest physicians, need, deserve, more time to complete the 100 yards. That was my main point.

One does not take on such large issues without confrontation. We had confrontation. Inside our own faculty, Lee Langley contested me at all points. One of my satisfactions was to note that his own special form of tutoring consisted of selecting students in academic difficulty, and through his special skills in tutelage, assist the student to pass this test. Lee went on to become a believer in what I had fought for—although I am still waiting for the public evidence of his late-life conversion.

Another satisfaction, a deep one, is to note that the purveyor of the test, the National Board, has now identified that it was a flawed test and is totally reconstructing it.

I knew a confrontation was inevitable. I therefore proposed to Chancellor James Olson that he appoint for a five-year period a panel of outside consultants. My thought was that an annual three-day visit by this group, as inspectors, would not only give him (Olson) an outside opinion as to whether I was taking him on a wild-goose chase—but at the same time provide us with an informed external witness of what we were accomplishing.

I use the word "accomplishing" because I hoped to make the issue that we be evaluated by the outcome, not by the process. The critics sought to fault us because of what we were doing to the system; the last thing they wanted to learn was that this alternative system might be a success.

We formed a Consultants to the Chancellor group. They came in October for three days each year (1973 through 1977). They were a rather spectacular group, and the only blemish was that they so much enjoyed each other's company at each yearly visit that sometimes it seemed difficult to focus them on Hospital Hill.

The chairman was the former dean of Western Reserve Medical School and Nobel laureate, Fred Robbins. With him were Norman Cousins, editor of the *Saturday Review-World*; Boisfeiullet Jones, head of foundations in Atlanta established by the Coca-Cola fortunes, previously Assistant Secretary of Health under Eisenhower; Monte Duval, former dean of the University of Arizona Medical School and former Assistant Secretary of Health; Kerr White of the Rockefeller Foundation; and Alfred Fishman, head of cardiology at the University of Pennsylvania and President of the American Physiological Society.

The next year, 1974, brought a series of losses, losses which when seen by the individual, were successes. Nevertheless, the end result was a painful feeling of loneliness for me.

The Cleveland Foundation, one of the largest of foundations, with resources in the hundreds of millions, stole Homer from Kansas City. Homer had given Kansas City a splendid gift of 25 years of his career. The Kansas City that he left behind bore the print of his creative mind. Painful it may be to say, but Homer simply outgrew the city. Mary D. and I gave a grand, black-tie farewell dinner for him. However, I felt like weeping, not celebrating.

My cup of bitter tea was still brewing. In July, Nathan was taken away to be the vice chancellor for Health Affairs of the University of Pittsburgh. Again a man gave a tremendous contribution to Kansas City and, in the very prime of his days, went on to a better reward. Later, Nathan went on to a very high position in government. He became Undersecretary of Health.

When Homer and Nathan left Kansas City, they each left behind 25 years of their career. All who knew Kansas City in those years, know what major contributions these two made. Kansas City, in losing them, lost the kind of talent that makes a city.

On the last day of October, Vern Wilson shook Missouri from his heels and became head of one of the largest federal health agencies. From his deanship and vice-presidency, he became the director of the Health Services and Mental Health Administration, HSMHA, known by all good Washingtonians as HIZ-MA-HA.

Before 1974 was done, the only music I could sing was that old song, whose words run something like this: "... I wonder what's happening to that old gang of mine ..."

We had the Medical School; the school building and hospital funds were assured. Their long efforts were, in truth, done. But someone had to stay and keep the tribal fire. I had now been in Kansas City six years. What had been a delightful team suddenly had changed. My concern for a seventh-year sabbatical leave was not in jeopardy; it was gone.

Progress for the year came in different size packages. On January 1, the Division of Nursing became official. That was one more objective done.

Recruitment for Docents continued and among them were Beaty Pemberton who went on to be chairman of Surgery, Ray Snider, also on to chairman of Surgery and associate dean, and Nathan Winer, who remained in the docentship as a steady quality. We even tried a pathologist, Robert Hawley, as a Docent.

In June, we launched our first Hospital Hill Run. My intent with this event was to combine it with a postgraduate course dealing with health and physical fitness. For the first few years, we combined the day with a Medical School picnic. A Kansan who had also gone out to the Scripps at the same time I did, took my idea and made it into a real success. Ralph Hall was, and is, a delightful internist, with a fondness for running. He also was an educator by training, as well as a physician. He was the perfect colleague for this endeavor. A huge trophy for men, named after the original physical fitness enthusiast of them all, Paul Dudley White, was established. Friends of mine created a more modest trophy, in my name, to acknowledge the woman winner of the Run.

This Hospital Hill Run deliberately was planned so the route would take the runners by many of the hospitals affiliated with the new medical school. These were TMC, Menorah, Baptist, St. Luke's, Trinity Lutheran, St. Mary's and Children's Mercy. The nursing department at each hospital organized first aid stations, to attend the runners.

Near the beginning of their route, the runners came up a long, long slope, immediately by *Diastole*. For many years, it gave me a surge of happiness to stand on the southwest corner of 25th and Holmes and see the thousands of men and women go by, many calling out a greeting.

The hope I had in the beginning was that the Docent Teams of the medical school would get caught up in the fun and competition, and every year there would be some degree of challenge, team to team. Our students did run, but the docent-team competition never came about.

For many years the Run was a distinct jewel in Hospital Hill's crown. Then, with Ralph's move away, and with differing priorities in the Hospital Hill administration, it slipped away from its founders. Trinity Lutheran was alert, and reached out. They seized it, contributing a little money, and smoothly inserted their name; it became the Trinity Hospital Hill Run.

In September 1974, Chandler and Dorothy Smith came from Washington; Chandler became head of Pathology. I include his wife in noting their arrival, for she was a delightful and devoted participant in Hospital Hill affairs. Chandler came, indirectly, because of Lee Langley. Lee was successful as a medical-text author and had worked with an anatomist, John Christensen. John came to us as head of Anatomy. He had worked with Chandler. He interested Chandler and they came, too. Langley begat Christensen who begat Chandler.

It is always interesting to look back and see how inadequate one's appraisal of people can be. Chandler stayed with us until his retirement and thoroughly, doggedly, resolutely, prosecuted his same series of lectures each year. He served well this role as a didactic pathologist. He and his wife were engaging dilettantes and enjoyed their daily tennis, tea dances, and ship cruises. Chandler's daily affect was one of semi-detachment, and one did not feel he was fully engaged in the dynamics of the place. He seemed to be a victim of hebetude.

A few years after his retirement, all of us on Hospital Hill were lifted out of the torpor of our day, when a novel was published by Chandler. The novel (*Path to Caduceus*, Forum Books, San Francisco, 1990) used, very perceptively and realistically, the story of the founding of the UMKC Medical School, and very thinly disguised participants in his novel could be matched against our real-life players. This slightly fey pathologist, using the license of a novel, told stories that made it clear he had been eavesdropping at all points. Those reading this book of mine who look for, and miss, the stories left untold, can rectify my omissions by scanning Chandler's novel.

There was much more life in our pathologist than we suspected. One of his paragraphs, when he is setting the scene, and speaking of himself, reads: "Sleeping with Dorothy is a comforting experience. I sleep in the nude, but Dor always wears a nightgown, often with sheer, see-through panels down the sides. 'Keeps your skin from sticking,' she says. We sleep like spoons, front to back and close together. At the beginning of the night, or when we turn, she habitually squirms gently about, as if to close all the little surfaces that still be apart. My arm comes over her middle; and often up to her breast...."

This interesting family memoir is unrelated to the novel, but Chandler felt moved to include it. It is a reminder one never knows the inner fires dwelling, seeking telling.

In his novel, he gives me the stage name: B. Elliot Porter. Homer is Harold Wagner; Nathan, Norm Stevens. The rest of the cast you will have to figure out yourself.

On October 27, 1974, there was a real event. We dedicated the new Medical School building. My old friend Ward Darley came and gave the address. We were not only an official medical school; but the message was now stated in bricks and mortar.

As I wrote the word "mortar" in the above sentence, I winced. An error in the construction of the building allowed moisture to slip behind the bricks. Between frost and heat, the bricks shattered and fell. We survived that awful event and the associated lawsuits. A red-picket snow fence was placed around the School to protect people from "the gentle bricks that falleth from heaven." The final repair of the building and the removal of the red-picket snow fence was finished in 1991. Thank heaven that I did not know this bit of the future on this grand day in 1974.

There was one omen that all might not be well. As the last of the dedication ceremonies ended, Ward Darley, Dick Noback, and I led the procession to the Medical School front doors, cut the ribbon, and entered. Just then a young woman handed me an envelope. I assumed it was a note of congratulations. That evening, as I hung up my suit coat, I found the envelope. In it was a message, "This medical school proves the existence of male chauvinism. I have counted the toilet facilities and there are more male toilets and urinals than there are for women." This was a useful way to reduce the size of my ego at the end of this special day.

For 1974, the dedication was one of the few bright spots to remember.

As the year ended, Mary D. and I went out to our ranch and I concentrated on sorting out what I wanted to do next. I was six years into the Kansas City project. The planning part was done.

But the real task was just beginning. The contest for the legitimacy of the effort was next. The effort to bury the past image of the old charity hospital was just begun. The intent of preparing physicians who were special did not end with getting the funds and initial acceptance of the academic plan. There had to be a sustained waving of the flag, a maintenance of the spirit, a convincing of those involved, both staff and students, that this was a superior school. This was not the time to ease off, not the time to celebrate, not the time to dream of sabbaticals.

The initial success was only postponing the inevitable challenges from the Establishment. I knew my job was not done; in fact, the real battle was still coming. Kansas City had been supportive all the way; the presence of the School was due to the backing of the people, in the truest sense. Our momentum had carried us to this level. The antagonists had been pushed back. But they were there.

We needed to continue the battle. Now was not the time to go.

Mary D. understood. Above all, she enjoyed a cause, a project with a moral purpose.

We agreed to sell our home on Ward Parkway. It had served its purpose. Our children were no longer home, the two of us would enjoy a simpler place.

My proposal for a move to the inner city, to build a house in an area in which no new home had been built for 70 years, to build immediately on the edge of Hospital Hill—this all found in Mary D. that streak of adventurer, enjoyment of risk, commitment to purpose that so much was a part of her.

Our plan therefore went into operation as soon as we returned to Kansas City in January 1975.

Stage one was to prowl the margins of Hospital Hill and see what was possible. This experience almost sunk the thought. The area was so deteriorated and so near general dissolution that it seemed impossible. Remember, Crown Center was not in operation. Truman Medical Center was not there. Abandoned houses, weed-grown lots, empty wine bottles in the gutters, sidewalks cracked, curbs crumbled, derelict cars—Mary D. was ready for adventure, but must we live in a battlefield?

We scaled down our intentions. We would build a one-bedroom home, surrounded by a seven-foot wall, no windows at street level. Was this a house or a fort? We sketched and talked and decided to have fun and build a California-style house. Of redwood, with openness inside, and a great deal of glass 30 feet up of from the ground. The view would not be the Pacific Ocean but the Medical School—the reason we had made this move here. We would have no other view, and when you entered the place you would forget the neighborhood.

Reality got ahead of plans. We put the Ward Parkway house on the market and it promptly sold. We were without a home. We had no children at home but we did have some space needs. We had two dogs, one a German Shepherd. We had two secretaries at home who needed space. Although the children were gone, they would be home on holidays.

We did not want to commit ourselves to owning another home at this time. Lucky chance brought an apartment at The Walnuts, a handsome place, on the market for lease. This was not a perfect solution for two dogs but it was doable. We moved into The Walnuts, a truly lovely apartment place to live, while the "town house" on Hospital Hill was further considered. This was a mistake. The Walnuts apartment was so comfortable, so civilized, so free of all stress, that both of us realized that any sane, logical, normal couple would withdraw from the eccentric, peculiar, slightly mad plan to move to the inner city.

We tried to acquire the land where the Ronald McDonald House is now located. It was not ideal for it looked at the Dental School not the Medical School. We decided to wait.

I found an architect, Tom McCoy, who enjoyed working with woods and modern design. He understood the size of our adventure, took our sketches, and drew us a house that could be conveniently lived in, yet, at the same time, was only one-third done.

Our intent would be to try it for a few years. If we were not driven away by vandalism and crime, perhaps we would finish the house. If that proved impossible, our loss would not be too great.

Our weekend pleasure consisted of driving down to Hospital Hill and trying to visualize living there. We then drove back south, through the Country Club Plaza, into the serene grounds of The Walnuts, into the elaborate underground parking, up on the gleaming elevator with its cheerful attendant, stepping into our apartment looking out on the Plaza. It was not a logical way to persuade oneself.

In late January 1975, a telegram came from the Philippines inviting me to come as a participant in the dedication of the Philippines Heart Center. The invitation came from Mariano Alimurung, the old friend from Paul White's lab and our host for the first circuit course of the American College of Cardiology. The invitation came from him, on behalf of Imelda Marcos.

The trip was a peek into the inner domain of excessive power. Twenty heart specialists were gathered up from all over the world. We Americans rendezvoused in Los Angeles and were flown out by Philippines Air. I won't detail the whole extravagant event, but it included my being met on the lawn of the Heart Center by helicopter after I finished my lecture, being flown to the Marcos' holiday villa on the shores of the Bay. Chris Barnard and his new bride, Denton Cooley, Charlie Bailey, all vied for surgical precedence; Imelda hovered over them. We poor diagnostic types had no charm. After a soiree of we cardiologists, Christina Ford, General Franco's daughter and son-in-law, President Marcos, the multimillionaire gentry of the Philippines, and other hangers-on, the Presidential yacht took us to Corregidor. There we were given the tour of drama and tragedy associated with the beginnings of World War II.

The evenings were essentially audiences with the President's wife receiving, and dining and dancing into the night. From the 14-hour flight, the time change, and the social calendar, I was dark-eyed with fatigue.

The event was programmed for a full week. At the end of the

third day, Mary D. and I knew, heart center or not, this was not the kind of show we wanted to be manipulated around in. We booked our own flight and went to Hawaii. We used the waters at Waikiki to cleanse ourselves of our sins.

Among the losses and gains of 1975 was the departure of Bob Mosser, who left for California, and Tom Glatter, another colleague from the Rancho Santa Fe course, who arrived as a Docent. Also, John Cashman, a former Assistant Surgeon General, came as a Docent. A surgeon from private practice came as a Docent.

This use of all fields of medicine as Docents was part of our learning process. Some, such as Beaty Pemberton, were superb. Beaty would have been superb in any teaching role.

We not only learned from this experience but we also learned that internists were the only realistic players in the docent role. This fitted the growth needs of the hospital and, over time, about half of the Docents would be representative of the subspecialties of medicine and about half would be general internists. With time, this tilted towards more and more specialists, simply because this was the direction the practice of medicine was moving. The hospital care of very sick patients became more and more demanding of the subspecialties; fewer and fewer physicians went into general internal medicine.

We learned another lesson, learned it by experience. The lesson was that because of the absolute newness of the Docent concept and the absence of any previous academic standard, we did not attract traditional academicians and the people we did attract were often middle-life men (and women) who were finding themselves willing to leave their previous practices or jobs. The idea of a secure position as a teacher seemed comfortable, almost a sanctuary. There were various reasons they were willing to leave their practices. Some were simply unhappy and not doing well; some were no longer willing to put out the energy needed; some were in between divorce and remarriage; some were having emotional problems; some were simply malcontents; some really wanted to be teachers. And of course, some were friends who came to help. In the first years, we had all of these. Because we were so very new and unproved, new graduates coming right out of residency were hesitant about putting their careers with us.

Although I am speaking of Docents in particular, there was a degree of the same truth in all areas of the hospital and School. This was a difficult time to weather, but from this melange of talent we wove a faculty. The ability to add to the faculty was directly related to the buildup in numbers of the medical students. We were given no seed money; money came to purchase "teaching time" only as the student body increased. This fact made it not only difficult to fill out the essential staff, essential to any hospital, but guaranteed we would exhaust the physicians we had.

The fact that our basic hospital took care of charity patients made a heavy burden for some who came with us. I was sympathetic to this feeling. From my own years of pleasure with the solid Kansas patients and the prosperous patients of the Scripps, I realized well that there is a daily attrition taken on the physician who tries to serve the absolutely downtrodden, often social rejects, of an adult-charity hospital.

Some very good people gave us three or four years of their lives; then their own goals became clear; they went on to other arenas. The practice of medicine in an adult charity hospital is one version of sainthood. Jim Mongan, the third dean, remarked in a press conference, "We are doing the Lord's work"—lovely Irish words.

From the time we began the School, it took about 10 years before we gained a reputation level that attracted young first-class talent. Even then, there is always a steady migration, just because of the fatigue of hospital life in the inner city—and the ease with which medical talent can move to better pay. There also is the continuing reality that many young people come to be in such a program as teachers; then, as they mature, they move on in their careers. I don't consider those as losses but one of the functions of a teaching institution.

This staffing problem on the hospital professional side was never true in terms of the staff who came into the Medical School. I have often used the phrase, "our secret weapon," to describe the caliber of medical students we attracted from the beginning. Also, from the beginning, the support staff of the

Medical School was superb. I include Jim Soward, Virginia Calkins, Marilyn McGuyre, Louise Arnold, Regina Chollet, Louise Gammon, Pat Gosney, Gloria Ragan, Connie Currall, Rita Leifheim, Betty Steinman, Tom Mueller, Lee Willoughby, Harold Glazer, Joan Salem, Francoise King, Roberta Epstein, and those I omit, I apologize to.

Just as Ginny Calkins was involved in the selection of the first 1,000 students, Marilyn McGuyre was involved in their lives after they entered the school. No one person is better remembered by the graduates.

The teaching of Pharmacology and Therapeutics by Doctors of Pharmacy was a major success from the beginning, again because of the quality of these professionals.

The Consultants to the Chancellor came in November 1975 for their third visit, and joining them was a new member, Homer Wadsworth. Homer may have moved to Cleveland, but we were not letting him get completely free.

As 1975 ended, we were still living in The Walnuts. Our courage had not risen to the task of life on Hospital Hill.

Chapter Twenty-three

THE FIRST SIX MONTHS OF 1976 went well.

Still another team came out to inspect our progress. This was again a group representing the American Medical Association and the Association of American Medical Colleges. These teams, called *ad hoc* site-visit teams, represented the Liaison Committee of the two parent organizations; "liaison" because they represented two organizations. The leader of the group was James Haviland, an internist from Seattle; the secretary and representative of the permanent staff of the Association of American Medical Colleges was James Schofield, a basic scientist; other members were Daniel Bloomfield, the dean of a new medical school, the School of Basic Medical Science at the University of Illinois, Urbana-Champaign; and Gustave Werner, a basic scientist and dean of the University of Pittsburgh School of Medicine.

Inherently, it was not what I would call a friendly group, with three of them strongly interested in the basic sciences. Pittsburgh was as traditional a school as one could find, and Werner was a classic basic scientist. Bloomfield was a clinical-investigator who was charged with running the basic-science years of a medical school, before the students went on to clinical experiences, elsewhere. Schofield had been a member of previous site-visit teams and had been a prickly problem, especially skilled at eliciting criticisms from our faculty. Haviland, although chairman of the group, was an internist in private practice and did not carry the "clout" of an academician. He also was a "traditionalist" in the sense of being committed to medical education as he had experienced it.

When their three-day visit was done, they gathered in the chancellor's office for their "exit interview." Chancellor Olson, Dick Noback, and I were there. They summarized the conclusions of the team and informed us of the recommendations they would make to their sponsors, the AMA and AAMC. Dr. Haviland complimented us on our efforts. He spoke well of the students' enthusiasm, of our progress, and the good internist-docents he had met. The visitors felt we needed to continue recruitment, both of docents and basic scientists. They were disturbed by our willingness to allow students to take Part 1 of the Boards several times, but knew that we had a different philosophy about the Boards. They would recommend continued approval to their parent organization. This was as positive a report as we could hope for and we therefore got on with the year's work.

I previously had received an invitation from the Minister of Health of China to bring a Medical School delegation for a month's tour. We would be in Guangzhou, Nanking, Shanghai, Jinan, Tienjin, and Beijing. This was exciting and I immediately accepted. The obvious major problem was that this was an invitation, but it did not include funding.

I was anxious to have a full mix of our education team, with students of all ages, as well as faculty and staff. To be certain the students represented the wishes of their peers, we had them chosen by vote, and I took on the responsibility of raising all the money for them. I did not want family resources to determine who got to go. The cost was $60,000 and, although not easy, we got support from the friends, auctions, testimonials, lectures—from the work of a lot of people.

When the full travel party was picked, Mary D. and I had them to our apartment and began a series of briefings on what they were to expect—and equally important—what the Chinese would expect from us in terms of behavior.

Our group, both students and faculty, were superb. The faculty was made up of old friends. Henry Mitchell, Ed Twin, Virginia Calkins, Jay Morris, Chandler Smith, Marge and Bill Sirridge, Harry Jonas, and one of the Doctors of Pharmacy, Kim Kelly. The students were Vincent Shen (his uncle, Han Xu, would later became the Chinese Ambassador to the United States), Oscar Schwartz, Nevada Mitchell, Mary Lee Heim, Bill Dennis, Marc Taormina, Jan Campbell, Sandra Katz, Dan Flavin, Jerry Alstott, Anne Sly, Jeff Zuke, Nancy Russell, Cynthia Kleppinger, Stanford Walker, Robert McCown, Craig Pratt, David Hayes, Betty Finnie, Robert Balk, and David John.

These all now carry our Doctor of Medicine degree, and their competences and successes are the reward one gets from this strange business called medical education. There is no bottom line of dollars and cents. One has no final victories, just the progress of each career.

I cite everyone's name in the 1976 China group because, in a sense, they are responsible for the later gift of *Diastole*, for the University's use. We had so much just plain pleasure from the planning, and the quality of each, that we made the final decision to go ahead and build our home on Hospital Hill. The quality of the talent coming to Hospital Hill made it a worthwhile place to put one's roots.

On February 7, the day of our departure for China, a farewell pep rally was held at the Medical School. A University bus came for us, and as farewells were being said at the curb, I pulled Wanda Strickland aside.

Wanda was the wife of the retired dean of pharmacy and a capable real-estate agent. We walked to the head of the bus and I pointed south, straight up the hill. A dilapidated old two story house stood there, exactly on the corner of 25th and Holmes, the closest piece of land in all the surrounding neighborhood. I told her to buy it for me. We had crossed our Rubicon and committed ourselves to raising the flag on Hospital Hill.

The China tour was perfect. The problems were all good ones. Nothing gave us warnings that the inner-team actors of the Chinese government were deep in a showdown war. The recent death of Zhou Enlai would be followed by the passing of Zhu de and Mao, all in 1976. Within days of the death of Mao, his widow and three other members of the Politburo were arrested, and are still in prison. Now we know the country was in turmoil; then we knew nothing and sensed nothing. The "foreign guest" in China always has a murky view.

We had an exciting month, warmly hosted by the Chinese, and a final banquet in Beijing, with George Hatem as our special guest.

Small vignettes which stay in one's mind are different for each participant. For me, I remember the immediate crisis of arriving at the Kansas City airport and learning that Chandler had forgotten his passport. And when we arrived in China, learning that he had left it in the drawer in his hotel room of the city we had just left. We assigned a handmaiden to him for the rest of the trip.

Another memory was in Bill Sirridge's room at the Tung Fang Hotel in Guangzhou, where I was introducing him to the famous drink, mao-tai. He spilled some on the green painted floor. We both watched in fascination as the paint smoked and slowly boiled up.

And the group's self-proclaimed photographer, Jerry Allstott, carrying a very expensive borrowed camera, hurried up to the roof of the Tienjin Hotel to photograph the city. He leaned out over the parapet, his hands miscalculated, and the borrowed camera, quietly, permanently, and gracefully, fell 11 floors.

On May 15, 1976, 11 of the original 18, the 18 admitted on a gamble, received their degrees. For the first 100 graduates, I felt I knew them each. Then, as the numbers built, I did not enjoy it, but it was impossible to know each by name. This group of the "originals" I felt I knew. For the next several years, I watched each move of their careers. I corresponded with their residency chiefs, and each up-and-down event provoked a parental anxiety attack. Finally they were old enough, and there were enough others, that I could relax. The ducklings were taking wing.

On May 21, the president of the University resigned and Jim Olson, our Kansas City chancellor replaced him. Olson was "interim" at first, then full president. I had been a professor of the University eight years and we were on my third president.

In passing, one must comment that the rate of passage of Arts and Sciences deans through UMKC did not make easy the effort to harmonize the double degree, A.B.-M.D. Even though I experienced it, I cannot remember all their names.

On June 30th, a full six months after the *ad hoc* site-visit team representing the Liaison Committee had given their favorable exit interview, and with no interim contact, we received a letter from the Liaison Committee on Medical Education. The long-anticipated attack was made:

"The Liaison Committee on Medical Education on June 16, 1976, recommended to its parent bodies that the University of Missouri-Kansas City School of Medicine be placed on probation, effective January 9, 1976, until evidence is presented to the Liaison Committee that solutions are forthcoming for the deficiencies outlined in the enclosed report of the visit of the *ad hoc* survey team."

The deficiencies cited were in our evaluation system, and in the docent system. The hostility and the intent, even if disguised, came in the last paragraph of the criticisms:

"Inasmuch as this school has been under planning for 10-11 years and in actual 'teaching' operation for six years without demonstrable success in recruiting the number and type of physicians required as docents to fulfill the 'Academic Plan,' alternate approaches to the education of physicians at UMKC need careful examination, at once."

The use of quotes around "teaching" and "Academic Plan" conveyed to any reader the suggested quaintness of what we were doing.

As the Ink Spots once said in song, "... into each life some rain must fall ..." And I think the words went on, "... why must so much fall in mine? ..."

Probation in academic life is about as dismal an event as can be generated. For a school to go under financially, as Oral Robert's eventually did, is infinitely a lesser level of wound. My ability to hate is as good as anyone's. As Churchill is rumored to have said, "Never trust a man who does not know how to hate." Although my hate level is first-class, my ability to settle down, understand the ultimate objective, weigh resources, and play life's chess game to a reward point, is in good repair, too.

Bill Martz told me not to take this action "personal." I shared this opinion with Mary D. Her answer was pure, wholesome, basic. "Not take it personally! What is it if it isn't personal! When someone shoots at you, it is personal!" I felt exactly the same way. This was personal.

I began my careful response. I spoke with our Consultants to the Chancellor. They confirmed their clear endorsement of the whole program, including evaluation and the docent system. I reread the evaluations that had been made by a host of visiting professors and the outside grant agencies who had been over us repeatedly. I reviewed the written, private analyses by the graduates and students. The areas criticized were not vulnerable.

We certainly knew the Docents did not yet match the potential that we knew would come. The Sirridges had been with us since the beginning, and were outstanding. Bill Martz, Don Santschi, Carl Schmock, and Nate Winer were honest, competent men. All of them were distinctly not the typical academic professor, but that was what we wanted.

Outside inspectors want to find that with which they are comfortable. The idea that the primary faculty person at our school must not only be a competent physician but an advisor, a confidant, a stimulus—but not a walking, talking, spouting oracle of information, was alienating. The inspectors were used to an aggressive, publishing, grant-getting, competing faculty of individual careerists.

They were not alone. Many talented people have come with us who, even after detailed briefing, found themselves intensely uncomfortable with the close student-teacher personal role we seek. They become uneasy. They are able to teach in the classroom; but one-to-one personal contact, over a four-year period, causes them to feel invaded.

Speaking of a larger issue, Franklin Roosevelt told of the difficulties he had in finding staff for his "New Deal." He wrote: "New ideas cannot be successfully administered by men with old ideas, for the first essential of doing the job well is the wish to see the job done at all." That is almost a summary of what we have experienced.

The pain comes from the fact that, over time, old ideas gradually move in. Unless the leader of the Docents is a cheerleader-coach, an excited and exciting personality, the word will remain Docent, but the work they do will revert to tradition.

In this new school, we knew this well, and we had deliberately taken a different route to find Docents. For the Liaison group, it was obvious that the concept of "docent" itself was alienating, not the Docents.

I checked with Nathan, who was intimately involved on the Liaison Committee. I contacted friends at the AMA. I gradually began to put together an understanding of the politics and personalities behind the attack. Evil is in the eyes of the beholder, to malignantly paraphrase. I saw evil.

An institution's responses to "probation" are limited. The local news media do what they are supposed to do, and make it a major story. There is little to be gained by responding, through interviews or articles. All you gain is a certain amount of satisfaction from at least doing something; in the main, you put yourself in the position of making excuses.

On many occasions, the "probation" status is useful to a school's administrators. In fact, sometimes one suspects that the designation of probation has been sought by the institution, in order to have leverage for more money at the State level. Probation in such a circumstance is a welcome crisis.

A direct political response is always possible. The school can organize an ethnic or racial group's backing, get the Governor, the Senators and Congressmen involved, and definitely, deliberately, not even delicately, get into behind-the-scenes-arm-twisting. With the local newspaper and media crying foul and bias, and with high-level politics, the two partners forming the Liaison Committee can be intimidated. In 1990-1991, this kind of response was mounted by a Florida medical school, successfully.

This had no appeal to me. I reviewed our progress and checked off the record: medical school building done, hospital near completion, Children's Mercy Hospital rebuilt, good, mature clinicians as Docents, a stable administration, $10 million in outside grants, negotiated contracts with all regional hospitals, durable financing from City, County, State resources, firm legal contracts binding all partners, very high-quality applicants for admission, happy medical students and graduates. It was clear that the attack was on our very education system itself.

The strengths already in hand were more than many medical schools ever achieve. In the ways that really count: physical resources, financial stability, and quality of students, we were better off than a very large number of American medical schools.

The attack was a major effort to force the University itself to jettison this irritating anomaly, this upstart challenge to the Establishment.

I formed my response; however, at the same time, I laid out my long-term plan. The short-term need was to stay calm, to avoid the media, to avoid a political response, and to avoid taking the issue on as a personal attack.

The ability of the Liaison Committee to make the designation "probation" stick was limited, I decided. The group of malcontents responsible for persuading the Committee to place this designation on us would soon lose their own credibility. What was being done at UMKC was too successful and too much witnessed to be ignored. The caliber of the Consultants to the Chancellor could not be brushed off. The other review bodies, who literally had crawled over the place, including successive *ad hoc* site-visit teams from the Liaison Committee, had all been too endorsing to be ignored.

Logic told me the probation would respond to time and the winning out of good judgment within the Liaison Committee.

More importantly, there was the clear signal that I, personally, must handle. That was the signal that I must separate myself from the issues involved. There were two parts to this "probation." The first was the threat felt by the traditionalists from the UMKC plan. This issue would be handled by the success of the School. In their anger, they had not read our hand well; we had a full house, not aces and eights.

The second part of the challenge was the personal attack on me. The personal image I had earned on the national scene was, as much or more, a part of their anger. The education plan alarmed them; the fact it came from me was the lightning rod.

From a chairmanship at a very early age, working with the independence of adequate personal resources, on to taking on the building of the American College of Cardiology, on to my repeated criticisms of medical education, to a highly visible base in Washington, to the actual founding of a medical school, to the publicity of the secret China trip—yes, I was the lightning rod.

My double response to probation was logical. First, don't change anything. Keep the integrity of the education system intact. Let success be the answer. Second, begin removing myself from all administration. The need was surgery, a clean division had to be made between myself and the School. This could not be done at once but I sketched out in my notebook how I would do it. The timing was right.

First, at the University level, a new chancellor was to take office. He would have his own agenda. It would be important to convince him of the integrity of his medical school; that would be a key issue, because his selection could occur while we were still on probation.

Second, one of the values I had built into the School was the intent to change the top administration on a seven-year basis. This was not a personal eccentricity of mine, but an honest belief that seven years is just about enough for the good of the School. An administration longer entrenched develops atherosclerosis. Too many favoritisms grow up; too many talents plateau. Rigidnesses and perks become the logic of the day.

Dick Noback and Ed Twin both had their seventh anniversaries in office in 1977. They should move into docentships, and new talent should come in.

I would stay until their successors were well launched, until the new chancellor proved supportive, then I would begin a disengagement. I would do this by steps, very careful steps, so that there was never a power vacuum to be seized, until one day I was not involved.

A part of the probation process is the right of appeal. This we exercised on October 25 when Jim Olson, now the University's president, Dick Noback, and I presented our side of the argument at a hearing in Washington. We did this carefully, reasoning that a very well-planned "paper trail" is important. Friends on the Liaison Committee would have grist with which to work.

The high point of this hearing was an unexpected reward. Present at the hearing, sitting across from me, at my right, was a very senior pathologist from a well-known southeastern seaboard medical school. He was there as an observer, we were advised by Dr. Schofield, who presided.

I was in the midst of my point-by-point rebuttal to the Liaison report. I noted the pathologist was leaning forward, quite tense, and clearing his throat nervously. Suddenly, he struck the table and demanded, "Just how long are we supposed to tolerate this harm you are doing the students out there?!" Dr. Schofield quickly rapped the table, and fairly harshly reprimanded the man, telling him he was not to again enter into the proceedings; he was to be quiet.

I relaxed. I had met the enemy. He was no problem. He was defending the past.

In October, using AHEC money, and with Ed Twin's leadership, we had an elective in primary and rural medicine in southwest Missouri. This we did by renting motor homes. The group visited practically every health facility in the region. The success was enough to warrant the same in northeast Missouri, a repeat in southwest Missouri, and then down in the Bootheel area.

These efforts to expose students to not only the varieties of health care but, also, to the pleasures of sharing an experience, were an important part of the School's spirit in the early years. I have already described the China adventure. Over the next several years, through the energies of Ed Twin, Henry Mitchell, Dick Noback, Ginny Calkins, and others, we had month-long student-faculty "health-care system" teams in the Navajo reservation; in Israel and the Isle Of Kos; in Austria, Czechoslovakia and Hungary; in Canada; and in northeast China. These were large, informative, joyful efforts.

The seriousness of this effort is spelled out by the calendar:

1976 China - 21 students
1977 Navajo - 11 students
1978 Israel, Greece - 22 students
1979 Ontario, Quebec - 11 students
1980 Austria, Hungary, Czechoslovakia - 19 students
1981 China - 30 students
1982 British Isles - 16 students
1984 Germany - 15 students
1985 Spain - 6 students
And then it ended.

Why cannot one find a million-dollar endowment for such important experiences? Call it 747 Medicine; it would add to the vitality and breadth of the whole organism. It needs to be endowed, for the opportunity must not be only for those who have the resources. Also, even a prosperous parent carries enough burden through the huge tuition. Such a gift would be equally far-reaching as an endowed Chair.

Two "building" projects were being finished in the latter half of 1976. On November 14, the Truman Medical Center was dedicated. This represented almost $40 million. With the Medical School building costing about $14 million, the new Children's Mercy Hospital, the Dental School, new construction at Western Missouri Mental Health, and the Brothers of Mercy building, $100 million of rebirth had occurred on Hospital Hill in one decade.

The second new building, on a very small scale, coming to completion in 1976 was *Diastole*. We moved in on January 1, 1977. In every sense, we meant for this move to indicate we were here to stay. Probation was not a problem. We would see it through.

I did not forget the shadow of probation, but I had decided we would change nothing. My exact words were, "We won't change one goddamn thing." The School was moving well. The students were our answer. Hold steady, and there will be no way to sustain the Liaison Committee's action.

April 12, 13, 14, 1977, saw the return of a new *ad hoc* site-visit team.

Membership of the team was numerous. The chairman was a very tough, hard-liner of basic sciences, Ronald Esterbrook of Southwestern Medical School of Dallas. With him were the secretary, Ed Peterson, a retired private practitioner from Evansville, Indiana; he was the AMA's staff person; Donn Smith from the University of South Florida; Robert Buchanan, the administrator of Michael Reese Hospital of Chicago; Harriet Inskeep, lay-person representative from Fort Wayne, Indiana; and Richard Magraw, dean at Eastern Virginia Medical School.

On July 11, 1977, President Olson received the Liaison Committee's formal report:

"The Liaison Committee on Medical Education, in its meeting of June 29-30, 1977, reviewed the current status of your School of Medicine and has recommended to its sponsoring parent organizations that the School of Medicine at the University of Missouri-Kansas City be removed from probation and be awarded full accreditation for a period of three years."

Deep in the report was the paragraph: "The school is to be commended for its recent success on recruitment, both in regard to the basic sciences and in the clinical fields, especially concerning the faculty members added to the Department of Medicine who will be serving as docents."

We had changed nothing. No grand new recruitment had been done. We were the same school, enjoying the expected normal growth.

Tucked away in the site team's report, there was the truth from which they could not hide:

"... the team enjoyed an informative discussion with [a] large group of students ... They indicated satisfaction with their educational opportunities at all stages. They were especially enthusiastic about the pairing system used on the docent teams ... This enables the senior student to provide some instruction for the junior, and also enhances case study follow-up ... The students have found the docent system to provide excellent counseling ... They feel their input into planning through membership on the various councils is excellent. ... They found that the variable roles they play in the course of their six-year educational experience compensates for vacation time, and also that the one month vacation each year is sufficient."

The students had been the evidence that could not be ignored. They have always been the strength of the School.

Leaping ahead, for it fits the story, it is satisfying to note the Liaison Committee's report of 1989:

"The University of Missouri-Kansas City School of Medicine six-year, B.S.-M.D. Program is viewed by this Team to fulfill admirably the requirements for the general undergraduate education of the physician. The Program effectively sequences and successfully integrates a baccalaureate arts, sciences and humanities curriculum, basic medical sciences, clinical sciences and correlative studies. It utilizes a Docent System to guide individual mastery of this subject matter and its application to patient care.

"...The Survey Team is particularly impressed by the following unique aspects of the program:

"The organization of the curriculum around a Docent System which delivers comprehensive general medical education effectively and compassionately."

The report continues in this laudatory manner. We were doing just what we had been doing since 1971. Nothing had been changed. I am sorry (seriously) that the good pathologist who worried about our students, has gone on to his reward. I would like for him to know that we were continuing to "harm those students out there" in the same old way.

Before I seem to be basking too thoroughly in the glow of success, I hurry again to comment that this acceptance does not mean we are an appropriate model for all other schools. We are a good model for the variables that were the reality of the time and place when we founded this school. Neither do I believe that the way this school is planned is forever. The scene changes. I hope the changes are made with a majority of the graduates of the school in harmony with the change. By this comment, I indicate that neither new deans in the front office, nor new chairmen of Medicine should have the deciding vote to change the system. Those who have been exposed to all the parts of the program, the graduates, should have the influential vote. No one else knows what the total experience is intended to accomplish.

Back to 1977. In May, we did an all-health-schools' elective in the Navajo Nation. Representatives of the Indian Health Service and of the Nation had come to Kansas City to help us plan, and Henry Mitchell went out to develop the details.

Again, we rented motor homes, and made the trip out from Kansas City, in convoy. Health care teams were set up in four locations on the Reservation (Chinle, Shiprock, Flagstaff, and Farmington), made up of medical-, pharmacy-, dental- and nursing-school students and faculty. We stayed a month. The members participating were Henry Mitchell, Bill Strickland, John Cashman, Brian Pope, William Sirridge, Richard Hellman, Edward Hesterlee, Walter Hemelstrand, Richard Waldman, James Ebberts, Gerald Wankum, Janice Abernathy, Mark Harris, Jon Julian, Mark Scarborough, Jeff Wright, Howard Schwartz, Christopher Sirridge, Lesley Schroeder, Carol Wiseman, Gail Stafford, Elaine Williams, Douglas Adcock, and Margueirite Lenzen.

If we, as an institution, had followed through, we could have developed a substantial long-range academic presence among the Navajo. It would have been exciting and rewarding. I don't fault anyone for this not happening; there was just too much to be done in Kansas City—and too few people to do it.

In June, Ed Twin resigned and became Senior Docent, responsible for the Gold Team. He realized, as did I, that his real work for the hospital was done. He had removed the old, brought in the new, and the Truman Medical Center was reality. The place no longer needed a reformer in pointing the way to honorable, humane care. Ed had done that.

Now the basic finances of the place needed solution. The excitement of building the new hospital had, in part, obscured the reality of crisis funding. He had done his part and had done what he was specially equipped to do. It was a considerable slowdown, a step down from tensions and crisis. and it took time for Ed to find himself.

He did, and Ed went on to his new role. I suspect, in the long spectrum of life and values, he would judge his time relating personally to the medical students as his real reward. Those students who knew Ed as Docent, can only treasure the experience and, of course, tell tales that will expand the story into a legend. They have shown this by forming an Ed Twin Society.

Ed lives, as do good teachers, through the lives of his students. Ed's reach was further than Hospital Hill. After his retirement as director of the hospital, he became infected with the China virus, the virus of wanting to help the Chinese as they reached out to the world.

Ed found happiness in what had been Manchuria. Now it is called Heilongjiang. The medical school in Harbin became his project. He took delegations there, and set about finding places for their young people in Kansas City.

In June, a new Docent came from Philadelphia. He was young, a bit insecure, but Ed enjoyed taking him under his wing. The man outgrew the "moniker" used by Ed, Stevie-Pooh, and went on to be a major strength as chairman of Medicine and associate dean.

In October, George Russell was selected as chancellor. He and

I began the mating game, at least the male half, characteristic of strong personalities. From the beginning, I enjoyed his directness and decisiveness. The University was not prepared, but over time, he began to shape the place. By the end of the first half-year, I knew I was on the right path with my intention to leave the Administration. Although I enjoyed George Russell and was comfortable with him as chancellor, I quickly recognized there was not room for both of us. Inevitably, if I remained in charge of Hospital Hill, we would clash. For the present, I would be comfortable if I had a free hand, or at least a firm input, into the successors of Ed Twin and Dick Noback. Beyond that, I would not try to reach.

In my first official meeting with Chancellor Russell, I outlined my own list of issues. These were:

1. The need for medical students to get the necessary Arts and Sciences courses in order to receive the double degree.
2. The need for a Life Sciences School.
3. The need for a combined Ph.D.-M.D. program.
4. The kind of new dean needed for the Medical School.
5. The need for the nursing program to concentrate on training Nurse-Clinicians, using the resources of Truman Medical Center.
6. The logic of terminating the Office of the Provost for Health Sciences.

In retrospect, it was a proper laundry list.

My urging about a school of life sciences was not new. When the School was founded, I deliberately separated the basic sciences from the clinical sciences, for all the reasons I have discussed, reasons dealing with two cultures.

My plan was only logical if the basic sciences had their own school, their own milieu, in which to prosper. Jim Olson understood the logic and, if money had been available, would have gotten this important piece done. The prolonged hassle to get the Medical School simply wore him down. With a new chancellor in office, and one who believed in research, I came back to the attack.

If the University had had the money, two schools would have been created at the same time: the Medical School; the Life

Sciences School. Most of the criticisms I faced, from both the local scene and national, would have been answered if real resources had been in hand. The extremely precarious origins of the Medical School become difficult to appreciate with the passage of the years. Twenty years after the opening of the school, the two schools are there.

In an effort to make clear this was our intention, the medical school building carries elevators and utilities for a full five more floors. These floors were intended to house the School of Life Sciences and the School of Pharmacy.

The logical place to put the physical plant for the Life Science School is on top of the medical school, on Hospital Hill. However, the players change, the scenario elaborates. George Russell has made a research park, the North Campus, the cornerstone of his tenureship as chancellor. He desperately needs physical construction as proof that his idea is valid. A new building for the life sciences is one he can perhaps capture. It is all a good example of what I have discussed earlier as the natural, inherent, unchanging nature of the two cultures, in academic life.

I had passed by my "sabbatical" time because of obvious reasons. Now, there was a proper time to have a sabbatical and still be useful. I asked the University for a total of four months, spread out over the year. I planned a month in Italy, a month in Israel, a month in China, with a month in between at our place in California.

The Rockefeller Foundation had awarded me scholar-in-residence status for five weeks at their Scholar's Center in Bellagio, Italy. This fabulous place is on a peninsula jutting into Lake Como. The home of Pliny the Younger had been on the same site. Early in this century, the heiress to the Hiram Walker Distillery fortune had married an Italian nobleman; in order to give this new status a proper setting, she had acquired the site and built an absolutely spectacular home.

If anyone reading this can ever find a reason to visit the Villa Serbelloni, at Bellagio, Italy, don't miss the chance.

And, of course, at the same time, inhale the beauty of the Lake Country of Northern Italy.

I had tape-recorded my many conversations with the American

physician who had joined Mao, George Hatem. With hours of these tapes, I needed time to transcribe them and make the material into a book. This was the justification for the Rockefeller award. The ultimate result was *Inside China Today* (W.W. Norton, 1983). Mary D. also was working on a book co-authored with Rewi Alley.

Five weeks in April in the Lake Country, with spring unfolding, was a delectable treat.

Other scholars-in-residence included people from all over the world, none a physician. It was the first time since I had entered medical school in 1941 that I had a period of such length in which all of my daily contacts were unrelated to the medical profession. Thirty-six years of full medical immersion was suddenly replaced by a privileged five weeks—of finding out what the rest of the academic world does. It was a revelation.

The director of the facility was Bill Olson, a political scientist. He and his wife, Betty, were ideal at the task. Robert Celli and his wife were their able colleagues. No place could have been more hospitable but, at the same time, conducive to scholarly work. There were musicians, authors, medievalists, law scholars, politicians—talent in all shapes and varieties.

During our stay, King Baudouin and Queen Fabiola of Belgium came to experience the place and see if something similar should be in their country. John Knowles, the head of the Rockefeller Foundation came. He had passed through the bitter time during which his appointment as Assistant Secretary of Health had been blocked by the AMA; he and I enjoyed exchanging stories about the organization. Within a few months from this time, he suddenly had toxic shock from a pancreatic lesion and was dead within hours. He had been so vital, so animated, at Bellagio.

One of the scholars was I. Bernard Cohen, the famous science historian from Harvard and a natural storyteller; his sparkling wife had been a heroine in the Spanish Civil War. A philosopher from England never appeared, whether dinner or picnic or hike, except in dark, pin-striped suit, vest, starched rigid collar—and brilliant red hair, uncut, uncombed, unforgettable. In the evening, he played classical music on the piano and, at dinner, no wine bottle passed him unemptied.

Each day was planned around breakfast in your room, a full morning in your study, a gathering of the group for lunch—then the afternoon free. At 7 p.m., all dressed for cocktails and music, then a splendid meal, always with the chef in attendance and taking bows.

On the free afternoons, I kept exploring wider and wider distances in the mountains above the lake. Although April, the mountains were not yet clear of snow. On one of my solo hikes, I attempted to cross a quite steep slope, perhaps an 80-degree slope. I slipped, fell, tumbled down until I was stopped by the trunk of a tree. The tree caught me across the back and I knew I was not right. I rested there in the snow, sat on my bottom, and slid down the rest of the slope. At the next village, I cleaned myself at the fountain in the square and tottered back eight miles to the Villa Serbelloni. If I did not have a ruptured intervertebral disc, I was a poor diagnostician.

Aspirin helped, and we went on to Israel. We were at the airport when the student-faculty team came from home. We spent three weeks and gained a full view of the health-care and education resources of Israel.

The members were (students): Ooch Cantrell, Shane Christensen, Robert Ferrara, Lawrence Friedman, Joseph Goldenberg, Cheryl Grey, Chris Haas, W. L. Harrison, Gordon Caplan, Kathy Lentz, Mark Molos, Karen Remley, Sally Prock-Rice, Craig Rosenfeld, Gary Salzman, Douglas Schwartz, Carlton Scroggins, Kathleen Bray-Shaffer, Stanley Shaffer, James Speiser, Pierce Vatterott, and Gary Wasserman. Faculty were M. Luisita Archer, Virginia Calkins, Mark Funk, the Richard Hellmans, William Strickland, Ed and Margaret Twin, and the George Devins.

A doctor friend, the same doctor whose thumb was bitten by a rattlesnake at the California ranch, took us under his wing. David Ruhe had become the international head of the Bahai faith, in residence in Haifa. He and his wife, Meg, took days off from their work to escort us. They not only taught us and guided us, but introduced us to exciting scholars, who took special effort to educate this mid-America group.

Israel, tiny but complex, stimulated our group and at the same divided us. For myself, with several dozen such overseas delegations in my bank of experiences, this was the most complicated in terms of maintaining harmony.

One small diversion came when our professor, Lee Langley, arrived with our medical student, his bride, Harriet.

After Israel, we went to the Isle of Kos, rented motorcycles and raced about, taking time to see the plane tree of Hippocrates and his healing temple. Then to Athens for the Acropolis and museums. If this is not a liberal education, how do you define it?

We returned to Kansas City with the group. On May 1, Dick Noback announced his retirement from the deanship and his desire to become a Docent. He had completed his successful role as the founding dean.

On June 1, 1978, John Ashley succeeded Ed Twin. John had degrees in medicine and administration. He had spent three years with us understudying Ed Twin before becoming State Health Officer for Idaho. I was satisfied that he was a good choice; although I was well aware of an underlying bull-headedness that sometimes complicated life.

On June 30, the Chancellor announced that Harry Jonas would assume the deanship, effective October 1, 1978. Harry had been head of our OB/GYN department and the head of the Doctors' Corporation. His move to the deanship left the Corporation position open.

On the same day that Harry assumed the deanship, I advised Chancellor Russell that I would leave the provostship on June 30, 1979. I would have completed all that I had come to Kansas City to do. I had become responsible for the Health Sciences Aug. 1, 1969. A full decade had gone into the life of Hospital Hill.

At the same time, I recommended that the Office of Provost for Health Sciences be closed. The deans of the respective health-science schools would be better served with this layer of administration removed. They should report directly to the chancellor. Ed Twin, Dick, and I were leaving a clear message to our followers. One should not hang on to title or power. Academic life was better served by change.

I sincerely felt the provost level of administration had served its purpose. However, it was clear to me that, at a future date, some one person must have an overview of the School, the Hospital, the Doctors' Corporation, and be the single person dealing with the main campus, the other health-science schools, the area hospitals, and Children's Mercy Hospital. I use the word "overview" because it is not an environment that can be managed by direction. Persuasion, through logic, is the only effective way to guide the unusually complex partnership. Persuasion, enlivened with imagination.

I took a long-range gamble and, for the present, urged a split leadership: the dean, the executive director of the hospital, the physician head of the Doctors' Corporation. I called it a troika. My gamble was that this was the best way to absorb the power, left free, when I closed my office. Time would choose the right leader. To do it by administrative fiat was not yet possible. There were too many incomplete issues. But at some point, it would become logical to place responsibility in one person.

Mary D. and I picked up our dogs, Lao Peng Yu and MaMa HuHu, packed us all in the motor home and drove to Rancho Santa Fe. We were there a full month and I finished the manuscript about Hatem. A considerable change had occurred in George's life. He had been diagnosed as having inoperable cancer. I felt it was an inappropriate time to publish about him. I therefore held the finished manuscript back for several years.

I tried to plant three eucalyptus trees and, on the third tree, had a jolting, crushing pain that took me to my knees. I convinced myself I had a back injury.

As it came time to head the motor home back to Kansas City, I could not tolerate sitting upright. I crawled into the back of the machine, to bed, and Mary D. drove us to Kansas City. I never left the motor home. It was entirely self-sufficient and Mary D. drove, walked the dogs, prepared meals and drinks, filled up the gas tank—and got us home.

My sabbatical was not exactly a joy; I still had major obligations before I could give up and get a work-up.

On August 2, 1978, I appeared before the Curators of the University. My purpose was twofold. I thanked them for the freedom they had given me. It had been just 10 years earlier that I had presented to them the plan for a new medical school. They had accepted it and, in the 10 years intervening, they had never called my hand, second-guessed me, or suggested any change. I then answered their questions, over a two-hour period. I knew it would be my last appearance before them.

The Chinese Medical Association had asked me to select a major team of American cardiologists for a lecture tour of Chinese medical centers. I had gathered a choice group of people, each with spouse. It was a commitment that I was fully obligated to do. The group was Jim Crockett and Marti from Kansas City; Bernard Lown and Lois from Boston; Ernie Craige and Hazel from Chapel Hill; Ed Haber and Carol from the Massachusetts General Hospital; Bill Parmley and Shanna from San Francisco; Tom James and Gleaves from Birmingham; Mary Allen Engle and Ralph from Cornell; Jack Collins from the Brigham, and Mary D. and me.

The Cultural Revolution was over, the Chinese were eager for information and contacts. The professional program went well. We moved from hotel to hotel, each room featured a bed with more sag than the previous. In spite of the very mature cockroaches one meets, I dragged the sheet and blanket to the floor every night, took my aspirin, and stretched out. My back was killing me. The nights were dismal, but a joy compared to the days.

On October 1, Harry took over as our second dean. Henry Mitchell had been chairman of the search committee. Harry was our first choice. Other men also had been on the list of possible candidates: Jay Morris, Ralph Hall, Jack Stelmach, and Bob Fairchild. We did not tell them and this may be the first time they know that fact. They were all able and the pain comes from wondering how things would have evolved under any one of them.

I finished out the two-week commitment to the Course for the Consultants, hosted a delegation of Chinese cardiologists at a Thanksgiving dinner at the Inn at Rancho Santa Fe, and we flew home.

I had a myelogram. The protruding little monster was found. Dennis Szymanski was the TMC neurosurgeon, and I told Mary D., "If we are willing to risk living down here, I guess I can risk having disc surgery at our primary teaching hospital." The surgery was done December 8, my birthday. It was a very good birthday present. I have had no pain since.

On the third day, I pulled on my pants, put on a tie, and tottered from my room, to the car, and home. The surgery was great; the constant interruptions, by friends sticking their heads in, was more than I could take.

My recovery was uneventful except for one problem. I had been taking 20 aspirins a day in the weeks ahead of surgery. I experienced a hemorrhage on the second day home and this produced substantial problems hovering on big difficulty. The body is a strong machine and time healed most of this damage. The back pain never returned.

Above the fireplace at *Diastole* there is a tile that carries this message, "Happiness is the absence of pain." The power and truth of that message takes quite a bit of living—and hurting—before it is understood.

PART SIX

Chapter Twenty-four

NINETEEN SEVENTY-NINE WAS A JOY. Not only did I end my primary administrative job but, recognizing that I had made the monthly cardiology tape for 10 years, I resigned as ACCEL editor.

My decade as provost was over. I remained the University of Missouri distinguished professor, and I returned to the title I had originally, Consultant to the Chancellor.

I continued my commitment to the Truman Medical Center Board and the Hospital Hill Health Services Corporation. My intention was to separate myself from the Academic Plan, to let it rise or fall on its merits. I resigned in order to depersonalize the issue. On the hospital side, especially with a new executive director, I wanted to still be at the table.

Ed Twin successfully had changed the heart and soul of the hospital. He had begun with a charity hospital and residency programs directed by powerful part-time men from private practice. These men were little kings, each controlling turf, prerogatives, and budget. The residencies were independent worlds, helping the poor, but not subject to supervision from the front office. Ed made the place into a primary teaching hospital, in partnership with the University of Missouri, controlled by a public volunteer board. This change has lasted.

The new director now would deal with the issue of solvency. To do that, it was critical to install a first-class administrative system. We believed we needed someone who had hospital-administration experience. Equally, it was our commitment that the person must be a physician.

I kept other interests: The Edgar Snow Memorial Fund, the Grenville Clark Fund at Dartmouth College, the twice-a-year Ran-

371

cho Santa Fe program, the monthly essay for the student newspaper, *p.r.n.* (this I have now continued for 21 years—try that sometime), two trips a year to China—and I began to work on a long-range project: to form a nonprofit corporation that would be the future owner of our home on Hospital Hill.

This corporation was designed not only to manage *Diastole* but also to provide a means of publishing books and educational material; organize and conduct travel delegations; provide a framework for visiting scholarships; and provide the business office for the Ed Twin Society. I wanted to launch a monthly audiotape, not on cardiology, but on the philosophy and ethics of medicine. I chose to call this corporation Diastole-Hospital Hill, Inc.

The audiotape, called, also, "Diastole," continued from 1980 to 1989.

I, also, was able for the first time to pay attention to the substantial California ranch and its commercial citrus grove. The land acquired from Dr. Billie Lieb in 1962, had become precious real estate.

Crown Center, our Hallmark Cards neighbor, had built an apartment tower. We put our name on the waiting list for an apartment. I assured Mary D. that we would move there after we added the second phase to *Diastole* and, in 1983 when I became 65, we would base ourselves between the new apartment and the ranch.

Many years ago, a physician, Alan Gregg, who had a major role in how the Rockefeller Foundation gave away its money, wrote a book, *The Difficult Art of Giving: The Saga of Alan Gregg* (Little, Brown, 1967). It is a quite ageless book and there are many who should read it—but don't.

One of his units of wisdom has stayed with me. He wrote that a career should be divided into chapters:

    age 20-32 learning
         32-44 doing
         44-56 directing
         56-68 advising

I missed some of these milestones by a little, but not much. I was 60 in 1978, and 69 when I left all Hospital Hill mainline duties.

As I had since 1968, I continued to organize and moderate the

Course for the Consultant, at Rancho Santa Fe. The participants had become such a league of brothers that it was difficult to conceive of the time and way for all of us to end the relationship. Mary Ann was the perfect hostess around which the entire group gathered; Jim Crockett had become so fond of Rancho Santa Fe that he, too, had a home there. Many of the men, almost all with their wives, had been there for 10 times or more (the tuition was $600, plus two weeks of deluxe hotel life, air travel, and absence from office; it was a large expense). When this long relationship ended at the end of 1980's, it was, for me, a painful parting.

These loyalists, men who came many times, men who formed a private, personal small school of cardiology, included: Arizona: Jim DeSando, Jay Silverman; Arkansas: Bill Holman, Keith Klopfenstein; California: Andrew Fitzmorris, Marshall Franklin, Irving Hirshleifer, Jerome Johnson, Rolf Koenker, James Lee, Tom Noto, Ben Rosen, Herman Sobel, Virgil Siebert, Ralph Truitt, Ted Welton; Colorado: Alan Rapp, Paul Smith; Florida: Ron Flam, Warren Lindau, Bernie Milloff, Selig Snow, Jim Strachan; Idaho: Tom Richtmeier; Illinois: Bill Cape, Norris Daugherty, Tom Glatter, Jules Last, Lamar Ochs, Paul Smalley; Michigan: Nathan Brooks, Omar Guevara, Vance Lancaster; Minnesota: Bill Bardsley, Bernard Cronwell (he attended every one of the courses), James Dahl, Tom Parkin; Missouri: Emil Miskovsky; New Jersey: Carol Kramer, Calvin Oyer, George Stoll, Irvin Sussman; Ohio: Martial Demany, Myron Fink, Matthew Mansuy, Stewart Nickel, Don Nouse, Bill Shafer; Pennsylvania: Peter Knibbe, Tom McGarry, John Wanamaker; Utah: David Richards, Bill Vincent; Washington: Gordon Hale, Paul Shields.

My enthusiasm in medicine, in teaching, was epitomized in the collegiality, goodwill, and commitment of these clinicians.

When I launched my "Diastole" audiotape, I soon found that my listeners were made up of former Residents and Fellows and the participants of the Rancho course. All the men listening were friends and students. More than anything I had done as a teacher, this nine-time-a-year audiotape became my recitation of what I really believed in. It is a rare privilege to have the right to take nine hours of a person's life, each year, and have them hear your solo propagation of your beliefs. After I had delivered 72 hours of this soliloquy, I felt I had had my fair share at the pulpit. I ended it in 1989.

I was involved in two diplomatic maneuvers in 1977 and 1978. The first was small, but satisfying; my part was real, direct. The second was very large, my part was indirect, only part of a piece, but satisfying.

On January 3, 1978, I had been contacted by Dr. James Sammons, the executive vice-president of the American Medical Association. He asked if I would work with the Chinese towards getting a Chinese-language edition of the *Journal of the American Medical Association (JAMA)*. I went about this, and on one of my Beijing visits got into full negotiations with the Chinese Medical Association. Things moved very well, and I telephoned my old friend, Bill Ruhe, at the Chicago headquarters and stimulated him into flying out to Beijing immediately. Within 48 hours (September 18, 1981) we had an agreement. *CLEJAMA* (Chinese Language Edition of *JAMA*) began publication in February 1982.

The second experience was, in every sense, a continuity of my relationship with Ed Snow, Paul White, and Grenville Clark. Richard Nixon had reversed the longstanding American policy of denying the existence of Mainland China, Red China, Communist China. By his 1972 trip and through the Shanghai agreement, the two countries had found a better way to live on this single earth.

It was not "peace," but it was better than sending our troops to Korea, to Vietnam, and maintaining a fleet in the waters between China and Taiwan.

With this new understanding, trade and exchanges got under way. During President Nixon's administration, official recognition of each country had not been accomplished; embassies, ambassadors, and full recognition were left undone. In 1976, at the end of the Nixon-Ford administration, the Chinese scene changed, too. Mao's death and the end of the Cultural Revolution put new leadership in power in China.

Ed Snow's interpreter, in 1936, at Paoan, the Communist headquarters, was a 24-year-old economics student from Yenching University. His name Wang Ju-mei.

Snow returned to Peking. Wang remained with the Communists. To declare yourself sympathetic to the Communists was certain to bring punishment, even death, to your family. There-fore, Wang changed his name to Huang Hua.

Huang Hua entered the Foreign Office. In 1977 he was the For-eign Minister of China, a considerable rise in the 41 years since his interpreter role with Snow.

In Beijing, over tea and in gentle, indirect conversations, many of them with Huang Hua's wife, Heliang, herself in the Foreign Office, we spelled out the steps that could lead to full diplomatic recognition and the conditions that would be palatable to the Chi-nese side.

From Tokyo, upon exiting, I sent the message to the White House and to the State Department. My foolishness does not allow me to magnify my role. Still, it was satisfying to be present in Washington, in February 1978, when Deng Xiaoping came. Full recognition was reality. The personal physician to the Chi-nese leader and I stood together and enjoyed what we had seen happen. Who was this personal physician? Wu Weijan—the same man who had met us at the Beijing Airport in September 1971, who had led the Chinese Delegation to the United States in 1972.

Life on Hospital Hill moved on, with ups and downs. However, the bad years had passed. Then, life had been made up of a series of crises, with occasional peace. Now life was an expectation of peace, interrupted by crisis. It was progress, but still not exactly a cruise ship.

Harry Jonas quickly found that life within a university is filled with restrictions and red tape. Things he felt should be done were contrary to the rules. This kept him at war with the new vice chancellor, Gene Trani. Within the Medical School, he had to sur-vive a small war with Lee Langley who had seized a degree of power in the dean's office in the interregnum between Dick Noback's resignation and the appointment of Harry. A major vic-tory for Harry, and a strength for all of us, was when he was able to get Russ Jones as his administrator.

At the hospital, the new executive director chafed under the unique conditions that forced him to not simply run the hospital in the best way he knew how, but to run it with equal attention to the needs of the Medical School. He was a TMC-Board appoint-ment but, equally, an appointment by the University's chancellor.

John found this difficult. He, also, had an additional stress source. Carl Migliazzo was not a hands-off board president. All of this made John's life complicated.

In 1980, we took our motor home to Cambridge, Massachusetts for the summer, rented a grand old home, and every day I visited the Cardiac Lab at MGH. Paul White's successor was Ed Haber. Ed was hospitable, and this time was good for me. It gave me a quick new-look into cardiology.

We continued our China commitment. In 1979, we were in Beijing, Inner Mongolia, Datung, Kunming, The Stone Forest, Jing-Hong on the Vietnam border, Si-Mao, and Guangzhou; in 1980, in Beijing, Beidaiho, Shanghai, Chengdu, Tibet, and Shanghai; in 1981, in Saudi Arabia and Turkey; in 1982, Beijing, Guilin, Nanning, Hainan Island off Vietnam, and Shanghai.

We were flying home in 1980, suspended in fatigue and champagne. I was quasi-dozing and barely heard, or comprehended, a remark. "I think you must know that I have adopted Wu Wei-jan's daughter." I "Uh-huhed" without much vigor; Mary D. repeated the statement and added, "She will be arriving at Christmas."

Wu Wei-jan had been one of those who had met us at the airport on our first trip; he had been chairman of the physician delegation of 1972. Each year, one of the nicest parts of our trips had been to meet him, his wife, and three little girls. His middle daughter was 13 or 14 when we first met; now she was a medical student and the family wanted her to have an American education.

Wu Tung arrived just after Christmas. As we drove away from the Kansas City airport, with the tiny, quiet little Chinese girl in the front seat between us, she said, very softly, "My mother says my name is Joan."

Mary D. had three daughters; I have three daughters. Suddenly we had a shared seventh. Life has unexpected moments.

This year also saw the death of one of the founders of the lay hospital board. Carl Migliazzo's efforts went back to the beginning; he had been chairman of the Jackson County Bond Fund Campaign. This bond fund was the major lever that had made everything else possible. He was one day well, and then one day was terminally ill with cancer of the kidney. He died in May 1981. He was on the Board from February 1962 until his death. All of us who had worked with Carl for so many years on Hospital Hill, and knew how much he had cared about the new hospital, caused a fountain to be placed at the entrance, carrying his name.

In July 1981, the Hyatt skywalk disaster occurred. The response of TMC was superb. There was no doubt that the hospital was first class. TMC's response was a direct result of the skills of Kendall McNabney, head of the emergency service.

One of our microbiologists, Tom Mahvi, was one of the 113 killed at the tea dance in the lobby. By only luck, we did not lose Dorothy and Chandler Smith; they were there "tea dancing" also.

At nearly the same time, another microbiologist joined us. Tom Hamilton (and his stellar wife, Bette) had been a part of that original group of chairmen I had enjoyed at Kansas. After what had been a long and useful career, deserving retirement, Tom and Bette chose to join our new School. They had team-taught so long that watching them perform in a classroom was a special, poignant experience. Tom was hurt by a stroke and needed a powered chair. This did not stop them; they continued on, adversity or not, to give students the lifetime knowledge they had acquired.

I had one last curtain call as a clinician in the middle of 1981. The Department of Medicine, the critical department in the Medical School's plan, had worn down four chairmen in a 10-year period. Bill Martz, Bill Sirridge, Don Santschi and Bob Conn had each taken a turn. Running a department of medicine in an indigent-care environment, without adequate money, and with the tensions of a new school in an old environment, had small reward. Most of the problems were over, but a stable period of administration was needed. I took on the acting chairmanship for nine months. I enjoyed this, and found myself doing things *deja vu*. It was all again Kansas, except then I was 33 and now I was 63. The burden of extra years was balanced by experience. One of the pleasures was to have as my chief Resident, Harriet Langley. Why? Because she was a full product of our system. She had come to the School directly from high school, and now, nine years later, I was able to bear witness to her competence.

The search process for a permanent chairman chose Steve Hamburger. Ed Twin and I were content. Ed's Stevie-Pooh had grown up. He took over the Department and gave it a reign of stability. It was my last role as an administrator-clinician.

In 1981, Nathan telephoned me to recommend a talent that he had seen on the Washington scene. I double-checked with others in Washington, both on Capitol Hill and in the Georgetown set, and verified the young man's qualities. We still had open the Doctor's Corporation vice-presidency. We brought him to Kansas City to take that position.

Jim Mongan and his wife, Jean, fitted in immediately. She had been a Capitol Hill staff person for a Kansas congressman but her roots were in Prairie Village; she had been raised there. With two quite small children, they had made a career move— but also a move to place their children in an environment trusted by the mother.

John Ashley solved his unhappiness and accepted an excellent job with the medical center at the University of Virginia. This was an amiable parting.

After thinking it over, looking at the alternatives, we chose to move a complete hospital-administration novice, Jim Mongan, into the executive director's job. Our thinking was threefold. First, he and Harry Jonas were getting along extremely well. After the tensions between Ashley and Jonas, this seemed important. Second, Jim had proved himself very intelligent, quickly able to size up issues, and third, perhaps a pure Irish genetic trait, he was a formidable politician. The hospital administration could be done by people trained in that area; handling the very complex partnerships relating to TMC required the kind of skills Jim had learned in Washington. Jim's appointment to the executive directorship of TMC began September 9, 1981. He had been acting director since June of that year.

We moved Ray Snider into the job at the Doctor's Corporation and the administrative troika was in effect.

Nineteen eighty-three was a special year. Mary D. and I began to talk about the reality that I would be 65 before the year was over. I was free of direct administration. However, I sat in with the troika weekly, made my monthly tape, was on the hospital board, and the Doctors' Corporation Board. Mary D. and I did our spring stint at the Rancho Course, did a lecture cruise for the Minnesota Academy of Family Practice, and made our plans.

Chapter Twenty-five

Although I have mentioned Mary D. in these pages steadily, I have not quite completed a portrait of her. Mary D. was different. She was extremely bright, wonderfully sensitive, unshaking in loyalty, and complex. Trying to search out two words for description, I select tenacity and rectitude. There, too, was a streak of derring-do in her; it was very unwise to challenge her. One night we walked out of an elegant California home. A large pool filled the patio. The night was salubrious. The host inhaled, lifted his head and remarked, "What a night! If we had any sense, we would all be in there swimming!" Mary D. looked up, her head cocked, and said, "Why not?"—sprinted to the edge of the diving board and swan-dived, clothes, shoes, watch, all, into the water.

Her love of her father was the strongest of all her characteristics.

Immediately after his death in 1968, she set about assembling his papers and, at the same time, began searching for the right place to put them. She went to Harvard, Stanford, Dartmouth, among several places. She finally chose Dartmouth. For several years, Mr. Clark's secretary was at Dartmouth every work day, codifying the papers, reporting to Mary D. At the same time, Mary D. founded a Grenville Clark Fund at Dartmouth to be used to award citizens of the world who had done much to further world peace, or civil rights, or used their energies as a private citizen for the good of others.

Through the years, this award was given upon the decision of the Grenville Clark Board. The meetings of the Board were a treat in themselves. Among the Board members were Kingman Brewster, Yale University president; Norman Cousins, litterateur; Anthony Lewis, journalist; Erwin Griswold, former dean of Har-

379

vard Law School; Leo Gottlieb, former law partner of Mr. Clark; Homer Wadsworth, old friend; and John Dickey, former president of Dartmouth. Each Board meeting was as an intellectual feast.

The awardees included Jean Monnet, Father Theodore Hesburgh, George Keenan, and a dozen other superb humans.

Mary D. was not a passive daughter. She knew her father was special, and she was determined that his work and hopes would not be forgotten. She devoted herself to being certain he was remembered. With the papers at Dartmouth and the Clark Prize established, she set about assembling a book: *Memoirs of a Man* (W.W. Norton, 1975). Norman Cousins agreed to edit it with her but, in truth, the finished product was all hers. She collected more than 50 essays from those who had known her father and added family photographs. She had an irresistible way of getting from people what she wanted. All the essays she sought, she got.

Even after her own book, she felt the story had not been adequately told. Gerald Dunne, of St. Louis University Law School, was commissioned to write a definitive biography. This appeared after her death. (*Grenville Clark, Public Citizen*. Farrar Strauss & Giroux, 1986.)

Still she was not done. She went about lobbying on Capitol Hill for the issuance of a postage stamp carrying Grenville Clark's portrait. A commemorative stamp, 39-cent denomination, was issued, May 20, 1985. Mary D. was not here to enjoy the moment; but she had put it in motion.

To be in Mary D.'s pantheon of heroes, one did not need to be her father. She could find qualities to admire in others, and, when found, she took them on as her special project. Ed Snow fit this image. The fact that he was our friend and that his death had occurred at such a bittersweet time, gave her the kind of purpose she understood. She immediately set about gathering Ed's papers and books. Working from her tiny, wonderfully cozy den in our home, she launched an attack on preserving the memory of Snow.

With the Collection started, she convinced our university that they should be partners in founding an Edgar Snow Memorial Society. University officials and librarians fell before the attack and found large amounts of space in their library devoted to a Snow exhibit. Kansas City, as his hometown, and the University of Missouri, as his school, were shaken up and reminded that they had a genuine hero needing to be recognized. Not only did the Mayor recognize a Snow day, but Lois Snow came from Switzerland to receive Ed's posthumous Doctor of Humane Letters degree.

Even with these descriptions, I do not quite convey Mary D.'s will-power, energy, and desire to do good. She carried on an immense correspondence and reaching out from our home on Hospital Hill, kept two full-time secretaries busy, and often needed a third.

China opened an entire new vista for her and, with thoughts about both her father and Snow, she made this another purpose of her life. One of Ed's friends in China was Rewi Alley, a New Zealander. Mary D. found him delightful; they carried on a steady correspondence. He sent her a very rough manuscript, titled *Six Americans in China*. Rewi was well into his 80's and pleaded that he just did not have the capacity to do the final draft. Mary D. did; she spent hours and weeks on this effort.

When a schoolgirl at Foxcroft, she had become interested in photography and during our years together, she took up this interest. Her eye for composition and color was masterful, and she assembled a collection of some 70 framed photographs. She organized showings of these and offered them for $500 each, all revenue to go to the Edgar Snow Memorial Fund. In one evening at Crown Center Hotel, she raised $8,000 from sales.

She had a way with a camera, but also with words. One evening we were sitting by a western lake, next to our motor home, coming back to the Midwest from California. It proved to be our last trip. She wrote this:

There is No Night Fall
Moon coming/sun going/thoughts slowing/heart resting
But not knowing/the new advancing/infinity
beckoning/sleep thinking/keep growing
Until——

During late 1982, Mary D. had a continuing upper abdomen distress. It was mild but recurring. We took her to the Scripps Clinic, a thorough workup was done, and they felt she had a mild gastritis. Medication did not help and, in early 1983, we took her to see Ed Twin, whose special field was gastroenterology. He did a gastroscopy and he, too, interpreted the observations as a gastritis. She complained occasionally of palpitation; exercise electrocardiograms were normal. Extrasystoles were frequent, but had been for years. Throughout these months she commented on her fatigue. However, when I was invited, as a speaker, on a Caribbean cruise by a medical society, she was energetic and participated in the women's part of the program by speaking and showing China slides. We came home by way of Buffalo, New York, where I spoke. Upon our return home, she was in full vigor, and immediately involved in putting on the first Edgar Snow Symposium.

This was a large production, with guest speakers sent from China and a considerable number of American China specialists. She enjoyed every moment of it and ran the whole show, competently, enthusiastically, and happily.

June 8, 1983, was a typical day. We wound up our work and met in the upstairs living room for a drink and talk time. She had her yellow legal pad and, as we talked, made notes for herself of things to be done. This was as much a part of her being as was wearing the diamond circlet that had been given to her by an aunt on her 18th birthday. Every morning began by an animated crying out, "Where is my pin! Oh, I can't find it." It was always found.

We read and talked after dinner, and were in bed by 10 p.m. She fell asleep with her yellow legal pad on her chest, her pen in her hand. I read on until 11 p.m., and went to sleep. I awakened in the night, noted the yellow pad and pencil were still there, and she was in the same position. Without a purposeful thought, I looked again and noted a strange slackness of her face. I brightened the night light and, in a moment, found there were no respirations and no pulse.

I called Ed Twin and he was with me within the hour. He shared with me all those suddenly logical, yet impossible, duties that come at that time. I went about reaching out to our families with the message.

We had had a wonderful 15 years together. We did many things we would not have done separately. We found a mutual strength in our late-life marriage. We laughed and lived and loved and had a lifetime of events compressed into 15 years. Every day was an exuberant adventure.

Chapter Twenty-six

LIFE GOES ON.
Several things were quickly apparent. I drove the motor home, with Lao Peng Yu and MaMa HuHu aboard, to the Ranch. The trip answered my questions. Motor-homing requires two people for pleasure; life at the Ranch, equally so. I returned to Kansas City and began the tidying up. The University added Mary D.'s papers to the University Archives. It took time, but I began shifting clothing, jewelry, furniture, automobiles, and family things to the children. I began the long, painful departure from the Ranch, my base for 30 years. I got the motor home out of my life. The San Francisco Towers apartment no longer fitted my needs.

I began taking each of the children to China, one by one. Five of the seven girls have now been there. They each made quick inspection visits to Kansas City to see if all was well.

Our shared Chinese daughter, Joan Tung Wu, became a graduate of our School and an ophthalmologist.

Another Chinese student, Robert Tung, had come as our ward. He, too, graduated from our School. He became a cardiologist. In 1991, he won the Young Investigator's Award of the American College of Cardiology. I had established this Award in 1961. Robert's achievement was my 30th-year reward.

Change is a constant. Ed Twin noted a node in his neck while shaving. I sent him to New York City to an old friend, a competent, careful internist. The diagnosis of lung cancer was confirmed. Ed died in the fall of 1986. Ed's death, and Carl Migliazzo's earlier passing, ended the transition era between the Old General and the new TMC.

Ed had brought from Harbin a young student, Li Gang. Li is

now in our Medical School and when he receives his degree, it will be a final reaching out by Ed.

A year after Ed's death, I took the task of escorting his ashes to Harbin. The medical university there had a handsome white marble marker placed among pine trees on the campus, with Ed's name in Chinese and English. A formal procession, on a cold Manchurian day, came out of the medical school, walked the meandering path to his grave site. There I spread my friend's ashes.

My daughter, Lea Grey, had two exciting years of life in Vienna and this gave me good reasons to enjoy Vienna. She returned to live in La Jolla and this, too, gave me ready excuses to visit that lovely place. My daughter, Lark, moved to Kona, Hawaii; more excuses for learning about a lovely place. My eldest daughter gave me company but, equally, the chance to take granddaughters on special trips. Mary D.'s daughters, Louisa and Claire, have been special pleasures.

Henry and Peggy Mitchell expedited a series of major delegations to China. The three of us did this for several years. Many of my old friends from the Rancho courses joined these travel groups. A special time was when my old, old friend, Herman Hellerstein and I were in China together on one of these Snow Delegation trips.

I continued my involvement in China and was there from 1971 to 1989, once or twice a year. In 1987 I was there three times. By chance, I was in Beijing when the Tiananmen disaster occurred. I have tried to see the episode from all sides but my final analysis was the Chinese leadership failed. It failed the test of ultimate responsibility. Yet we Americans also fail if we do not understand the basic, overwhelming desire of the Chinese people for stability. China's experiences over the past 150 years have given them their own definition of liberty. It begins with stability.

Harry Jonas, as second dean, served the important role of validating our efforts on the national scene. His major contribution was that and, it makes me smile to report this, when he finished his tenure, he went on to be the permanent staff person at the American Medical Association for our old friends, the Liaison

Committee. We have come a long way—from suspect, to seated at the table.

At about this same time, our graduate, Dr. Eva Frazer, became a curator of the University. Again, we have come a long way: from curators seeking to ignore the possibility of another medical school to the president of that group being our graduate.

The bright young man from Washington recommended by Nathan prospered with us and, as I write this, is ending his tenth year here. Jim Mongan has effectively, competently, taken on the overall leadership that I felt Hospital Hill should have. This has been done by gradual, incremental, earned reward, just the way it had to be done.

One of his achievements was to carry through to completion an affiliation between the Medical School and Saint Luke's Hospital. This brought Saint Luke's into a new role as one of our major primary teaching hospitals. Here again, this gave evidence of the hard-won recognition, even endorsement, of the School.

A School of Basic Life Sciences was created. The battle over the site of its future building is still fought. The original plan for an additional five floors on top of the Medical School tells how we, from the beginning, thought it should be done.

The ability of the medical school to control the content of the basic science curriculum was laid out carefully when this new school was formed. But as with most things in life, well-laid plans need human interpretation. The plan was bold; now the administration of it tests the human factor.

Residential apartments, attractive and affordable, after 17 years of trying, finally are under construction on Hospital Hill. An elegant Eye Foundation brought an unexpected verve to The Hill. Children's Mercy Hospital worked its way through an internal Board discontent and elected to stay on the Hill. Old General came down and Mercy expanded to the site.

The law profession continued its generous contribution. From the very beginnings, back when Homer and Nathan proposed to Mayor Roe Bartle that the City hospital be run by a lay board, skilled legal help, always contributed, guided us. Bob Fizzell, Jr. of Stinson Mag began the generous gift of time and talent. Frank Sebree, Don Chisholm, Ron Spradley, Joel Pelofsky, and Ned Holland, lawyers, not physicians, have done as much for the medical welfare of Kansas City's poor as the physician staff.

In 1985, under Ginny Calkins' able leadership, we did a bit of bragging. We held a nationwide symposium titled, "A Look Back by Our Graduates." We had a full day of presentations by graduates, analyzing the parts of their education experience with us that they felt had been special. We had on the program, also, the original Consultants to the Chancellor. We gave them a chance to see their investment of time had been of merit.

The lives of the Linvilles and myself continued to intertwine. My daughters had grown up knowing them and became semi-children for their childless marriage. When Ralph died, Eve gave their stein collection to *Diastole,* where it is permanently displayed. On the first shelf, at the left, is my mother's stein. My interests, and Ed Twin's, in China had a completely unexpected dividend. Living with Eve is a full Harbin family, complete with NaNa, age 5. Eve, as she nears 90, is the doting "grandmother" of a Chinese child.

Using a gift from my old friend and patient, Armistead Carter, the University had a Carter Courtyard placed at the entrance of the Medical School. There we put the names of those who had been the happy warriors: Vernon Wilson, Nathan Stark, Homer Wadsworth—and because she had in every way shared the campaign—Mary Clark Dimond. The names of the Consultants to the Chancellor, the deans: Richardson K. Noback, 1969-1978; Harry Jonas, 1978-1987; and the associate deans, Lee L. Langley, 1973-1981; Charles Wilkinson, 1980-1987; and W. Ray Snider, interim dean, June 1987-August 1987; are there, too.

Justice Oliver Wendell Holmes summarized his advice for leadership in just four words. He defined leadership as a four-stage event: Organize, Publicize, Deputize, Supervise. My role on Hospital Hill fits Holmes' thesis. However, there is a fifth stage. On July 1, 1987, the year I was 69, I resigned from the last positions in which I had supervising "power." I ended my place on both the hospital Board and the doctors' Board. I was back to base-zero. What is the correct term for this fifth stage? Vaporize? Depersonalize? Neutralize?

I felt comfortable making this last separation. The Doctor's

Corporation was well-run, still guided by Jerry Stolov, its finances and purpose well-understood by all participants. The hospital board had evolved through logical change until, as I looked around the table, I realized I was the oldest person sitting there, and the longest in service. It was time to leave the scene. Nothing can stifle fresh thinking more than to have someone present whose memory is too long. New people need to air new ideas, without someone at the table who may grump, "We tried that before."

How lasting are the things that I came to Kansas City to do? The primary objective was to create a medical school. Universities are permanent things. The Medical School, as a degree-awarding institution, will be here as long as any other structure of our society. The School can be called "permanent."

The hospital seems permanent, but one remembers the decayed Hospital Hill we took over. One cannot predict the future. Medical care evolves. The hospital built in 1905 seemed to be built "forever."

The academic plan, so much a part of my time and effort, cannot and should not, be "set in stone." How to educate a physician for the future must be determined by the future. The academic plan was my answer to my life and times.

We all have plans. All of us have dreams. All of us have duties. I had the special satisfaction of combining all three in building the medical school. That has been the rare privilege. What is good about what I did here and is worth continuing, will be decided by time.

Walter Lippmann, speaking about Franklin Roosevelt, said, "The final test of a leader is that he leaves behind him in other men the conviction and will to carry on...The genius of a great leader is to leave behind a situation which common sense, without the grace of genius, can deal with successfully."

Lippmann speaks of another level of action, one dealing with the national masses, political issues, and world policy. I have been involved with a smaller world and a world in which one does not lead—but stimulates. I ran a certain course and carried a certain message. My victory will come not from what I led or did—but from those who ran on beyond me.

My single hope would be that those who earned their M.D. degree here would voice their opinion about their medical education experience. No other group quite earned that right. From them should come the validation and opinion about this academic plan. Through the years, I have often been asked when I would write about this medical school. When would I write about why it happened, how it happened, and what were the results. The "why" and "how" I tell here.

My answer about "results" has always been that the story of this school will be visible in the careers of its graduates.

The piece of driftwood I had carved on the beach at Carmel in 1952 was cast into bronze, titled "Take Wing," and placed in the center of the Carter Court Yard. The bronze was dedicated to the graduates of the Medical School. For they are the end point of this entire story. Mary D. and I had our shared daughters—and the graduates of the University of Missouri-Kansas City School of Medicine are, surely, equally, our shared family.

E. Grey Dimond, M.D.
Diastole—Hospital Hill
June 1, 1991

Index

Abernathy, Janice, 359
Academy of Health Professions, 273-274, 290, 296-297
Acapulco, 194
ACC International Circuit Courses, 174
ACCEL, 183, 233, 371
Achya, Endot, 84
Acropolis, 365
Adams, Forrest, 178
Adcock, Douglas, 359
Adson, 58
Afghanistan, 84
Aizawa, Toyozo, 84
Akre, Phil, 152, 210-211
Alimurung, Mariano, 65, 107-109, 175-176, 343
Allen, Max, 87
Allenbaugh, Kelly Grey, 31
Alley, Rewi, 308, 363, 381
Alpha Helix, 154-155
Alstott, Jerry, 349
AMA Residency Review Committee, 290
American College of Cardiology, 91, 131-132, 138, 166, 170-171, 173-175, 184, 232, 236, 254, 273, 321-322, 329, 333, 343, 354, 383
American College of Physicians, 131, 157, 273-274
American Heart Association, 111, 124-126, 129, 131-132, 138, 173-174, 178, 180-181, 254
American Heart Journal, The, 43-44, 125-126
American Medical Association, 18, 165, 169, 226, 290, 293, 322-324, 327, 347-348, 353, 357, 363, 374, 384
American Physiological Society, 337
Anacapri, 101
Anache, Mario, 82
Anderson College, 6
Andrews, Thurl, 139
Andrus, Dr. Cowles, 131
Annals of Internal Medicine, 44
Archer, M. Luisita, 326, 364
Archives of Internal Medicine, 44
Armistead Carter Courtyard, 168, 386
Army, 6, 42, 49, 51, 53-54, 56, 70-71, 92, 140, 191, 314, 323
Army Specialized Training Program, 42
Arnold, Louise, 276, 346
Ashley, John, 365, 378
Association of American Medical Colleges, 169, 293, 334, 347-348
ASTP Program, 42-43, 52
Aub, 64
Austin, Texas, 66, 68, 70, 72-73, 103, 143, 159
Azeem, Mohammad, 84
Bacci, Alex, 272
Bailey, Charlie, 215, 343
Baja, California, 194
Balk, Robert, 349
Ball Hospital, 47

389